Baby Momma Saga:

Part 2

Baby Momma Saga:

Part 2

Ni'chelle Genovese

www.urbanbooks.net

Urban Books, LLC
300 Farmingdale Road, NY-Route 109
Farmingdale, NY 11735

Baby Momma Saga: Part 2
Copyright © 2017 Ni'chelle Genovese

ISBN 13: 978-1-62286-597-0
ISBN 10: 1-62286-597-9

First Trade Paperback Printing December 2017
Printed in the United States of America

10 9 8 7 6 5 4 3 2 1

Distributed by Kensington Publishing Corp.
Submit Orders to:
Customer Service
400 Hahn Road
Westminster, MD 21157-4627
Phone: 1-800-733-3000
Fax: 1-800-659-2436

Prologue

My fingers were wound up so tight in the belt of my trench coat they were starting to go numb. Bright as day, yield sign yellow was the best way I could describe it. Angelo had taken it upon himself to pick it out for me, and I hated it the second I laid eyes on it. *"Think of it like a bombshell-meets-video-vixen look," he'd said, smiling proudly.*

All I could honestly think was 'Where in the world is damn Carmen San Diego.'

Hours ago he came home from an urgent family meeting and after a quick hushed phone call he was draggin' me off to God knows where in the middle of the night. *The better to see you with my dear, that's the only reason why I'd ever pick a glow in the dark jacket. The family probably told him to escort me somewhere secluded so I could be put down like a lame horse.*

The moon was the fullest I'd ever seen it and I couldn't help wondering what Mimi would say it meant. I hadn't thought about my grandma since the night she'd found me unconscious in her bathroom floor. One minute I was fine, listening to Avant in my room. The candied scent of Pear Glace' body splash, my signature fragrance, filled the air. I must have taken some bad oxy, because next thing I know I was retchin' into blue toilet water and then everything went black. When I came to, Mimi was hovering over me, rambling about a mirror breaking on its own and a bird on the roof making a nest out of hair, both signs of bad luck and death. She was probably still superstitious to the point of insanity; superstition was Mimi's religion of choice.

Angelo looked over at me and the bluish silver light from that moon did un-humanly things to his gray eyes. I knew him, but I ain't really *know him*. You could have the most well-kept pet in the world but if it was dangerous to begin with you always worried about it reverting to its baser instincts and turning on you. Angelo claimed to love me, but we never made love. He was a collage of rough rushed sessions that usually ended in me peeling his hand from around my throat before I passed out. Sex was never about me, but I'd just let him get his and consider us since he was helping me stay out of prison.

We'd pulled to a stop in front of foreboding wrought iron gates.

"How are you feeling?" he asked, brushing a cold finger along my cheek, feather-light, faint like the salt in the air from the ocean.

"I'd be better if I knew what was up. And why you so cold all the time? I think your ass is anemic, you need to get seen about that."

He scoffed, "I'm fine. And all yous need to do is play your part. Here, I brought ya' a present." He pulled a little vial of white powder out of his pocket and I looked at his ass like he was crazy.

"You know I don't –"

"I know and that's why I'm not askin'. The family is involved now, so ya' gonna have to trust me on some things. Take it, can't have you up in there acting all nervous. *Andiamo.*"

"Well?" the voice called out.

Startled at the interruption, my little imaginary Q-bert who had been hopping around the three-dimensional Parquet wood flooring vanished as I glanced up. Angelo was out in the car and here I was alone with this stranger and probably not supposed to mix coke with pain-killers.

"Well, what?" I asked the pale fiery red-headed man.

"Do you have it? The one in the car said you'd bring it in. I have the money but I'll have to sample it first. You are a funny acting one. You aren't wearing a wire or anything, are you?" He lifted his head, narrowing his eyes at me suspiciously.

Oh, thanks Angelo, get me high and bring me on one of your drug runs. Appreciate that a bunch.

Sighing, I tried not to zone out again as I stared at the blazing halo of flames on his head. My fingers tingled at the thought of touching his flaming locks. I swore I could almost hear them crackling and sizzling in the air. Instead, I reached into one of the pockets of my jacket. Yep, just as I expected, little vials clinked and I walked toward the ginger freckled-faced man. He didn't take them as I expected. His rhinestone-encrusted smoking slippers were soundless as he padded away. The white satin of his shirt billowed behind him like the sail of a ship. *He's either a Gingy Geenie or a sultan of Satan with all those red flames on his head. And I'm the yellow submarine coke queen.*

There was a blur of shiny wood paneling, marble flooring, bronzed busts on pedestals and winding staircases. The private rooftop patio was dizzily breathtaking, plus all those steps had me realizing how out of shape I'd gotten. Gingy pointed for me to sit down on large chocolate and red cushions in the midst of his rooftop garden. White awnings covered the seating area with yellow and green teacup lights. They twinkled and winked overhead like little Tinker Bells.

I handed Gingy his product and frowned when our fingers touched. Static sextricity, I mean like some other-other kind of sexual charge shot all the way down to arches of my feet. The cushion sank beside me as he sat down and I felt like a sensual heat-seeking missile. It wasn't even like he was that fuckin' attractive. The heat coming off of his skin hit me in radiating waves. I naturally leaned closer to warm myself by the hearth of his head fire. *See, this is why I don't mess with this shit. Vicodins don't make me wanna mount a damn stranger. Why would Angelo send me up here high and horny as hell?*

"Woo, you can tell Angelo I agree, he's definitely got the best shit in all of Miami," he shouted. "And your angel-face has a look worth dying for. Why haven't I seen−"

He paused and we both looked down. There it was, in the crease of his expensive, satiny white lounge pants. The welcome party had come out—the happy tee-pee—and he turned 'bout as bright red as the hair on his head.

"Fuck uh, that doesn't happen like−" He'd started to explain, but hell, I understood what he was feeling and I was already pissed Angelo had sent me to do his damn job. We hadn't even discussed the particulars about this shit. *Mmm, might as well earn myself a "tip".* My skirt cinched up as I slid over onto his lap and I didn't know if all Gingy felt was that damn electricity or if it was just this one in particular. He untied my jacket and reached inside, locking his arms around my back. Just grinding against him through my panties had us both gasping and panting. I didn't care if Angelo was outside waiting. This is exactly what the hell he got for forcing my ass into the coke game. I'd make something up. I just needed to get this out of my system, and Gingy's lips were gettin' real close to figuring out my kitty's password as he purred along my neck.

Reaching down, I unzipped his pants and gasped. *Damn, Gingy, lemme find out I picked the wrong other white meat. Big ass dick. Access granted. Thank you for entering your password and pussy ID.* I slid my drenched panties to the side and all but gasped in shock against his ear. Either he was a freak of nature or I'd just been dealing with Angelo so long my ass was a born again virgin.

"Pull my ears, tug my ears, I can't . . . unless you, I need you to," he chanted breathlessly.

The hell, this ain't the time for Simon-fuckin-says, pull on what, and tug what? Ears? Ugh, I just want to cum. I started tugging anyway and he let out this deep guttural moan. The sound traveled through my body like notes vibrating through a harp. All five of my senses were now erogenous senses. Sounds like gasping and moaning, or wet skin sliding even smells like Bonne Belle cotton candy Lip Smackers were all pinging my 'oh em gee' spot dead on. *What the hell kind of Spanish-fly roophie-colada coke did we do?*

"Ally?" Someone shouted from behind me.

Gingy frantically pushed me off his lap. Frustrated, I sniffed my upper lip confused, because I sure as hell didn't wear cotton candy lip gloss.

"Jasper. Jassy, baby it's not what you think I promise." Gingy approached a very pissed off little man with his hands raised apologetically and he was speaking so . . . so *effeminately.*

Completely miffed, I wiped the damn lip gloss off my lips and straightened my skirt and jacket. *He sure as hell didn't have all that flair turned on five seconds ago.*

"Really Al? It isn't what I think? So, you're gonna tell me you weren't just fucking that . . . that hi-ho school bus prosty? She was tugging your ears, Al. *She was tugging your fucking ears!*" Jasper's interrogation ended in a high-pitched shriek and my hands too flew up apologetically when I saw the gun he'd whipped out. *Oh, Bonne Belle and butt-fucks really?*

"I have had enough, Al. You're like a puppy with your little pink lipstick hanging out. Every time I let you out to piss, you're wandering around and you've got your *G-damn lipstick* in or on some . . . . some *tramp*. It's supposed to be *my fucking lipstick*," Jasper wailed at Al and I cringed. Poor little guy, but it was so less dramatic when he kept calling it lipstick. I imagined him crouched in front of Al trying to *put it on* like some lipstick and it almost made me burst out laughing.

The gun exploded and I jumped as Gingy crumpled. Bright red stained his pristine white garments as well as the deck beneath and shit just got so serious.

"You-who, old-yellow, yeah you. I'm gonna help rewrite the manual for all your Stepford-Goldy-Gold Digger, boyfriend fuckers in training. Chapter One: Never Touch Another Bitch's Lipstick."

Jasper turned the gun on me and my eyes widened. I threw my hands out in front of me.

"Angelo, wait, he didn't know," I shouted.

Jasper turned to see who was there. That was the play I'd chosen out of the split second coke-cocktail induced options that I had to choose from. When the ball snapped in my head, I got low and charged, hitting him with my shoulder in his midsection. His back thudded against the white sandstone of the balcony, where he teetered with his arms flailing wildly. We locked eyes and for an instant and I felt sorry for him as he tipped over and fell the four stories onto the rocky private beach below. His neck broke amongst several other things from the way he was unnaturally sprawled on the outcropping rocks.

I walked out the front door and climbed into the car.

"The family needs to know how well you handle certain uh, situations to see how you'll fit in. Was that your gun I heard, or do I need to get the boys to clean up?" Angelo asked quietly.

"There's no mess. I didn't even know I had a gun, or that I was supposed to kill or get someone killed. Thanks for the heads up," I replied as sarcastically as possible.

"Anytime, bella. *Anytime*."

"What do you mean *replacing me?* You don't replace Sadira Nadesche."

Her voice rang through one of the studio monitors where most of what looked like around forty people hovered, watching anxiously. They appeared to be in various states of excitement, awe, or shock.

"We're mid-production. I'm the highest paid actress in this industry, voted number one on all the lists. Pick a list. Get me my manager and my lawyer. *Now*," she said.

The click clack of my electric-blue, peep-toe Badgley Mischka heels echoed loudly across the cement flooring of the set. The camera feed, which must have been another area on set, quickly flickered off. Everyone turned and Angelo, who'd promised to stay by my side the entire time, squeezed my arm gently as what felt like a million eyes focused on me. To the average observer we looked like the perfect couple. He wore a black Henley long-sleeved shirt that clung to his lean and thinly-muscled frame, Cavalli shades, tousled hair, and Diesel jeans. Clean, simple, and sexy. Me? My stylist, Sir'Tavius, put me in a little black dress and a Paul Smith blazer that matched my favorite new blue and black Dior purse.

Rumors of a fresh-faced starlet surfaced out of nowhere. A favor Angelo asked from his father. The price for that favor was atrocious. When I made my debut I couldn't show up lookin' like a ragamuffin, so Angelo hired me the best stylist in the business.

"Oh, wow, she's gorgable," someone whispered.

"Don't matter how adorable or gorgeous she is, Sadira is going to murder that ass," someone responded.

Ignoring their comments, I pressed a tight, nervous smile to my new face and tilted my chin high. Oh yeah, my new face. I guess good things do come from foul circumstances.

It'd taken three surgeons, almost a year of healing, and at Angelo's prodding some etiquette and refinement classes to get me ready for the world.

Last August when Michelle broke my nose it gave Angelo the idea of a lifetime. He paid his father to help re-invent me. Yes, I was still hiding in a sense; I was just doing it in plain sight and armed with everything from a new identity and credit cards all the way down to a damn near perfect credit score.

A short woman, way shorter than me, with large, thick, square glasses that made her eyes look enormous, walked up to me. She extended a shaky hand, blinking her alien-esque eyes rapidly.

"Desivita Dulce', I presume? I'm awestruck. I mean, my name is Frankie and wow, you are a minxer. They didn't show us any pics, which was weird. Not that you're weird, just that it was weird. Directors just said they had a better header, and *ta-da* here you are, and I'm rambling. Um, we . . . I . . . well, we weren't expecting you until tomorrow. Uh, so your trailer isn't ready yet," she said in a flurry of nervous head nods and hand gestures.

"That's fine," Angelo said, stepping forward to speak on my behalf. "We just wanted to meet everyone. Hone . . . I mean Desi was just curious about the set. It is her first movie. She wanted to get a feel for it, have a look around before the big day. See what her marks are, or are there marks on the set or whatever? I mean, I don't know what the fuck it is you call it." Angelo too, blabbered like a nervous idiot. He'd been making me write and say my new name over and over, and in the first thirty seconds he almost dropped the ball.

"Oh, well, then let me show you two around. We're really good at adjusting, especially with the way the first producer . . . Uh, hopefully you watched the first movie right?"

I was glad I'd taken one of the extra Vicodin I had left over from my surgery. The movie was a wack-ass horror film called *Revived 2*. The script was easy to memorize because all my parts were "Daisy running," or "Daisy screaming topless." That bullshit made me laugh so much I hurt my new cheeks. Angelo threatened to take it away during my recovery, afraid

I'd burst my stitches or whatever he'd said. However, being on set and overhearing the gaffer and key grip asking the best boy about butt plugs and magic fingers had me thinking I'd walked into a sex shop. *Maybe I'd misread that shit and we were shooting a horror-themed porno?* When Frankie saw my expression she calmly explained that butt plugs were stand adapters for the speakers, and magic fingers were a type of mount.

The first movie was apparently a box office hit. According to Angelo's logic, this one would be a good fit for my introduction into the world of bright lights and even brighter stars since it was predicted to do three times better. Angelo already had his own self-made fame. He wasn't wanted by U.S. Marshals and on watch lists for escaping prison. Trenisha, aka L'il Miss Honey, was. With his help and the family pitching in I could covertly push coke as an industry insider and I would be untouchable. Instant fame where I could pick up and go anywhere, do anything I wanted, and on top of all that I'd have *star power*.

"So, are you ready for this or what?" Angelo asked once we were back in the car and on our way to get ready for some kind of celebrity all-star party.

I didn't answer immediately. Instead I stared at the face of this almost-famous movie star's reflection in the window. It was weird how little I could see of my old self. Desivita was raised in a group foster home that was paid to doctor up fake records. She graduated from high school in Fayetteville, North Carolina. She'd relocated to LA, auditioned for roles, took acting classes, and had been working part-time as a Hooters waitress. This stranger stared back at me, with her high, perfectly flushed cheeks and these bright, mysterious eyes. Sir'Tavius had given me a ring to wear and I fidgeted with it anxiously.

"Always wear one accessory," he'd said as he exaggerated a yawn. "That'll make ere'body go snaparazzi with their little camera phones and whatnot." On his finger sat a black angel's wing with Swarovski crystals in the feathers. He'd batted his long, perfectly placed lashes before handing over this ring that engulfed my entire index finger. Twirling it in place, I sighed, wondering how I'd get Paris if Honey technically no longer existed. How would I, as this famous actress person, actually approach Michelle and convince her to give her up? Angelo probably hadn't even considered that since he was more concerned with having an "us," and then having us make a family.

It just meant that I'd have to do some creative tinkering on my own damn time and my own damn dime. That's what the hell it sounded like it meant.

Angelo looked over at me. "It's kind of late to be gettin' scared, *bella*."

"I'm fine, baby. You know I stay ready, so I never have to worry about gettin' ready," I told him.

Chapter 1

Self-Destructing Hearts </#

(Six Months Later)

I could probably tell you the time every half hour on the hour throughout the night because I woke up at the slightest thing. Every time I'd shift or turn over, the house settled, or if one of the kids so much as sneezed, my eyes would fly open and my heart rate would shoot to threat level "imminent danger." The only good thing about sleeping as lightly as I did was that I heard everything, which was also the bad part. Something had awakened me, and with my sleeping habits, a mosquito could have burped, thus sending my brain into panic mode. *Okay, October. I know your signature move is bumps in the night and whatnot, but this is not how I want to start things off.*

I'd left my window open and the wind picked up the scent of the gardenias outside. It cooled my face and, as I sat up, made my sweat-soaked sheets feel as though they'd been doused in ice water. It was still unclear if I'd heard feet shuffling or if I'd dreamt about it and immediately my thoughts turned to Larissa. Confused, I'd started to call out, but stopped as the hazy, restless cobwebs cleared in my mind. Secretly I wished it were her coming home late. That used to be her usual bullshit reaction to "nothing." Okay, granted, what I would call "nothing" was most likely someone or something I'd done. Larissa and I had a long history of drama and an even longer history of unhealthy solutions.

Regardless of how much it hurt, every time I opened my eyes I'd have to remind myself that she was gone. I was a widow now, with a late wife, and there was no changing that.

Realization would sink in and my throat would feel like I was trying to swallow a dry handkerchief whole. It didn't matter where I was. I could be lying in bed or at a grocery store with the kids, or just daydreaming. Because, when I say every time I opened my eyes I felt like crying, I meant every time. Since she was gone, a noise in the night was definitely not a good thing.

The house alarm was beeping at sixty-second intervals; it only did that when it was running on the backup generator. The power was out; or worse the power had been cut. Just the simple thought of someone cutting the power made me cautious. I reached into the nightstand and grabbed my handgun. It felt cold and foreign to my fingers, but it made me feel safe. The bedroom was painted in a combination of eerie shadows from the battery-powered air freshener in the corner.

Everything always looked strange with shadows attached to them at night, especially people. Some people could stand with a shadow over even a little bit of their face and look like monsters. Rasheed was one of those niggas who could wear a shadow and exude pure sex. Whereas Larissa, my late wife, would look like the very devil himself.

Sometimes I'd slip and absentmindedly think of Rasheed. He was my heartworm for life, even after his death. He'd gnawed his way in, latching on. I'd gotten so used to living with him and the pain and our illusion of love that I felt borderline guilt and misery at having him removed, permanently. He was murdered because of me. Now Honey was trying to murder me over him. Well, over the daughter she had with him. Honey, Danita, Diamond, the list could go on; they were only a few of the many reasons why my heartworm had to go. I shook my head at myself and frowned. You stay with someone for years and over the course of time they seep into your pores little by little, day by day. The craziest thing happens and suddenly, you can't make lasagna anymore because the smell reminds you of one person. You can't drink a certain kind of champagne because the taste reminds you of the other.

It's been said when a relationship is over, you should remain single six months for every year you were with that person. I got with Rah at sixteen, Ris at eighteen, and I was twenty-seven now. Based on that theory, I wouldn't be fit to deal with anyone until my ass was damn near thirty-two. Add in the fact that Ris had a drug habit and Rah had children with two different women, one of whom was trying to kill my ass, and I'd probably be better off staying single for the rest of my damn life.

Rasheed was like a drug. I could never tell if I was sprung off good dick or just stuck on dumb love, but we had this hardcore yo-yo "relationshit."

I mean, the harder we fought, the grimier and lower he got with the shit he did. In turn, that's how much higher the highs would be when we bounced back and how much harder his love would seem to be magnified. It was addictive and it was mind-blowing. It's a damn shame that it took me having a baby and some years in order to learn how to tell the difference between ships and shit. Some people are ships and those are the ones you build your relations and connections with. They'll help you carry your burdens and your dreams, and they won't let you drown. Others, as in Rasheed's case, are just shit. Larissa just happened in the middle of all of that.

I quickly surveyed my things, trying to make sure nothing was moving or, worse yet, creeping up on me. I was too damn old for nightlights, but with everything going on I could admit that I was too damn scared to sleep without one. Safety light was the best name I could come up with when Trey asked why Mommy's nightlight had "smell goods" in it and his didn't. As far as anyone was concerned I just had it because it smelled nice, and it just so happened to have a safety light on it.

When I heard it, it was faint yet distinct, like "hungry in church and hearing someone trying to sneak a piece of candy out of their pocket" distinct. Someone was trying to get into the house. Throwing the sheets aside, I grabbed my phone and put my Bluetooth in my ear.

I fought back memories of that night that forced me to become a slave to preparation. The night Honey dragged me out of my own house and almost killed me. It made me stay on high alert, always sleeping fully clothed or in my robe over full pajamas. I couldn't remember the last time I'd slept comfortably, let alone the entire night.

I've always had a fear of guns. Guns and cancer, and if you grew up in my house you would as well. My mother passed away from cancer when I was ten and I was raised by my father, who was shot in a hunting accident two years later. Even still, I'd never get caught unprepared or unprotected again. If you've never had someone stand over you ready to end your life while your son is crying, calling out, "Mommy", you wouldn't understand.

Weighing the small Luger in my hand, I disengaged the safety and inserted the clip in mechanical motions. The gun range was my weekend getaway. Towanna would watch the kids so I could familiarize myself with my new gun. Some of the folk up in there looked shady; it always made me nervous to be around so many strangers with weapons. Then I'd remind myself I had a weapon too, and was damn lethal with it. Sliding it into the pocket of my robe so it'd be easily accessible, I speed-dialed three. My car keys, credit card, and cash were already in my pajama pocket in case we needed to get on the road. Three packed bags stayed in the trunk of the car in the garage. I kept everything on standby at all times because at any moment someone could come for us or for me and I couldn't risk not being ready.

"Michelle? What's wrong?" Towanna answered on the first ring.

"The power's out and I think someone's outside. It sounds like the bay window downstairs. I'm getting the kids." The words tumbled out of my mouth in a rushed whisper as I padded soundlessly out of the bedroom toward Lataya's and Trey's rooms.

They were like little sponges, soaking up every detail of even the smallest things. I'd just enrolled Trey in what everyone said was the best private school in the area. He'd only been in the school for three days before I was called in over his behavior. On one occasion he told a little girl to sit her ass down before he sat her down and, again, when he tried stabbing a boy with a jumbo pencil over a toy. It was bad enough there were only a handful of black kids in the school to begin with. I couldn't have him being the poster child for the single-parent household.

"Okay, get the kids and go back to your bedroom. I'm on my way right now. Are you all right?" Towanna asked.

"Yeah; scared, but I'm okay."

The kids' rooms were directly across the hall from each other and not more than two feet from mine. Afraid to stay by myself and tired of months in the hotel, when Towanna suggested we stay here with her I was all too eager to accept. Don't get me wrong, I still didn't trust cops, VA cops specifically. However, my choices were staying on my own, or staying with Towanna. Living with a cop was the safest thing I could think of until I could come up with a solid game plan. Towanna'd been more than patient with my "just a little while" that turned into a little over a year, but we split everything and she swore she loved the company. I took the easy way out as opposed to finding a new house right away, but I couldn't help thinking that Honey was out there and eventually she'd be coming for Lataya.

Walking into Lataya's room I gave her a quick once-over. She was sound asleep, her thick lashes fanning over her pudgy little cheeks like delicate, dark brown palm fronds. She squirmed a bit but didn't miss a single soft snore as I scooped her up into my arms. She'd been teething and was being all kinds of fussy with the rest of her teeth finally coming in. I eventually had to resort to rubbing the teeniest bit of rum on her gums and, voila, problem solved. She was happy as a jaybird and of course snoring like a drunken sailor not long after that.

I pressed her head full of soft curls onto my shoulder beneath my chin and turned to go get Trey. Even now, a shadow of a smile curved my lips and I shook my head, trying to repress a memory of a conversation I'd had with Ris. I'd come home one night and she'd played around saying she'd gotten Trey drunk. Tears burned my eyes and threatened to spill down my cheeks as they always did when I thought about the good times I had with Larissa. They were glowing embers in the fireplace of my mind that never seemed to completely go out. Thinking about something as simple as her laugh, or how she tried to kill Rasheed for me would act as fresh kindling and the fire would—

"Y'all good? I'm not more than five minutes away."

Towanna's voice broke through the silence into my earpiece, almost making me drop my poor baby.

"Shit, woman, you scared the hell out of me. I forgot you were there. I've got Taya, and I'm going to get Trey," I replied in a hurried whisper, hoping I wouldn't wake up Lataya as I tiptoed across the hall.

My mind was a hornet's nest of activity, buzzing with a swarm of thoughts all at once. Aside from thinking about Ris, I was also hoping whoever was downstairs took just long enough to get in for me to get back to my room, even though I'd have rather been heading for the car in the garage.

Think . . . just calm down and think Michelle. There's no way she could have found us. Where have we been, who have we talked to? Stores, parks, work, school, fuck I don't know. It didn't even matter; I was ready to fight until the death for my babies. Would she?

Lord, I hoped Trey wasn't in one of those sleeps that an earthquake couldn't shake him out of, and even if one did, he'd move at glacial paces, dragging his feet and whining. As I entered his room, his nightlight cast its familiar glow across the floor, illuminating my way. It carved shadowy halos around Ironman and Thor action figures along with his discarded pajama top and half-eaten Oreo cookies. Everything was scattered along the plush beige and brown carpet in a path that ran from his toy chest toward his bed. That mess definitely wasn't there when I tucked his ass in, and I made a note to get his behind good for playing and sneaking snacks after I'd put him down for the night.

"Trey, baby, wake up." I spoke his name softly, gently pulling back his comforter. He always slept like a little mole and there was no telling what part of the pile he'd be buried underneath. Something creaked downstairs. It was much louder this time, echoing throughout the house like a cannon blast in an empty auditorium.

"Trey?" I threw the blankets off his bed in a panic. My stomach dropped and I was about three heartbeats away from hyperventilating as I stared down at nothing but The Hulk's animated angry green outline on the sheets.

"Towanna, he's not here. Oh my God." I scrutinized every inch of his room from the toys to his pajama top, and immediately my thoughts went to the worst.

"Michelle, calm down. I'm pulling up now." Her voice was calm and controlled.

As comforting as it was knowing Towanna was outside, nothing was gonna reassure me until I could physically see and touch my baby. After all the drama with Honey and Rasheed and even Larissa's murder, I just wanted my kids to have as normal a life as possible. I'd have given anything to make them forget all the bullshit they'd seen. From the petty arguments that I know they'd overheard between Ris an' me all the way down to the bloodshed. Lataya was hopefully too young to be affected by it, but Trey worried me the most with his random questions about his daddy and Ris.

It had taken everything in me not to skip the conversation and just kiss all the little confusion lines out of his forehead when I tried explaining the concept of death. He seemed to grasp certain points but his behavior and his anger toward other children made me wonder if some things were indeed hereditary. When it came to Larissa and Rasheed, that boy had a barrage of questions from "Do you have to get hurt to go to Heaven?" all the way down to "Why would Jesus want my daddy if Jesus already has a daddy?" It was definitely a little more than I was cut out to handle. That was the only reason I'd fought every ounce of motherly instinct within me and forced them to sleep in their own rooms instead of in bed with me. My babies needed to not be forever traumatized or afraid of the past. That was for me to lose sleep over, not them, and now I was kicking myself for that decision.

His room faced the front of the house, and the blaring red and blue lights from Towanna's police car flashed through his window, turning it into a gut-wrenching crime scene kaleidoscope. Thankfully they were shut off before my imagination could do any more damage.

"Michelle, do you have Trey?"

"No, I . . . I don't know where he is," I replied in a barely audible whisper as I glanced down at his pajama top.

"Then I need you to . . . oh shit . . ."

"Towanna? Hello?"

Tapping the Bluetooth to redial her number, I cursed silently and crept back toward my bedroom. The line wouldn't dial out at all and I could feel the sweat beading on my upper lip as sheer panic set in. Towanna had gone over at least a thousand different scenarios after we'd moved in, but none of them were like this. I went back to my room to put Lataya down in the middle of the bed, piling pillows on either side of her in case she rolled. I'd just started to go check Trey's room one more time—the closet, under the bed—when the hairs on the back of my neck stood up. It was that sixth sense you develop from playing hide and seek in the dark. Where you can just feel when someone or something is around a corner or in a darkened room.

My feet moved in the direction of the Lataya's room, even though my brain said to be still. I was making my way back to Lataya's room.

"Michelle, where y'all at?" Towanna called out from downstairs.

"I'm up here. I don't know where Trey is." I was on the verge of a complete meltdown, and my voice cracked.

"Get Taya; come here."

I did as told, making my way toward Towanna. Her heavy-lidded eyes were wide and disturbed, her cheeks flushed. The crisp black uniform she always took so much pride in was wrinkled with dirt on the knees. Gone was the calm and reserved officer I'd spoken with on the phone. She actually looked frazzled and worried with her pistol drawn and her back pressed against the wall by the front door. The domino effect took place. That's when one person freaks out or runs without saying a word and then everyone runs. She looked flustered, so in turn I got even more flustered.

"What is it?" I pleaded with her, "Please don't tell me what I think it is. Did someone take him? Is he okay? Is he outside? Just let me see him," I rambled at her wildly.

"Calm the hell down. The window was pried open around back and the panel box looks like someone fucked with it. Ennis, my partner, is out front calling it in now. Can't figure out why the hell the alarm ain't go off."

"Where's Trey? Towanna, did someone take my child?"

"Calm down, babe. I need you to focus while I sweep the house. Go get in the squad car; you'll be safe while I check shit out. I'ma find him, okay?"

All I could do was nod. My heart was hacking away at my breastplate like a painful pendulum. It banged harder and louder by the second. I watched Towanna do something for me not many people would be willing to do. She was doing her best to stay brave and calm when my own hands were sweaty and shaking. In those quiet, painful seconds I came to the official conclusion that God punished Eve when she bit into that apple, and it wasn't by giving her a monthly cycle or direct knowledge of good and evil. God's specific punishment to Eve and all women was our hearts. Our hearts are our natural defects, our self-destruct buttons. We give our heart to a person and they have the power to destroy us with it or they can bring us back to life. Childbirth is a painful process that bonds us with our children. Yet it's still possible for us to have spiritual, emotional, even heartfelt bonds with children who aren't our own.

Shit, at the moment, my heart was damn near imploding from fear and simultaneously melting at the sight of Towanna taking care of me and my kids. I swore whoever or whatever was in the house wasn't gonna have to lay a finger on me. At any moment my heart was gonna bust right out of my chest and kill me in the process. Oh, yes, hearts could also kill hearts. God gave Adam a little this and a little bit of that but he got Eve real good.

My ears rang like a silent fuse and I shook my head trying to clear it as I shuffled past her, trying not to wake up Lataya. A million crickets chirped in greeting as I made my way to the squad car where Officer Ennis sat waiting inside. My senses were on high alert. Everything from the stillness of the air to the lavender baby shampoo that lingered in Lataya's hair bombarded my frazzled nerves. I gave Officer Ennis a soft, nervous smile as I opened the passenger side door of the squad car. It was a little embarrassing to meet him, as we'd never been formally introduced, and here I was in my damn robe with my hair all tied up. He was a cop; he probably met a ton of people looking this way though, if not worse.

He was focused on typing something into the laptop in the patrol car. The scanner in the car was going crazy, blaring so loud I was worried it'd wake Lataya up. She could sleep through a tornado, and with the rum I'd given her she wasn't budging, but that shit was overly annoying. Instead of sitting down, I opted to stand beside the car where the door could still shield me. Nervous and fidgety, I tried to make small talk.

"Hi, Officer Ennis. I'm Michelle. Officer Towanna said to come wait out here. Any idea how long before backup arrives?"

Something brushed up against my ankle and my nerves were so shot I screamed, waking Lataya in the process. She instantly started wailing. A white Persian kitten with cotton ball–fluffed fur purred up at me. I glared down, debating on kicking the living daylights out of its little ass. Towanna came running up behind me.

"What the fuck is it? Michelle? Ennis? What's wrong?" she demanded.

I couldn't answer. My eyes were glued on the ribbon tied around the kitten's neck.

"Oh no, Ennis! No. No. No. Michelle, take Trey," Towanna screamed, but her words fell on deaf ears.

There was no way in hell this could be possible. That Persian was Sodom and Gomorrah and at the moment I was Lot's wife. I stood there, nothing but a useless pillar of salt punished for daring to look at it. Attached to the blue ribbon around the damn cat's neck was a little card; even from where I was standing I could see the bright gold letters. Towanna's voice was panicked and frantic in the background; she was in the squad car calling in Ennis's murder. His throat was slit.

Trey quietly scooted past me.

"Ooh a kitty, Mommy." He kneeled down to pet her.

Tears fell down my face as I was motionless, afraid to move, afraid to look around, and even more worried about the fact we were all outside in the open, exposed.

Trey continued to admire the tiny fluff ball. He was determined to pick her up. "Is dis for my birfday tomorrow, Mommy? It says my name, see?" He pointed to the card and went back to cooing at the kitten. "You can sleep with me under Taya's crib. I don't like my new room."

Somewhere in my head I was screaming for him to get away from it, afraid that it'd blow up or try to claw him to death. As if Honey had actually sent some kind of trained attack kitten. How could she possibly even know when Trey's birthday was and how the fuck could she have found us? My knees felt like they were about to give out and my stomach was queasy.

There was no way in hell Rah could be—

"Michelle . . ."

Towanna's strained voice broke through my cluttered thoughts.

"Get Trey; we need to get inside. *Right now.*"

I barely nodded, grabbing Trey by the hand. He cradled his newfound fur ball from hell like he was carrying a football. I didn't feel like arguing with him over that damn cat. There'd be time for me to launch it out the back door or chuck it down the garbage disposal later. Right now, my main concern was getting us inside safely.

Chapter 2

The Miami Blues

The view from the window of our penthouse on the top floor was depressing. It was a "tired after a long day, going to check your mailbox and getting a postcard of a beautiful beach at sunset" depressing. I got the honor of having an upper-level front-row seat to one of the most beautiful attractions in the world. Yet, I wasn't allowed to feel the sun and the sand or smell the salt spray from the ocean on the breeze. This had to be one of hell's third dimensions. It was like baking chocolate chip cookies without eating a single one, or hitting a blunt without inhaling.

In my jealous state of envy I'd started calling the little shadowed figures in different stages of beach enjoyment "sheeple." I'd combined the words sheep and people. That's how all the little blotchy outlines looked from where we sat. The sheeple always followed all the rules and did as they were told. The sheeple didn't break laws. The sheeple bought the movie tickets and were instantly in love with me. The movie premiered a week ago and its instant success made me feel almost like being an escaped convict again. Cameras were starting to appear everywhere we went, and I had interviews lined up all over the place. Angelo had already accepted another script on my behalf. He didn't ask my opinion or anything. Since the directors didn't want a reading I wasn't sure if he'd paid them off or if they'd requested me. I'd had the script for a month and only half-assed studied my lines. That was pushing it with filming set to start in a day or two. It was whatever; they could fire me for all I cared. I thought I'd be flying around the world actually doin' shit. Here I was *still* stuck up in my glass cage, Angelo's little identity reassignment program sucked.

Watching my sheeple be boring sheeple was slowly helping me get over the anger I felt every time I thought about it. Instead of stressin' over movies and appearances I could be making sure Michelle was getting dealt with.

Yeah, but the sheeple's asses are down there enjoying the beach while you up here.

"Jimmy One Side is the only person I got who'll vouch for yous right now. We still need more of the family to speak up in your favor so she'll forget about all this retribution foolishness." Angelo sat across from me at our little dinner table, jabbing his fork in my direction to get his point across.

I hated that fork pointy shit; it made me feel like he was subliminally stabbing me every time he jabbed it into the air. "Why do y'all call him that anyway? Wait, I know. It's because of those burgers that he makes at all the barbeques. They all charred black on one side and still mooing when you flip 'em over?" I giggled at my clever observation.

Every time we went over that fool's house I had to make sure I ate beforehand because nothing that man cooked was edible. The macaroni and cheese would be crisp on top with half-cooked noodles halfway toward the bottom; fried chicken would be smellin' all nice and when you bit into it, ugh. It's a wonder he didn't get married just so he'd have someone to cook for him.

The sound of Angelo's fork clattering to the table made my laughter stop. I'd done gone and pissed him off again.

"No, lucky for yous they call him that because he only gots to hear one side of a story before he decides to body a man or not. The rest of the family ain't been so keen on losing blood over . . ." His sentence trailed off as he sneered at me across the table and my appetite was immediately gone.

"Over what? Go ahead and say it, Angelo. It ain't like I can't figure the shit out. Over a black woman? Because aside from you and Mommy dearest I think eight-tenths of your family's in the system, so I know they can't have a problem with that part of my background."

Sliding my chair out from the table I threw my napkin down on my plate. I'd barely touched my baked ziti and garlic sautéed zucchini I spent half the day making. Yep, I'd learned a thing or two up in the kitchen. Boy, if Mimi could see me now she'd cluck her tongue and ring a bell to get rid of the demon she'd say I was possessed with. The old me would have never stepped foot in a kitchen unless it was to fix myself a plate or look in the fridge. What else did I have to do with my time these days? Once we wrapped filming, if we weren't at a club hosting an event, I was here online socializing and gossiping with Sir'Tavius pointing out who's who. There was only so much of that I could do in one day. Sir'Tavius would then come by and force me into umpteen different outfits and show me what went with what so my look would "stay ahead of the game."

Angelo refused to order out from Olive Garden or IHOP, even though they were still my favorite spots. If it wasn't home cooked he'd scrunch his face up, calling it "overpriced airplane food." The cooking network was my best friend and my ass was getting fluffier by the day. Angelo's ungrateful behind was getting spoiled, too. I never got a "thank you" or "the food's good," nothing. Even now, he just sat there anxiously pushing food around on his plate, and when he wasn't doing that he was air forking me to damn death.

I'd learned that you never got up from dinner without being excused. These folk took meals serious as all hell, and walking out in the middle was rude and beyond disrespectful. "I'm gonna take a walk; I need some fresh air, Angelo. We've been up under each other too much. I really just need to get up out of here for a few minutes."

Rumors had started circulating within the family again about Angelo's mom holding his half brother and sister Lania and Key's death over my head and it was absolute bullshit. Angelo got all prune-faced when I asked for details about his last conversation with his mom. It couldn't have been good if he'd actually refused to never speak to her again afterwards. It wasn't my fault. It was Angelo's decisions to solicit their help in dealing with Michelle and then Keyshawn being a typical man had to go get his dick caught up in the spokes of Michelle and Larissa's love triangle. *They* got sloppy doing their part with Michelle, not me. Yeah, some fresh air would really do me good right now.

"And what if someone recognizes you? Been starin' at that TV so long it's done started to addle that brain of yours? You forgetting yous not a regular person anymore, huh? Come back here," he shouted, kicking his chair from under him. He marched over and planted himself in front of me, blocking my path.

Angelo's little temper tantrum didn't mean shit to me. I was undersexed, under stress, and so over his ass at the moment I didn't even care. His eyes were dark and turbulent like the underside of a thundercloud. They always got that way when he was excited or irritated, like right before we fucked or moments before he had to kill someone.

His voice was now cold and unemotional. "So, no talkin', jus' like that? We have a disagreement and this one needs to take a walk, huh?"

I ain't pay him any mind. The only reaction he got from "this one" was an eye roll and a smirk.

I pulled the door closed behind me, tilting the brim of my fitted baseball hat so low it touched the frames of my sunglasses. It felt like I hadn't been outside on my own in ages as I took in the sights and sounds of Miami nightlife like I was seeing it all for the first time. For October it was still humid as hell so I tied my jacket around my waist, loving the feel of the moist air as it kissed my skin.

At least something was kissing my skin. Angelo won't doin' a damn thing for me except workin' my nerves.

All the boutiques on this part of the strip were flashy and crowded. The storefronts all seemed to be fighting with each other for attention. There were plenty of pretty sundresses and heels that caught my eye. But Lord knows I had more Michael Kors, Marc Jacobs, and brands in my closet than I knew what to do with. The only reason I stopped at one particular spot was because I wanted to relax and stay low-key. It seemed conducive to both. After debating whether I should go in, I found myself in the small parlor, staring down into a pond filled with the prettiest fish.

"Those are Japanese koi. The gold ones are the most popular. They're called *Yamabuki*. They represent wealth."

I turned to address whoever had spoken to me and froze. He looked familiar as hell, and faces ran through my brain as I tried to remember every man I'd ever seen or spoken to. He narrowed his eyes at me suspiciously.

"Um, Honey?" He pointed at me, waiting.

My mind went blank, like I literally couldn't think of a lie or an alibi, so I slowly started to shake my head no like a mute fool. I began backing away with my heart in my throat.

"Oh, sorry about that. The tattoo on your shoulder, I thought it was your name and um, I knew a stripper with that name. Not that I'm calling you a stripper or anything, ma'am. I'm sorry. Let me shut up."

Oh hell on hot wheels. Does this mothafucka know me from the Hot Spot? Did I dance for his ass or something? The door wasn't but four steps behind me. I could've been out of it and on my way when my adrenaline finally slowed down enough to let his words register. *How the hell could I have overlooked my tattoo?* My mental Rolodex finally kicked in and I was so excited all the refining and training flew right out the window. I debated for a hair of a second on whether or not I should say something, but I was just so excited at seeing a familiar face.

"Hold the fuck up . . . ain't no way," I blurted out, staring up at him in complete shock.

He nodded and smiled in confusion, his rough lumberjack features softening as he broke into a slow grin.

"Big Baby, what in the hell? I thought you was locked up! It is me; well, a new me. I go by Desi now. But yes." I threw my arms out like I'd just flashed before him like ninja magic. "It's me, Honey, or the actress known as Desivita Dulce'."

"Well, look at yo' li'l escapee superstar self. Congratulations, girl. You've got to tell me how you did it," he responded before scooping me up into a tight bear hug.

It felt so good to see someone from home; hell, Big Baby felt good as a bitch, too. The thin fabric of his clothes didn't leave much to the imagination. His body was like a rock wall pressed up against mine. They looked something like doctor's scrubs except they were all black. My mind went to some domination bondage shit. As soon as my feet were back on the ground I took myself back over to look at the damn koi. I needed a dickstraction, as in something to distract me from the "bad touch" thoughts I was suddenly having about Big, even though I needed some kind of distraction from Angelo's sudden lack of not knowing how to put it down at home. *I hope this next movie has some love scenes or something gracious.*

"I'll tell you what I can tell you one of these days. You just have to swear that you'll neva eva eva in your long-legged life say you've seen Honey. You can't remove tattoos up in this shop can you? No, I'm messing, but I wanna hear about you. What happened to you? How'd you get out? You feel goo . . . I mean you look good. You look really good. The beard is mad Paul Bunyanish on you but I kind of like it in a 'chop down some trees' kind of way."

I realized I was nodding nonstop like one of those big-headed bobble thingies on a car dashboard and settled on frowning at him to keep myself still. *Umph, lookin' like thaaat, he could ride all up on this ass. Call me Babe the got-damn Blue Ox . . .*

Big chuckled, thankfully interrupting my cyclone of dirty thoughts, which were probably spinning all over my face. He made his way behind the counter and started fidgeting with some paperwork. "Girl, long story short . . ." He briefly looked up in my direction. "Yo, you okay? You look upset or something."

Ugh, okay, don't frown. Straight face, girl, just keep a straight face. I waved for him to continue. "Keep going, you're . . . I'm fine. Just shocked at seeing you that's all. It's been crazy as hell, but that's another story."

"Well, somehow Rah was the only one who went in. We all got picked up and questioned, of course no one talked, and then all the charges got dropped. Sad shit, my boy took the heat for everybody. Having my life on the line like that, knowing that I could have lost everything . . . it changed me. We all had rainy-day funds; every real hustler does. This what I did with mine. I got my life right, started eating right, working out, meditating. I've got ten of these spots and Miami is lucky number eleven." He waved his arms around the small, dim, jasmine-scented parlor and smiled.

"I'm proud of you. You did good, unlike some of us I guess. So you ain't the massage person, you're actually the owner? Why this, though? That just seems so not you." I stared at him, confused and relieved because he could've been a snitch, thankfully that wasn't the case. This was so not like the Big Baby I remembered. Then again, look at me. We were both in completely opposite directions from where we'd originally started, on some type of yin-yang self-discovery adventures. From the koi pond to the white paper lanterns and dark brown leather sofas, everything looked sophisticated and relaxing.

"Miami won't be on the radar. I thought there'd be too much competition, but a couple of investors saw how good I was doing and approached me about this area. Starting was easy; you remember Shiree? Ah man, she used to love my amateur back and ass massages."

"Ass massages, really, what the hell kind of mess is that?" I was cracking up at that one.

"You laughing; why you think she used to fuck with me so hard back then? It wasn't 'cause I was pretty. We both know that." He chuckled. "But nah, your boy is handy. I knew how to do a lot of out of the ordinary shit before I even knew how to cook."

"What the hell? I forgot all about her; where is she now?" I tried to sound nonchalant. I couldn't believe I'd forgotten about her ass. Seeing as how she was Larissa's sister, she might be someone I'd have to check in on for info about Michelle and Paris.

"Aw, I messed up bad with her, ain't never hear from her again after I got picked up. I actually went to school, got my degree and everything because of how good she told me I was with these hands. I don't have any staff in here yet, so I'm the staff right now. But Honey . . . I mean um, Des, we were doin' it all wrong. It's to the point now where I don't even use my hands for nothin' but countin' paper. Legit, clean, 'ain't gotta watch my back' paper."

He'd walked over and stood next to me and I couldn't believe how big his ass was. I kept giving him the side eye. He was like Andre the Giant, and all I wanted to do was wrestle.

He could put me in his sleeper choke hold, million-dollar dream . . .

"You can get a massage on the house if you don't believe me. You ain't gotta get naked or anything like that unless you're comfortable. Trust, I ain't tryin' to lose my license over no foul shit. I've got the hot stones for stress and tension relief. We can start you off with a rosehip oil and lavender mix. Come here see for yourself."

Big led me to an area that smelled like a field of wonderfulness in the springtime and I was impressed. There were so many extracts and infusions, each one smelling better than the last.

"What is this one? Oh my goodness, I kind of like it." It was like those Atomic Fireballs I used to get when I was little with vanilla and a little bit of cherry.

"I make them myself, all natural. You should try this lemongrass and mint oil one for energy. I promise it'll be worth it." He winked.

"Marcus Latharium Bello, oh shit," I whispered in an excited little voice whipping out my phone playfully. "I gotta take a picture. This nigga got a *real name*. Boy you don't even know how we used to bet dollars on you. All them nights where you ran the club the goal was to see how many shots it'd take to get you to tell your real name. This is your business license right?" I laughed.

"Well, as far as you know Ms. Desivita, my name is Big or Big Baby, so we're even as far as the name game goes. Now, pick out an oil."

His tone was reassuring as he stared down at me, his expression saying "why not."

Ooh, why had I not done something like this sooner?

A few minutes later I was lying face down in a cozy, dim room, wearing nothing but a soft black cotton towel. My face peeked through a hole in the headrest that Big had adjusted so it cradled my cheeks perfectly. I tried to focus on the small stream that ran under the clear glass tile flooring. Just like the Ritz Hotel, there was something about the people of Miami and their fascination with putting wildlife indoors.

Tiny fish darted in and out of the rocks beneath me as the lighting in the water shifted from shades of purple to blue. I'd never seen anything like it. As much as I wanted to enjoy the view, I couldn't have forced my eyes to stay open once Big's hands started working the tension knots in my lower back.

He wasn't lying. If it wasn't the size of his hands, because they were huge, then it had to be their sheer strength. Big could easily break or bruise any part of me if he wanted to, but under the heat of his hands I felt myself relaxing. It's a wonder I didn't just slide off the massage table into a melted puddle like a crayon left outside in the middle of summer.

Paris should have crayons now, she is old enough. Those fat jumbo ones and probably some chalk, too, so we could draw on the concrete. I wonder if she can draw?

"You know you're all knotted up right in here," Big grunted, pressing deep into my lower back and it wiped my thoughts completely from my head.

Maybe it was the excitement of having another man touch me with hands that weren't always cold. It might have been the peppery-woodsy smell of the cologne he was wearing that had me wanting to climb off the table and climb him. My stuff was throbbin' and there was probably a puddle up underneath me. He hit what I'd have to call an "oh shit" spot and before I could even think to try to stop him or distract myself, it was done and I didn't even know how the fuck he did it. I ain't never in my life tried so hard to fight my own body.

"Ooh fuck," escaped through my clenched teeth while I tried to hide and enjoy the small ripples running up and down my legs and through my back.

"What's that, are you okay?" Big paused and leaned down next to my ear.

"Hmm, me? Yeah." I was damn near out of breath. "I thought your li'l fish down there was fuckin' or fightin'. I don't know; it was weird. They stopped though. Whew, I'm good. Get back to rubbin'."

He went back to work and all the while I was damn sure my nails were going to leave little half moon–shaped marks in the leather of the massage chair.

This nigga actually made me cum without dickin' me down or even going near my pussy, what the hell? No wonder white folk fly off and get this shit every damn week.

"You got a frequent flyer card or something like that?" I asked later, jokingly, but serious as hell.

Big laughed, handing me a shiny gold and white card. "After your fifth massage you get a free deep tissue or a facial with a seaweed wrap. It's up to you."

Mmm hmm, I'll take a free deep anything you're offering. Realizing I was just standing there stuck in a post-climatic-day-dream, I snapped myself back to reality.

"So how long will you be in town? I ain't trying to let no strangers rub all over me."

"I'm here for another month or so. Winter is probably slow so I'll head back to VA and relax. Come through sometime; we need to catch up. You need to work out or look into some serious stretching. That area around your S4, S5 lower spine felt a little tight."

We exchanged numbers; and to hell with that Big Baby foolishness, I saved his shit under Big Daddy.

Chapter 3

It's All Fake-Believe Anyway

Shame on me for putting my phone on silent, I'd missed a million texts and calls from Angelo's ass. He was just gonna have to learn that I wasn't the one for that whole "text tracking" bullshit. Text tracking is when a nigga calls or texts every ten minutes and then waits to see if you reply in "ain't fuckin' somebody else" amount of time. No, we were not about to play that game. I had enough on my mind as it was.

I Googled S4 and S5 on the way home. Those were discs in the spine that controlled sexual function. The smile that spread across my face was damn near impossible to control from that moment forward. I walked up into our penthouse, trying to erase the smug grin off my face.

Big must have gone and enrolled himself in Game 101 while he was getting that massage degree, because he used to have zero.

Leaning up against the door, inhaling the rose oil and mint still on my skin, I closed my eyes and just stood there for a minute. He'd looked so damn good, and his hands—

"Look who finally decided to waltz in. We've been waiting for you."

My eyes shot open at the sound of Don Cerzulo Campelli's gruff voice. He was actually in our living room, propped up on our couch with a brandy snifter in his hand. I'd have known that voice anywhere. He was one of the most famous actors in the world and he was here, talking to me. Sir'Tavius would kick my ass if he ever found out I met Don Cerzulo Campelli and I didn't have on not one piece of snaparazzi or any makeup. He was probably here to consider me for another role, and here I come all sweaty, mismatched, smellin' like straight-up wet padussy. Thanks to Big my panties were soaked, and I wasn't about to walk all the way home like that. They had to come off, so in my jacket pocket was where they sat soppin' wet and everything.

Suddenly feeling embarrassed and beyond self-conscious I looked down and kicked myself. *Out of all the days to wear flip-flops with my polish chipped and lookin' crazy, I'd pick this one. Smooth move, real smooth.*

"Honey, I tried callin' like, I don't know how many times." Angelo came in from the kitchen.

"Yeah, my phone died *sweetie.*" I emphasized that shit and gave him a funky, fake smile stare down, praying Don Cerzulo would think we were just calling each other pet names. Angelo was gonna make me take to burning his ass with cigarettes or something. Maybe the negative association would help him get my damn name right.

"Well, I'd like to introduce you to my father. He helped make all of this happen and now you know why it was easy, but not so easy."

Don Cerzulo's expression was unreadable as he inclined his head gradually in acknowledgment of our introduction. Angelo's father, aka the head of the family, aka the fuckin' Angel of Death in the flesh, was in my living room. His second name was because he stayed on some straight-up hermit shit, hiding from every agency on the planet. The story Angelo had told me about his father's name was that the only time anyone ever saw the Angel of Death . . . well, let's just say he was the last person they saw. How he managed to hide that part of his life from the world was a mystery to me, but I guessed that's why he was who he was.

Angelo walked over, his face furrowed up in a frown. "You shouldn't have left the way you did. I was tryin' to—"

"What Angelo is trying to say is, money isn't everything, but in this day and age time is our most valuable commodity and sweetie, *my time is money.*" The Don's fat fingers slid his suit jacket away from his watch and he tsked at it in disappointment.

"Waiting on you has cost me more than you'll ever be worth in this lifetime."

My throat tightened and I felt lightheaded, my stomach knotted up and that zucchini I'd fixed for dinner wanted out of my stomach, but I couldn't tell which end it wanted out of. The Angel of Death didn't make special appearances, and Angelo was just standing quietly, looking pale and sweaty. In the time it would take me to open the door a bullet could be in my head. I ain't escape prison to go out like this. Paris was going to see me and know my name, touch my face. I was a cornered Rottweiler ready to rip their throats out with my teeth if I had to.

"Angelo, son, get over here and be done with this. I told the family I'd see this business through and here I am. So *andiamo*."

Reaching behind me slowly, I began to pull down on the the door lever. It was the only chance I had. Angelo moved closer to me as Don Cerzulo began to stand.

I twisted the handle, and had barely turned to pull the door open when it hit me like a tidal wave.

"Honey, my Desivita, will you marry me?" Angelo dropped down on one knee and stared up at me through nervous, pleading eyes.

My mind could have been playing tricks on me, but I'd have sworn his hands were shaking when my eyes focused on and confirmed what was, in fact, a ring. Wide-eyed and caught off-guard, I quickly looked over at Don Cerzulo in a panic for help, or advice, or I didn't even know.

Marry him? Marry Angelo? I can't, we don't even know each other that well. You're supposed to know a person for years before you marry them. Be in the love, see stars and fireworks, and hear orchestras when you kiss.

Don Cerzulo gave me a quick, tight nod and I'd have been a damn fool if I ain't think he wasn't telling me to say yes or else.

What the hell could I do?

"Of course, baby." I gave Angelo a crazy smile- grimace combo as my thoughts drifted to a man I hadn't seen in ages, with hands that could give me goose bumps and make me moan.

"Mmm, I don't wanna fight. I love you like I've never loved anyone. *Il mio cuore*, you have my heart." Angelo stood and nuzzled my neck before smiling down at me, and I tried to my damndest to smile back.

"What is this on you that smell so good? You buy it today?" he asked.

Still flustered, I could barely piece together a lie. "Uh, just something I saw at one of the boutiques. It was sold out. Um, I just tried it on."

I broke away from him, removing my jacket and setting my things on the stand by the door.

"Tell me which boutique and I'll get it for you; nothing is sold out to us." Angelo was following me like a puppy.

"Never mind all that."

Don Cerzulo smoothed his silver-tipped sideburns as he came up to me. Do you know what money smells like? No, I don't mean them dollars fresh from the bank, but real money. It smells like sweet cherry pipe tobacco and the Wilson's leather jacket shop at Christmas time.

Don Cerzulo had it unconsciously flowing off of him in waves like some kind of high frequency luxury radiation. I wanted that. My body didn't have a price anymore. No more pullin' the G-string to the side and fuckin' niggas on the low during lap dances. If I played this shit at the right angle, Don's paper could easily be my paper.

Don Cerzulo spoke softly. "Just so we's clear on a few things, I don't feel any particular way about the death of the boy's half siblings. His mother's a spiteful cunt; her elevator may not go all the way to the roof." He jabbed his finger into my temple for emphasis. "But, still spiteful. And yes, you're protected now, but she's a ruthless bitch. Watch your front, side, back, 'cause she don't respe—"

"Hey now, Pop, nice to see yous two chattin' it up. Feels good."

Angelo walked over grinning, and I damn near screamed at his bad timing.

"Yeah, well, this old man still has to go dig in the dirt. Got a few money trees that need bodies underneath 'em to grow. Finish that drink for me, son. I'm sure you two want to celebrate." Don Cerzulo winked at me, straightening his suit jacket.

"Ah, maybe later. Give me a ride out, Pop. I need to see a man about a horse." Angelo took his glass and handed it to me, smiling mischievously.

Huh, this fool ain't want no ass? What the hell kinda shit is going on up in here?

Confused, I just stood there as he gave me a quick peck on the cheek before grabbing his things and leaving. I stared down at the rock on my finger, admiring it and hating it at the same time.

How the hell did I get myself into this bullshit? I wasn't trying to marry this fool and have his babies. There was only one nigga I thought of like that and it was Rah. Only reason I even entertained Derrick's ass was to show the nigga that somebody else would take care of home if he didn't. I needed a Percocet or a Vicodin, somethin'.

My cell rang on the stand by the door. "Yeah," I answered without looking.

"Are we meeting or not, my dear?" a woman cooed seductively in my ear.

Confused, I pulled the phone from my ear. Of course, the number was unavailable.

"Meeting? I ain't meetin' nobody. I think you got the wrong number," I snapped into the phone.

I scrolled through my contact list looking for Big's number. I for real needed to talk to someone about all this marriage foolishness; maybe he could give me some kind of advice.

Psssht. Whatever, you know yo' ass just want that nigga to give you a reason to run away or creep on Angelo. All he gotta do is say the words.

Smiling at the thought, I paused, trying to remember what the hell name I saved him under. When I realized I was past the Bs my heart stopped and restarted itself. I cursed so loud the people on the street probably heard my ass. This wasn't my phone. Angelo's dumb ass picked up my phone by accident on his way out. Why did we have to have the same exact fucking model? I gulped down the drink in my hand. When that ain't make me feel any better I launched the empty glass against the wall.

He never left out this late at night, and he never mentioned a meeting with no damn woman. Cheatin'-ass motherfucka. We could have gotten a third wheel if he wanted to
play. I'd done a couple girl-on-girl strip parties back in the
day. It'd been nothin' to get a cute plaything for a few nights;
hell, it'd take some of the boring sex stress off me. But this . . .
this mistress shit wasn't happenin', not on my watch.

Even though you was ready to let Big get it, that's ironic.
Karma maybe?

No, Angelo was fuckin' with the wrong one.

Chapter 4

Warm Kitty, Soft Kitty,
Little Ball of Fur . . .

The house had been buzzing with activity, and the last officer had finally come and gone. Trey was upstairs in my bed. He'd finally worn himself out crying over not being able to keep that damn cat. I'd have to go find him a puppy or a goldfish as soon as possible to make up for it. The chance of that thing being microchipped with a tracker or something crazy was too much of a risk. It was almost four in the morning and Towanna was about as frazzled as I was, if not more so.

"Towanna, you gonna be okay?" I approached her timidly. She was sitting in the darkened kitchen, nursing a drink. She rarely drank, but you'd never know that from looking at the half-empty vodka bottles on the table.

"Fuck if I know. Been in damn near twelve years and I ain't never lost a partner before."

She wouldn't even look at me and it made me feel a hundred times worse. I'd forewarned her about taking us in. Death and danger had been my damn best friends these last few years.

"What's in the glass?" I nodded, trying to move to something lighter since I was too choked up to apologize for her loss and too stressed to think of more to say.

"Pixy Stix. Cherry, grape, and watermelon. Three Olives. One and some change parts each."

"Damn, that sounds a little too potent for me; can I just tap one of your bottles?"

She scooted one toward me and I tipped it to my lips, frowning and gasping because that mess tasted like straight-up Robitussin.

"You such a fuckin' lightweight. Go get ya ass one of the kids' juice boxes out the got-damn fridge. Wastin' my shit," she growled, snatching the bottle right out of my hand.

"The hell I am; you just an angry-ass somebody when you drink." I snatched the bottle back, ready to smack her ass with it one good time if she kept this bullshit up. Her anger set off my own temper and I went from sad to furious in a heartbeat. "You can't hold this shit against me, Towanna. Yes . . . I'm sorry about your partner, I really am. But don't you go turning into no asshole over something you volunteered for. I ain't come to you for help, you came to me." I scowled at her and took a long swig. Visions of glass shattering all up the side of her head made me feel a little better as I imagined using it to literally knock some sense into her. How dare she cop that kind of attitude with me?

"Michelle, why you gotta be so damn selfish and shit?" Towanna sprang up out of her seat. Her hands were fisted at her sides and I gripped that bottle, ready to go to war. Everybody handles death and alcohol differently, and in my opinion, she wasn't handling either one well.

She was fast. Even intoxicated she managed to lash out and get the upper hand. The heffa moved with Bruce Leroy–esque lightning speed. The bottle was wrestled from my fingers before I could even raise it. She was also stronger than I imagined. A picture of me in the emergency room trying to explain two broken wrists flashed through my head as she bent my wrists back in a painful vise grip, wrapping her arms around me, pinning my arms behind my back. Tears welled up in the corners of my eyes from the pain.

"I risked my life and Ennis gave his!" she yelled in my face, spraying tiny speckles of Pixy Stix–scented spit onto my skin.

"Really, you think I don't know that shit? Let me the fuck go, Towanna. You have a right to be upset, but you need to shut up. The officer they've got posted outside might hear you, and you're gonna wake up the kids," I replied quietly, setting my own anger aside to give her a wide-eyed look of warning.

Towanna didn't pay me any mind; she just replied in outrage, "You think you the only one with kids? What about Ennis's kids?" She shook me, her face twisted in anger before pulling me into a tight python death squeeze of a hug. "Man, you so damn selfish. He could have kept that kitten. You can't even see when someone in love with your ass. When someone would do anything for you, risk they life for you and your kids." Towanna's voice had transformed into a warm whisper against the side of my neck.

Her grip loosened on my wrists, but she kept my arms pinned behind me. My breath caught in my chest. I struggled to wrap my angry mind around her avalanche of words and feelings.

Just keep piling it on there, buddy. I already feel like shit about Ennis and now we're gonna add love into the equation, too.

"Towanna, you don't even know me well enough to be in love. If so, then you'd know my auntie had a black cat named Lucky that tormented the hell out of me when I was little. He could open doors and everything, would pee on me when I was asleep. I hate cats. My favorite color is sky blue. And I like girly drinks that make me feel pretty when I say them: Bellini, Tequila Sunrise, piña colada . . ."

The liquor, the drama, her closeness were all overwhelming. How was I even supposed to respond to something like that? Who the hell dropped a love confession in the middle of an argument? Confused and tired I dropped my head onto her shoulder for lack of anything else to say. I wasn't ready to think about love or talk about love. When the time was right I just wanted to fall and have them fall right back.

Larissa could barely reach my neck unless she was standing on something or I was sitting down. Those were my exact thoughts as surprisingly soft lips brushed against the side of my neck.

You can't cheat on the dead right? Then why did this feel so wrong?

Her fingers massaged my wrists in the places that she'd most likely bruised. I was still a little pissed off, and scared, definitely frustrated beyond reason.

I shook my head against her shoulder. "Pin them back like you had them and bite my neck."

Maybe it won't feel like cheating or I won't feel as bad if it hurts.

My breath hissed from in between my teeth as she did as directed. I closed my eyes, the world went spinning, and I let myself enjoy that sinfully erotic feeling that comes with a little bit of pain. When she alternated sides I moaned and bit her back, smiling against her neck when she gasped in shock. Towanna leaned back and looked at me, surprised at my brazenness.

Yes, sweetheart, momma can get rough too. Don't let the look fool you.

My expression was guarded but my thoughts were X-rated. She was so close I could see the light dusting of freckles along her cheeks, and the copper flecks in her eyes. I made the mistake of letting my gaze drop down to her lips. I had the worst weakness for some pretty-ass lips.

Completely giving up and giving in, I kissed her. She tasted like plums and Pixy Stix, and if I wasn't tipsy yet her lips were getting me the rest of the way.

"Fuck all the misery out of me." I actually moaned that into her lips. I didn't mean to say it. That wonderful thought bubble slipped out of my head and hung in between us like a fog cloud.

I might as well have said "abracadabra." No sooner had the words left my mouth, than my robe came off, her belt buckle clinked, and our clothes vanished.

She sat down in one of the wooden kitchen chairs, pulling me down to straddle her lap. We both giggled when it teetered under our weight. The legs were uneven thanks to Trey's handiness. He'd taken all the screws out of the thing one day when he was supposed to be taking a nap. I'd put it back together but it just wasn't exactly the same after that.

The giggling stopped when Towanna's lips made a journey from my earlobe down my neck. She blazed a hiking trail with her tongue. Goose bumps rose like the tiny marks hikers leave on trees. If she lost her way in the dark she could always follow the trail back to my lips. I couldn't stay still, and I damn sure couldn't be quiet. Parts of me were waking up that had been lying dormant for months. She went from my neck to my nipples as her hand slid down in between us.

Fuck, when was the last time I shaved? She's probably gonna think I'm some kind of hippie cavewoman.

"Mommy?"

The sound of Trey's voice snuffed all of the flames in a small whisper of cold water. Thankfully the power was still out so the kitchen was dark. I got dressed with lightning speed and snatched up my robe before scooping him up, heading toward my room.

"What's the matter, baby?" We were almost fully up the stairwell.

He was already dozing off on my shoulder. His voice was quiet and groggy from sleep. "I woke up an' you were gone. Da man in my room said go find you."

My foot slipped and I almost missed a step. Fear shot through my chest, stopping me like a brick wall. "Trey? Baby, were you having a dream?" I whispered shakily next to his ear as I stood frozen in place one step away from the landing.

"No," he whispered, shaking his head into my neck.

A chill ran down my spine and my ears rang from straining against the silence in the house. Warning bells chimed in my head. In those seconds it felt like I was torn in half.

Get Lataya or go get Towanna? Pull the gun out of my robe pocket or leave it concealed just in case?

Something rustled at the bottom of the stairs and I turned slightly, thankful Towanna had pulled it together. The warning was on the tip of my tongue when those warning bells jumped out of my head and manifested in front of me.

"Snowball." Trey squirmed, suddenly wide awake as we both laid eyes on the kitten. It tiptoed out of the shadows of my bedroom, and instinctively I backed down a step. We'd sent that cat off with the cops. There was no way it could have gotten into the house. The blue ribbon had been replaced with a small golden bell attached to a red collar. It jingled softly but in my mind it was as loud as bells ringing from a church tower.

"Towan—"

I called for help but it was too late. Pain exploded in the back of my head and the world lit up in a burst of bright flashes before everything went dark.

Chapter 5

Houdini Who?

"Chelle? Michelle . . ."

Towanna's voice was a faint murmur against the jackhammer trying to crack through my skull as I came to. Something, a pillowcase maybe, was thrown over my head. Panic flooded back over me. My hands were tied together behind me and from the sting in my ankles my feet were bound too.

"Did you see who did this? Where are they and where are the kids? Please don't tell me they got the kids," I whispered anxiously into the darkness.

"Don't know. Someone must have come up behind me right after you left. One sec I'm watching you walk away, man, and then it was dark and shit. I heard voices earlier, been quiet for a minute though."

"If they hurt my babies I swear . . ." My words were cut off by the tortured wail building up in my throat. I groaned as an alternative to screaming my frustration.

"You been out for a good while. I started countin' when I heard the front door close. 1,320 seconds. That's about twenty-somethin' minutes right?"

I waited for her to say more, and when she didn't, I prepared myself for the worst. No one would go through this much trouble just to tie us up and leave. Trey was in my arms what seemed like moments ago and now this.

"Michelle, I need you to stay calm, okay?"

"Towanna, am I not sittin' here calmly right now? You ever seen a woman get assaulted, wake up with a sack over her head, kids MIA, and be as fuckin' calm as I am right now?" I'd been clenching my teeth and fightin' one hell of a headache. The harder my heart beat, the more it hurt.

"No, see, I kind of overheard some shit. They was whisperin' about you comin' up off some drug money you stole or somethin' like that. Man, I think the plan is to hold the kids and ask for a ransom."

Did she just say stolen money and ransom in the same sentence? I ain't steal a dime of what I took from Rah. That was my money; hell, most of it was even in my name. I worked, cried, and bled for that money.

"There wasn't no drug money. I don't know where they would have gotten that info from."

She sighed from somewhere beside me and I could tell she was frustrated and probably more scared than I was. Her partner had already given his life and she was probably worrying about following in his footsteps.

"Shit, Michelle, man. If there ain't any money you're . . . we're gonna have to come up with something. I can't do this by myself, yo. Think about it, is there anywhere that nigga might have hid the money?" She sounded frazzled and on the verge of panicking.

"No, not that I can think of. I've got my own money. I can pay damn near whatever they ask."

I sure won't about to tell her what I'd done. Those grimy little details went to the grave with Larissa and Rah, and I wasn't about to unbury them for anyone. Not even Towanna.

She got quiet for a minute, so quiet that I thought she might have passed out or died on me.

"You hurt? You are okay, right? I didn't even think to ask you earlier. I'm just so worried about my babies. I'm sorry." Speaking into the pitch black, not being able to see her reaction or condition, felt awkward as hell.

"It's cool, I understand. Think I'm still tipsy and that knock upside the head ain't help. Everything's catchin' up with me. Gonna close my eyes for a sec."

"You can't go to sleep. What if you have a concussion? You might not wake up. They might come back any second and—"

"And, I ain't gonna be any good if I'm tired. Just too much adrenaline for one day, man. Count to a thousand and then whisper or something. That'll wake me up."

I'd started to tell her again that sleep wasn't a good idea but she had a point. If we couldn't do anything at the moment, she could at least get some rest. Straining against the silence I contended with counting the beeps from the alarm system every sixty seconds. Somewhere around 3:19, the front door opened.

"Oh shit, Towanna, I think they're back."

My heart was in my throat and I squeezed my eyes shut to block out the feeling of helplessness. There was a presence beside me. I could feel it there staring down at me. It didn't make a sound and I felt lightheaded from holding my breath listening. The air around me shifted and I could tell it'd moved away. The beeping from the alarm system felt like sonar. It pinged crystal clear, and whenever the person moved in front of me the sound was deadened just slightly.

If they gonna kill me, let 'em do it and get it over with. All this waiting was pissing me off just as much as it was scaring me.

"Hey, hey don't fuckin' touch me! Get your hands off me. I ain't got nothin' for you and neither does she." Towanna's shouts went silent with the sickening thud of something connecting with flesh.

Lord, let her be unconscious and not dead. This isn't going to end this way; it can't. Not after everything I've been through.

It was so still and quiet in the house. I couldn't stop the scream that shot out of my throat as rough hands dug into my skin. The small metal buttons from my pajama top sounded like jacks as they scattered across the floor. It might as well have been ten degrees in the house from the way I was shaking. Air whooshed against my exposed skin as my shirt and robe were slid off my shoulders.

Is a gun on me right now? Stay calm, gotta stay calm. The worst they can do is hurt the kids. I can handle anything anyone does to me as long as they're safe.

I bit the inside of my cheek so hard I tasted blood as my bottoms were yanked down to my ankles. Bracing myself, I waited for what I knew was coming.

These niggas won't gettin' the satisfaction of seeing or hearing me beg for mercy or my life. I'll scream and cry in

*my head before I do it out loud. God, why couldn't I just have
a fair fight at least once in my life?*

My chair was tilted back and I could hear the rustle of plastic being slid underneath me before I was lowered to the floor.

I could see the headlines in the papers already: MICHELLE LAUREL FOUND BRUTALLY RAPED AND MURDERED IN POLICE OFFICER'S KITCHEN. All the years I'd lived secretly fearing how or when I'd die. Wondering what day God stamped over my life like an expiration label. It wasn't like in the movies. There's no superhero or heroic neighbor who bursts in to save your ass at the last second. No bomb goes off and no fights break out. There's no random act of kindness by your captor that suddenly sets you free. It's all you, and for the first time through the entire ordeal, I quietly cried.

Something feather soft brushed up against my cheek, sliding around my shoulders and across my back. There was a soft meow beside my ear and I knew they had Trey. Something moved along my feet in the plastic. They were teasing me with a damn kitten, really? I was hurled back into bed at my aunt's, trapped staring up into Lucky's demonic yellow-orange eyes while he sat on-top of my chest growling. The sound of plastic over my head had me waiting for a knife, gunshot, or the raping to start.

The air was starting to get stifling hot all around me and I thought I'd suffocate when I heard Trey's voice beside me.

"Mommy, where is the money?" His little singsong voice made my chest heave.

Pinned beneath my own body weight, my arms began to throb and ache.

"Mommy, they don't like closed bags." Someone had to be coaching him. There was a click and I thanked God it was some kind of recording and he wasn't there in person seeing me like this as the first question was played back for me. Shaking my head, I refused to answer. *They might as well kill me now.*

And then, a hiss split the air so close to my ribs I could feel it on my bare skin. Another hiss responded on the opposite side of me, like one you'd hear at the zoo or on National Geographic. It was very distinct, unmistakable, and sheer, absolute terror set in.

Oh, dear God, please help me. Please don't let that be a snake, it couldn't be. I could barely breathe. Fear sent tiny darts of pain to the center of my chest every time I tried to inhale. I was so tense I flinched out of reflex. Something moved, making the plastic crackle underneath it as it brushed up against my side. It slithered against me with cool rubbery winding motions, touching and moving away as it traveled along my body. *There are snakes in here! God, get them out, get me out. Please don't let them be poisonous.*

"Mommy, they don't like closed bags." Trey's voice was almost my undoing. It was an eerily familiar and loving soundtrack to my gruesome execution.

His voice played over and over, yet I still didn't speak. I couldn't make a sound; terror had frozen my vocal chords, capsized my lungs, and locked all my muscles. My worst nightmare had come true and the living hell of reality made my dream seem like a fairy tale in comparison. The bag rustled like someone'd hit or kicked it and I jumped as if I'd been shocked. Pain tore through my side as my skin was slashed open. I screamed. The snakes were . . .

"Mommy, where is the money?"

There were at least three different hisses. There was so much movement on either side of me and I screamed again as something slid across my chest and something else . . .

My arms were going numb beneath me. All the danger, the slithering and hissing, was getting closer and closer to my neck and shoulders. There was more movement around my feet. Fur brushed against my toes.

Snakes and cats? What the fuck? Who the fuck does something like this?

Hyperventilation set in when there was slithering across my neck and shoulders as well as in between my legs. Without my clothes I was vulnerable, exposed to every claw and strike. The cat hissed, or it could have been the snake as my shoulder was ripped open. Stress made my body heat rise. It turned the inside of that plastic bubble into a plastic hell as Trey's voice resonated all around me.

"I took the money. I did." I sobbed softly, afraid the cats would taunt the snakes and I'd get clawed or bitten again. "Invested it into my business and put the rest away. It'll take me at least a day to withdraw it all from the different accounts."

Gut-wrenching sobs shook me down to my soul. The bag was cut open and my chair was pulled up off the floor. My skin stung from where I was bitten or clawed and my arms felt like they'd been stomped on repeatedly.

"I luh you, Mommy. See you later." Treys voice clicked off and the front door closed. There's no telling how long I'd sat there, scared a snake or something would still be coiled up at my feet. Towanna was possibly dead. I had no idea which animal attacked me, if it was poisonous or anything. My nose started bleeding. The blood trickled down to my upper lip, tickling my face. My nose itched and it wasn't one of those nice easy-to-ignore itches either. I squirmed uncomfortably, trying to lean my head so I could rub my nose across my shoulder. The chair rocked and hope swelled up in my chest, making me forget all about my injuries and the snakes.

Bending my wrist as far as I could I grabbed one of the rungs on the back of the chair and twisted. It yielded quietly and I almost shouted to the rooftop. This was the chair I'd half-assed put back together. I'd managed to twist both rungs off and was holding them behind my back when I realized I needed to let them bitches go in order to untie my hands. Excitement and trepidation coursed through my veins. Hopefully I could get out before they got back. With any luck they didn't leave a watchdog or a guard out there.

I let the chair rungs slide down my hands slowly until they stopped moving. Giving up a silent prayer I let them go and they fell soundlessly. My chair must have been just on the edge of the area rug under the kitchen table.

After undoing my wrist, I yanked what I discovered was in fact a pillowcase off my head in a "swish moment." That's what I call it when you celebrate with yourself for doing something extraordinary. It could be catching your phone midair before it hits the floor, or tripping on stairs and keeping your balance.

My celebration was short-lived as the familiar ocean of dread swept in and washed away my smile. Towanna wasn't sitting beside me anymore. She was nowhere to be found. I pulled my clothes back on as best I could and I crept into the living room on wobbly legs. She protected me when I needed it, welcomed me and my kids into her home. It was my turn to return the favor and find and protect Towanna.

Chapter 6

Always Beware of the Jellyfish

The streetlights filtered in through the blinds in the living room, making yellow-orange slashes across the floor. The clock on the wall ticked like it was attached to an amplifier. Relieved there were no blood trails on the carpet, I looked for any other signs of Towanna as I made my way toward the main window. Her eyes followed me as I passed pictures of her with her family. The bright gold R for "Respect" winked at me at the bottom of the frame. It was her mother's favorite song, Towanna told me. She and her brothers didn't look anything like their father. They were all replicas of their mom; she was beautiful.

My plan was simple: find out if these assholes were still around, and how many of them were in between Towanna, me, and the kids. Okay, so maybe that really wasn't a plan. It was more of an outline, because I wasn't exactly sure how I'd get to or past anyone, but it was a start.

I parted one of the blinds with shaky fingers. The sky was turning violet-blue and birds were just beginning to chirp here and there. I guessed I was expecting to see black SUVs and BMWs lining the driveway. Yet they must have rolled out pretty quick because there wasn't a single car—

"Michelle? What the hell you doing out here?"

Jumping at the sound of my name I turned, excited and alarmed at the same time. Towanna was sitting up on the couch looking perfectly fine and confused as hell. I hobbled over, intent on giving her a hug.

"Towanna, I was worried as hell about you, woman. When I heard you get hit and then I got loose and you were gone . . ."

I stopped not five feet from her as my brain caught up with what I was seeing. We analyzed each other, both of us trying to sum up all of the events.

"How did you get out here, Towanna?" There was no point in even trying to hide the suspicion in my voice.

Her shoes were off and tucked side by side neatly beside the couch, there wasn't even a visible bruise or scratch anywhere on her.

"Man, I just woke up on the couch out here and saw you over there lookin' out the damn window and shit." She shrugged. "Head hurts like a bitch though."

"Why would you be out here all cozy on the damn couch, when you were just tied up in the kitchen with me, Towanna?"

"Man, what the hell you tryin' to say?" Towanna threw her hands up in frustration and sat back, glowering at me.

It wasn't like we just went through hell together and I was giving her the fifth degree. No, no, no. I went through hell and walked in on what looked like her taking a nap. Something was up, and it was making me want to throw furniture at her ass. *Ten, nine, eight.* I counted down to keep myself from trying to choke her ass out. I knew I was being irrational, especially since she could take me down with a wrist-grab. If she had anything to do with what I just went through, on my life, I'd make her pay. My insides shook as I paced the couch in front of her staring her down out the corner of my eye.

"Towanna, where the fuck are my kids? I'm not playing with you."

"Man, Michelle—"

I was so over this shit. "Trey!" I shouted his name at the top of my lungs and headed for the stairs.

There was a noise behind me. It was a mixture between a war cry and a bloodcurdling howl. The full brunt of Towanna's weight crashed into my back, knocking me off balance with the impact of a battering ram. She must have built up a ton of momentum, because I swear she collided with me in a thunderous crash. The sound ricocheted throughout the house. It left me dazed and knocked the breath out of my lungs. Pinned beneath her weight with my face pressed into the carpet, I could hear the kids crying for me from upstairs.

It was all over faster than a knife fight in a phone booth. Towanna didn't seem to be moving. My gun had gone off when she knocked me down. I pulled myself from underneath her and she moaned softly.

"Anyone up there wit' them I need to know about?" I asked, my voice breathless and shaky from fury and fear.

I kicked her when she didn't answer, but she didn't move. In the future I'd have to remember to be a better judge of people. Nobody's willing to help you for free. She probably knew about Rah's money the entire time. I should have known better than to put my trust in someone in law enforcement. The world is full of jellyfish, and even though you think you'll be able to see right through their fake asses, you still have to be careful. They'll sting the hell out of your ass the second you let them get too close.

I stepped over her lying ass and I couldn't even feel sorry for her. I'd lived with her for a year now and not once had she used "man," "shit," and "yo" more times than when she was obviously lying to me. I tsked at her like I couldn't believe she'd killed her own partner and tried to play me for a damn fool.

No one would have ever believed what happened up in here. Not in a million years. It was time for me and the kids to make moves.

Chapter 7

Listen, Time Will Tell Every Time

The sky outside was fading from black into the soft blues of morning. It was almost five a.m. when Angelo crept in. I'd gone through his entire phone, e-mails, voicemails, texts, and all. Either he was overly cautious, or actually up to something, because everything was empty or deleted. His contact list didn't even have real names. I'd searched for my number first and it was listed under Acts 5. Jimmy One Side was the only other number I knew because I'd called him a few times. He was under 2 Judges 16. The list went on and the more I scrolled the more creeped out I got. Angelo didn't even own a Bible. He was raised Catholic but never went to Mass.

Reluctantly, I'd given up and set his phone back on the stand by the door. I prayed Angelo hadn't gone through my texts. Hopefully Big hadn't tried to call or anything while he was out with my phone. It would have been easy to cover up the text he sent earlier if that shit ain't come from "Big Daddy."

It took everything I had not to get up and go off on his ass. He'd gone straight to the bathroom and gotten in the shower. Suspect. When he finally decided to ease his ass up in the bed I pretended to be sleep. As expected, Angelo wrapped his frigid limbs around me, tryin' to steal my body heat. He started grindin' on my ass and I rolled my eyes to myself. I knew he ain't think he was about to hump all up on me after he'd been who knew where.

"Where'd you go? You never stay out this late," I quietly grilled him.

"Nowhere for you to be worried about. I had to take care of some things."

He nuzzled my neck and I brushed him off.

"We can't right now, think my cycle's about to start. I got cramps."

"Want me to go get the towel?" He winked at me, and I just rolled my eyes and rolled over. No, I didn't want him to go get no damn towel. I don't know how much time passed before he finally fell asleep. But it was the only thing ticking down in my head with the clock on the mantel piece in front of the bed as I waited. I slid out of the bed and found his pants. This fool had the pocket mentality of a five-year-old. It took me four tries to find my phone among the clutter of a pocket knife, casino token, zip ties, screws, a slip of paper that listed every poisonous plant in Florida and its side effects, and spare gun clip.

Add a dump truck, Yoo-hoo cap, and a lucky dinosaur and I got two kids . . .

He shifted in his sleep and I flattened myself out on the floor, not even taking a breath. I was on straight-up ninja assassin mode trying to get to that damn phone.

I went into the kitchen and checked my texts, e-mails, and incoming and outgoing calls. Thankfully there was nothing there from Big Daddy, and Sir'Tavius had sent thousands of outfits that he wanted me to consider for my next public appearance. I did a double take as a new messages came through.

Desivita, picking you up at eight p.m. Wear a nice skirt or dress and heels. We are going to an audition. I will meet you downstairs. Don

Des Call Time 8 a.m. check your e-mail for directions Do Not Be Late

It was cool outside and felt more like early spring instead of late fall. Since all they were going to do was take me out of my clothes and throw me in wardrobe, I just threw on a sweatshirt with some jeans and my winged high-top Adidas. Angelo threw on an instant attitude at having to be up so soon after getting his "sneaking around doing what the fuck ever" self in the bed. I'd told him to give me the keys. I didn't need him chauffeuring me all over the place.

As a matter of fact it was time I got a car of my own anyway. *It would be easier for me to deal with Michelle, among other things, without my real-life stunt double following me around.* Angelo acted all kinds of insulted, offered to get me a driver and whatever kind of car I wanted. He wasn't fooling anyone though; he was paranoid about who or what I'd do if I could get around without him and it was obvious. We didn't speak the rest of the way to the set.

The set was a warehouse beside a boat marina that they'd transformed into several scenes. We passed through a club dance floor, next to a back alley that looked like it was plucked right up from outside with manhole covers and a dumpster. There were swarms of actors, extras, and stagehands all over the place.

"My Queen Midas has graced us with her golden glemmied presence. You will win me a Globe and an Emmy? You will Glemmy my movie?"

I could only nod yes at this mountain of a woman who reminded me of an Amazonian warrior goddess. I immediately regretted not studying my script, because she looked like she had a bull-whip or a cattle prod hidden somewhere to torture disobedient actors. And she'd enjoy it, too.

"Don't feel special, newbie, she says that shit to everyone," Sadira called out.

She prowled toward us like a wanton alley cat. Angelo's scent, shit any man's scent probably, grabbed her attention within a ten-mile radius. It took all the refinement and etiquette training I had not to whoop her ass right then and there as she basically eye-fucked my fiancé. Angelo tensed beside me before letting my hand go and that almost sent me over the edge. I rolled my eyes behind her back as we fake hugged one another.

"The two of you need to go get into hair and makeup. Your first scene is dirty dancing and a boat chase," the director called out as she went to speak to a cameraman.

Angelo had all but vanished into thin air by the time I turned around, and I wasn't about to ask Sadira any damn questions. Sir'Tavius showed up just in time and we almost broke our necks simultaneously. The cause was about six feet three inches in bright yellow swimming trunks. His nomadic desert skin was oiled up and down, covering every muscle, divot, and dip. I didn't even know I was holdin' my breath until his large, bushy, barely tamed ponytail was out of sight and I exhaled.

"Uh, two questions. What the hell was the director talking about dirty dancing for, and who was that?"

"Bye, girl, because I see you ain't read ya script. A: twerkin'; and B: Kai, your stupafine costar, the one you lockin' lips with on the speedboat." Sir'Tavius gave me an "I love you, bitch, but I'm so jealous I hate you" twisted glare.

Oh wow. The twerkin', strippin', dancing, whatever they want me to do won't be a problem, but um, Kai and that body, oh, my damn. Did Angelo read my script and know about this kiss? He couldn't have.

My nerves were all over the place while I looked around for Angelo, who was still nowhere to be found. We were in such a rush I'd left my purse in the car, and my phone and my pills, everything was out there.

"What's the matter, Desi? You lookin' a little flustered, boo," Sir'Tavius asked, patting my arm.

"Nothing, I just need to calm down. Too much stress and it's too early to drink."

He nodded like he understood and took off, leaving me stranded.

"We'll be ready for you on set in an hour, Des."

The director sailed past with that announcement as Sir'Tavius reappeared, pulling me into my dressing room. He looked like he had a mouthful of feathers and was gonna burst if he didn't get to tell someone something and fast.

"Girl, I got you some happy pills." He handed me two long, oval-shaped pills.

"What are they?"

He looked down at his hand and then back up at me without blinking. I took them, swallowing those things without water like we used to do back in the day. I quickly dressed in a red cocktail dress and sat myself down. Sir'Tavius quietly worked on my hair and makeup while I watched in the mirror. Even with all the surgery, movie makeup still made me look like a completely different, different person. *Michelle would never recognize me like this. Never in a million years.*

"That's better; now you look you an actress. Um, is everything going okay? You ain't goin' over your lines or doing vocal exercises. Things all right with you and the boo?" His hands stilled in my hair and he locked eyes with me in the mirror.

I wanted a real friend outside of Big. Someone I could tell about Paris's and Angelo's funny ways.

"It's all right, he might be cheatin' he might not. Life will go on."

"Karma kicks ass. Oh, and you ain't get those from me. I stole them bitches from Sadira's purse."

"What the hell? You gave me somethin' her crazy ass takes?" I swiveled around and glared at him. "What if she saw you?"

"Pssst, please, she too busy fuckin' your man to seesaw anythang but that dang-a-lang."

"Too busy doin' what?"

I was up out that seat and dressing room so fast it's a wonder I ain't create a spark and combust from all the spritz in my hair. I planted a tight-lipped smile that said "go to hell" on my face as I marched past faces I didn't know. They all knew me and spoke or nodded in greeting.

"The director and everyone's down there; you're going the wrong way," someone pointed out.

I just nodded and kept going. The opposite of where everyone was meant I was going exactly the right way. If I'd have been thinking, I might have asked Sir'Tavius exactly where he'd seen them and why he'd waited so damn long to say something. Maybe he was waiting to see if I knew or wanted to know first; that's how some folk do. They feel you out before they give you dirt, because all they're really worried about is being held responsible if you have a complete meltdown after you find out.

I knew I had to be going full speed ahead, but the floor and even the air around me seemed to be in negative warp speed. Blinking felt like I was taking these erotic micro-naps where even though I was pissed the fuck off, my angry pulse felt good. Every time my eyes closed my heart would send a thump that shimmied down my entire body. I had to lean up against a wall for a moment to get my bearings. My ears picked up the sounds of low gasps and whispering.

Peeking around the corner I could see Sadira and Angelo on a couch. *Maybe I should let her have him and then I can get more of whatever the hell these pills are.* No, I'd just have to remind myself to ask who her supplier was after I whooped that ass. It took everything in me because gravity was working against me, but I grabbed a metal bar leaning against the wall and charged.

That's how it happened in my head anyway. What really happened is I was too woozy and uncoordinated to actually charge or attack anything. I tripped over my own feet and ferociously spilled out onto the floor in a slow-motion tumble of big hair and bright red.

"What the fuc—" Sadira shrieked.

"Cut. Cut. Did I say improvise? I didn't tell anyone to improvise. Why is she improvising? Is this how she Glemmies? Someone tell her to turn her fucking Glemmy off and stick to the script before I come out there and knock it out of her. Ruining my fucking money shots." The director's voice boomed through an overhead intercom.

I looked up as the room swayed and Kai climbed off the couch from where he was lying to help me up to my feet. Not about to be upstaged, Sadira rushed over and started making a big deal out of having her scene interrupted. They were on a closed-off portion of the set that had cameras in the ceilings, so the director could watch off screen. It was perfect for love scenes or really emotional moments. Mmm, and Kai had a mole on the left side of his neck. The lighting made his pulse flicker under his skin, and he had these teeny tiny sun brightened hairs all over his body. He seemed to be quietly studying me just as closely as I was studying him.

"We're all hanging out in my suite later. You should come by when we wrap." My eyes floated toward that fine mouth of his and I nodded. What I wouldn't give just to be that nigga's teeth. I'd get to spend all mothafuckin' day in between his lips and his tongue; you couldn't convince me that wasn't heaven.

I was about to unleash my so-called exorcised inner demon named Honey all over his fine ass. "Only if you let me climb that—"

"Um, Desi, come here, boo." Sir'Tavius snatched me up, putting his arm around my waist, quickly twirling me in the direction of my dressing room.

"I thought you said she was with my man." I glared at him out the corner of my eye.

"Okay, um if you don't know how to get in character or read scripts that's your own fault. He's your man in this movie, heffa; she tries to steal him."

"Mmm, Sir'Tavius, I don't know how or when, but I'm gonna get his ass," I shouted, suddenly amped about my new mission. *Go, team, get that ass.*

"Is that so? And who might this be?"

Sir'Tavius and I had the same exact look on our face at the same damn time, when we heard Angelo's voice. He'd been MIA all this time, and of course he'd show up now.

"She jus' going over some lines, Angelo; don't pay us no mind." Sir'Tavius to the damn rescue.

Angelo looked between the two of us with an eyebrow raised before chuckling and wandering toward the catering area.

"Tavius, I need you to help me get that ass. I'm gettin' that ass. Look at me. I grabbed him by his shoulders and stared past the swooping silver tipped lashes he was wearing. "Look in my eyes, you see this? This is my serious face, I need that ass. I need *some ass*, or I'm gonna take it from someone." I gave him a good up and down glance for emphasis. "Your legs lookin' a little muscular in them jeans, Tay. You been workin' out?" I teased him.

"Ho, no. We gonna make sure you have your purse and all the fixings from now on, because them pills got you some-where else."

"You see what I'm stuck with, though?" I pouted.

We turned and examined Angelo's departing frame, both of our heads tilting to the side.

"Ugh, him just so skinty. Do he even have a booty girl, what do you grab? Ain't no meat on the chicken. I'd break that all to pieces. Wouldn't be no more good."

"Tay, he's already been broken." I giggled, pointing myself out as the guilty, skinnny boy breaker.

Chapter 8

Red Box

Sir'Tavius promised to take me home once we finished shooting for the day and Angelo reluctantly left. We were actually done by four, and it gave me more than enough time to relax before meeting Don Cerzulo later. I borrowed a form fitting green cowl-neck dress from wardrobe to change into since I didn't have time to go home.

"Tavius, I just want you to know that I'm like five feet two-ish and my knees are in the dashboard. I still love you and your mini, golf-cart car."

"It's a Fiat, bitch. Recline the seat. I can't help that I'm always hauling Queen Etheria's wardrobe across the damn state."

We laughed and joked all the way to the hotel. By the time we got there, the crowd that had gathered out front was an apparent sign most of the cast was already inside. Sir'Tavius got me as close to the main lobby doors as possible. The last thing I needed was for Angelo to see my picture popping up all over tabloids.

"You're here, your boy Tavius hit me and said you were outside." Kai walked over, smiling. I immediately decided whatever trouble I was getting into was going to be so worth it.

He led me to a reserved elevator with double-wide golden doors. It needed a key card just to get them to open. It was strictly for access to the wing with the suites and penthouses. We went up to the one just beneath the top floor and the elevator opened up to the devil's playground.

The shades were all drawn so that even during the day it looked like it could have been midnight. In the center of his

suite was a large glass room. It glowed in a dull red. That red
room wasn't as fascinating as the people inside it.

"They can't see us. It's a sauna. Inside there's music and
they're watching themselves in mirrored glass," Kai informed
me in a soft whisper.

He grabbed my hand and led me toward it. My heels sank
into the carpet and I passed ivory furnishings with violet
lighting underneath. Whoever designed this room needed to
design some strip clubs, fertility clinics, and marriage coun-
seling offices, because from the second the elevator opened
I'd been on ten.

I stood less than four inches from Sadira, the world's
number one actress. Her face was pressed down into the
marble bench. Some big-ass football playing-looking nigga
with shoulder muscles on top of his shoulder muscles had
her pinned down by the back of her neck. My eyebrow shot
up when I thought about how bad I wanted that to be me. Kai
had walked over to the counter, and it was like watching a
calendar model twenty-four-seven.

He walked in sexy confident steps, stopped, and that sexy
unruly man ponytail of his swayed as he winked and smiled
at me. His thick pink lips wrapped around a neon green pipe
and he exhaled, ab muscles flexing as he took off his shirt.
Rewind. The nigga was behind the counter, hitting something
out of a pipe. It definitely wasn't marijuana. I'd never smelled
anything like that before. Not crack, or that fake weed salvia
shit. I had no idea what he was smoking.

I glanced back into the red room, and almost walked myself
right up in there. Shit, they wouldn't notice. There were like
four different couples going at it, and at the moment, I didn't
know if Sadira even knew she was eatin' a nigga's ass and not
pussy. No, no, she definitely looked up at him. Smiled and
stroked him with one and sucked her finger to get it nice, wet,
and wow.

"Kai, come here, boy. What the hell you in there doing?"

He jogged his ass over to me. "DMT, baby. I had to get
ready for you. You should try it."

I ain't have time to be playin' with his uber-high ass. I was
on a schedule. I wrapped my fingers in all that damn hair and

pulled him down. *Mmmm, damn.* He felt good, and I backed him up against the glass so I could watch everyone else at the same time. I licked a salty layer of sweat off his skin and he groaned. I did the same thing to the opposite side of his neck and he slammed his fist back hard against the glass.

"Shut the fuck up. I can't focus," Kai yelled, and I jumped my ass the hell back.

What the hell was this fool on? Real talk, you could practically hear grass growing out here; that booth was damn near soundproof.

He looked at me apologetically, rocking back and forth on the balls of his feet. "Not you, it's not you. They wanna show me God, Honey. He knows everything. Sees everything."

"What did you call me?" I stared at him, frozen, confused and paranoid. This had to be a joke or a set-up. *Did Angelo put him up to this?*

"I'll get one for you."

Kai walked back toward the counter and I just stood there staring at the red box in front of me. They looked like one of those paintings from Dante's *Inferno,* minus the demons. They didn't need demons to torture them. Sadira, Kai, me, we tortured ourselves. I squinted when the lights came on and waited for Kai to explain whatever he'd found to show me. The panicked screams made my feet move before my brain could process what the fuck was happening.

"Look, look up there. Who is that? She pushed Kai," people were screaming.

I quickly ducked back into the room, trying to blot the image of Kai's body sprawled across the pavement from my mind. I didn't push him. I wasn't anywhere near him. There was no way in hell I'd go down for a murder I didn't commit when I'd been getting away with real fucking murder. Panicked beyond reason, I called the only person I knew could help me.

Don Cerzulo was reclining in the back of a luxury car with limo-black windows. He gave me a warm smile as I climbed in.

"Desi, stuff like this happens all the time. DMT is some hard shit, makes you hallucinate and all kinds of stuff. Everything will be fine. I've handled it. Forget about it, okay? It's done.

We have bigger things to deal with, not even going to ask why you were at one of Kai's hotel orgies."

My eyes almost bulged out of my head. As if it wasn't bad enough that I had to call my fiancé's father to help me, the dude I was with was known for throwing shit like that.

"I had no idea that's what it was. The cast was going and I went too, Don. That was it." I shrugged, and helped myself to a glass of champagne. Twirling the stem between my nervous fingers, I stared off into space, thinking about everything and nothing at once.

"It's a sad thing," Don said quietly.

I looked away from the palm trees and whirring lights of the city flying by my window. "What's a sad thing?"

"That you can be anyone, go anywhere, and do anything. People do anything to get it and just as much to protect it. But, after a while, it all gets boring."

He looked out his window and I gulped down the rest of my champagne. *It sounds to me like someone has way too much money and too much damn free time on their hands.*

"Let's make this game interesting." Don Cerzulo sat up with a clap, rubbing his hands together. "It's time that face of yours earns its keep."

I waited as the car slowed to a stop. We were somewhere near downtown Miami, but I couldn't figure out where. I had an eerie feeling that this was going to be a little more than an acting class.

"The best actors are method actors, Desivita. They get into their roles; they live them."

The driver opened Don Cerzulo's door before I could ask him to explain, and I was speechless after that. We walked along carpet that was such a bright shade of red I was surprised a flock of jealous cardinals didn't swoop down and attack. It led us up stark white steps into an Italian-style villa that had to be the set of one of Don Cerzulo's latest movies. This romantic storybook palace had majestic arched ceilings with glistening antique chandeliers and ornate tapestries. I was in awe, and Paris would have loved it; any girl would. My ass was in love with it. All I needed was a princess dress and I'd be in business. There were a few men wandering here and there in expensive suits, looking at the art in different areas.

"All of this was done by hand. It took one man two years to duplicate the paintings from the Sistine Chapel," Don Cerzulo remarked.

I hadn't even noticed that the walls were painted and not wallpapered. Every inch was covered with an angel, cherub, or a cloud. Marble staircases with intricate gold and black leaf carvings on the railings divided the massive foyer in half.

"What in the God's name is going on in here?"

A wizened little gray-haired man came rushing in, looking around frantically. He took one glance at us, stopped cold in his tracks, and tried to turn and leave. All the men who seemed to have been so preoccupied earlier were immediately occupied with dragging him over toward me and Don Cerzulo.

"You're supposed to offer me a drink. Ask how I'm doin'. But no, thanks, and I'm doing a lot better than you're lookin' right now." Don Cerzulo chuckled.

"Business is business, Campelli. You don't break into a man's house over what goes on in the meeting room. I—"

"You, my friend, are going to make the news tomorrow. Producer-slash-movie-director Raul Scanetti commits suicide in Miami home. They're gonna find you upstairs in your little dick-complex, California king-sized bed. Pea-sized brain matter splattered all over the ceiling. Your movie is now my movie. I am the next bidder who can actually afford to produce it. By the way, this is the new star. Say hi to the man, sweetheart."

Scanetti sputtered unintelligible, gut-churning, "about to die" pity moans, and I was a nice brewing medley of "shock and what the fuck" stew. Don Cerzulo glared at me, nudging my arm, urging me to actually speak when I honestly ain't have a clue what to say. I managed to squeak out a weak "Hey," without making eye contact.

"We can fifty-fifty, seventy-thirty? Anything, it's yours," Scanetti pleaded.

Don Cerzulo nodded to one of the men, who pulled out a pistol with a suppressor on it and a set of gloves.

"Desivita, take the man upstairs. One bullet in the temple, arm fully extended or you'll get blood splatter on you. Don't touch anything on the way up or down. You will earn your keep in this family. Now go." He nodded toward the stairs.

"No, wait, please no. I've got kids and my wi . . . wife, what about her? Desivita, don't do this; you don't have to do this. I can help you." Scarletti fell to his knees, pleading with me and crying.

I looked at Don Cerzulo and shook my head no. I couldn't do this kind of shit. There wasn't any reason for me to kill this man. If it had been Rah or . . .

Don Cerzulo's face twisted into an angry snarl as he leered down at me.

"What do you thinks gonna happen to you if I don't have a use for you? Either you work for me, or you die here with him and be all over the news tomorrow as a junkie actress turnin' tricks for work."

Don Cerzulo's voice made my blood run cold, and I could feel the winds whirring of some dark, malevolent storm in my chest. It's a wonder my teeth didn't break from grinding them as hard as I was. Two men pulled Scanetti to his feet in front of me. He stood with his shoulders shaking, tears and snot hanging from his quivering chapped lips. The stench of coffee-tinged urine hit my nose full on as he pissed himself right there. I slapped on the black latex gloves while Don and his men in black snickered and laughed at him.

What I wouldn't give to be regular ass, catching a-ride-to-the-Hot-Spot Honey right about now.

Chapter 9

There's No Place Like Home

"Mommy, whose house is this?" Trey wandered aimlessly around the small, modestly furnished front porch, touching everything. Two wicker chairs sat on either side of a tiny wooden table. An old-fashioned flower can filled with dirt sat on top of it. He had that look that all little boys get when they're seriously searchin' for something to unintentionally fuck up or break. He'd settled on poking a rotting cantaloupe with a stick.

"Trey, get over here and be still. And don't you touch nothin' when we get inside or I'm wearin' that behind out. You understand me?"

He nodded, trudging over to stand beside me just as the front door opened.

I smiled my brightest smile. "Hey, Momma."

"Da hell are you? Another one of them Jehovah's Witnesses? 'Cause I told the last ones not to come back 'less they was bringin' red wine and tata chips. Look like you ain't get the message."

"Momma, it's me, Michelle. Rasheed's, um, ex-fiancée. Um, you remember our son, Trey? Your grandson?"

"Oh, Lawd, hey, baby. I'm so sorry. Time's been hard on this ol' mind. You heard what happened to my boy? Them county folk came through here askin' all kinds of questions. Couldn't even have an open casket." She sulked while looking at me through cataract-clouded eyes.

I almost broke down, apologized, and begged forgiveness for everything I'd done. It never crossed my mind how Rasheed's momma would suffer without him. I didn't kill him, but I may as well have for getting him locked up. Her nightgown was stained and frayed around the edges and her hair was haloed around her head in a short salt-and-pepper afro. Momma had always kept at least three fancy wigs with a special one for church. Without Rah paying for her medications and her bills, and left to live off the system, she looked the worse for wear. My ass should have been sending her something, even if it was anonymously.

Unfortunately, this was the only game plan I could come up with. It was a long shot. A pitch-black, blindfolded, "with no wind to guide me" type of shot but I was taking it. Virginia wasn't even on my list of relocation options, but that meant it would also be the last place anyone would ever think to look for us. If anyone did come looking, Rasheed's Momma wasn't one of the first people they'd question, and I highly doubted Honey would even risk the trip. She was, after all, a wanted woman.

For every mile I put between myself and Florida, a new question formed concerning Towanna. Things just weren't adding up, like why she'd wait over a year of establishing a fake friendship if she was after Rah's money. After I'd shot her, there'd been no news on the radio; I hadn't gotten any phone calls. I should have checked her body. Trey needed to be in school, and my business couldn't run itself. I could probably home-school him. *And strangle him in the process.* It wouldn't take long to find an acting manager to run my real estate company. I could hold web conferences to manage and check in on the manager once I got one in place. I just needed to keep my head down until I could find Honey and get her locked up again or taken out for good.

"Child, you gonna stand there and stare me down or you and my grandbaby . . . wait, you had another one?" She was staring down at Lataya, who'd just woken up in her car seat sitting near my feet.

"No. Well, I mean Rasheed did. Just not with me."

"That little red heffa ain't come from my son. Yella an' cocoa, yella an' yella, hell yella an' pitch black don't make no red baby. Was the heffa a white girl?" She furled her face up and I almost laughed out loud.

I chuckled. "Her momma is a little reddish-yellow if I recall correctly."

"That ain't Rasheed baby. I know what a White look like. Done birthed, burped, an' outlived 'em. She ain't got the White nose or the ears." She sighed heavily before continuing, "Come on in anyhow. Wit' your imposter crumb snatcher." That last part was a grumpy mumble under her breath.

"Um, Momma? Why is that rotten cantaloupe on your porch over there? You want me to throw it away for you?" I couldn't help offering; flies were buzzing around the thing and it was stinking up the entire corner where it sat.

"Hell no. It showed up one day. Don't know where it came from because I damn sure ain't ask for it. I ain't touchin' it, and don't you go touchin' it neither." She leaned in so close I could see the gray rings around her cataracts as she whispered, "I think it's a body snatcher."

All I could do was stare at her, waiting for a laugh or the punch line, but she just turned and hobbled inside ahead of us. She was dead-ass serious.

The carpet was so worn down I could barely tell the difference from being outdoors to stepping inside. It was as if I'd stepped into a dumpster with ambient lighting. I sidestepped empty soda cartons, stacks of newspapers, and piles of old lottery scratchers and empty bingo markers.

Trey tugged at my leg, put his hand around his mouth, and whispered, "Mommy, is this Oscar the Grouch's house?" His little face was all scrunched up in confusion.

I couldn't even get mad; that was a better description than what I was thinking. At least he'd asked quietly. Aside from the old newspapers and cardboard, there was the overwhelming smell of cigarette butts.

She closed the door behind us, whispering, "Child, I don't know if it's safe. Ever since they told me my baby passed, I been sensing things. Hearin' folk creepin' around outside. They are tryin' to get in my house. You saw it. They leavin' pods out there, hoping one'll snatch me up. Body snatchers and peepin' Toms. The Illustration been watchin' me."

I needed a damn minute. Here I was worried about real people and real-life threats and Momma was worried about . . .

"Wait. Momma White, are you talkin' about the Illuminati?" Our situation was bewildering enough as it was. I needed to get this craziness nipped in the bud, fast.

"Shhh. You know that pod can hear you, girl. That's exactly who I'm talkin' about."

She waddled her way through the clutter and sat down in the only clear spot on the couch. I couldn't figure out where to set Lataya's car seat and I for damn sure wasn't about to take her out of it. It was hard enough keepin' an eye on Trey's busy little fingers.

"Now, lemme see the baby toes. All the White babies have stubby, fat, li'l Flintstone-looking feet wit' a baby-dick second toe," she said matter-of-factly, crossing her arms across her chest.

Trey gasped. It was too late to cover his ears.

Shaking my head at him, my eyes silently said, "Boy, you'd bet' not repeat that." He'd better not add any of this to his already-colorful vocabulary. We'd have to get a child-friendly filter on Momma White's mouth, and soon. I was sure I'd heard her and scared to ask for clarification.

I cleared my suddenly dry throat and asked, "A . . . a what for a second toe?"

She snorted in irritation. "A baby dick, like a monkey finger, a damn cobra-clutch grabbits long as hell second toe," Momma White responded, and with an attitude on top of that.

She even added terms for toes that I'd never even heard used in reference to a toe in all my adult life, as if they were medically defined terms I should know.

"Mommy, do I have monkey fingers?" Trey questioned.

Shit, he definitely had a long as hell second toe, but I wasn't about to give him a complex about it. I ran my fingers across my eyebrows, mentally wiping away all this toe business.

"Okay, yes, Momma, she has a long toe. Now, how about we get you away from the Illustration, and go to a nice hotel? I'll let you hold Lataya and you can examine her for yourself all you want."

"No. I ain't goin' anywhere. Mona be done came up in here and took all my shit. Shit I worked for. I've got to be a vigilante."

I sighed, wondering what on earth I'd walked into. "Vigilant, Momma?"

"And that, too," she replied, twisting her mouth up at me.

Lord, please build up my patient, side because I'm sure there ain't nothin' right about chokin' out an old woman.

Chapter 10

Shot at and Missed, Shit at and Hit

Me and the kids spent the night at the Hilton. I'd been doing all kinds of mental gymnastics trying to come up with ways to get Rah's momma up out the house. Aside from setting fire to it or flooding it, she wasn't budging. The least I could do was get off my bourgeois ass and pitch in with cleaning it up. There was no way I could leave her with it like that. She'd have these hacking painful sounding coughing fits that would leave her doubled over wheezing for air. It was probably from years of smoking, and I'm pretty sure there were all kinds of dust mites and mold spores making it worse. I couldn't help but feel sorry for her, my own momma sounded somethin' like that when the doctors said they couldn't do anything more for her. They just sent her home telling my Daddy to make her as comfy as possible.

The timer on the oven went off, and I opened it to see the oven cleaner eating through all the black crud on the racks. I'd nearly asphyxiated myself with bleach and scrubbed through a whole box of Brillo Pads. I don't know what I was thinking when I'd decided to tackle this cleaning job by myself. Momma White needed Molly-maid, Super-nanny, and an extraction team up in here. We could finally see a hairline of a dent in all of the filth she'd accumulated. For every spot I'd managed to clean, she'd be right behind me, taking something out of the trash or pulling an item or two back out of boxes.

It took a carton of Newports and a bottle of Merlot but I'd managed to bribe her into letting me clear one of the bedrooms for me and the kids. All we really ended up doing was shuffling items from that room to other parts of the house. The woman was a bona fide hoarder of empty cigarette cartons, cup noodle cases, and little else. There were no pictures from when she was growing up or when Rah was little. Nothing was left of value because her sister had squandered all of that for heroin or whatever else.

This particular morning I found Momma staring out of the kitchen window.

"Momma White? What are you doing?"

She was so still she could have been a wax sculpture. I'd have named it *Rebellious Domestication*. Momma White was holding her coffee mug full of wine with a lit cigarette perched carefully between her fingers. The ash hanging off the end looked almost as long as the cigarette itself. She was staring intently at the trees in the backyard. Thankfully the kids were still asleep, but I wanted to get to the sink and wash dishes before they were up and all in my way. She didn't seem to be paying me or the dishes any mind.

"Momma? Are you all right? Is something wrong?" I gently tapped her shoulder.

"Shush, girl. He gonna hear your loud ass, and then we all gonna be dead."

My pulse raced as a memory of my last night at Towanna's created a massive pileup of emotion in my throat. I swallowed past the lump. "Who are you talking about? Who's gonna hear me?" I whispered cooperatively.

She gave me an annoyed glance, briefly curling her lip in disgust before pointing at a tree closest to the house. "Right there in the corner. He got that shit turned on though, guess he call himself hidin'. Damn Predator sitting right there. I see him. Camouflage don't fool me. See the leaves movin'?"

I followed her withered finger through the smoke burning my eyes and stared at the few remaining Reese's Pieces–colored leaves that were barely hanging on the tree branch. I was looking and thinking, you know, hunter, apex predator, and then my shoulders slumped. I rubbed my eyes in aggravation and looked at Momma White, who was still staring, fascinated with this tree.

"You mean *Predator*, like on TV?" I couldn't keep the disbelief out of my voice.

"He obviously ain't on the TV if he in my damn tree spying," she snapped back, taking a sip from her mug.

Left with nowhere to go and stuck with my ex's bat-shit crazy momma.

This had to be God's way of punishing me for all the fucked-up shit I'd done in my past. I'd have pointed out the fact that it was just a squirrel, but that would turn into another one of her "Illustration" arguments and I wasn't even in the mood for it right now. On more than one occasion I'd started to ask her if she was on something. I was thinking maybe Mona wasn't the only one doing "the hard stuff." The house would be dead silent and Momma would start yelling for everyone to shut up. She even had Trey convinced the walls melted every day when the sun came up. He'd sit on her lap and they'd whisper about where they thought the drywall came from when it grew back at night and what color it might be.

I noticed a trickle of blood down the back of her leg.

"Momma, did you cut yourself?" I asked her.

"Hmm? Oh no girl. It's a boil. Put fatback on it and a few home remedies. It's fine."

"Oh, okay. Well, let me have a look then, you don't want it to get infected."

I'd already figured it was infected because it was the leg she'd been limping on. She reluctantly walked over and slightly lifted her house dress. She had a huge mean looking hole on the back of her thigh about the size of a soda bottle cap. I'd gotten a rag and some peroxide to clean it with.

"Momma, you've got to go to the doctor. Um . . ."

"Spit it out child."

"You have maggots, in your leg Momma."

"Oh, girl tell me something I don't know. They only eat the bad parts. They making it healthy. How you think they got there. That's why I let you look. Do you think they done yet? You gonna need some tweezers to take 'em out, some of them little buzzards'll latch on good and won't wash out."

There weren't too many options since I wasn't exactly her kin. Momma wasn't going to be happy with me, but hopefully she'd thank me one day.

The hospital wasn't exactly what I expected for a mental institution. After seeing Trey and Lataya settled into a quiet, guarded play area on the main floor, I checked in and went to see how Momma was handling herself. You'd have thought we were sentencing her to life in prison when they came by the house to speak with her and diagnose her condition. Her stay in here was completely contingent upon her cooperation. Turned out she was schizophrenic and in the early stages of Alzheimer's. I'd already agreed to take care of her once she agreed to get with the program. I'd found a ton of unopened Risperdal prescription bottles littered around the house. At some point, she'd decided to start boycotting her meds. It made me wonder if that mess was a dominant or recessive trait in the gene pool. I'd need to start watching Trey and Lataya's asses, because shit like that always skipped generations.

I was escorted through at least five different checkpoints by a well-mannered, broad-shouldered guard. My cell, keys, and belongings were left at check-in, as nothing could be taken inside. Hate to say it, but it was all very reminiscent of visiting Rah in prison. There was a rundown of do's and do not's. Such as "do not leave the visiting area, do sit quietly, and do not be alarmed if other patients randomly join your conversation." Oh, and "do not stare."

All the visitors were corralled into a large dining area with bare ocean-blue walls. A row of barred windows let in sunlight, greeting us with a view of the concrete walls. They surrounded the entire building.

Well, isn't that a cozy sight to see. They could at least put up some shrubs or rose bushes; these folk already depressed enough as it is.

Momma wasn't at the stage in treatment yet where she could have unsupervised visits in her room. That would come later. I sat down at a long cafeteria-style table and waited. A few patients were already seated in the area. It wasn't like on TV where you'd see people wandering around in raggedy hospital gowns. I was instructed to pack warm, comfy clothes for Momma, and to be sure not to put any belts, razors, or mouthwash in her suitcase. All the patients wore brightly colored hospital bands and clothes of their own choosing.

I questioned that logic when I saw an awkward-looking, pale, middle-aged man sitting slouched in a corner. He wore nothing but biking shorts and brown penny loafers with no socks. Blinking seemed to take a conscious effort as if he were snapping himself awake from a quick nap. He was giving me the thousand-yard stare down with his dark, beady eyes in between blinky jerks.

Humph, but it isn't okay for me to stare, though?

The guy seated next to him slid out of his seat and began holding an intense conversation with the chair. He started crawling and sliding it around the dining area. His sister or wife sat by, watching sadly, and I gave his crazy behind a cautious side eye.

Momma was finally led in, strolling like a regal mafia matriarch. A short, stocky woman, who made a Shih Tzu come to mind from looking at her, bounced along beside Momma. She had a pinched face and stubby little legs with a pink bow in her hair. They were followed by a hunchbacked old man with graying hair, and a towering, serial-killer Green Mile–looking somebody.

Shit, I should have been allowed to at least keep my cell phone, my Mace, something. Momma rolled her eyes at me and sat clear at the opposite end of the table. She promptly folded her arms across her chest and sat gripping her upper arms with a sour look on her face. Sighing, I got up and walked around to pull out the chair beside her. If she wasn't going to come to me, I'd just have to go to her. Regardless of what she thought, putting her in here was my way of helping, not hurting.

Green Mile had been giving me his version of the thousand-yard stare from where he stood. Before I could plant my ass firmly in the seat, I gasped as something cold and wet splattered across the front of my blazer. The room erupted into chaos as Green Mile decided it was just time to go ape shit ballistic. He flipped the table and started launching chairs at the orderlies with missile-like precision. I was literally watching *King Kong* live and direct. If there'd have been something in there for him to climb, he'd have scaled it and been roof bound in a matter of seconds. Panic alarms went off and a squadron of orderlies, guards, or whatever you call them, stormed in. I stared down in disgust at the brown ooze ruining my cream Marc blazer, and I shut my mind off.

Lord, please don't let this be what I think it is.

I fought back a gag. Figure the odds. I'd been shot at and missed, shit at and fucking hit. Momma glanced up at me with a smirk on her face.

"Ms. Laurel, I am so terribly sorry. Please come with me we'll get you cleaned up."

A gorgeous, thick-hipped nurse with dimple piercings manifested in a mango sugar-scented cloud. Giving me a reassuring smile, she took me by my elbow and led me through one of the side doors into a maze of hallways.

I will not ask for her number. I will not ask for her number. Hmm . . .

But, what if she asks for my number? No. I will not give out my number.

We are on a break. Mentally chastising myself for even thinking about cheating on my sexual diet, I continued to follow along and keep my eyes above hip level. I was sure these were the areas they left off the tours when they solicited you for your money. The friendly dark blue walls gave way to a more institutional-feeling, split-pea, soup-colored green. We passed rows of rooms with "fit your face" sized square windows. They lined the hallway on either side. People screamed or cried nonstop like they were being tortured behind the stark white doors. My nosey ass tried to peek in, and every now and again I could see people curled up in their beds; sometimes they were strapped down.

And this is supposed to be the place where we send depression and mental illness to be cured? When I went through shit with Rah, I'd tried to sleep the pain away, sometimes for days at a time. And then Ris would save me. Bowling, jogging, drinking, dancing, and fucki—

I could hear what sounded like a life-sized bug zapper humming at the end of the hall. "Is that . . . ?"

"Electroshock therapy? Yes, some people actually need it," she answered before I could even get my question out.

She led me into the women's locker room. "You can get yourself cleaned up in here." She smiled sweetly and disappeared around the side of the lockers to go get me a fresh shirt.

Stripping down to my bra, I did my best not to smell or come in contact with the filth on my jacket and blouse.

"Mmmph, aren't we nice."

That either had to be the fastest trip in history or this locker room was the size of a broom closet. I bit my bottom lip as she brushed the towel across my shoulders and down the center of my back. She walked around and stood in front of me, pursing her lips as she handed me the towel, staring down at my barely covered breasts. I couldn't remember the last time I'd bought a new bra, and the cups weren't exactly a perfect fit anymore.

So much for covertly checkin' out another female, Michelle. No more looking at anything for you. Ever.

Thankfully she just handed me the towel, giving me another calculated up and down with her eyes that I read like an erotica novel.

"Unless you need some help, I'll let you to get cleaned up. And again, I'm sorry." She quietly added under her breath, "But, I'm not."

I gave her a tight-lipped smile. "I'll be fine. It's okay, it wasn't your fault."

I hated to be the reason for the look of disappointment on her face as she walked out of the locker room but, oh well. My hiatus had just barely begun, and after Keyshawn and Ris I needed to do some serious soul searching. I was only happy with Larissa when Rasheed was acting up, and I was happy with Keshawn when Ris was stuck on stupid.

Maybe I need to look into that polyamourous stuff, get myself a . . . No, I need to look into my own place. Where did I pack that damn vibrator? All this Honey business . . .

Honey probably needed to be up in a place just like this. From what I could remember and from what I'd seen, she was always a little off. Maybe something like this would be better for her than prison. I rinsed myself off and toweled dry quickly over the sink. There was a gray T-shirt lying on the bench beside the lockers, and I aimlessly slipped it over my head. I didn't see her bring it back in. *She had better not be watching me wash.* Pulling the collar to my nose, I sniffed it just to make sure it was clean. They weren't about to have me walking around in a funky, dirty T-shirt. It smelled wonderful, like Gain detergent, warm vanilla, and cardamom.

They needed to knock some dollars off Momma's bill, that's what they needed to do.

"So do you always sneak around locker rooms, sniffing and stealing things that don't belong to you?"

I jumped and whirled around, my eyebrows raised in shock and embarrassment. I'd been so lost in thought I hadn't even heard anyone come in. My mouth plopped open and I was pretty sure it was stuck in the shape of either "oh, shit" or "oh, no."

I'll take "oh, shit" for $800, Alex.

Old King Kong himself was standing calmly just inside the doorway of the locker room.

Now you already know this fool's crazy. Do you do or do you don't make eye contact?

Clearing my throat, I brought my eyes up no higher than neck level, and then I chickened out and looked off at the lockers to the left of him, focusing on them instead. "Do you always walk up in women's locker rooms? Because, thanks to your king-sized temper tantrum back there I needed a new shirt, so I'm adopting this one. And just so you know, I'd have plucked my son's face clean off his head if he ever pulled what I watched you pull out there, and he's only five." I prayed I could keep up the small talk long enough for the nurse to come back.

"Well, I apologize for the unfavorable first impression that I'm sure I made. It's nice to meet you," he replied casually. His voice had a husky deepness to it that made it seem bottomless.

Why, oh, why do the crazy niggas always gotta be the ones with them deep-ass voices? And you know this fool can probably back that shit up with some crazy deep-ass dick, too. Girl, shut up!

He gave me a large, beaming smile as he came over, extending his hand toward mine. Timidly, I returned the gesture, afraid my ass was about to get yoked up as his baseball mitt of a hand engulfed mine.

Aww hell, here we go. I can see this headline now: WOMAN
MURDERED IN AN ASYLUM LOCKER ROOM BY KING KONG PSYCHO
MOTHERFUCKA.

Satisfied he nodded down at me and sauntered over to one
of the lockers.

"I don't think you should be messing with that. Are you
even supposed to be um, roaming around at your leisure? I'm
Michelle by the way."

*Um, hello? Why you tell this fool your name? What if
his crazy ass done killed everybody and now he's trying to
escape? This shit happens on TV all the time. He threw shit
and lost his damn mind up there not even five minutes ago.
Why isn't he in the crazy solitary? This can't be good.*

His long, tapered fingers maneuvered the combination on
the lock until it popped open with a click. "We do drills twice
a month to see how well the orderlies are following procedure.
Patients are supposed to get checked before each visitation
to make sure something like today doesn't happen. Darren
will lose a day's worth of pay. It could have been real fecal
matter instead of chocolate pudding and peanut butter. I'm
Dr. Harrington by the way."

He turned from rummaging around in the locker and
handed me his badge. A smug smile lingered on his thick, full
lips. Embarrassed at reacting the way I reacted to some damn
chocolate pudding, I couldn't help blushing.

*Now you know you've been elbow deep in diapers worse
than that. You should've known better, woman.*

"Oh, yeah, and the locker rooms are unisex. It's a psychology thing. The hospital will gladly compensate you for your
clothing, and I'd be more than honored if you'd let me take
you to dinner, as my way of apologizing for scaring you." He'd
turned on that bottomless-pit voice of his again and there I
was teetering on the edge.

*Oh, no, no, no. I'm not ready for this dating nonsense. And
he seems too sweet and way too stable to even fit into my
crazy-ass lifestyle.*

"I . . . I'm sorry, but I can't. I just moved here and I've got a
lot going on. Like, a *lot*. Don't get me wrong, you seem really
sweet. You just really don't want to get mixed up in my life."

He gave me an inquiring look, like I was something to be queried or studied on his couch. "Thirty-two seconds ago you looked like you were praying I wouldn't chop you up and stuff your little ass in one of these here lockers."

I scoffed. "I did no such thing. You obviously imagined the hell out of that look." We both chuckled at my obvious lie.

"Riiiight. You were up in here subliminally threatening to slap off faces and now you think I'm too sweet? You do remember me saying I'm a doctor? A damn good one, too. I can fix anything." He winked, and I felt my cheeks flush variations of pink and red that Crayola probably hadn't even invented yet.

"I don't need fixing. I just need a damn break." My wistful reply was a combo-meal whisper of hopelessness and hope-fulness. It could've gone either way.

"Oh . . . Dr. Harrington, I didn't know you'd be in here. I found Ms. Laurel something to wear." The nurse came barging in, holding a scraggly-looking set of old, used scrubs.

"She's fine, Denise. She uh, 'adopted' my T-shirt. Show her how to get back to the dining hall."

Giving Nurse Denise a smile, I then nodded good-bye to the fine doctor.

How the hell was I supposed to know the T-shirt was his? And on top of that, he caught me smelling it. I can't lie; if it were up to me, this shirt would never see the inside of a washin' machine. It smelled like a bald, honey bun–hued King Kong of a bottomless pit. And all worries aside, I wanted to fall in that bitch fifty ways from Sunday.

Chapter 11

No Harm, Your Foal . . . Fowl . . . Foul

I stared at the umpteen-whatever-count threads in the pillowcase so long my eyes started to cross. This was the second time he'd pulled that coming in late shit, and I was fed up. When Don Cerzulo dropped me off, as much as I didn't want to see Angelo, I kind of needed to. We'd never discussed the terms of my surgery, fame, or hell, my life for that matter. It was one thing when it came to doing shit to get Paris back, but this was . . . was slavery. Do or die. How long would I have to be Don Cerzulo's puppet before we were all squared away, and what if I got caught in the process?

It couldn't be that hard to suffocate his snorin' ass. Angelo snorted and sawed logs in his sleep. That's exactly what it sounded like. *Them hoes on* Snapped *do that shit, hold the pillow over his face and—no, wait—they shoot the niggas through the pillow. Men suffocate hoes with pillows. Must take a lot of muscle to do that shit. Look at my ass, already tryin' to murk every-damn-body for no reason. The Don's methods already rubbin' off on me.*

When I couldn't take the sound of the air whistling out of his nostrils anymore, I quietly eased out of bed. My bare toes touched the cool gray marble tile, sending rivulets of pain from my backside down my legs and I cursed him. Angelo came home, took his "wash away the evidence" shower, and got in bed. I pretended to be asleep just like I always did, even though I'd just had a really good Skype call with Big. Angelo started kissin' on my shoulders, grindin' on my ass, and I just refused to react. I ain't sign up for this shit. Who wanted a relationship with an absent man and some bullshit no-foreplay quickie morning sex all the damn time?

So what did Angelo do? He decided he's just gonna lick his hand to lube up and slide in. Shit, I still ain't move. If he was hoping that was gonna get me in the mood he missed the mark. Askin' if I could feel it, and if I loved him. He was breathing his hot-ass toothpaste breath all up the side of my head. He eventually wore himself out, and my skin was cracked and dry. Dumb ass, I guessed he was one of those kids who liked to hit the Slip 'n Slide without water.

Talking to Big definitely made me reassess things. He wasn't gonna be in the area for much longer and I was feeling pressed to find Paris and haul ass. Marriage to Angelo was sounding less and less appealing the more I thought about it. After pacing a hole in the living room carpet, I finally made up my mind. It was always easier to ask forgiveness than to ask permission.

A woman in a sweaty red tank top jogged past me as I made my way down the street. Pulling my hoodie tighter over my head, I looked around to make sure I wasn't being followed or recognized by anyone and quickened my pace. Granted, Don Cerzulo's ass said don't touch anything; something good did come out of that situation.

Scarletti's wife had a pharmacy of pills beside the bed. I didn't even read the labels. I just emptied a bunch into one bottle. I shook out a light pink one and a pretty light yellow one. They'd either wake me up or make me calm; either way it'd be interesting.

Walk through a deserted carnival ground in any state and it'd feel just like Miami at seven a.m., minus all the beautiful joggers of course. I'd decided to press my luck and text Big to meet me for coffee. He was actually awake and agreed to meet me at a spot close to his shop.

"Look at you, looking all good this early in the morning."

I got up from the table to give him a hug, again amazed at how big he was.

"They got some bomb-ass chai tea up in here; it's better for you than coffee," he told me.

"I have a confession to make: my ass don't even like coffee. I jus' wanted a reason to see you. But, I'll try your tea."

"So what has you out and about this early in the day, unaccompanied by your man?"

His tone went dry when he added the last part, and I wondered if I'd said too much in our Skype conversations.

"It's hard to explain. On one side I'm grateful to him for his help, but that shouldn't mean I owe him shit forever. He proposed and his daddy was there and I ain't know what else to say. And now I feel stuck, when all I really want to do is find my baby and be happy."

"And Michelle got her, right?" He reached over and rubbed my shoulder. I nodded. "Would I be your favoritest Big hero if I told you I think I know where Michelle is?"

I couldn't tell if he was serious or playing. "I'll stab you in the eye with this spoon if you fuckin' with me right now." I grabbed one of the spoons off the table, giving him my version of Angelo's pointy stabby, poking his hand for emphasis.

"Damn, okay, Tonto, calm down. Yes, I'm serious, I wouldn't play with you about something like that."

My hand started shaking as I set the spoon down on the table. The room swayed and I blinked several times. I looked Big directly in the eye and slid my hand up his leg under the table. Honey was officially back, well, mentally anyway, and she was ready to handle business. I was the baby-voiced seductress with the womanly curves that drove niggas insane, and now I had this silver screen siren's face to complete the picture. They'd do anything to make my pouty lips smile and hear me say, "Yes, daddy." And in that moment, I turned it all on for Big.

"If you tell me where Michelle is and where my daughter is, you would be my Big Daddy and I'd do anything for you."

He swallowed hard and shifted in the booth. "My homeboy looks in on Rah's ma every now and again. We all know she always been a little off, so he make sure she got food and smokes. Just leaves stuff on the porch most of the time, because you catch her on a bad day and you liable to get taken hostage or shot if you can't convince her why you there. Said he rode past last week and saw a woman with a little boy and a little girl in a car seat up on the porch. The car been there every day since."

I couldn't believe my ears. Even if we were sitting in the middle of ten o'clock service on Sunday, it wouldn't have kept me from climbing on his lap and kissing him. Up until that moment I didn't have the slightest clue where to even start looking for Michelle. I'd have asked Angelo what he thought if he were ever home long enough. I was pretty sure he'd seem more interested in making a baby than finding mine.

I leaned back and smiled; my chin was probably red as hell from Big's beard, but I ain't care. "Let's go back to your shop; you can give me a celebratory massage." I winked. The number one rule of runnin' any man is to keep they asses working for you. As long as they feel like they earnin' something, you hold all the power. Because, everyone knows that anything worth working for has value.

Big grinned and paid our tab; he even offered to carry my backpack, but I declined. My emergency cash and a pistol were in it as always and it never left my hands.

"You know I'm leavin' in a few days, right?" he said over his shoulder as he fed his fish.

"I thought it was gonna be at least a few weeks."

"Nah, the season here is slower than I thought it'd be. I wanted to tell you in person."

Good news and bad news. Up and down in the same day. I was instantly depressed as hell. Big wiped his hands on his jeans and turned to face me. Worry lines creased his forehead.

"What do you plan on doin' about your baby girl?" he asked.

I shrugged suddenly realizing how overwhelmingly, hopelessly impossible my situation seemed. She was right there and I had the means and everything. Except flying to Virginia and just taking her wasn't really an option. Anything I did now would draw tons of media attention, so I had to be careful about how I got her. Angelo and all this murder, death, kill business was a hurdle I wasn't ready to jump over or knock down just yet. I didn't need to tell Big any of that though. I was pretty sure he could tell from the bags under my eyes, or from the way my skin was starting to break out. My ass ain't never been big on wearing a bunch of makeup, but at this rate, I'd have to look into some foundation or face powder. Eyeliner and lip gloss wasn't really cutting it for me anymore.

Big's arms circled around me and he somehow managed to duck down, propping his chin on top of my head. He sighed and it pretty much summed up the moment.

This is damn nice. My very own live-action teddy bear and he's leaving me. What am I gonna do?

Big felt solid and safe; he was an invincible pillow fort against all my believed and make-believe monsters. He even came equipped with his own extra-large black Maglite.

"We gonna figure this out, Little Bit, okay?"

I buried my nose into his chest and nodded. He always smelled so damn good, too. I just wanted to breathe him in so I could remember it later. I inhaled warmth and sandalwood.

"Girl, you makin' my nipples sweat." Big broke my concentration, sounding like he needed a dang church fan.

I actually stopped breathing and leaned back to stare up at him, scrunch-faced and everything. "What in the world are you talking about, boy?" I asked him.

"All that nose breathing. What in the hell are you doing? It's makin' my chest hot."

Big scowled at his shirt, then leaned down, grabbing me by the shoulders. This fool started rubbing me back and forth across his chest so vigorously I was surprised we ain't catch fire.

I yelped, "Negro, what the—"

"You was tryin' to wipe a damn booger on me. I know how y'all women folk do."

We both busted out laughing.

Somehow laughing turned into us kissing. And kissing turned into me in the air with my legs wrapped around his waist, moaning against his lips.

This is what the fuck passion is supposed to feel like. This feels like front-row seats to a fireworks show over the ocean with an orchestra playing dramatic music in the background. And this is the kind of feeling I'd be more than happy to settle with for the rest of my life.

He held me up with one hand, pulling my hair from its ponytail with his free hand. Fingers in my hair never felt so damn good. I groaned. Every part of my body was alive and begging for his undivided attention like it was all jealous of my hair and my lips. We'd backed up against the far wall.

How or when he got my shirt and bra off I didn't know. I'd never wanted to be out of my clothes so bad while trying to stay in them.

Of all the days for Big to make a move and then tell me he has to go somewhere. We can't do this, not today. Not after Angelo done ran and splashed himself all up in there no condom no nothing. That would just be nasty.

We could do this any day except today. Intent on telling him just that, I broke my lips free, placing my hands on his shoulders. "Big, I need you to lis—"

He pinned me back against the wall and made figure eights, grazing my bare skin with his course beard. I'd just gotten my mouth tooted up to call a time out when he decided to go all hungry wolf cub on my ass. Big growled and bit me on my side. I squealed and pinched him. It wasn't bad, he just caught me off-guard. Before I could do more damage, his mouth made a swirling ball of heat around my nipples. I didn't want to breathe anymore. Air in my chest would expand, drawing him closer, but eventually I'd have to let that air out. I didn't want my skin to be any farther from his lips than it had to be. Forgetting where I was, I had one of those "throw my head back and be cute" moments. My head smacked the wall and I squeezed my eyes shut, hoping Big didn't catch that very unsexy Kodak moment.

"Um, was our meeting cancelled? Because, I didn't get the message."

My eyes fluttered open and were met with Big's. He gave me an irritated "get you later" stare down as he slid me gently down the wall. Standing behind him for cover I clumsily put my top back on. I didn't hear the door open or anything.

"Nah. My bad, T. I got sidetracked. You know how it goes. Why you ain't hit the cell?"

"I did, several times actually. Figured, what the hell, I'd just roll through."

"Shit. Um, Desivita." Grinning, he glanced back to see if I was dressed. "Let me introduce you to my business partner."

I nodded at Big, but I couldn't bring myself to look Angelo in the eyes. It was easier to talk to the floor in between us. "We already know each other, Big. That's my fiancé, Angelo."

"Wait, Testa is ya man? King, the boss of Miami. Oh, fuck." Big ran his hand over his forehead and sat down hard on the leather couch.

I glanced at Angelo. It was like looking at a shipwreck survivor, well, a rich one anyway. He'd rolled through all right. His ass rolled right out of bed, into his wrinkled-ass man capris, Ralph Lauren button down, and them preppy boat shoes that I hated. He could have rolled through a shower and a brush first.

"Yes, King Angelo Testa, *the* Boss of Miami," Angelo snapped at Big.

I looked down and rolled my eyes. Was he really standing here in his Carrera shades, looking like a spoiled brat, spouting his name, when he won't nothin' but a daddy's boy?

Angelo leered at me. "All I've done for you and you'd cheat on me?"

"You're mad, because I'm out here doin' exactly what you've been doin'? Late nights and early mornings, huh? That's not what the lyrics mean, Angelo, you were doing it all wrong. Climbin' in our bed from Lord knows where for what? Some stale-ass morning dry humps. Fuck outta here with that."

There's always that point in an argument when you know you've gone too far. The words leave your mouth and you know they should have stayed in your head. They hit the air and the other person's ears and they're the kind of words that change your life forever. Yeah, his dick game was wack, but I didn't have to actually say it out loud, especially not with Big right there. I'd heard Angelo and his boys say that "get outta here" or "fuck outta here" line at least a hundred times a day. Hearing it from me was just salt and vinegar in an open wound.

"I ain't been doing anything, Honey, except meeting with this one"—he nodded at Big—"to go over investment business models, and then catching red eyes back and forth to Key West. I've been spending money planning a surprise wedding so you'd be able to walk around for a weekend without feeling like a fish in a fishbowl." Angelo reached into his pocket and threw hotel reservations, snippets of cake pictures, and business cards onto the floor in front of me.

He was really serious about that marriage thing. Why wouldn't he be? You said yes to the man, in front of his daddy, and you're wearing his ring. What the hell did you think would happen? Maybe one of us would die first and I wouldn't have to be bothered for real. Or something like what's happening right now would happen.

Why couldn't the floor have just opened up and swallowed me. His lips were drawn in a grim, thin line, as his nostrils flared angrily and tears ran down his cheeks. There wasn't even a "sorry" I could give him, because I wasn't sorry. I just wasn't in love and had never been in love with him. If anything, I was sorry he'd fallen in love and had decided to go all in with me.

Time felt as though someone had laid an hourglass on its side, stopping the sand all together. The room seemed quiet—too quiet. Waiting for Angelo to react was like watching lightning and counting the seconds waiting for the thunder. I couldn't tell if the storm was going to move on, or just quietly building up energy.

"Desivita?" a woman's voice called out from the shop door.

The muscle in Angelo's jaw was ticking. I looked around him to see who or how someone had even seen me. Either them pills were kicking in and I was hallucinatin', or there was an entire fucking studio of paparazzi outside. Big got up and stormed over, locking the door to keep more of them from getting in.

"Hi, Desivita, so is it true? Are you the Angel of Death?" she asked, waiting for me to answer her dumb-ass question.

"No, and this is not a good time for any kind of an interview. I'm sorry." I tried to sound polite but her question rattled me to my core.

"You made your movie debut in *Revived 2* after the original producer, Albert Meekins, was found murdered by his lover who committed suicide. Sadira Nadeshce had already completed over eighty percent of the movie when you replaced her under mysterious and unexplained circumstances. There were even tweets about you trying to attack Sadira, the star of your current film on set with a metal bar during a scene with your on screen love interest."

I gasped and looked at Angelo, who surprisingly hadn't stormed off yet. No way? Al and Jasper weren't a drug deal? But, I'd never heard anything about a producer dying; no one ever made a peep about it during filming. *Unless they were too scared or threatened not to talk. Fuck, Don Cerzulo, what the fuck did you start?*

The woman continued, "First there were sketchy rumors of you being spotted on the balcony and leaving the hotel of co-star Kai Nimako after his alleged "fall" from the sixteenth floor. Now, not moments after the release of Scanetti's alleged suicide, Sadira announced via Twitter that she's being replaced on yet another film. Her replacement in the leading role is none other than you, Desivita Dulce'. So again I ask are you the Angel of Death? Is that nefariously dark angel ring more than a fashion statement? Is America's new 'it girl' killing her way into our living rooms? What kind of woman are you?"

Angelo spoke this time without looking at me. "I'ma tell you something my pop told me. He said a woman can only be one of three things: foal, fowl, or foul. What that means is she's either gonna be a bird, always waitin' on you to throw her some crumbs, with no real values, flyin' from coop to fuckin' coop because she don't know better; or she gonna be a fuckin' thoroughbred, loyal 'til the day she dies. You might have to put that crop to her ass to show her who's the boss. But, end of the day, she a winner." His voice got scratchy and he cleared his throat. "Or she foul. Fouler than . . . fouler than the stench of a slaughterhouse, in the middle of a heat wave, with a jilted freezer, and no power."

With that, Angelo turned on his heel and strode out, letting in the mass of people who had been dying to hear what was being said. His insults lingered, burning my ears, weighing down the atmosphere. They always say angry words are the truest words. They just don't say how much it'll hurt to actually hear them. Both rings on my fingers felt heavier than usual; one was suddenly an ugly, embarrassing reminder of my fake-believe engagement.

The other sparked my fear that Don Cerzulo Campelli was using me for something else, something big and wrong as fuck. Now that I didn't have Angelo in my corner I had no way to predict or defend myself against him. I had to have done something, said something; maybe Angelo found the texts from Big that very first night. None of it mattered; what did matter was getting myself away from Miami and this fairy tale bullshit. People were yelling and snapping pictures all around me, and all I was thinking about was how long it would take me to get to my little girl.

Chapter 12

All of Y'all Crazy

(Back in VA)

I was sitting at the kitchen table leaving a voicemail for the office. I needed to get a few properties sold and I needed someone to start sending me listings so I could find something somewhere that felt safe. The kids were down for their afternoon nap when I heard a floorboard creak behind me.

"Trey?" I quietly called his name before stuffing the rest of the chocolate chip cookie I was trying to enjoy in private in my mouth. I folded the bag back up as quietly as possible and slipped it back in the cabinet. These were mine and yes, I snuck and ate them. Sometimes I even hid them in my clothes and took them in the bathroom. Trey and Lataya had enough snacks to fight over. It was probably selfish of me, but I couldn't help it. Mommy had to share everything from her bed to a cup of water, which became their cup of water after they'd put backwash in it. The only things I wanted right now were peace and quiet, and my damn cookie.

The house actually felt like a home again. Without Momma there to clutter it up I was able to throw everything away that didn't have a social security number on it. If we could just keep her on her meds maybe it would stay this way. I peeked in the living room; seeing nothing I went down the hall. The door to the kid's room was cracked.

If that boy is wandering around not answering me I am gonna wear him out. I know he heard me calling him.

Both of the kids were still in the bed sound asleep. Poor Trey, my baby ain't have no covers on his behind. Kissing each of their foreheads, I carefully unraveled the blankets from around Lataya. I didn't know how that girl did it. To be so tiny, she always managed to burrito herself up, stealing every inch of the comforters and sheets. I made sure the pillows beside the bed were still stacked nice and high and left just as quietly as I went in, pulling the door closed tight behind me.

The wind made the branches scrape wildly against the siding on the house and I tried to familiarize myself with the sound. I'd pulled my gun on that sound the first few nights when I'd heard it in the middle of the night. It reminded me of the sound I'd heard that night I was tortured.

Counting down no longer worked when I was anxious or afraid. Not after being nearly suffocated with snakes slithering all over my neck and in between my legs. Sample a small piece of your worst nightmare, and see if it doesn't change you. Because, in the beginning I always thought the worst that would happen was they'd kill me. I never considered all of the sick and twisted things that a person would do just out of revenge before the killing actually happened. Things that I'd have no control over if I got caught off-guard, and the thought alone made me feel frustrated, angry, and nervous.

Making my way back toward the kitchen I choked on a scream as we collided in the hallway. Something hard and metal slammed hard into my chest and rattled loudly. I fell back, checking myself for a stab wound or blood.

"Shiiiiiit. You can't see where da hellllll you goin'?"

If Wild Irish Rose, blunt smoke, and fried chicken grease could talk, it would look exactly like the little withered woman croaking up at me in the dim hallway. The voice belonged to a skeleton-thin, slightly older version of Momma White. I did a mental up, down, and sideways double take on her. This heffa was actually wearing skin-tight pleather leggings with a tube top. She was busy adjusting the tangled 1B/27 bird's nest propped on top of her head, giving me an irritated look. If you asked me, I might've knocked it straight because she repositioned it into some kind of crooked craziness.

"I'm Michelle; um, how did you get in? I mean, I didn't hear the doorbell or anything like that. Do you have a key or something?" I asked as politely as I possibly could.

Where the hell did I put my purse and car keys? Rah always said his auntie was a crackhead, and even Momma said she comes in here takin' . . . *Hold up, is that my toaster she's holding?*

"Don't need no key. Mona ain' neva nee' a key. Keys are why y'alls is slaves to the sys'em now. Stop believin' in keys an' you can go anywhere you wanna go. Like me." She slurred all her words together as she stumbled, turned, and began walking in the complete opposite direction of the front door.

"Where are you going, Mona?" I called after her, worried she was about to march herself through the kids' room. The only thing in that direction was Momma's room and the bathroom.

Let me find out I need to hide the shower rings and soap dishes, too.

I got up and followed to see where she was headed. She mumbled as she walked into Momma White's room, crawling across the bed toward the open window that I knew was closed and locked.

"Goin' out the way I came. An', let my Reena know I'ma see if I can borrow 'bout ten dolla's from her damn illegal natives."

Her illegal natives?

"Umm. You're talking about the Illustration?" The fact that I even knew the right wrong name to correct Mona with almost irritated me a little.

"Mmm hmm. An' her toaster," she muttered as she shimmied out the window.

I sighed, calling down out the window after her, "Ah, that's my toaster, Mona."

It wasn't like I was expecting her to say, "Oh sorry," and bring it back or anything. I could always buy another toaster. Guessed that's why Momma was adamant about staying. Mona would get in somehow and someone needed to be vigilant, or "a vigilante" as Momma had put it. I could see Mona coming back with a shopping cart next time.

"Oh. Well I'm borrowin' yo' toaster, honey. Tell the 'ministration to pay me for you. I mean you for me. Ah, hell ask for yourself, they parked right there on the corner," Mona called out over her shoulder, pointing as she jogged down the street, toting my brand new toaster under her arm. She stopped at the corner next to a black Altima and I watched her tap frantically on the window. It rolled down and a woman threw out a few bills that fluttered wildly into the street. I ran to get a better look out the front door, but it sped off with the tires squealing and smoking. Mona was there and gone so fast I thought I might have imagined her.

If Mona could get in and out, hell, anybody and they damn momma could. Lord, I needed help some kind of bad right now. Who the hell was that in the car? It had VA plates; she could have rented a car, it couldn't have been her. Did Mona tell her anything? Who would believe Mona? That woman acted about as nutty as Momma. Nutty or fiending and willing to sell someone out . . .

I went back to Momma's room and closed and latched the window. When I pulled to make sure it was secure, it wouldn't budge.

She must've used something to get it open. This house, this arrangement, just wasn't gonna work. I needed to find us all a place fast.

"Trey, baby, don't slurp the noodles; you're gettin' sauce everywhere. And eat your toast. You asked for it, so eat it."

I'd made spaghetti for dinner because it was quick and easy, but with the mess the kids were making I immediately regretted it.

"This not toast, Mommy. You put it in the stove, and toast go in the toaster. Oun't like it," he whined, dropping it square in the middle of the table.

"No nost. No. no. no nost, No no no no no," Lataya chimed in singing and banging her empty sippy cup on the table. She was all grins with spaghetti sauce all over her little cheeks and chin. I tried to get her to at least stop clanking the cup. Trey was frowning, tapping the table with his fork.

He'd barely taken one bite out of it and was already complaining. I always made garlic bread in the oven, which he didn't like, so I'd make him buttered toast instead. Without my damn toaster, I had to make Trey's buttered toast the old-fashioned way.

"Boy, it's still butter on a piece of bread. So eat it before I butter that ass. Your sister's eatin' hers without a problem."

"Eat, eat, eat. Eat . . ." she sang, silencing herself with a fistful of spaghetti.

Trey dropped his fork and slumped back in his chair. "G-ma and the walls said she not my sister and when my daddy—"

"Lord, help me," I actually groaned out loud. This boy and all his G-ma talk; and when did he decide to shorten grandma to G-ma? I didn't even know. I wanted to wring both her and Trey's necks at the moment. He was saved by my phone.

"Ms. Laurel? It's Dr. Harrington."

I smiled into the phone, thankful for the distraction before I snatched Trey up from the table. I'd been secretly hoping he'd call and ask if I'd reconsidered. My nerves were still on edge from dealing with Mona and that car. An adult conversation would take my mind off things, even a brief one; it would make me feel so happy right about now. Even though I'd coached myself over and over to tell him no, I could feel the cogs spinning in my brain.

"Yes, this is she," I replied sweetly.

Damn, I'd need a sitter. Maybe he'd consider a child-friendly date. No, that would be awkward. Trey would ask too many questions and Lataya would get fidgety. We wouldn't get any kind of conversation in. I didn't have anything to wear. We couldn't even do happy hour anywhere because I didn't know who to trust with the kids. Not after that car earlier. No one knew I was back in town. I could have called one of my girls from the bank. But if Honey was having me followed, they wouldn't know what to do if confronted—

"Your mother's had a small stroke. She's stable and asking for you."

His words sank into my ears and settled in the pit of my stomach with the rest of the gloom that seemed to be hovering over my life, and my shoulders slumped. "I'll be right there," I replied, disappointed and worried about Momma.

The hospital took up the first two floors. They'd obviously had enough drama with patients self-inflicting wounds, having heart attacks, and enough seizures to require one on site, and for that I was thankful. It was also a relief not to go through half the security I went through on my last visit. I felt naked leaving my gun in car, and if I'd known it was going to be so lax I would have kept it in my purse.

Dr. Harrington was waiting beside the front desk when I arrived. I had to admit he handled the transition from rugged brute to sexy intelligence extremely well. His lab coat was most likely a size too small on purpose. His biceps completely filled out the sleeves, and I was pretty sure if the man so much as sneezed he'd completely rip his way out of it.

When he glanced down at the floor, clearing his throat, I realized I'd been staring and I finally opened my mouth. "How . . . How's Momma doing? Is she gonna be okay?"

"She's asleep now. It was minor; they don't see any permanent damage. She was lucky she was here taking it easy and not at home alone."

"Good. Well, I don't wanna wake her up. I'll just get the kids—"

"The kids will be fine in the playroom. Come sit with me, have a drink. Someone gave me a bottle of Cîroc Amaretto. It's been sitting in my office and you are gonna be my guinea pig. You can even talk my head off for free."

"Who says I want to talk? And I have to drive. Plus I've got the kids."

He flashed that disarming smile of his before answering me. "You show me a woman who doesn't like to talk, and I can guarantee it's because she's mad, or she can't stand the person she's sitting next to."

I was trying hard to keep from laughing. Call it a control thing, but I knew he wanted to make me laugh, and I was just refusing to do it. The result was a crooked, twisted-mouth smile. He did have a point, because I couldn't count how many silent dinners I'd sat through because I was mad or Larissa was pissed off. I finally answered once I had my humor fully contained. "Touché, you got me. I will drink to that. Just one though."

The sound of ice clinking into two crystal glasses was the background music to the look of me in awe. His office was impressive. It was about half the size of a hotel ballroom and breathtakingly masculine. Several rich walnut bookcases lined one of the deep blue diamond-patterned walls. One was filled with volumes of psychology books and journals; the other one had a signed football by Redskins players, and his various degrees. Two large flat-screen TVs were mounted to the far back wall facing his desk, which was made of the same cherry finish as the bookcases.

That would be just like a man. Who in the world needed two TVs?

The sun shot golden glittered arrows off the corners of buildings as it set. I stood in front of monstrous floor-to-ceiling windows overlooking a view of downtown from the top floor. He handed me a glass and leaned beside me on his oversized mahogany desk.

I smirked. "So what kind of doctor doesn't need a computer?"

"Aren't we the observant one. It's all wireless and the flat screen on the right is my computer screen; the one on the left is my TV. Even though I will have two games goin' if I'm stuck in here on a slow day, don't tell anyone though."

He nodded toward them and I was in "wow" for a moment. I needed that all up in my life; working with the guys and staging the houses usually kept me up to date on those types of things.

I have definitely been slacking on my techie game something serious, and that is so not like me.

"So, Harrington, what's your first name? And don't tell me it's Doctor."

"That's a good one. I'll have to remember to use that. It's Devon."

I sighed. "Well, Devon, I'm in the wrong damn line of business. I've got a company in Florida and my view was just the Realtor's ass in front of me." I pouted. "It wasn't a good look, trust me. He was a big boy, always managed to have a 'man camel toe.'" Seeing Devon's confused look I clarified, "You ever seen a fat guy in really tiiiiight pants? Now imagine him bending over and his balls—"

"No! I refuse to picture any dude's sac in any format." Devon made the "blech" face along with sound effects.

"I'm just sayin'. I looked directly at it once by accident. It's like a freaking solar eclipse. You know you shouldn't stare but you can't look away. The vision still hasn't been fully restored in my left eye." I did a dramatic hiccup sigh.

"Aww, there there. I'm a doctor remember. Let me have a look at it." He playfully took my chin in between his thick fingers and stared curiously into my eyes.

Our gaze locked and I instantly became hypersensitive to everything. Heat waves rose from his hand, radiating into my skin, making me wonder if they could do that everywhere. He had the thickest, curliest lashes I'd ever seen on a man. I wanted to laugh and ask if they came that way out the pack, insinuating that they were fake, but I couldn't stop looking at them . . . at him.

Mmm, and what gorgeous eyes you have, Doctor . . .

Suddenly uncomfortable, I blinked, ending the transmission and locking him out of my head. *Oh no, sir, you ain't about to glamour me googly-eyed with your Dr. Wonder Sex Care Bear stare down. Tighten up, girl. One drink and carry your ass.*

Frowning, I shooed his hand away, clearing my throat. "You ain't even an eye doctor. You might break it."

"Why are you so guarded?" His voice was low and pensive.

"I'm not guarded. I'm just careful. If I told you even half of what I've done or what I've been through, you'd probably have me thrown out of the hospital." I took a sip from my drink to try to cool me down. He needed to turn on some AC.

"And she actually murdered my wife. Did you hear me? Murdered her and the guy I was seeing. Not seeing like cheating, because we were about to divorce anyway, I think. It was bad. But, honestly, would you ever drug your own wife?"

His drink stopped midway to his lips and he stared at me, wide-eyed.

"Don't answer that, you're a damn head doctor. You'd probably have just as well had us all strapped to your bug zapper downstairs." With the attitude of a queen dismissing her court, I waved off any excuse he was about to try pitching in my direction. "Anyway, so this cop comes along; next thing I know I'm tied up living out my worst nightmare. Traumatized me, trust no one."

I'd started with how I met Rasheed all the way to how I ended up staying with his mom. Devon sat completely motionless. The only things that moved on the man were his eyelids. He blinked, and finally sat up like he was coming out of a trance.

I gasped. "Oh fuck, you're probably thinking I'm like the worst kind of person. I'm really not. I can't believe I told you all of that. Am I gonna have to kill you now? The way my luck has been going you're probably gonna try to kill me or just randomly die and I . . . I don't even know." I sobbed into my hands.

A sip had obviously turned into me having a drunken meltdown moment. I could hear him laughing and I frowned, peeking at him from between my wet, teary fingers. This fool was sitting there just grinning, running his index finger back and forth across his bottom lip, looking conceited as hell.

"So, I take it that you like me, huh? Because that was quite a bit of talking," he asked in between grinning and biting his bottom lip. He was referring to our conversation downstairs.

I shot daggers at him with my eyes.

Devon looked down at his watch. "Why don't we take the kids out and do something fun while Mommy sobers up? I'm sure they're hungry by now, and unless a DUI is on your bucket list . . . I don't know. Let me see if I can remember you saying anything about that in your adventures." He couldn't stop laughing, and I couldn't stop feeling mortified.

Okay, so I could add funny and disarming to the list. I had to give him points. He could have taken advantage of my emotional breakdown and tried to get me butt-ass naked on his desk. Hell, he could have let me sober up in the visiting area with a pot of stale coffee and pretzels after everything I'd told him. Maybe there were some good guys out there, because not once had he been anything less than a gentleman when I'd been doing all the mental Olympics.

Even if he is a good guy, then what?

Chapter 13

Almost Doesn't Count

"You sure this is Rasheed momma house?" I asked, looking out the corner of my eye at Big, trying not to get irritated. He hadn't stopped eating since we got in the car. This fool was the textbook definition of a stress eater. It took all of my will-power not to open my mouth and point out that that's proba-bly how his butt got big in the first place. If he wasn't stress-ing about how much money he might lose without Angelo as an investor in Miami, it was only because his mouth was full. Every time we passed a rest stop or a gas station, he was out the car looking for tuna salad, Swiss Cake Rolls, and Jujubes. It didn't matter how many times I explained and re-explained, Angelo was not worried about him. If anything, I needed to be worried. I'd managed to get on everyone's list on both sides of Angelo's family. He wasn't gonna want anything more to do with Big, and had enough money to not be pressed about the chump change he'd loaned him.

"Yeah, girl, I'm sure. All the homies pretty much grew up here hanging out with him. It's the one right there with the burgundy shutters." He spoke around a mouth full of Hot Pocket.

"Why ain't the porch lights on? There ain't even a car in the driveway. What time is it? Eight forty-three p.m. on a Thursday; someone should be home this late, Big."

"Maybe she took her to Bingo. His ma was always crazy about that shit."

The car was smellin' like a stuffy mobile canteen. Since it was last minute the only thing at the rental place was a compact Prius hybrid. I'd had to do most of the driving since Big was obviously on his man cycle. Y'all ain't know men had cycles? Shit, they get moody, pissy, sentimental, and be all touch me, touch me not. At one point he actually tried talking me into turning around because he didn't properly tell his fish good-bye. We made it to VA just in time. He would've contracted some kind of deadly food poisoning eating all those random gas station snacks, or I'd have killed his ass. We could have flown, but the chance of being spotted by Don Cerzulo or any of Angelo's people was just too risky. Besides, I didn't want any more people questioning me about that Angel of Death business.

I gave Big a wary look, patting his shoulder. "Okay so, you just stay in the car and um, guard your snacks. I'm gonna go look inside and see if they've been here."

I parked far enough away that no one would notice the car and got out, pulling the hood of my jacket over my head. I walked around the side of the house, glad all the windows were low to the ground. There was one around the back of the house that didn't have a screen on it. I pressed in and pushed up on the glass. When it slid up I celebrated and waited to see if an alarm or anything went off. When nothing happened I pushed the window up and climbed through, landing on an old, musky quilted bed. The house was pitch black. Sliding my phone out of my pocket I used the flashlight app for light and cracked the bedroom door open. If I'd had a weak heart I'd have died on the spot. She was standing there like a damn ghost. Reflexes made me drop to the floor drawing my little handgun out of my pants leg.

"Who the fuck are you?" she whispered down at me with her pistol aimed at my nose.

"Desivita, and your ass?" I snapped back, my gun pointed at her gut.

"Oh shit, the little murder actress. I'm Towanna." She put her gun away, reaching out her hand to help me up.

I took it, brushing myself off, looking at her warily, and asked, "Why are you hiding in here in the dark, Michelle fuck you over too?"

Her eyebrow went up, and I realized where I'd messed up before I could even fix it.

"Too? How does Michelle know Desivita Dulce' and how she fuck you over?" she asked, and I wasn't answering I'd already said too much.

"A'ight, well I think she saw me. I was out in front watchin' the house and a crackhead come out the house through the window you just came in, and straight out to my car. Carryin' a damn toaster. Anyway, Michelle came to the door so I pulled off in a panic. When I came back, the house was empty."

No, no, no. I started shaking my head back and forth. This hit-or-miss, "a day late and a dollar short" bullshit had to stop eventually. Tears shimmered in my eyes and I sat down right there in the hallway. I actually had a breakdown in somebody else's house. I couldn't think of what I was supposed to do next or where I was supposed to go. My life was all fucked up, and the only thing I wanted was with the one person who fucked everything up in the first place.

"She's mine, Towanna, and I'll miss her first words. I ain't never heard her laugh or kissed her check and it's tearing me up inside. How do I walk away? If someone could just tell me how, I'd do it. Michelle took her from me, and I just want her back."

Towanna surprised me when she didn't ask any questions. She just sat down beside me and wrapped her arms around my shoulders. She leaned her head against mine and rocked back and forth with me.

I leaned my head back against the wall, staring up at the dark ceiling. Teenage Rasheed probably had all kinds of nasty little girls up in this house when his momma wasn't home. The metal upper half of a pull-up bar was stuck to one of the doorframes, and I immediately knew that was his bedroom.

My chest got tight and the hole in my heart with Rah's name carved around it slowly started to ache. I had to get my mind off him and on to something else. What me and Rah had wasn't nothin' but a stripper's dumb fantasy. When I got him out of prison, I saw him for what he really was with my own eyes. I took a deep breath to calm my thoughts, but something Towanna said made me pause.

"Towanna? Why would Michelle and Rah's momma leave the house if she thought she saw you?" Wiping my tears on my sleeve, I turned to look at her. My eyes were adjusted to the darkness, but now I felt like I was literally in the dark about something. I knew Michelle couldn't have possibly made a new stalker ex-girlfriend already.

Towanna let out a long sigh. She dropped her forehead down to rest on her forearms, which were propped up on her knees. The short poofy ponytail at the back of her head swayed a few times like she was wiping her eyes or her nose before she quietly confessed to the floor.

"I can't help this shit. I'm a protector. And, she got this thing where it seem like she's cold and invincible, but she's not. It makes you feel like Atlas. Like you could do or be anything for her when you finally get Superwoman to take off her damn cape. I fucked up though, on some other shit. Trying to be fast, rushing shit. Anyway, long story short, Chelle's gun went off, it was an accident, just hit me in my vest. She ain't know and I was stunned. She thought she'd killed a cop and she ran."

Towanna was sniffling and wiping her eyes, her head still down.

I couldn't believe my damn ears. She could have said she hated Michelle. That the girl gave bad head, had stank-ass garbage-truck pussy, and gave her the herp. Anything would have been better than what the hell she'd actually said.

Hitting her in the back of the head with my gun I pulled hers from her waistband and stood over her. The blow should have knocked her out, and I cursed when it only stunned her. She rubbed the back of her head and looked at her hand to see if there was blood on it.

"The fuck you do that for?"

I didn't answer her. My gun was aimed between her eyes while I called Big. "I need you in here now!"

I was motioning for Towanna to walk so I could go unlock the front door when this nigga decided to just Donkey Kong barrel crash his ass through it.

"Yo, where you at?" His voice boomed through the house.

So much for being covert.

I rolled my eyes, calling out to him, "Back here, just follow my voice."

He fee-fi-fo crashed through the house, knocking shit over in the process.

"Big, this is Officer Towanna. Officer Towanna, this is Big," I introduced them.

"You ain't say you had a cop."

"Because if I'd said that, Big Daddy, would you have gone all Mighty Joe Young on that door to get to me like you just did?"

The "Big Daddy" and doe-eyes routine wasn't gonna work for this. He was not happy.

"What the hell you think you gonna do with a cop? I can't get in this kind of shit right now. I'm a businessman." Big's tone was short and sharp while he scowled down at me.

I shrugged. "She's not just any cop; she's Michelle's ex–fuck buddy super cop or something. She'll probably come in handy."

Chapter 14

Knights Like This . . .

"And you call yourself a what kind of doctor?" I scolded Devon on the drive back, thankful the kids had fallen asleep in the back seat.

"I'm sorry. A haunted hayride sounded like something fun. I didn't know we'd get chased by axe murderers and zombies. I was thinking more like spooky ghosts and goblins."

"As if that's any better. You definitely don't get to pick anymore child-friendly activities. Your administrative privileges have been revoked. They're probably gonna have nightmares about this." I giggled, unable to stay completely serious.

"Ah, anymore? So that means I get a do over date. In that case, I'd suggest we expose them to gambling and mass amounts of junk food. There's a Chuck-E-Cheese somewhere around here," he laughed.

I slapped his arm playfully.

After my "never to be spoken of again" meltdown in his office, we'd grabbed Lataya's car seat out of the car and I was able to sneak and grab my gun case from underneath the seat. I'd have felt vulnerable without it in my purse. We'd driven all the way out to Podunk middle of nowhere to ride on a haystack through a "haunted" cornfield. Even though the kids were scared shitless, I did have fun.

"Michelle, wake up."

I didn't even know I'd dozed off. I looked around, trying to get my bearings.

"Are we at Momma's? How'd you know how to get here?"

"GPS; her address is on all her records. It's late. I was gonna drop y'all off and just pick you up in the morning to get your car, but you might have a problem."

I looked past him at the front door standing wide open. I sat back quickly and stared straight ahead. "Go, now. Just drive, please."

You've got to be kidding me. What makes this so bad is I don't know if it's Mona or someone else. If they're waiting in there for us or if it was a robbery. Good thing my laptop is in my car. Shit, it's a good thing we aren't pulling up in my car right now.

"Shouldn't you be calling the police right now?" He gave me a concerned look.

"No, you don't ever go to the police unless you know which ones are dirty. My ex had half of them on his payroll back in the day. If they're dirty and the person who did this wants to get away with it, there's nothing you can do about it. I don't know why I even bothered coming back here." I wanted to angry-slap myself repeatedly in the forehead in frustration, but I settled on rubbing my eyebrows.

We rode, with me lost in my thoughts, for what seemed like hours before the car stopped. There was no way in hell Honey could have possibly been able to find me. I hadn't seen anyone, hadn't talked to anyone.

Did she have a tracking device implanted up my ass? If I were her I'd never in a million years think to look for me with Rasheed's momma of all people.

The sad part was that I couldn't even sit down and rationalize with Honey. What she and Rasheed did was between them. I didn't get Honey locked up, but she was so hell-bent on revenge and avenging Rah's murder that she couldn't see the forest for the trees. She could visit Taya, call her, talk to her, but as long as she was a wanted felon, giving Lataya up was not an option.

We'd pulled into an oversized garage filled with four-wheelers, dirt bikes on one side, tools, toolboxes, and a couple of motorcycles on the other.

Assuming this is his place, no one will ever find us here that's for sure.

"I've got four guest rooms upstairs that I never use. This is the kitchen." He pointed quietly so as to not wake up Trey, before turning on the alarm at a panel on the wall.

I nodded and followed along, carrying Lataya's car seat. There were several doors that were bathrooms on the first floor before a laundry room that also somehow connected to the kitchen. I was just relieved when I saw stairs. It meant I could finally lay my tired ass down.

After seeing the kids tucked in, I told Devon I'd be fine sleeping with them after I showered. They would most likely wake up and have a fit at being in a new place otherwise. I wanted to be nearby.

We were standing in the hallway outside a bathroom. The recess lighting was dimmed enough to keep you from running into the cream-colored walls in the middle of the night. Devon pulled me into a hug and was telling me everything would be fine. And there it was, that cardamom, warm vanilla, masculine scent that was all him. Devon started to draw back, but I didn't want to let go. I needed to be comforted and I needed to hear exactly what he was saying. His warmth and closeness . . . *ten, nine, koalas' fingerprints* . . . I couldn't mentally block myself this time. Instead I directed all that fear, anxiety, and panic into pulling him back, burying my face into his neck and letting him hold me. I was probably squeezing the breath out of his lungs, but he didn't complain or protest. His hands stroked methodically up and down my back until I relaxed against him, drawing in deep, even, Devon-scented breaths.

I wanted that smell all over my skin, like his T-shirt I secretly slept in every night since we'd met. I loved my babies to death, but I was tired of technically sleeping by myself. My brain decided to shut down that section that thinks and worries too much. All thrusters set to go, and umpteen thousand volts of pent-up "get him, girl" energy surged in between my legs. I'd worry about tomorrow, tomorrow.

Lightly pressing my lips against the side of his neck, I paused, waiting to see if he'd object. I had to know what that smell tasted like, and I flecked my tongue over his skin. He drew in a sharp, quick breath and my own breathing sped up. I lifted my head, waiting for my kiss, because that's how it works. He let me hover there not more than a breath away. Thinking he was playing some kind of game, I frowned and started to pull away, and he shook his head at me. Those oversized hands of his slid down my hips, igniting my skin underneath my jeans. When he roughly palmed my ass I gasped.

Our lips weren't more than a hair apart, and that's where he kept me, suspended on the edge. One of his fingers slid a little lower than the rest. Instinctively I arched, wanting to feel more of it, grinding against him, and he smiled, teasing me. We were in some kind of psychological war that I didn't know the rules for.

I reached down the front of his slacks and we bit our bottom lips at the same time. It wasn't too big and it wasn't invisible. He was perfect, and I was so excited I forgot all about his Jedi mind fuck or whatever he was trying to prove. I started stroking him through the fabric of his pants, and he closed his eyes and moaned in response. That's what I was used to: being able to break a man down with one hand. All the staring games to see who blinks first or breaks first, that wasn't my territory. It was the thrill of making anyone, man or woman, bend, melt, cave in, react at my will. For the first time in my life, I said, *fuck it,* and I made the first move.

Soft red and yellow lights refracted off the ceiling and walls. Walking into the bedroom was like getting away from the city and standing beside a gently churning creek in the forest. I'd seen them in the lobbies of hotels and restaurants, but never in someone's house. There were two massive marble wall fountains that had to be at least six feet tall on either side of the bed. Water slowly trickled down the slate, rust, and auburn-colored surface gently splashing into the basin at the bottom.

"Devon, that's crazy . . . beautiful," I whispered, awestruck.

He walked over and posed beside one and my jaw dropped. All this fool's clothes had vanished, and he was crazy beautiful too. The bedroom door was wide open and I shook my head. Poor thing definitely wasn't used to having kids around.

"You gonna need to close that, lock it, too." I pointed at the door and undressed.

We met in the middle of the bedroom, our naked bodies collided, and his skin felt like smooth, searing heat and muscle over steel. He kissed me and a surge of intense want and need went through me. Biting his bottom lip, I moaned and reached down to stroke him into action, but he stopped me.

"No. I've already figured out Michelle's problem. Michelle always wants to be in control." He went to get something from underneath the bed. I stood there, completely confused and suddenly a little nervous.

It was hard to see with the meager light from the fountain so I had no idea what he had until he'd slipped some kind of Velcro handcuffs around my wrists. In a single motion, he simply lifted my arms and had my wrists attached to a little thingamajigger hanging from the ceiling before I could even say the word thingamajigger. It was low enough that my feet were still planted firmly on the floor.

"Devon?" His name was a whispered plea from my lips.

Aww hell, I've gone and done it now. Sure, Michelle, go home with the resident Dr. Psycho serial killer and decide to do something you never do. Oh worry about tomorrow, tomorrow? What the fuck about tonight?

When he didn't answer me I became a human cocktail of random emotions. It consisted of about 2 parts scared, with equal amounts of frantic and pissed as I started yanking at my wrists. There might have been a dash of hope somewhere in there, but it wasn't enough to keep me calm. "Devon? What the fuck is this? We ain't even on this kind of level. I don't even know who else's wrists been in these nasty-ass things. I will kick the fuck out of you, just step over here. I swear if you don't let me out," I hissed at him swingin' one of my legs in his direction for emphasis. He easily side-stepped it.

He started laughing. "I do my sit-ups with that. My ankles go in there."

I scoffed and he moved behind me, pulling me back until I could feel his skin pressed against every inch of mine. He wrapped his arm around my waist, filling his hands with my breasts, spreading out his fingers so they touched all but my nipples. When he placed himself in between my legs, my pussy turned traitor to my brain and she throbbed, aching for more attention. It was all the sweetest torture, and not being able to do anything, or anticipate what he was going to do next, was making me feel crazy.

"You are so beautiful to me. Do you know, I thought about you every day until I saw you again?" His words were a warm caress against the back of my neck.

My eyes closed, and I rested my head back on his shoulder. I rocked slightly, rolling my ass back into his hips, simultaneously sliding the length of him against my clit, and I all but purred. My eyes damn near crossed when he rolled my nipples in between the heat of his fingers. Without any warning, he pressed upward. Clamping his hand over my mouth, he buried every inch of himself so deep I instinctively bit into the fleshy part of his palm. If it weren't for his hand I would have screamed.

Damn, I must have forgotten what this felt like. Try to swear off what for how long? My knees felt shaky as hell. Devon was stroking it so good I'd have been on the floor if I weren't attached to the ceiling. Devon had me up off the floor and I didn't even know what that shit was called, but I just wrapped the back of my legs around his thighs and held on. I did my best to be quiet, but it'd been a minute, and I was right there. My pussy started to clench up, and I held my breath because I knew I'd yell or scream. All the pressure, and aching, was building up in that one spot, and he then just stopped.

What the fuckin' fuck kind of bullshit . . .

"Devon, please," I begged him.

He reached above my head and undid my hands and carried me over to the bed. I was breathless, shaky, and getting more pissed off by the second. He smiled down at me and I couldn't see why. I wanted to explain that he was supposed to let me finish before he did all that damn cheesing. Then I saw the light; how many colors are in a fireworks display? Devon kissed his way up my body like he was saying hello all over again, and then he went in. Like "choking me so good I forgot I changed my last name" went in. "I'm marrying this Nigga" went in. I'd already made up my damn mind and everything.

Exhausted, I snuggled into his side and started falling asleep, listening to the water splash in the fountains beside us. I had to admit that shit was extremely relaxing, and sexy.

"You and the kids will stay with me for now. I've got more than enough room, and I feel like it's time to have my life disrupted by two little people and their mother's craziness." Devon's voice loomed in the darkness.

I quietly rolled his words over in my head. *How would a new house and a new person affect the kids? Especially Trey? Could I actually trust this man with my kids under his roof?*

Releasing a long, drawn-out sigh, I looked up at him, trying to figure out his character, worth, and values at a glance. It was one thing when it came to me; it was a completely different matter when the kids were concerned. I considered getting Jim Bartow and the security team, but that shit had cost me an arm and a leg, and at the end of the day more people had died, Honey had lived, and I still wound up getting abducted.

Suddenly anxious from thinking about Honey, I squeezed Devon. I needed to get settled into a routine with the kids and fast. The image of Momma's front door kicked in quickly made me switch from long-term safe to right-now safe.

"I don't like being told what to do." I huffed against his chest.

Devon shifted and leaned over me. "I can always make you beg."

He was giving me a sly, sneaky grin, and I quickly shook my head. I was too damn tired for any more of that; he'd completely worn me out.

Chapter 15

All Good-byes Ain't Gone

"My nigga? Man, I know you ain't cryin'.".”

I climbed in the car and Angelo was sniffling like a little bitch. He called himself mannin' up or whatever, flying through the city on some Nascar shit. If I had to hem this fool up and get behind the wheel so be it. My ass was Makavelli right now. We couldn't afford any heat from a speeding ticket.

"Rah, man, she was fuckin' him. I mean, about to fuck him. Right there in broad daylight. Anyone could have walked in. I walked right in. Then the fuckin' bloggers, paparazzi walked right in like they were supposed to. No, I'm not . . . yes. Yes, I'm good, man."

Angelo slammed his hands against the steering wheel before wiping his nose on his sleeve. I looked away and focused my attention on my phone, acting like I didn't even see that nastiness. He wasn't taking this as well as I thought he would.

I asked him, "When I was locked up, I sent you kite. And if I recall correctly, my exact words to you in that letter was that—"

"Your exact words were that I had what you'd call an anybody getta. That I shouldn't feel special for having her because anybody could get her. And, Honey would fuck me over if I wasn't careful," Angelo sounded off. He squared up his shoulders like he was getting some of his bravado back.

"Right, right. Remember, I told you, she did the same bullshit to me. Had me thinkin' she was locked up with my seed, knowing her ass was Triple H. I'm just glad you seen it before you wifed her up." I dapped him on the shoulder. The kid definitely needed to toughen the hell up before we hit these streets hard and moved into VA.

He snickered, glancing over at me through his pretty boy shades. "Triple H, man, what the hell is this, a code for somethin'? I'm lost," he muttered in his Guido Italian-American "run all the words together" accent.

"Triple H? You know, three Hs? Honey the homie humper. That's her MO, her title. She went from me, to my boy, to my other boy. Need to get her some embroidered panties wit' a big-ass H on them shits like a . . . a damn super she-ho." I slapped the dashboard, cracking up.

I could see Honey's little ass bustin' up in bedrooms. Her hands on her hips, wearing one of her barely there lace pieces from the Hot Spot and some knee-high boots. That image sent me through a slideshow of forgotten memories. Memories that I thought died the day Michelle turned her back on me and walked out of that prison. Smiles, steak sauce, hotel rooms, Trey's first word, and—

"What about your boy Big though? You needs to let me get Bad Apple Sims to handle him," Angelo pressed impatiently, pulling me from my somber thoughts.

"He can handle Big Baby for half of what anyone else would cost. And he can do it just as good."

"Ah, man, Big, he ain't know better. He thinks I'm dead like everybody else. It's guy code. Man law. I'm out the picture. I mean, who could blame him? She cute, probably called him 'daddy' wit' the baby voice. Y'all gave her that fame power. She still got that fat ass?"

"Shut the fuck up already! It ain't power it's quicksand. Had she stayed in line, she'd have floated. She acted up and started moving around, trying to creep and be a sneaky whore. She stirred up the muck and now she's gettin' pulled under by her own actions."

Angelo swerved across the lane and I let it go. Ain't nobody tell him to go pull that whole bended-knee routine. All it did was made him feel worse when the real deal came to light. I'd been in that boat myself. My baby momma found out and stole my paddles, life jacket, and she drilled holes in it, knowing my ass couldn't swim. In my little black book payback was definitely a bitch, and her name was Michelle.

They put niggas in prison not realizing it's concentrated criminology, gangland, and law school combined. You learn who's who, how to do what better, smarter, and more efficiently, because if there's one thing we all have down to a science it's how to get caught.. When I found out Honey was mixed up with the Miami Italians, I heard an easy way out. There was so much talk about Angelo bein' nothing but a pussy-whipped shadow of his father. They called his ass "the joke wit' good coke in Miami." Shit, it ain't take me long to realize the perfect storm would knock his boat right out the water and into my dry dock of a jail cell.

I planted small seeds, sent him a letter telling him about Honey and how she was messing with my master at arms. He was like second in command of my team and my best friend, Derrick. Mind you I was just lookin' to earn his trust so I could push product inside. Imagine my shock and awe when I found out Honey was on a vigilante mission to get me out. So I did the unthinkable. I let old boy know if I escaped, his first mate Honey would jump ship. It was a no-brainer to a calculatin' nigga like myself. I got Angelo on the phone and flat-out told him what the dudes inside thought about his cartel, his fam, shit, kids he ain't even had yet. Dead ass, I even put a couple of Guidos on the phone for validation. He was probably heartbroken, hugged his pillow, cried, I don't know.

But, if there's one thing I did know, you never dead-end a man's ego without offering him a road to redemption. In return for my freedom, I'd be Angelo's redeemer, his savior, so to speak.

He got the official braggin' rights for murkin' my ass; it was a start. It only cost me a few teeth and a burnt-up body. Now all we needed to do was erase the Angel of Death's shadow and handle business. Yeah, payback's a bitch all right, but I was about to play her and everybody else so hard for this paper. My new fake ID needed to say Parker & Parker. The game I was about to run would put the Parker Brothers to shame and make me five times richer. No more living hand to mouth, hustling to get rich. Angelo's people rolled in that old-world money that got inherited and trust-funded.

I met a few dudes on the inside who told me how some of the biggest movie production companies began with startup money from Angelo's pops. This kid didn't even have a row of the Rubik's Cube figured out. In my book he wasn't anything more than a glorified distributor.

"Get your head together. The best way to get over a ho is to get under a better one. You need to throw a party. Invite only, password to get in is 'wet dream.'"

He started to protest, but I kept going; this was my show. "Make sure all the somebodies who push product are there, including your pops. I don't care if you pay him to show up; just make sure he's there. I'll handle the rest. Drop me off at the barber shop. I need to get cleaned up for this shit."

Back home I could walk in any shop from Campostella to Five Points, E.O.V. to Berkley Commons, sit down and they'd do a nigga right. Out here was a different story. I went in the shop looking for the dude who hooked me up last week and he done bounced, phone cut off and everything. The new cat looked sketchy as hell, but we had that party so I tested it out.

Sitting in the barber chair, I planned and ran through every way all the roads could intersect. The record in my head kept skipping, and my first order of business quickly became finding a new barber. This nigga kept fuckin' up my train of thought by putting his stank pinky on my upper lip to balance the clippers. When he wasn't doing that, he was completely disregarding all the personal-space boundaries every man is supposed to abide by no matter what. He was straddling my legs or pressing his meat up against my forearm. My head was on my shoulders; how hard was it to reach across and cut? I shifted so many times it was a wonder my shit wasn't fucked up by the time he was done. I'd go back inside the joint to get a trim or edge-up before I'd go back to this dude. The only reason he even got a tip was because I didn't fuck with a working man's paper. I told any and every one that. You always take care of the working man.

I still managed to walk up out that barber shop feeling clean as hell. Violated yes, but I was still ready to get my Denzel on. Know you can't tell a dude nothing when he got a fresh cut and edge-up hair smelling like Motions oil sheen.

I had Angelo run me past a flower shop. I wanted to get real flowers, not the ones from the grocery store that come in them flimsy bags like some penny goldfish. Twenty minutes and $135 later I climbed back in the car with a damn bush of purple orchids.

"Aww, Rah, you got me flowers." Angelo batted his eyes at me, laughing.

"Shut the hell up, and take me to the crib."

I'd been put up in a condo not far from his. His family owned the building, so most of the tenants were connected, or they came from stupid money. I kept to myself and they assumed I was a rapper or a basketball player, paying me no mind.

"Hey man, you look out and get me lots of cheerleader's numbers right?" The door man Ernesto grinned up at me. I just chuckled at him and shook my head as I walked past him into the building. Looking down at the flawless black marble flooring, I checked my reflection outside the door. I could smell baked chicken with gravy and yams coming all up out the condo and my stomach growled.

"Oh, Rasheed, these are beautiful, baby!" Shiree gasped, her eyes brightening up at my gift.

I puffed out my chest and smiled. "I picked 'em out myself."

She closed her eyes and buried her nose in them, and I let her have her moment before taking them out of her hand and pulling her in close.

She put her hands underneath my shirt and raked her nails along the skin on my sides. I loved that shit. My boxers and jeans were getting more uncomfortable by the second. Shiree had a way of looking at me. Her eyes would turn into these deep, loving pools of chocolate syrup. I know I ain't the most emotionally expressive person in the world, but that look would make a nigga chest tight. I'd have to look away or drown on dry land from staring.

Shiree came to see me and apologized months after Michelle's confession. They'd thought Big gave her an STD, so on some revenge shit they set her up with my pistol. Truth is, his dick game was wack and on top of that he was playin' her. She just went along for the money. She felt like shit for takin' part in it and even used some of her paper to get me a lawyer to help appeal my case. He did what all them legal liars do and took her money, but I appreciated her effort. She'd sat there goin' to pieces over me, and what they'd all done. Now, I'd tear through anyone with nothing but my bare hands if they fucked with her.

I nibbled her bottom lip and let it go. "I missed you."

She ran the tip of her tongue across mine. "You didn't miss me. You missed big Shirley." She rolled her eyes. "You betta tell her how much you missed her."

I hoped whatever she had in the oven was off or had a ways to go. As soon as she got that aggressive tone I got rock solid. There's nothing wrong with being a soft, yielding woman, but nobody wants to be playin' keep-away with your grown ass all the time.

"Dick me down now, daddy." Go ahead, say it. I'll give you time to practice. Now, ask any man out there what the most beautiful sound to the human ear is. Remember you're asking a man, so it ain't a symphony in whatever minor or any of that other foolishness. Those words are it, and the "daddy" at the end is optional.

I kissed her, sucking on her bottom lip hard. She tasted like Riesling and pineapples. I reached down and lifted her sundress, laughing when she ain't even have on panties.

"You think you slick, huh."

She shrugged in response and bit her bottom lip, waiting for me to continue. She was already slippery wet and ready. I parted her lips and watched her eyes barely flutter closed while my finger hovered over her clit, barely touching her.

"Go get me some peppermint tea and daddy'll take care of you."

She squealed and took off for the kitchen, clothes and ass cheeks flying everywhere.

I'd gotten off my shoes, pants, and boxers. My shirt was barely over my head when my eyes crossed and toes curled. Shiree dragged her nails across my bare ass with one hand and cupped my balls with the other. She had a mouthful of me and hot tea, as she slurped, tightening her lips around my dick, pulling me farther down her throat. I yanked my shirt over my head and watched her work. Knowing Shiree, she'd already had that shit on standby, and it was beautiful.

I growled, pulling her up, bending her over the couch. Looking back at me with her head down on the back of the couch and her thumbnail in her mouth she gave me a little evil grin. She knew she was in trouble and loved it. I drank some of the tea, letting it warm the inside of my mouth before swallowing it. I didn't swallow the next sip. I leaned over her back so my dick was rock solid right in the crack of her ass and I slid a hot kiss down her spine. She moaned and pressed back into me. I took another sip, spread her ass open, and ran my tongue from her tailbone down to her asshole and dove in. She moaned like she was possessed, locking her ankles behind my back locking me in. Peppermint tea and ass eatin', be careful how and when you use that shit. If you've ever wondered what makes perfectly normal women turn into crazy, "kill your ass if you try to leave" psychos, there's your answer.

When the tea got down to room temperature, that meant it was time to handle business. Shiree grabbed the back of the couch for leverage and threw all that ass back at me. I tensed and started thinking about how many grams it takes to make an ounce. How many ounces mak—

"You fuckin' me or am I fuckin' you huh?" she shot back at me, sounding all breathless.

I exhaled. My body back under control, I leaned down and pressed my chest against her back so she could feel my skin against hers. Grabbing her hips for leverage, I pulled out and went in so slow and so deep she looked like she'd stopped breathing.

"I'm fuckin' you, baby," I told her quietly.

See, Shiree always fucked with these short-stroke, "no dick game" niggas she could out sex in the bedroom. All she needed was to sense a weak moment, and I'd have to remind her who was in charge less she go trying to pull a damn plastic dick out on a nigga. I have to admit, every now and again that shit did get to feeling good as all hell. But, I never slipped up though, to hell with that. I'd just pull some fuck-crobatics on her. Flip that ass over, give her one of them deep "I love you" kisses and go-go gadget drill-her until she'd tap out. Literally.

Chapter 16

All Over a Wet Pigeon

The spot Angelo found for the party was on some next-level shit. It looked like a meatpacking plant from the street view, but once you got inside, it was perfect. Four themed levels broke up into smaller areas. It had pool tables, two areas that we were gonna use as dance floors, and a bar. I saw an investment opportunity. The place would make a killing as an after-hours spot. I made a note to check into the property owner.

I wasn't exactly sure what kind of turnout we'd have, so I got there mad early to get everything set up. If Angelo did his homework like he was supposed to, we shouldn't have a problem. I kept it simple, balancing some black leather Giuseppe Zanottis with a blazer and some Balmain jeans. Shiree was all over me when I tried to get out the door, so I know I looked good and smelled even better. She refused to not work and I loved that about her. Shiree wasn't the type to take handouts or live off a nigga. I refused to let her get back on a stage. We compromised, and she found work doing hair and makeup for a major modeling agency. She had to be at a shoot tonight out at the beach with some dude who wore more makeup than she did. I let her do her thing, get that money.

Everybody who goes inside the way I did, usually come out broke. Not your boy. One day out in the yard I seen this dude scaring the hell out of a cat. He was a big, ugly somebody with one of those crazy brashes. A brash is a beard so long it could brush his ass. "Trying to collect cat piss," was what he said when he saw me staring him down. It was prison; people did all kinds of weird shit, so I ain't ask why. The cat he was scaring to death was one I'd been feedin' scraps to. Since she liked me, I knew what spots she liked to mark. I helped him set up bottle caps to collect piss with, and he asked if I wanted to get high as his way of saying thanks. Me and this crazy white dude, who went by the name Scorpion, was tight after that.

Lo and behold, him and his boys were making their own versions of powder by cuttin' down and refining the stuff that came in off the street. Cat piss was only one of the additives they used to tweak and mix shit down. They had a makeshift lab rigged up with butane lighter Bunsen burners, and soda bottles for beakers. I'd never seen anything like it. You walk up to a dude to buy an eight ball or whatever, and then he turns around and asks you what you wanna feel. I remember standing there like, "Um, high."

There's levels to that shit like the levels to medicinal marijuana. There's clean high, which is your normal coke. Then there was the extreme left-field stuff like face melter, mind warp, wormhole, chest expander, and body rock. None of those were for amateurs. I'd sent some samples out to test the water, and let's just say I'ma leave all that to the dudes inside. We don't need no more zombie apocalypse scares. Then you have lines like the phantom limb, where random body parts go numb or magically manifest. One cat swore up and down he had a damn tail. It was funny as hell, but I'm sorry, prison is not the place to run around thinking you gotta ghost appendage attached to your ass. Heaven's gate was on some "so beautiful I'd never do it again" type shit. Have you seeing angels and talking to God.

Scorpion helped me tweak the fuck out of this one line though. I called my new baby Indican wet dream, and she wasn't nothing but the truth.

"Rah, yous already here. Lookin' Ginsu sharp." Angelo walked in with a smug smile on his face. He was boasting like a boxer before the big fight, walking around the ring with his arms spread out yelling at the empty room.

"What you think, it's like Kitchen Stadium up in here or what? We's gonna flambé these bitches tonight, Bobby Flay style."

The smile instantly fell off my face. "We gonna what? No. Don't ever say that again. Where the couches and them chaise things I asked for? We only got a couple of hours."

"My bad, dude. Honey used to keep me watching the damn Food Network . . ."

I glared, and looked for something, anything, to throw at this kid.

"Okay, chaise lounges, I'm on it. Password wet dream."

Four hours later we were all set up and every major anybody who did anything started making their way in.

"Yo, what's up with me telling them a password and then you don't even make 'em use it?"

I didn't tell Angelo everything, because just like a woman, he'd ask too many inconsequential questions. I'd end up pissed off and not answering anyway, and we'd still end with the same outcome. I just sipped my Henny and Coke, waiting for the crowd to peak, hoping Don Cerzulo would actually put in an appearance. Some of the finest women in Miami showed up, fighting with each other to get our attention. I ain't gonna say I settled, but I could look at every last one of them and know they weren't worth half of my Shiree. She came to me when I was dirty, broke down, and hopeless. Stayed with me, gave me hope, and I refused to mess that up. I decided to text her to pass the time.

Hey, you. I stared at the screen. Secretly I was waiting to see exactly how long she'd take to respond.

Hey, baby. Is everything going okay?

When she replied immediately, I was relieved. If she was texting me then she damn sure wasn't fucking somebody else. Yeah, I put it down, treated her like my queen and all that, but I'd done a lot of wrong in my time, told a lot of lies to a lot of women. It was hard for me to completely let my guard down. I was a changed dude, but I damn sure ain't want to go all in and throw on the blinders called love and then have someone runnin' game on my non-seeing ass. I tried to think of something cute that would make her smile.

Everything's good. Up here waitin' when I rather be home with my heart.

Again she hit me right back. Aww. Well your heart is still at work, baby. This shoot is running over. I'm on standby for touchups.

I read that shit twice and looked at my watch. It was damn near midnight. Shiree hadn't worked late in a minute. On second thought, she hadn't even been flying out for any shoots with the girls. At one point it seemed like she was working late or hopping on a jet almost every other week. All that stopped once I got her locked down though . . . or so I thought.

My fingers were going a mile a minute. Why you ain't get somebody else to fill in? It's late. What time you gonna be home?

I waited and after five minutes I'd finished my drink and ordered another one. Angelo was all over the place like a Chinese spinning top, and I was getting more irritated by the second. The first floor was packed, standing room only, and that was my cue. I signaled the DJ and the music lowered as I made my way up to the second floor. Reality nodded, opening the solid metal door that led to my showroom. Reality was one of the guys I'd recruited for the night's security. A dreaded, six feet six-ish, purple-black brick wall of a motherfucka controlled my door. If anyone tried to act stupid, they'd get a Reality check.

The guests were all being told to consider using their password carefully. Once they came upstairs, there was no going back downstairs or changing their mind. You'd be surprised how many people in this lifestyle hear something like that and push forward all gung-ho and shit. They'd seen and done everything so if you've got a novelty, you'd better use it to your fullest advantage. The first wave came in and stood under the black light, gripped in a state of frightened anticipation. To add some dramatic flair I'd found a Phantom of the Opera mask that covered half my face. The second floor was nothing like the club we had downstairs. Couches, chaise lounges, and oversized pillows were from one end of the room to the other. I opened a case covered in black velvet and the black light made the vials inside glow. One was incandescent pink and the other was bright blue. The room broke out in ooh's and aah's.

"Choose tonight's experience. Would you like to have a wet dream, or become a wet dream?" I asked them, feeling like a damn ring master.

They came up and started making their selections. Wet dream was the prison favorite and the most hated. For a woman, it was the equivalent of turning on every sexually arousable nerve ending in her body. That's how Shiree described it anyway. She said even her toes felt like they could actually cum if I touched 'em just right. It's a sexually explosive buildup that'd have you hangin' on a door humpin' the hell out of a doorknob. All the while it's feeling like you got ten niggas with ten dicks with lips on each dick going to town.

There honestly wasn't any difference between that pink shit and the blue one. As a businessman I just knew you always need an option, and it's always a plus if it's pink. Women tend to gravitate toward anything pink. So it honestly didn't matter who picked what.

"Come over here and play with me, sexy. I like the mask."

Grinning at my handy work I quickly peeled a topless Dominican chick off my chest, shaking my head at her. The no was more for the head in my pants than for her.

You stay down, boy. Yes, I seen them pretty-ass dark exotic nipples too, but we can't play.

It was all going exactly as planned. I checked my phone and still no response from Shiree. Angelo was nowhere to be seen. Making my way up to the third deck, I spotted him on a couch with two brunettes and shook my head. I specifically told him to wait until after we handled business. Of course, Reality would hit me at that exact moment to let me know Don Cerzulo was on the way up. I made sure the third floor was completely empty before posting G and Fallon outside the door. Stuffing the mask behind the bar, I checked my reflection in the mirror.

Oh well, all or nothing, this is it.

"I don't think we've met, Don Cerzulo, I'm—"

"Not my son. Where is Angelo?" He dismissed me and looked around suspiciously.

"Angelo is downstairs, sir. I was going to partner with him, but seeing as how he's in the middle of a naked orgy with the customers and we haven't done any business, I'd like to rethink my options. It seems as though you might be the better businessman?" I waited.

"You don't have anything I don't already have. Whatever it is, I can get it."

"What I'm selling you don't have, and can't get, because I created it," I replied smugly, setting two vials of wet dream on the bar underneath the black light.

Don Cerzulo rubbed his chin and took a seat on the sofa facing the bar. He stared at them, frowning, tilting his head from side and then to the other. I wasn't sure what the protocol was for something like this, so I went behind the bar to freshen up my drink while he stared or whatever.

"What the fuck kind of laser-light show cockamamie magic shamrock shit is this? You take me for a fucking fool?" Don Cerzulo's breath was a hot hiss into my ear.

I had to give him his props. He was quick and freakishly quiet on them old feet of his. His pistol was pressed hard up against my junk and I could feel a lonely tear burning in the corner of my eye.

"It ain't a joke. I learned to make it locked up in VA. My name is Rasheed White; your son fake killed me for street cred. Tomorrow, every dealer in the area is gonna be lookin' for me or wet dream, because right now, they on the second floor fucked up and fuckin', and I need my dick and a truckload of shit to sell them."

"Atta boy, no man alive'll lie on his Johnson. Fix me a gin and tonic. How much are we talkin' about?" Don Cerzulo dropped his gun and walked back over to the couch.

"Two mill for my time and the supplies and one major supplier. Guarantee I'll have your investment back to you with interest faster than a hummingbird fuck." I handed him his drink and took a seat, quickly sipping from mine to calm my jacked-up nerves.

"Gotta sample it. You do half first to make sure you ain't trying to poison me."

After the stunt he just pulled, I wasn't about to tell him that we shouldn't be doing this shit together. But, Don Cerzulo was not the kind of guy you hesitated around when it came to business; it made you look sketchy. I uncapped a vial and lifted it to my nose, inhaling quickly. The powder numbed my nostril, making my eyes water.

"Let me just tell you now, Don, shit hits harder than wood-pecker lips, my dude."

I handed it to Don Cerzulo as the hairs on my head began to pulsate, sending throbbing vibrations down my back that made my eyes feel like they were dancing in my skull.

"We're gonna need to get a girl up in here, man. Trust me."

I stuck my head out the door with my body throbbing and I looked G and Fallon up and down. Fallon had scuff marks on his shoes and a ketchup stain on the bottom of his shirt. If he ain't care about his appearance, who knew what kind of women he'd come back with.

"G, go find me some girls." I relayed the quick order and popped back into the room, trying to stay as far away from Don Cerzulo as possible. I'd seen dudes do some fucked-up shit to each other inside, all because they touched and had a "it felt good" moment. No, sir, his old ass was not about to have me *Brokeback Mountain* up in this bitch. I made the mistake of looking in his direction and almost gagged. He was in the chair with his eyes closed, doing some kind of geriatric air humps. Sounding like a drunk gorilla.

The girls came in just in time, and Don Cerzulo almost jumped out of the chair he was so excited. I busied myself on the other side of the bar, rubbing my junk along the counter with my eyes closed, thinking about Shiree. My phone vibrated in my pocket and the sensation traveled all the way up the back of my neck.

Do I ever ask you when your ass is coming home? No. So don't ask me.

That was her answer, damn near an hour later, and that's what she had to say. What the hell had she really been doing?

"Why you over here all by yourself, sexy face?"

I didn't even argue when she unzipped my jeans, wrapping her pretty lips all around me. And she was a hummer. A song came on downstairs and she got into it humming with the faint music. Even high as hell, my conscience was fuckin' with me. I kept hearing Shiree's voice; it detracted from the mean sucking and slurping effects this chick was making.

"Yo, ma, you gotta stop." My words came out in a painful groan.

"Mmmm, Mr. Pretty Dick, does that mean you ready to fuck?"

She still hand my dick in a viselike grip and I gritted my teeth trying to hold back.

"I know you're not done already. What's the matter, your girl got wack head?" Don Cerzulo called out from over his shoulder. He had his chick bent over the couch. The chick on her knees in front of me turned to see who the hell was calling her head game wack. In the process of her turning, her hair swept across me like a thousand fingers, and that combined with her hand sent me over the edge. I exploded with a growl, clutching the counter behind me to keep my balance and she screamed.

"Eeew, you got it in my ear. Really? Arrrgh. It's in my ear!"

Don Cerzulo hooted, "Wet dream? You need to call it wet pigeon. I ain't wet pigeoned a broad since grade school. My partner, the wet pigeoner. I likes this kid; meet me here tomorrow, three p.m., two million."

All I could hear over my heart beating in my ears was Don Cerzulo telling his girl to get up so he could wet pigeon her, and Shiree, yelling.

Pulling my phone out of my pocket, I squinted at the bright white letters that said Call in progress 00:6:48 and still counting. I didn't even bother lifting it up to my ear.

Chapter 17

Tell Me Somethin' Good

After my night with Devon I woke up practically singing. He seemed like such a good man and he was so easy to get along with. Even though he had no sense when it came to kids, I giggled at that haunted hayride fiasco. He even challenged Trey to an ice cream eating contest when he got off work. I'd have to run interference on that one, because the last thing I'd be doing is playing nurse to two bellyaches. I made his bed and straightened up, wondering if I could ever think of it as *our* bed. It was kind of soon yes but, all these kinds of things made me think about having a real, normal life again. Not always running around scared of everything and everyone. I missed that, and there was only one person keeping me from it, and it wasn't Honey. She couldn't be my boogey-man forever.

Devon had already made breakfast and left for work. That one was still a jaw dropper. He got up and actually cooked real food from scratch, not some microwave heat-up crap. He'd brought me chocolate chip pancakes, turkey bacon, strawberries, and two little people covered from head to toe in flour. All I could see were Lataya's eyes. I was shocked they didn't have a fit and come screaming and kicking the door down when they woke up in a new place. Devon asked if they wanted to make Mommy breakfast, and they were all in.

He'd called to tell me he rode past Momma's house and it looked like someone had already put the door back up. Mona or one of Momma's neighbors must've done it, I couldn't think of anyone else. The kids had enough clothes in the bags I always kept in my car to last for at least a month, so I wasn't too worried about anything we had in the house. After lunch I decided to get the kids dressed and take them to see Momma.

I was sure she'd enjoy having Trey there, and she probably secretly missed her "imposter crumb snatcher," too. She was still in the intensive care unit and giving all the male nurses hell, grabbing their asses and making kissy faces at them. When she wasn't doing that, she was complaining: it was either too cold, or the food ain't have any flavor, the blanket was scratchy, the lady on the other side of the room sounded like she was getting more channels. It might be good for her to see a few familiar faces. Maybe she'd hurry up and get better.

"You just stick me in here like a potato plant, waiting for me to sprout roots to this bed," Momma whined pitifully as soon as we walked in.

"Hey, G-ma." Trey climbed up in her bed, geared up to show her his new iPad. That thing was Devon's idea not mine. Trey picked it up and Devon told him go for it, saying some mess about extra ones for the hospital. Yeah, well I hope he had an extra, extra one. I could just see it falling and cracking all over one of the many tiled floors in that house or outside on the sidewalk. But, he insisted, and it'd been fused to Trey's hands ever since.

"Hey Grandma, suga'. I could just eat ya all up, nam nam nam."

She was making chomping noises and he was squealing, but still determined to show off his new present.

"What in the world is this? An i-what?"

I let them have their time and I wandered off to see if I could find Devon.

"No. I can't come see you. It's not because of anyone, it's because I don't want to. You'll survive I'm sure. I honestly don't care what she thinks."

I found Devon in a corner of the admittance desk having an intensely heated conversation.

I'd started to back away. I didn't want to get caught eavesdropping.

"Mommy, G-ma gave me money for the smack machine."

Trey slammed into my leg going a mile a minute about the snack machine? I was pretty sure that's what he meant. Normally I would have corrected him, but Lataya's car seat was getting heavy, and I just wanted to disappear.

Devon called after me, but I just wanted to get outside and get some fresh air. This shit was impossible; these men were damn impossible.

Was that a woman? And why was his ass whispering?

I walked out the front door, trying to get my mind together. "We'll go get candy in a minute okay, Trey?"

I must have looked upset or something, because he simply nodded, and he rarely did that. Devon would be out here in a minute, and I needed to figure out what I'd say if I should ask anything, how to explain my reaction. It'd only been but a blink, here I was about to make myself look like one of those women who go all insane stalker over some good dick.

It was just a'ight dick anyway. Psssht. Whatever, that shit was good.

Not in the mood for thinking, I just took some breaths, cleaning my mind. I'd read a pamphlet on his kitchen table that suggested you try breathing to alleviate stress, so here I was breathing instead of counting, and I still felt stressed. At least counting down from ten kept me from thinking about all the other crazy shit going on in my head. So what if I never made it past eight? I just needed to slow my roll, not define anything; he did tell whoever she was he couldn't see her, so that was a start.

And that's when I damn near had a real-live on-the-spot panic attack. We locked eyes as she walked past me. I couldn't believe she was alive, even though I hadn't been sure she was dead to begin with.

"Hi, can't really talk. I've gotta get someone checked in," Towanna said and quickly walked by, dragging a young girl in handcuffs up the stairs toward the entrance.

The wind blew, and I stood there staring at the back of her black windbreaker, slack-jawed and dazed. The girl stared back at me with demented crazy eyes and let out an eerie cackling sound of a laugh. I sighed. I really needed to figure out which pet cemetery or Indian burial ground they were sticking everyone in so I could go bless or whatever the hell you do to destroy those things. What was Towanna even doing in Virginia?

"Momeee, can we go to the smack machine now?" Trey piped up with his perfectly aggravating timing.

I walked back into Momma's room a complete flustered mess. Devon rushed in after me.

"It's so nice to see you two together all in love. I'm in love myself, with these murses," Momma announced with an ecstatic shimmy as she fanned herself, peeking around for another nurse to harass. "Is it football season? 'Cause I've been watching tight ends all day. Whew, these male nurses running around here with these tight behinds, murses got my love oven getting moist and it ain't did that since—"

I turned to Devon. "Sweetie, can you please run Trey to the snack machine right quick before he asks again?"

He quickly obliged, happy to not have to hear whatever was about to come out of Momma's mouth.

"So you're feeling better, Momma White?" I sat down next to her on the hospital bed, noticing that for once she wasn't talking about predators or body snatchers; she was her normal self. The woman I remembered meeting ages ago.

"Oh, I was lyin' here last night and I remembered so much, it was refreshing and hellishly scary. You ever rode a wild man or a rollercoaster backwards? It was like that." Momma nodded.

"It was like what, Momma, really?" I gawked at her and started blushing because I'd definitely ridden a wild man backwards, standing too.

"Child, I ever tell you what I did for the first three years after I had Rasheed?"

"No, ma'am. I don't even think Rah ever mentioned it."

She patted the pillow beside her. "That's because he ain't neva know. Get comfy."

Chapter 18

Momma's Maybe

Me and Ray always tried to find a way to see each other despite his parents foolishness. Even with the DNA test proving he was the daddy, his parents made him go through hell to get out the house to see me. One night he was walking me home. Sometimes it was just easier to visit him at work than to try to see him after hours. We heard all this noise. It was like a rusty trombone sounding off against an angry pirate. Hurt your ears something terrible. Frankie Diamonds was laying into some poor girl. He was stomping and beating her; blood was splattering all up against the side of that pretty Cadillac of his. Ray wasn't going to just stand by and watch something like that.

He marched over and asked Frankie what the problem was, and of course, Frankie put him off.

"You ain't gonna keep that nose if you keep sticking it in traps to see if they've snapped. This ain't got nothing to do you with you, young blood. Go tend to your woman before I decide to tend to her, too." Frankie Diamonds looked around Ray, blowing a kiss in my direction.

My baby whooped his ass right then and there. He went to help up the girl Frankie beat, and she was pretty much at the point of just giving up. She wasn't going to make it and she knew it. She told Ray where Frankie's clip was at in the car and he went for it. Came back across the street and showed me what had to be at least $30,000. Back then that was a lot of damn money. We decided we were gonna take that and move away together.

A shout split the silence. "Them motherfucka's right there. They snatched my shit." Frankie's Cadillac pulled up at the end of the alley, and we could hear him circle around. I took Rasheed; he was all I could carry, and I ran like the devil was chasing me. I ran through front alleys, back alleys, slid through puddles, ducked around trash cans. I splashed through what I could only hope was mud or puddles.

"You'd better have a bank roll of bills strapped to that baby's ass, or I'll kill everything you've ever known and that ain't a forecast, it's official," Frankie hissed at me as he climbed out of the Cadillac.

I wasn't fast enough, and damn sure didn't hide well enough. Raising my chin and squaring up my shoulders I stepped out from behind the corner of the Dumpster where I'd been hiding.

"I don't have your money, so best you just g'on ahead and kill me then," I told him defiantly.

My head snapped around. I saw Frankie, brick, that dumpster, and then Frankie again. I could feel my cheek split open from the spot where his ring connected with the skin. He stood there in the alley with all of them diamonds glittering and glistening, sneering at me like I won't nothing but shit on the bottom of his shoe. Somebody'd gone and rubbed the lamp his daddy called a dick one day, and this evil genie of a man floated into the world, promising all of these riches and treasure, claiming he could make all your troubles go away. The only thing you had to sell was you.

He looked over at this tall, lanky black thang beside him. "What you think? Should I put her on the track, she look like she got thirty grand makin' snatch, plus my commission?"

They stared me up and down, assessing my street value, while Rasheed whimpered in my arms.

"You down one ho anyway. Lexy ass is done for. Might as well make her work off that roll; the kid gonna be an issue. Dead that."

Even if Ray gave Frankie that money back, I knew he'd still kill him, Rasheed, and Mona for taking it. Something like that wouldn't go unpunished, and if word got out, it'd make Frankie look weak. Police wouldn't do nothing about it except lock Ray up for stealing if I went to them. I did what I had to do to save my family.

"My sister can keep my baby. Put me on that track and I'll make you six figures. Please don't hurt anyone." I was out there begging for lives that ain't even know they were in danger, tears running down my face and falling on Rasheed's. He stopped crying, though.

"You make six figures and I'll give you my Caddy, throw in some girls, and make you a damn partner, shit." He laughed and jabbed the other guy with his elbow. "Tell Smoke where your sister stay and he'll take your brat to her. Understand one thing ho, my repumatation, yes you heard me right because I'm never wrong— my repumatation is imperial. I won't be known for peddlin' or maintainin' dirty sewer shit-stain pussy. Those are the kind of accusations I'd get if niggas saw or smelled yo' ripe alley cat lookin' ass right about now. I'm the hand of God as far as you're concerned, cross me and I will smite thee. Your shift starts once you are cleaned up to my liking, and you are on my clock."

That was the night Frankie the Ambassador Diamonds became my pimp, lover, husband, confidant, and my employer. When it was time to take me up out that alley and show me my new home, he'd actually said out his mouth that I wasn't ready to ride in his car yet; that I'd funk and fuck up his interior. This nigga took every side street and back road through the city, and I had to walk while he followed along beside me. He said it'd toughen up my feet, get me conditioned for long hours of standing. Teach me how to get out there and properly do that ho stroll.

It's a big deal when a pimp adds a new girl to his roster. All the other girls that want and chose to be there are instantly jealous and catty. There were eight women all cramped up in this small three-bedroom house. The master bedroom belonged to Frankie, and the only way you got to sleep in there with him was when you were earning stupid money. It didn't make a lick of sense to me. If he had so much money, why did he have us all up in this little-ass house, and why would he want a ho that any dude could run up in on any given day? I never said that shit out loud though. Just kept it to myself.

Frankie had the girl he called his "bread winner" show me the ropes and explain how everything worked. His reasoning behind that was that if I was trained by a "bread winner", then maybe I'd become one. Royce was a pretty, round-faced girl. I heard him call her a black and tan. She had a nice brown skin complexion with long, shiny black hair. I didn't know what black and tans were, but I was determined to figure it out one of those days.

"Hand jobs is ten dollars, blowjobs is twenty dollars, sex is fifty dollars. Always use a rubber and don't go anywhere suspect with more guys than you can handle. Stay away from the other pimps or they'll think you're choosing. That means like you're looking for a new pimp. If you get locked up call Frankie, he gonna take it out cho' ass if he have to bail you out, that's what happened to Lexy. Rule number one, have Frankie's paper, and rule number, um, one . . . don't get busted." She rattled off rules like she was reciting her bedtime prayers. I wanted to ask if both of the rules were number one because they were that important, but I left it alone. Royce talked in a spaced out, breathy little voice like she was in a galaxy far, far away.

Hours later, I was out there with thoughts flying through my head, driving me crazy at around 145 mph. All I knew was that it was gonna be a helluva long way before I saw $30,000. My first hand job was easy as hell, and after that I kept getting those left and right. Lacy walked over to ask my secret.

I shrugged. "I just stand there like y'all do and tell 'em it's ten dollars; ain't no secret."

She looked dumbfounded. "Ten dollars! Ho, is you crazy? Hand jobs are twenty dollars. Frankie is gonna have your ass if he finds out the only reason you makin' any money is because you out here giving discounts on your first damn day." She rolled her neck at me.

I almost popped her smart ass in the mouth for threatening to rat me out, and Royce for telling me the wrong prices. Spacey or not, she only did that shit because she was ruthless and wanted to stay the top earner. Showed me to never trust nobody no matter what. Just to show them hoes I wasn't playin', I waited until all they asses went to sleep and any nasty douche bottle left sitting in the bathroom got dipped in toilet water. Nasty-ass heffas ain't know better, then I'd show their asses better.

After about a week I was the top earner and everybody except Lacy was up in the clinic with they snatch smelling like a sewer rat's ass. That week, Frankie Diamonds took me to see Rasheed for the first time. He cried when I tried to hold him like he didn't know who I was, and Mona clucked her tongue, taking him back from me.

"Mona, you seen or heard anything about Ray?"

"He moved from what I heard, don't know where. His ass win the lottery or something?"

I smirked. "Yeah, or something." I couldn't believe he'd just leave without even looking for me or trying to help me. He didn't even have the nerve to face Frankie, and here I was selling myself to pay back the money he was out enjoying? I changed the subject. "How you been doing, though? You okay with the baby and everything?"

"Me and little man here is good. He get gassy at night and wake up fussy, but Auntie Mona taking good care of you ain't she?" She cooed at my baby and he smiled up at her. "Oh, sis, let me borrow about ten dollars. I'm gonna need to go get Rasheed some more formula."

I gave her ten out of the money I had to pay out to Frankie; it'd be nothing to make it back up. Frankie beeped, and I kissed Mona's and Rasheed's cheeks.

After working for Frankie Diamonds for three years, I finally decided to ask him how much I'd made him. He was sitting in the bathtub in the master bedroom at the house. It was one of the few times he actually stayed there during the week. The other girls were in the bedroom fighting over the clothes he'd brought us. He liked to keep us pitted against each other. Normally, I'd have already picked mine out and left the rest for them to fight over since I had the top spot. I had more pressing matters to deal with than cheap clothes.

"You ain't the tally keeper, you the tail. You earn the tally and I run the tally wagon. When you hit your mark, I'll give you your letter." Frankie smirked at me.

He tried to brush me off, but I wasn't having it. I handed him my notebook wrapped in a towel so he couldn't complain about his hands being too wet to take it.

"I know, baby. You love your Diamond Ambassador pimp, and you wrote me a poem or song or some other beautiful sonnettical form of self-expression and shit. I'm relaxing in my bath. I'll look at it later." Closing his eyes, he laid his head back on the rolled-up towel on the ledge, mumbling, "Y'all hoes kill me thinking you worth a nigga every waking breath."

"That's because I am worth it. This year I started tracking every dick I've had to touch for a dollar. I've made you a total $115,200!" I screamed at him, throwing my notebook at his head.

You start to touch so many twenties and hundreds in a day and then you see a man with all these diamonds, watches, and furs. It makes you start to wonder what it all adds up to. The other girls didn't question shit, because as long as they had their dope for the night, or Frankie got them that bottle of whatever they liked to drink, they were fine. My ass got out there every night. More sober than a got-damn saint. I seen what that shit did to Mona, and I wasn't touchin' none of it.

There was a particular Friday night when I got out on that corner before sundown at six p.m. and didn't get in until the sun came up the next morning at seven. During those thirteen hours I made $975. That was in one day. Made me wonder where ol' Frankie really went when he stayed gone days and nights on end. He took me on a run with him once, to get dresses. He told me to go try shit on while he paid. I watched through the slats in the fitting room; he leaned 'cross that counter, running his mouth. When he was done, we were pulling around back and the bags went in the trunk. That register didn't ring, ching, or nothing. Our money wasn't even going toward us.

It had gotten dead quiet outside that bathroom, which meant all ears were probably glued to the door.

"Look here." Frankie sat up in the bathtub, adjusting the shower cap on his head. "What I tell you about trying to count higher than what you can hold in one night? Ho business

is yo' business and dough business is mine. Unless you got receipts, I don't know what the fuck you talking about. Matter of fact, if you made that much and it ain't cross my palm"—he slapped the palm of his hand, spraying bubbles and straw-berry-scented water into the air—"bitch, you betta go find my motherfuckin' money! Delusional ass. Hey, hey now! What the hell y'all give this ho to smoke before you . . ."

I didn't think about it. It was one of those things that you just see in your head over and over every day. Especially when you're laid up under some stranger and he's just sweating and gruntin' over top of you. Or someone's got you by the back of the head and they're mashing your face into they stank balls for a measly fifty dollars. This is life day in and day out because a nigga says he'll kill you and everything you love.

One day I pulled that fantasy out of my head and made it happen. I turned to walk out of that bathroom knowing for a fact that I'd made this clown-ass poor excuse of a nigga well over $100,000. I'd lost my family behind it, and sad to say, for all that, I barely had more than three grand to my name.

The curling irons sizzled when I knocked them off the edge of the sink into that bathtub. I could never put in words the way Frankie the Ambassador Diamonds smelled as he stewed in his own excrements in that tub. Burning flesh has a smell that's all its own. It's kind of like how bacon smells exactly like bacon, you can't describe it, you just know it. He got fried to a crisp, knocked out the power in a four-block radius. And it all smelled like salvation to me.

I took his car keys and drove home to see my baby.

Chapter 19

Burn Bitches Like Bridges

(The Other Side of Miami)

There's only two times that a man is actually scared to walk into his own house. One is when you don't know who in there. That morning, I'd stood in front of the door trying to perfect my game face before I walked in on that second moment—a pissed-off woman with Lord knows what as a weapon. I'd driven around the rest of the night hazy as fuck, piecing together exactly what I thought she'd heard, but the shit was fuzzy. There wasn't gonna be any lying my way out of this; she wasn't the one to play with like that.

Exhausted, I gave up and went home when the sun started hurting my eyes. I'd gone up in there, ready to face damn near anything except an empty house. Shiree sent my calls straight to voicemail, so I privatized my number and started calling. She turned off her phone. I kicked myself for being so damn stupid. Last thing I remember was laying my ass across the bed, fully clothed, still buzzing from the long night.

Hissing woke me up. Shiree hissed in my face; her nose was so close to mine I actually jumped when I saw her.

"Shiree, baby," I started to explain, wanted to explain everything to her.

She held her finger up to my lip and shushed me. "You could have at least taken off your nut-stained jeans nigga. Don't even try to start a lie. Worried about me at work and you out doing you." She sneered.

I'd started to sit up; maybe I could reason with her or plead, beg her to stay, I didn't know. She laid her hand on my chest, motioning for me to lie back down. I ain't know if we was about to angry fuck or what. Tense as hell, I did as directed. My head wasn't flat on the pillow before she was floating a damn Mason jar right above my forehead.

She looked down at me out the corner of her eye. "Ah, ah, ah. Don't do that or you might make me spill it," she said in a calm quiet voice.

"What's going on, Shiree? What the hell is that?"

"Shhh. Acetic acid can eat through skin. You'd be amazed at what I have access to in the lab, Rasheed. I'd do worse to you, but karma is comin' around and it's gonna fuck you over better than I ever could. You've got me confused if you think I'm about to have this baby myself."

Baby? I ain't even know she was . . . was it mine? Of course it was mine. The cool glass bottom of the jar felt like a lethal iceberg resting on my forehead as Shiree removed her hand, letting it balance itself out. Holding my breath I watched her out the corner of my eye as she slowly backed away from the bed. I wanted to cuss at her ass so bad my lip twitched.

"I packed all my stuff while you were in your drugged-up, hoed-out coma. See how much the world loves you, when you and your pretty dick ain't so fuckin' pretty."

I heard her call out in a petty voice from the doorway, but all my focus was on not breathing, blinking, or moving. Shit, she was probably bluffing and that shit wasn't nothing more than bleach, but I didn't want to take any chances with hit. The smoke detectors were going off and I could smell smoke, even see it out the corner of my eye. If I ain't think of something quick that shit would have me coughing and it'd be a wrap.

I prayed every prayer I'd ever heard or read and I smacked the jar off my head, rolling to the side simultaneously. It shattered against the closet, sizzling and fizzing.

That crazy bitch really set a jar of acid on top of my fuckin' head!

I'd be mad about it later; first I had to figure out what the hell was smoking. The couch in the living room was completely engulfed in flames. All my clothes were up there, my kicks, my dress shoes. I couldn't have slept that hard.

Grabbing the fire extinguisher out of the kitchen, I got the fire put out. The fire department still showed up because all the smoke set off the alarms in the building. I lied and said a cigarette fell. Couldn't risk throwing her crazy ass under the bus out of spite; she was liable to throw the bus right back at me. After the fire department left, I checked my voicemail and tried to find something clean to put on. She'd actually managed to fit every piece of clothing I owned on that damn couch. I was reduced to washin' the crotch of my jeans in the sink until I could roll out to buy some more.

That made me think of car keys. I panicked. Thankfully, they were still on the table by the front door. I checked my car and it didn't seem like she'd tampered with it, so I was good. It felt like a piece of my damn heart was missing, and it was my own fault. She ain't even want to hear anything I had to say. On top of all that, she was havin' my baby. How far along was she? Man, Shiree couldn't get rid of it; that wasn't an option. She'd come around; she'd have to come back around and hear me out. I returned Angelo's call to get my mind off Shiree's craziness.

The phone didn't even ring a whole ring before he picked up.

"Angelo, what, was you sitting on top of your phone waiting for those chicks from the club to hit you back?" Hopefully he'd be able to get me out of this foul-ass mood I was in.

He shrieked in my ear, "You cut me out and cut a deal with my pop?"

Or not. I grimaced. It hadn't crossed my mind that Angelo would eventually find out and that he'd be pissed when he did. Shit, Shiree messed up my planning process. I'd have normally sat down and figured something like that out.

"You act like I can't still cut you in as a partner. Shit like this happens when you run off and get buck-naked with the natives when you're supposed to be in the skybox discussing politics. I keep telling you that it's all about opportunity and preparation."

"Opportunity and preparation? That's what it's about you say? Well, I'm prepared to find other opportunities and I hope you have a backup plan. We are no longer equals; you will bow."

The line went silent, and I sat there trying to figure out what the hell to make out of that shit. Why did these Italians have to be on that damn emotionally dramatic shit? On the corner, a dude would just be like, "Yo, I'm mad you cut me out of that deal. I ain't fuckin' wit' you no more, watch your back." At the end of the day, it was over and you knew exactly where you stood. *You will bow? What the fuck was he on with that?* I looked at the clock and jumped into action. Half the day was already gone, and I still needed to meet Don Cerzulo.

The plan was to get there an hour early and park around back. That way I'd know if anyone sketchy showed up, or if anyone had eyes on the building I could hopefully see when they arrived and set up. Don Cerzulo walked up to my car and tapped on the window.

"You'd have to have been here yesterday to get a jump on me, wet pigeon." He cackled that old man version of a witch's cackle, and I got out of the car laughing.

"I was just trying to make sure we were good. I don't do these kinds of large transactions often." I told him.

Don Cerzulo slapped me on the back hard before throwing his arm around my shoulder like we were old drinking buddies. "Well, Rasheed, today is your lucky day. Hey, Joey." Don Cerzulo whistled through his fingers and a heavyset guy in black sweats wobbled over. He was breathing heavy, and I was hoping it was from carrying that heavy briefcase full of money, because it's not like he had that far to walk. He wheezed as he handed it over and then turned and wobbled back in the direction he came from. Don Cerzulo opened the briefcase, and the smell of crisp, clean legal tender filled the air. He handed me a sheet of paper. I unfolded it, reading the neat handwriting before placing it in my pocket and nodding.

"Now you show us this works so I know it's not quack science and we're—"

Don Cerzulo stopped midsentence; he stood there with a circle of blood forming on the front of his white dress shirt. Since our backs were turned to his guys it would only be a matter of seconds before they figured out he'd been shot or before I got shot as well. Snatching the briefcase I jumped in and started my car as Don Cerzulo fell to his knees.

"He shot Don! Get him, he shot Don Cerzulo!"

I didn't shoot any damn Don Cerzulo. I just saw an opportunity and I'd taken his damn money. As soon as the thought crossed my mind, I realized my own words had come back and bitten me in the ass. Angelo couldn't have shot his father over some petty business shit. Not only that but he was trying to make it look like I was the killer, *Angelo was trying to run me out of Miami.*

My phone went off and thinking it was a text from Angelo or Shiree, I flipped it open only to see a message saying my momma's house was in bad shape. Any other time Angelo, would've had a fight on his hands. But I needed to go figure out what the hell was up with my momma. I didn't even think about it, I just got on the nearest highway ramp and started heading north. It rang in my hand, I glanced at the number and started to ignore the call, but I knew I couldn't.

"Yeah, this is me," I snarled into the phone.

"Right now I'm looking at a little blue marker on a screen. That little blue marker is heading north. Now, where could you possibly be going, Mr. White?" he barked into my ear.

Special Agent Harper was a poorly socialized evil Rottweiler of a motherfucka who talked to anyone and everyone like they were plotting on his nasty-ass chewed-up lamb bone. And frowned like it, too.

I ain't have time to be a crook turned rook in the damn alphabet boys' chess game anymore. "I did what y'all asked. You got the deal on tape and on film ain't nobody ever got Don doing a deal."

"Wrong, you cocky son of a bitch! We got Don Cerzulo Campelli, the famous actor, handing you a got-damn piece of paper which could have been nothing more than a got-damn Kool-Aid recipe for all we know. The plan was simple. You get his trust, get inside, and get us his damn suppliers, find out if he's behind the SAG murders and director killings. Lucky for you, the boys upstairs hit the kill switch on good old Donny before he could have you shot on spot as planned. We picked that bit of intel up from one of our informants who overheard the hit man complaining on a phone call at a gas station around three a.m."

Rolling my eyes at the phone, I scanned the rearview to see if my ass was being followed. If Angelo hadn't put the hit on Don Cerzulo, then he and everyone would definitely think I'd killed his pops. There wasn't anything worse than a spoiled brat with an honest grudge.

Agent Harper finally decided to share why we were having this friendly little chat in the first place. "Your objective has changed. We need you to work an angle on Angelo. As Don's only son, he's most likely going to take over the family's cartel. I need clean bodies on him, clean suppliers—"

"You need to come back to reality. Y'all just made it look like I shot and robbed this dude's pops. Miami, hell, all of Florida, will be lookin' to hem me up on sight. That shit is impossible."

"We didn't make it look like anything. If your ass hadn't picked up that briefcase, you wouldn't look like anything. No, son, you made you look guilty, and unless you want to go back inside with Scorpion and your buddies, I'd better see this blue marker on my screen busting a U-turn and heading back toward Miami. That paternity test you requested for your cooperation came back."

I could hear paper unfolding in the earpiece and I waited.

"The little girl, Paris, born to Trenisha in prison is not your daughter."

The line went silent and I pulled over to the side in the emergency lane of the highway. I was so furious my insides were shaking. Fuck you Derrick and double fuck you Honey for whatever Angelo does now. Never in this lifetime did I ever see myself walking free with ties to my freedom.

I'd been in for about a year when they dragged me into solitary for no reason and sat me at a table. It was normal for Officer Reynolds to pull me away and do kinky shit on her breaks. I hadn't seen her in a minute, and I was ready to wear her ass out something decent.

I'd stripped down to my boxers when the door flew open and in walks this big Magilla Gorilla nigga in a fresh black suit.

"This ain't that kind of party, son. Put your fuckin' pants on and have a seat. I ain't come here to fuck, suck, or stare at your ashy-ass knees."

I ain't never put my shit back on so fast, feeling like I'd just got caught by the principal trying to sneak behind the school with the class freak. A long brown file folder landed on the table in front of me, with a loud slap.

"Go ahead, open it up," he commanded.

It was like looking at my entire life on film. There pictures of me as a shorty with moms. Some pics of mom dukes from way back with an old pimpish-looking motherfucka. I chuckled at that shit. This cat had a li'l curly mustache and pretty curls in his hair. Moms had never said nothing about whoever he was. Seein' me pause on that particular picture Magilla Gorilla started barking.

"That was Frankie the Ambassador Diamonds. Murdered in 1989, electrocuted in his bathtub. He was wanted for the murder of over thirty-eight women up and down the East Coast, and they almost had a solid case against him until he was murdered and robbed blind."

He continued, and I flipped over a picture of the dude laid out on the coroners table. There were puckered blisters from his chest down and you could see the network of veins running under his skin in this eerie deep dark purple color.

"They couldn't find a single solitary one of his girls to question except your mother. Couldn't figure out why she had a dead pimp's car. Mona, your aunt, said she'd stolen it. Since they couldn't pin either one of them at the scene for murder, your aunt with her theft record would have still gotten locked away for a long time. But, the judge was lenient, because honestly Frankie wasn't shit so Mona got away with a warning."

I'd flipped through a few more pictures and got a feeling in my gut I ain't like. "What does this have to do with me?"

"We've got more shit on you than a pig trying to keep cool fresh out of a pepper patch in summer. Last month we picked a woman up. Over the course of thirty years, she's married and killed five men, clearing out their accounts every single time. For a reduced sentence she's pinned your mom in the Frankie Diamonds case, has a notebook of hers hidden away. She says it puts your mother under his charge, dated and everything to the day he died. Combine that with that Cadillac, and even in her old age, she's looking at some time."

My mouth dried out like I'd been sitting there holding a wad of toilet paper in it as I waited to hear the "but" or the "what." I didn't have to wait long.

"Your ex-girl Trenisha? She's managed to get out and align herself with one of the biggest coke dealers in Miami. We'll give you back your freedom, but the you sitting here right now has to die. After you've accomplished your goals, you go on with your new life, far away from Virginia. And well compensated for your time."

At the time, it seemed like an easy out. Take water from a man until he's almost dead, hallucinating, sick, and dizzy from thirst. He can hear the slightest trickle of a stream. He won't care if there's garbage, syringes, and dead fish floating in that bitch. He's gonna follow the sound, fall to his knees, and drink. That deal was water, free water, and I'd been dying of thirst on the inside. Locked up, counting tiles, and going damn near insane.

A car whizzed by so close it made my shirt flap like a flag in its wake, snapping me out of my memories. Staring down at the cracked, broken concrete, scattered glass, and cigarette butts, I considered my courses. Regardless of what them special assholes said, it was never my complete intent to just forget about my son. I'd imagined waiting until he was older and better able to understand my absence. We'd sneak off on weekends when he was a teenager and I'd teach him about the world. Get him drunk. Just dumb shit that a locked-up nigga got time to sit and daydream about.

I looked at the text, wondering what could be going on with my momma. Her house phone and cell were tapped, I was sure of that. My cell was obviously tapped and Momma ain't know nothing about texting.

I was out because of Momma; without that case against her I probably wouldn't have done shit for those agents. They probably didn't have anything better to use against me other than her.

Climbing back into the driver's seat, I clicked the seat belt and sat there, staring at the road behind me in the rearview. *Nigga, you'd better haul ass. All of the FBI is about to rain a shit storm down on your ass, and you ain't got a raincoat, umbrella, and you for damn sure ain't got toilet paper . . .*

The tires squealed and the tail lights illuminated a trail of rocks and dirt as I threw the car into sports mode and floored it. Throwing my cell out the window, I started looking for the nearest rest area. It'd take them longer to find me if they couldn't trace me. Fuck stealing a car; somebody was about to sell me their shit.

Chapter 20

A Monster Is Still a Monster

When Momma had finished telling me her story I just stared at her in complete awe. I would have never guessed she'd been through and seen so much.

"Aww, Momma." I hugged her, clutching her side, unable to say anything more.

"Girl, don't aww me. If you wait for the walls to melt they'll show you all the secrets." Momma's voice had changed dramatically, and she'd started talking like a little girl staring up at the TV in the corner in somewhat of a daze.

My brow puckered and I shook my head and sighed. News reporters were going crazy about a murder. Some crime boss or something of another named Don Cerzulo. He was a murderer, drug dealer, just more bad news if you asked me.

Here they go glamorizing the murder of someone dying by the sword he lived by. Typical bullshit.

I changed the channel to a soap opera and fluffed Momma's pillows. It was the Alzheimer's. The doctor had given me pamphlets to read and it said she'd come and go. One minute she could seem perfectly fine, and the next she could be like she was right that very moment. My cell rang and I stepped outside, hopefully the office was calling me with some good news. Looking around for Devon and Trey, I answered.

"This is Michelle."

They should have been back awhile ago. Devon was probably teaching him how to X-ray his foot or something crazy, knowing him.

"Michelle Roberts?"

Frowning, I paused, afraid to answer to a name I didn't use anymore that definitely wasn't attached to this number.

"Michelle Roberts, my name is Special Agent Harper. I'm with the FBI. We have reason to believe Rasheed White is on his way to or already in Virginia."

I quickly leaned against the wall beside Momma's room, my hand over my mouth. I couldn't tell if I was gonna vomit or pass out. "No, Rasheed is dead," I whispered in a barely audible, shaky voice.

"No, ma'am, he's very much—"

Urgh! I swear I need to switch carriers. If I wasn't outside or standing on top of a got-damn cell tower, I stayed dropping fucking calls. Why couldn't I just buy my own damn satellite? This couldn't be happening. It was all a bad dream, and at any minute I'd wake up. Towanna decided to spring up on me and now this? It's a wonder I didn't march my ass up there to the insanity ward and check myself in. I debated whether it would be good to even mention something like this to Momma. Probably be best to wait until after I spoke to this special agent. I wiped the tears from my eyes and fixed my face.

Walking into her room I quickly blurted out, "Momma, sorry to cut this short, but we've gotta go." I tried to sound as chipper as I could so she wouldn't get suspicious and ask too many questions.

Momma wasn't in her bed and Lataya wasn't in her car seat where I'd left her. I flipped the curtain, looking over on the other side of the room. There was a grizzled old woman lying in her bed with nothing but the sound of her oxygen pump. She barely turned to acknowledge me.

He's already here. I can feel it.

A single window was open next to Momma's bed and I picked Lataya's pink and red sock monkey up off the floor. My feet were saying to run outside, but my head was telling me Rasheed had them and he'd kill me if he saw me. If I took one step near the window or the door, I could feel my heart screaming from inside my chest, "I'm going to explode."

"I knew you'd be out here," Momma called out.

"Whew, momma, you don't even know—"

My chest felt like a mule had kicked me, caving it in, and my heart somersaulted at least five times. I screamed, and I screamed so loud it brought half the hospital down on that single room in less time than it'd take a SWAT team to raid a crack house. Someone pushed past me, grabbing Lataya's tiny limp body out of Momma's arms. They put her on Momma's hospital bed, yelling for doctors and intubation tubes and crash carts. A few nurses fought to get Momma restrained and out of the room. They pulled her past me and she looked at me, but it was like she didn't really see me as she reached for me. Sobbing, I backed away from her and she started yelling at me.

"I baptized her, Mirna, just like you told me to. Ain't no man gonna ever hurt her. Ever."

Her eyes were wild and dazed. She didn't know who I was or where she was.

One of the nurses grabbed me by the shoulders and pressed me out of the room. I kept trying to look around her and over her shoulders, clutching that damn sock monkey to my chest pitifully.

"I'm her mother. I need to be in there," I begged her through my tears, but she just ignored me as they're trained to do.

I was left to wait miserably outside the door, feeling helpless and irresponsible.

"Michelle? Me and Trey were watching TV in my office I heard a code three to your mom's room?" Devon's voice was filled with concern and alarm.

He was holding Trey, trying to look over my shoulder and I couldn't get past the emotional bubble in my throat to even tell him what happened.

"Mommy, why you crying? Where's Taya? I got gummy bears for her out the smack machine." He held up the little yellow bag, shaking it at me.

Hearing Trey ask for her, and not knowing whether she was okay to even answer him, shattered what little composure I had left. I bawled, throwing myself into Devon's chest.

"Nurse Denise," Devon called out over my head, "take Trey back to my office if you don't mind. Cartoons . . ."

"I shouldn't have left her in there. She seemed fine and was talking. The special agent called and I was looking through the door until he said Rasheed was here. I wasn't thinking, I just wasn't thinking."

My shoulders shook. My whole world shook from me crying so hard. The doctor walked toward the door, his expression unreadable. I tried to see where she was, if she was awake, and I couldn't see anything past all the nurses in the way. It felt like I couldn't breathe, like an elephant was sitting on my chest and my heart was exploding, and then everything went black.

I opened my eyes and the room swam dizzily in front of me.

"Easy now, that stuff's got a kick." Devon's voice floated over to me.

I was lying in a hospital bed and my head was killing me. The hospital bed jarred my memory and all the misery I'd felt before surged back over me in an instant. I looked at him, unable to ask, but the question was evident.

"You got so upset; you were hyperventilating. I'm sorry. I just sedated you so you'd breathe, sweetheart."

He sounded so sincere. I didn't want to point out that this would be the second time I'd wakened in a hospital bed, drugged by someone I was sleeping with. The "first-time award" goes to Larissa for using me as her voodoo lab rat while experimenting with cocaine and anal sex play.

"Chelle, Lataya," He shook his head unable to actually say the words. "She had a lot of water in her lungs. Her head had been held under in the sink for a while. Statistics show drowning is one of the most peaceful ways to go though. She didn't feel a thing . . ."

His voice droned on and on as the doctor in him took over and he tried to explain how peaceful death is. Like he'd drowned and knew firsthand. She didn't know what was happening to her or why, and I wasn't there to protect her like I should have been. The hole in my heart opened up all over again and I started crying. I tried to wipe my nose and my hand wouldn't go any farther up than up to my chin.

"Why am I strapped to this bed?"

Devon gave me that pitying look that I'd seen one time too many. "You were talking about a secret agent calling you. The entire hospital heard you. It was a murder. I had to report it. They filed that on the report. Michelle." His voice took on a tone of seriousness. "I have to keep you for observation."

"Keep me for what? Where's Trey? Devon, let me go please, this isn't funny," I half whined, half pleaded with him. When he didn't look like he was going to even help me anger at everything welled up inside me. "For the record, he was a special agent, and he said Rasheed isn't dead and he's on his way to Virginia."

Devon sat back in the chair beside my bed and put his chin on his thumb. He looked deep in thought.

"I looked this Rasheed White up while you were sleeping. I couldn't find so much as a birth certificate on him. Called and even got online looking for a Towanna James, Miami PD and Virginia, nothing. I even looked in your phone and there aren't any secret agent calls. I'm trying to figure out if you and Mrs. White are sharing a delusion. It would explain why you'd be at her house living out of suitcases and why you'd both share this Rasheed person. I can't help you unless you help me help you, Michelle."

A guttural animalistic wail escaped my lips and I yanked against the taught leashes on my wrists. He had to be joking. There was no way this could be happening.

"They erased it for some reason. I don't know. Where the fuck did my kids come from, then?"

"I'm not even supposed to tell you that the real police are running Trey through their database of missing children. They wanted to take him. He's okay to stay with me. Denise has offered to help me watch him. I'll let you rest. I know it's been a rough day."

Chapter 21

Wheels of Steel

I didn't sleep as lightly as I used to. If I did I would have known this crazy little girl was in my room with a knife pressed to my throat. There was so much grief and so many drugs in my body I couldn't even feel afraid, and could barely feel the blade. My body was practically numb. Instead, I cried and pressed my throat farther onto it.

"You let her die," this girl spoke to me in a breathless whisper and her eyes only spoke of vague drugged sadness, pain, and death. They were Lataya's eyes and I didn't know if she was a ghost or an angel or a real person, but staring into them made me hurt even more..

"I didn't let anything. How do I live every day of my life loving and protecting someone else's child and then one day, just one day we're fine and she has pancake flour everywhere and then they wouldn't even let me hold her hand. She didn't have her sock monkey . . ."

The pain I felt at losing Lataya was like nothing I'd ever experienced and I let the dam that had been holding back all the helplessness and hurt break. I was flooded with drugged hazy thoughts of what Lataya might have felt, what she might have thought, the fact that she probably looked for me or reached out for me and I couldn't get to her haunted me. I closed my eyes and waited for that knife to cut into my throat.

"At least you got to hold her. Your life, for her life," she said in the faintest whisper.

Her voice was frightening and haunting, especially since I couldn't figure out if she was real.

I didn't care. I was tired of running and fighting. Always looking over my shoulder and not being able to trust anyone.

It would be more like self assisted suicide than murder because in that second death sounded like a peaceful option.

"Take it because if you don't Rasheed will, since the agent said he's somewhere nearby." Exhausted I waited for the blade to tear through my neck. Trey would finally be safe. I'd put money into a college fund and a trust fund for him. He was his daddy's son after all, he could survive anything.

Voices stopped outside my door and I opened my eyes. I looked around as best as I could but my damn restraints only let me lean so far. She had to be in this bitch somewhere, unless I was dreaming. *That wasn't a dream, that was a straight up hellafied nightmare.* They were giving me so much shit to keep me "sane" it was making me crazy. Devon walked in staring intently at his clipboard.

"How are we feeling today sweetheart?" He asked.

"Did you see . . . anything on the news about kidnappings sweetie?" I asked smiling sarcastically. I'd started to ask about the girl with Taya's eyes and quickly changed my mind. No buddy, he already thought I was deranged. Even though she seemed kind of real and I think that knife felt real as hell. It was hard to say but my throat seemed to hurt from where the tip was pressed against it. There was no explaining how she'd gotten in and out without him seeing her.

"I did not. But, I did ask how you were feeling?"

I was beyond miserable. They gave me miserable flavorless food and I wouldn't eat it so they shoved IVs into me and fed me that way. I honestly just hoped Rah would just show up and prove to them all that I wasn't crazy. Even if he killed me, at least I'd die with everyone knowing I was a sane woman who did not kidnap her children. Devon would sit beside the bed and talk and talk. Whatever drugs they gave me kept me so mellow I could only look at him at times; blinking alone seemed to drain ounces of my energy. I didn't even know what day it was or how much time had passed.

On this particular day he was extremely chipper. The sound of his voice made me want to do nothing more than stab myself in the ears with anything I could get my hands on ear-hole size. They wondered why people lost their minds and lashed out? It was because of overzealous doctors who sat in your face and their very presence was a slap in the face.

They made you remember passionate kisses and warm smiles, made you angry because they should have fought for you. Even if they were the only ones who believed you.

"Michelle, are you listening?" Devon sat there looking at me expectantly.

I shrugged in response since I had no idea what he'd said.

"Good, I'll have you escorted in as soon as everything's set up."

As soon as what was set up? I sat there staring at the closed door, trying to figure out what the hell was going on. Moments later Denise came in and sat me down in a wheelchair.

She spoke so quick and hushed I had to strain to under-stand her. "Your boy's doing fine, Michelle. I don't know what all's going on but I promise I'm looking out for him. He's at a homeschool my nieces run out of their place right now. They good people don't worry. If it was me and this shit happened I'd want somebody looking out. Shit, with the way they scoot folk in, out, and around on the fifth wing fuck that. I don't make enough money up in here to catch a charge over some uppity actress they check in for killin' folk who checks herself out before she even sees the doctor. Especially when regular folk like you catchin' the third degree. Anyway, he's been asking for you, and I told him you were at mommy daycare, resting up. So once you finish resting, he's waiting for you."

I had to look down at my hands in my lap so no one would see the teary smile on my face. Every now and again we still get angels to look out for us and I was so thankful for Denise's words. Devon refused to talk to me about anything relevant until I rewarded him by acknowledging any of my story as made up.

Denise wheeled me into a dim room. "Sorry boo-boo, I imagined strappin' you up but not like this," she said in a soft whisper, giving me a weak smile.

She strapped my forearms down onto the arms of the wheelchair and secured my ankles as well before turning to leave the room. The lights came up and I saw Momma sitting across from me in another room, strapped to a wheelchair as well. She stared at me through the thin pane of glass and seeing her for the first time since Lataya's death made me realize why I was strapped to the chair. Snarling, clawing, and growling, my hair flew wildly around my face, spittle hung off my lip as I looked at her through that glass. She'd taken Lataya, and now I was up in this hell because of her ass.

"Calm down, Michelle." Devon's voice sounded overhead on the intercom.

Chest heaving, I stared at the clinical pea-green tiled floor in front of me. Everything was pea green from the floor to the walls, even the toilet was that macabre shade of squished caterpillar, sea-sick green. As much as I hated looking at the tile, I refused to make eye contact with the woman across from me and I damn sure refused to cooperate with anything Devon planned.

"Chelle? I been wondering why I ain't seen you in a while." Reena's voice rang into the silence.

I stared blindly at the floor, trying to turn off my ears the same way I seemed to have turned off my eyes.

She isn't even sorry for what she did. Hell, she probably doesn't even know.

"Don't look like we going anywhere anytime soon, child." She paused like she was thinking or remembering something. "I ever tell you about the time I decided to become a madam?"

Chapter 22

Minding Madam Business

After everything blew over with Frankie I'd sold his car. Well, what I mean by that is I gave it to the Mexicans who ran the chop shop down the block. That was decent money to live off of for a while. At least until Mona came across Fink her ex. She called him an innovative misunderstood dreamer. He was a penitentiary pioneer. I called him that because every idea he had landed his ass in prison. Fink was definitely innovative. If that's what you call a fool that hides in a custodial closet at the bingo hall until everyone's gone so he can creep up on Mabel and Ms. Sarah countin' out the money. Only to be standing there holding the gun when his bowels creep up on him, fool was going through withdrawal so bad he had the shits. Police caught him in the bathroom of course they had to wait a good twenty-minutes or so until he was all clear. But you get my point. He'd just gotten out again and he had Mona on some hard stuff. Couldn't tell you what because she had a cocktail of whatever you could think of depending on which day of the week it was.

I'd stomped into her filthy bedroom and stared down at the mattress on the floor. I picked a naked leg and started kicking. "Mona, wake your trifling ass up. Wake up, girl." I was screaming at the top of my lungs and wasn't nobody moving.

The rent was already a month late and I'd come up with the back end of it donating plasma and selling some of Rasheed's old clothes. It would have put us in the clear for a minute. Mona had found my cash by pulling out my bottom dresser drawer and looking underneath. What the hell she was doing down there I'll never know but she ran right

through every dime. If we got put out we ain't have any-
where else to go. We ain't have any options left, no favors, no
nothing. I'd used every last one, at least twice a month for
something with Mona staying up in the house.

I decided that one time, I'd do the only thing I knew I
would bring me quick money. I sat Rasheed on the floor in
her room. "Watch Rasheed, Mona. You hear me?"

"Watching," was the muffled response I got back.

I started on the side of the track closest to downtown. That
time of day the shipyard workers would be taking lunch
breaks. It'd be easy to make a quick $500, $600.

My first customer was Tim Washington. He pulled up in
an old blue pickup. It squeaked and rocked to a stop in front
of me.

"What can I do you for, baby?"

"What can't you do for a hundred dollars?" he croaked out
the window.

If you heard Tim Washington's voice and a croak coming
backward out of a bullfrog's ass, I swear you wouldn't know
the difference. I'd climbed up in that old toe-jam, corn-chip-
oil refinery and sweat smelling truck and when he dropped
trow I had a mind to charge him another hundred for having
a third leg. There is such a thing as too big and if a woman
ever said otherwise I'd let Tim say hello. That voice was the
sound of his donkey dong pulling on his tonsils. Just think of
the "camel through the eye of a needle" scripture. He gave
me an extra fifty dollars for being a good needle.

I was climbing down out of his truck when he started
looking all sheepish.

"Reena? I know that ain't little Ms. Top Seller herself. You
stole my man from me and now you out here stealing my
customers," Royce snapped at me.

"Your man? A pimp ain't no man for any woman, sweetie.
He married to and respect money. You were just a way to get
it."

She swung all that hair like she was about to do somethin'
to somethin'. "That's why I'm married now anyway. Got me
a good man."

I laughed in her face. "Royce? He so good, why the hell are you out here? And where is your married nah rock." I mocked her, throwing her words back at her when I didn't see a ring.

That's when I noticed Royce didn't have all that dazzle to her, not like she did a few years back. Her black and tan was looking a little more like ashy and burnt.

"He's rich, and he took my ring. He don't give me shit because he worried I'll shoot it up."

That had my full attention. "How rich, Royce?"

Her eyes got as wide around as footballs. "Filthy rich, Reena."

That shit gave me an idea so big I birthed the Northern Lights on the other side of the world. In order for it to work I'd have to keep Royce just high enough so she could function normally during the day. I'd started turning a couple extra tricks but I knew it'd be worth it in the end. Even ran into Lacy and offered her a percentage of everything overall if she cut me in on her earnings so I could keep Royce good. Royce's husband was used to her fien'ing or so high she couldn't see straight. Once we got her to a middle ground everything fell right where it was supposed to. She got the insurance policies changed over, the wills. She knew all the bank information. It was time.

I'd gone and seen this lady over at the African shop once when Rah had whooping cough and I couldn't afford a doc-tor. All I had to offer her was a peanut butter jar I'd started collecting change in. It won't even halfway full but she took it and cured him.

"Reena. Long time no see. How are you, my queen?" She greeted me soon as I walked in and I couldn't remember her name.

"I'm all right. um, you know it's been a while I'm sorry," I apologized because I should have known.

She laughed and waived me off, "You wouldn't pronounce it right even if you did remember it gal. Balifama tamu-nominini Bello, but call me Fama."

"You right, about that one. Girl that's a mouth full. I need something Fama, and I can pay. I'll pay extra if I need to." I

strolled through, looking at the shelves by the counter. There was shea butter, black soap, coconut oil, nothing that I could use.

"What is this somet'ing?"

I put two hundred dollar bills on the counter and she snatched them up, making them disappear somewhere underneath the long sleeves of her tunic.

I made sure no one was standing down any of the tiny aisles before leaning across the counter and whispering, "I need to make a man die and it has to look like an accident."

"Hmmm. Are you sure?"

She'd just gotten $200 of my money. Hell yeah, I was sure. I nodded. "I'm very sure."

She went into the back and came out with a little box of powders and oils. My $200 bought me a bottle of oil that couldn't have held more than a thimble full of whatever she'd mixed up.

"Two drops in their bathwater for three nights; after that massage one drop on the soles of each foot. That's it."

That's it? Royce had a hard enough time remembering the instructions to boil a damn egg.

I gave Royce the bottle the next day and on the fourth day she gave it back.

"Did it work?" I asked her.

Me and Lacy were about to gnaw each other's hands off in anticipation.

Royce in all her splendid, ditzy wonder said, "I don't know. I didn't check. Was I supposed to check him or something? I mean, I just came to out here. I didn't think."

"Royce, where was your husband when you got out the bed this morning?" I asked through my teeth.

"In his bed and I got up and took my morning poo, and showered and had coffee, and put on my not going out - going out face, and I walked Kimpy our Kane Corso and then when I . . . Oh, I think it worked."

Don't forehead slap her, was the look Lacy was giving me.

"Don't you think it's going to seem strange that you got up, went in and out the house and did all that, and ain't call 911? Go home and call now please."

We waited to hear back from her and waited, and waited. A week passed and finally we went to catch the bus out to that old ritzy rich million dollar homes neighborhood. All the houses looked like castles and if I were Royce I'd have just kicked my damn habit. We went by the address on one of the forms she'd messed up when I was helping fill out the insurance paperwork at a restaurant. Something told me to keep one just in case, and I was glad I did. We walked up just in time to catch this heffa hopping into a shiny little Benz and speeding away.

We were leaving and I was scheming, looking to see what other eligible paychecks lived in the area. I looked over at Lacy. "I think we found another one and this time you are gonna do the marrying and hoodwinking."

Lacy took a little more work to refine. Royce already had all the beauty school guidance any single head could possibly hold. It would explain why her flighty ass couldn't retain much of anything else. I put Lacy on a diet, got her eating right so her skin would stay bright. She had high cheekbones and one of them beauty marks. That's what she called it. I'd call it a dern mole if you ask me. But, from the way fools acted when they saw her, she's the reason that model girl got famous, I'm telling you. The one with the big old big-ass mole on her face. I can't even remember her name.

Anyhow, we'd taken our money and gotten her hair permed and cut into one of those little bobs with the bang that's pointy and long on one side. It framed her face, accenting that big-ass mol . . . I mean beauty mark. I remember stepping back, looking at my baby-doll-faced perfection on many an occasion. No one would have ever guessed she'd gone from a hooker to a looker.

It took two years for her to woo that man and get married. But that was two years of extra money so we was off the street. We were enjoying gifts and all the luxuries that come with dating rich men. I had her treat this one the same as the last one. Slowly made sure she had all the details, got everything changed into her name. I wasn't worried about Lacy skipping out on me like Royce did. Lacy was loyal.

Another one down and unlike the first time Lacy actually came through; she only missed a couple of minor details but we still had a payout of hundreds of thousands each. We had a way to take a life with nothing pointing to foul play. It'd looked like he'd had a heart attack, no chemicals in his blood stream, absolutely nothing.

However, I wanted millions and so did she. Anyone who's ever gone fishing knows you've got to follow the tide and venture out if you want to catch bigger fish. We went up north to Philadelphia, following the money flow. Rented out a place and in less than a week's time I had four girls working for me in exchange for a place to stay, protection, and bail money. I always remembered the look on Royce's face the day she took off with her millions. Lacy and me didn't have that look just yet though. No, if we actually went out and bought the mansion we wanted with the fleet of matching Mercedes we'd be broke.

It took me drawing her a pie chart on paper before she barely understood how millionaires got that way. A mansion cost millions and we only had hundreds of thousands. Million-dollar property came with a million-dollar property tax. She was addicted to all the diamonds, champagne, and flashy parties. I'd modified Frankie's business practice, only taking a fair percentage of my girls' money and Lacy was blowing through it like Kleenex.

We lived like this for years. The entire time my sister thought I'd just found a job out of state. I could never send her more than enough to scrape by with at a time. If she knew anything she'd have blown through it, or run her mouth in the streets and raised suspicion. We were making so much off the girls I started stashing money to keep Lacy from finding and running through it. When Lacy came and told me she'd run across a wealthy widower in the steel industry I was thanking my lucky stars. Then, I sat there and plucked every last one of those stars out of my unlucky sky. She came and told me the man's mother passed the very day before he was set to die. Lacy stuck me with his spoiled, miserable heathen of a child. I had no choice but to get rid of him. Told her she'd never pick her own mark again. That child was something that'd been on my conscious to this day.

We all packed up and went to Jersey near Alpine after that. A lot of good years were spent there. Think we had two or maybe three weddings in Jersey. Then there came a time when Lacy thought she was just too grand to be living with me and the girls. She even thought she could pick her next one. She pointed out five and I said no to them all, showing her who I liked instead, better targets. She went ahead anyway and I couldn't work with her anymore. Not like that.

"Dr. Harrington, how well did you like your stepmother? I don't think she goes by Lacy though. By the time she met your daddy she was probably calling herself Melanie Mal . . ."

Chapter 23

Psychics Get Called Crazy—Until They're Right

"Melanie Malia." Devon's voice was barely above a childlike whisper coming through the loud speaker. Static crackled through it and then the intercom went silent.

I didn't know what to think of Reena's story; the woman could have told me she was a royal cat burglar for the Queen of England and I wouldn't have batted an eye. None of it was gonna bring my little girl back, though. All this story time and power-hour crazy house shit was pointless. I wasn't crazy; everybody, including Reena, was. The lights dimmed and I could barely make out the other side of the room. The panel window had gone dark, showing nothing, reflecting nothing. Reena was still there, singing at the top of her lungs. It was her rendition of "Amazing Grace" and "The Star-Spangled Banner."

"No one would know my stepmother's name, let alone her maiden name; how'd she do that?" Devon asked the question from behind me.

I shrugged. "Maybe because she obviously knows what she's talking about."

"No one could know what she's talking about. I didn't even find out myself until a little over a week ago. They'd told us she was suspected of murdering all her late husbands. They couldn't press any charges because there was no murder weapon, nothing linking the deaths except her being their widow. It hasn't gone public yet, but it's only a matter of time."

He undid the straps on my hands and kneeled in front of me.

"I don't know what's going on, but the first thing you told me was don't trust the police, and I turned around and trusted their word about you, over you. I'm so, so sorry."

He put his head in my lap and I argued a vicious inner battle with myself.

It's not like we've known each other forever, he was just doing what he felt was right.

Leaning down, I kissed his ear softly, saying, "I thought you were completely insane too when we first met. On that, we are even. But just so you know, I do get to drug you at least once in this lifetime, and you can't be mad."

He smiled up at me as he unlatched my ankles.

"You can drug me whenever you want and I wouldn't complain. Let's get your clothes and get you out of here. We can go get Trey, and then you can rest."

"So by letting me go without the police or anyone's permission, that doesn't make me a criminal, does it?" The last thing I needed was more drama to explain later down the road; wake up and my whole identity was gone, except for this one visit to the psych ward.

"I wrote everything up before I even came down to get you. You are fine and clear to go, per the doctor's orders. "

Clearing my throat, I hesitated. "Have, um, arrangements been made for Lataya yet?"

Devon got that clinical look that he used to break any news he felt would be negative. "I made all the arrangements and took care of everything; it's scheduled for tomorrow. I wasn't sure how to tell you, or not to tell you."

"Just get me to Trey. I'm ready to get out of here."

We rode out to an area near Campostella; it was mostly Section-8 housing and a few overlooked trailer parks. It definitely wouldn't have been the top of my list of choice areas to send Trey to on a day-to-day basis. Devon went inside to get him while I waited in the car, on high alert. I'd been around Rah and his boys enough in the beginning to know what corner boys looked like. They weren't anything to worry about unless you bothered them. I was, however, worried about that agent who had called me. I knew I hadn't dreamed or imagined that phone call. I'd checked my phone, and just like

Devon said an incoming call didn't even register during that time frame.

Something was going on, and I didn't understand what or why, but I felt uneasy and anxious knowing Rah could be anywhere. Trey came outside, and I got out giving him the biggest watery, squeezy hug. He eventually whined to get in the back so he could finish watching his movie on his iPad.

"Chelle, you hungry?" Devon put his hand on my knee and squeezed.

"Can I have cake?" Trey yelled from the backseat.

I wasn't, but I tried to perk up just a little for Trey since he hadn't seen me in a week. "I think Ruby Tuesday's has cupcakes. Devon, does Ruby Tuesday's have cupcakes?" I asked in the most serious tone, like it was up for major discussion.

"Well, since I'm driving to Ruby Tuesday's, I think they have cupcakes." He screamed and Trey screamed.

"Mommy, can we save Taya cupcake too?"

I knew it was coming, he'd ask and I'd start crying.

Devon's squeezed my knee. "We can do Ruby Tuesday's another night, Michelle."

Shaking my head at him, I wiped my nose and my eyes on my sleeve.

"Trey, baby, do you remember when we had that talk about Heaven and Daddy—"

"Michelle, can he have his cupcake first?" Devon tried to stop me.

Before I could finish asking, Trey answered, "I 'member, Mommy, and G-ma told me that she was gonna have to send Taya to Heaven. When the walls melt away you can see all the secrets. Did Taya go to Heaven already?"

We pulled into the restaurant parking lot and me and Devon were staring at each other, not knowing what to make of Trey's words. Some minutes later we were all inside seated in our booth. Trey insisted on sitting by himself like a big boy. I was just trying to keep it together. I let him have his way for once, so long as he promised to behave.

"No. You know you wanted this dick." Some teenagers behind us were making me rethink the seat and the restaurant all together. There was so much coughing, snickering, and inappropriate chatter going on.

Frowning, I leaned over and turned Trey's headphones up on his movie.

I fiddled with the straw in my soda, debating something that had been floating around in my mind.

I nudged him with my shoulder, not looking up. "Devon, I have a question."

Nudging me back he responded, "I have an answer."

I stopped using my straw to pop bubbles in my soda and decided it was time to woman up. Looking him in the eye I said what was on my mind. "I heard you on the phone at the hospital, with a woman that day after I came out of Reena's room. Who were you talking to?"

Devon frowned with a look that could have been confusion or, maybe, he was a bit taken aback. He'd started to answer when our waiter came back over. I was about to ask for a new seat when I realized it wasn't our waiter.

He slid into the booth next to Trey. One of his hands was underneath the lapel of his jacket. He stared at Trey for a moment in a look of joy or shock before turning to me with those memorable embers of anger and hatred still burning in his eyes.

"Hey, Michelle, how've you been? No letters, no postcards, no forwarding address. It's like you were trying to move on without a nigga. Scream or draw attention, and it's happening."

He nodded down at Trey, who'd barely glanced at him. He was a toddler the last time he'd seen Rah. I never showed him pictures because I wanted him to forget, in the event they ever met again, like now. I wanted Rah to see his son, growing up without him, unaware of him as his father. Trey was watching his owl movie for the fifth time in a row, not paying any mind to the adults at the table.

Rah put his arm around Trey, sliding off his headphones, tapping at his iPad. "What you got there, li'l man?" Rah asked Trey, his voice cracking, choked up with emotion.

"My iPad," Trey whispered.

Rasheed started tapping on the screen. He put his head against Trey's. "You know what that word says?" he asked Trey, sniffing quietly.

Trey shook his head up and down and his eyes got wide. "That's 'daddy.' My daddy is in Heaven and—"

"What are you doing here?" I quickly snapped at him, destroying their bittersweet moment. The last thing I needed was for Trey to get talkative.

"I'm trying to find my moms. A little birdie pointed me in the direction of that fancy mental hospital. Imagine how exciting it was to see my favorite person in the passenger seat at the light beside me when I was tryin' to find it."

"No. You just high as fuck, and technically both y'all were fighting over this d-i-c-k," the guy behind me bellowed and laughed.

The teens in the booth were getting loud, and a few restaurant guests were casting annoyed and disgruntled glances their way. I was praying it would be enough of a distraction to get a manager or a waiter over.

"Big!" Rah jumped up, looking over our heads, but his hand was still too close to his gun.

Damn, is that Big Baby? Guess they're just gonna have themselves a reunion up—

Devon nudged me and I looked down. I took his cue and slowly reached underneath the table, blindly feeling for his hand. He handed me the car keys.

"If I can take him, you go," Devon mumbled, his lips barely moving.

"Hold up, Rasheed? Dawg." The guy in the booth who had been making all that noise behind me addressed Rah, sounding excited.

"I know that ain't no motherfuckin' Rasheed, triflin', hoing, nasty, druggy, dopin' ass."

I didn't recognize the hoarse, raspy woman's voice coming from directly behind me.

I looked at Devon dumbfounded; he shrugged in return. Neither of us could see over the high-rested back of the booth seats, but I was able to lean just enough to see through a small gap between the booth walls. The raspy voice was Shiree.

"You left me to run back to Big Baby? Really? Did you get rid of the baby too? I actually loved your ass." Rasheed actually sounded hurt. I stared at him in awe, no this fool was not still making damn babies.

"Oh so, nigga, you loved her ass, huh?"

I mouthed the words "oh no" to Devon. I knew that voice just as well as I knew my own. That was Honey, and she did not by any means need to see me up in here with Trey having dinner without Lataya. I tried to peek and get a glimpse of her, but there was no way to do it without drawing attention to myself. The sound of her voice jarred me back to that night in my hospital room, but the sedatives they'd given me were so strong I could barely remember it now. It felt like a dream, and the girl I'd seen and heard didn't even look like Honey. She might have been a cousin or someone I didn't know if she was ever even there. But, Honey was right here, right now, and God help me, because I didn't even have the one person she wanted back from me.

"Look, you high as fuck, we don't need to handle this right here, just let it go girl," Big said.

From all the stories Rasheed's momma had told me, I was pretty sure she had a million and one "oh, shit" and "oh, no" moments. It explained why her hair had grayed all the hell out. I couldn't help wondering if it was a gradual change, or if after one too many the whole thing just sprouts.

"Nah, this is exactly who I need to be handling. This is why it all started. So this is where it's ending. Right here, right the fuck now. Because even though I'm the one who got locked up behind yo' ass, had your baby, and then got you out of prison, you're gonna stand here and say you loved her?" Honey shrieked at Rasheed.

Please just don't let anyone come around this corner, look down, and see me. I'd rather take a gun and shoot myself than have to say what happened out loud if anyone asks where the baby's at right now. It would just be too much for me to answer.

It was as if the director had yelled "action" and we were dropped smack in the middle of a bad Western. The cold metallic clink of guns cocking behind our heads was unmistakable. Customers started running out of the place. The most I could do was hope that we got out of there with a mild flesh wound. If you've ever heard an M-80 go off in the middle of a packed hallway in between classes, that's what a gunshot in a restaurant sounds like. The sound hurt my ears and Trey cried out, throwing his hands over his before crawling under the table and into my lap. It was akin to raindrops on unsuspecting ants. The people and staff who hadn't started fleeing ran, ducking and screaming, scattered in various directions toward exits.

"Pull a gun on me over a kid who ain't even mine? That's that bullshit. Get y'all asses the fuck up, take me to see my momma."

We rushed out of the restaurant to the sound of sirens wailing in the distance.

Chapter 24

Hit the Brakes Like Errrrrrrrrrrr

We drove in silence, me sitting in the back with Trey. I wanted them to have as little contact as physically possible. The less the better; he'd just accepted the fact that his daddy was in Heaven. I couldn't just *Pet Cemetary* Rasheed back into his life even though everyone seemed to keep jumping back into mine.

Devon led us in through the admin entrance so Rasheed wouldn't get asked for ID and go on a shooting spree to get to his mom. I couldn't figure out where the hell the special agent was now who had called me earlier. If they had so much intelligence out there and they were that worried, why weren't they watching the hospital the moment his momma was brought in?

We followed Devon up through the back entrance, and I was hoping he had some kind of plan. None of the nurses were aware that we were walking hostages. How the hell do you blink a distress message at someone?

"Every now and again, I'll have high-profile patients or people who need to get in or out without a ton of publicity. They'll be in an area where the rules will need to be altered a little. I'll have your mother brought up to the 5th floor you'll be fine; the staff is used to it."

Devon's words reassured Rasheed, simultaneously squashing any hope I had for a random act of assistance. Rah paced the length of floor until his mother was just outside.

"Is that my momma? Why she strapped down like that? Let her in," Rasheed growled at the door like a wounded bear.

"She's dangerous and unstable. She might not know who you are."

"Man, fuck outta here with that. That's my mom; she knows me."

Devon nodded and she was rolled in, he then dismissed the nurses. It was a bittersweet reunion. Rasheed was teary-eyed trying to hug his momma; she was doped up and strapped to the bed.

"Rasheed? Boy, they'd told me you passed on. Second saddest day of my life. Where've you been, what happened?"

"Yo, take her out of that shit. She don't need to be in no shit like that," Rasheed barked at Devon and he obliged, undoing the straps and letting her free.

"Why they do this to you, Momma? Was it because of me? Is this because of something I did? I ain't dead. Look, I'm right here. This ain't because of me is it?" he asked her pitifully. He sounded like a scared and worried little boy talking to his momma. Like my old Rasheed, not the angry shell of a man I'd gotten used to dealing with.

"No, my love, this is all me. Sometimes my memories are as crystal clear right in front of me, happening right now, and I can't tell the difference between what's now and what's past. Everything look like it's supposed to and feels real as you and right as rain baby. Other times I can't remember how to brush my own teeth unless somebody shows me where or what a toothbrush is first."

He looked at Devon like he wanted an explanation and he explained, "She'll need to be in an institution or a full-care senior living facility. We had one slip-up here where she didn't take her meds and"—he hesitated—"she drowned Michelle's daughter in the sink in her bedroom."

Actually hearing the words out loud to describe what had transpired made tears fall down my cheeks. Rasheed looked at me and seemed completely bewildered as to how something like that could happen. I didn't have an answer.

Rasheed pulled his phone out of his pocket. "Yo, this is me." He answered and paused, his face getting darker and angrier by the second.

"How did you get this number? It's a prepaid phone," he demanded angrily.

"What do you mean mixed up the swabs? You was only supposed to swab one."

My eyebrow went up on that. The tone of his voice had gone to furious in a matter of a few words. I didn't even want to know what the person on the other line had said but I had a feeling I was about to find out.

He slid the phone into his pocket and stared at me like he didn't know me, like he'd never seen me before and he still hated me.

"Life or death, were you cheating on me before Trey was born, Michelle?"

Shocked as hell, I quickly shook my head back and forth. "I don't know who just told you that, but they're lying. I never did anything."

"You never did anything when? You was doing shit with that bitch remember? So, I'm gonna ask again and I'm gonna let you think about it. Because, my people swabbed Trey and Paris, he ain't mine and her swab . . . Aw, fuck! Ma."

It was as if the realization of what happened didn't hit him until he was saying it out of his own mouth. I'd already been feeling what was just now hitting him head-on. Even though the part about Trey not being his was all new to me.

"Momma, what did you do? What did I do, Honey aww fuck, Desi . . ." He fell to his knees crying, crippled by pain and reality.

I'd never seen him or any man cry like that. It made me want to put my arms around him and kiss his shaking shoulders. What he was feeling he didn't deserve, none of us did; at least Honey wouldn't have to find out. Not one time had I ever cheated on Rah with another man.

Oh, shit. Ris, what the fuck did you do?

I felt like I was about to throw up as I thought about Ris underneath me and what I thought was Keyshawn behind me. How mortified I was when I realized he was just watching. Thankfully that one time it was Lania with a strap, but she hated Rasheed, maybe that it meant blind-folding me and getting me knocked up. There was no way I'd ever know who the hell it was with unless he came out and told me. Trey was still my Trey, it just meant I didn't have to worry about Reena's mental health history affecting him and—

All the air left my lungs in a sickening sharp thud. I wanted to vomit and breathe at the same time. Crashing to my knees, clutching my stomach, I gasped for air. He'd gotten up and out of nowhere and stormed over, hitting me with the butt of the pistol.

Devon roared and charged Rasheed, knocking him off his feet, and they both sprawled across the floor in a tangle of limbs and angry grunts and growls. Trey started crying. The only thing going through my mind in those seconds other than trying to breathe was trying to get to Trey and shielding him.

The gun exploded again and again. The sound was deafening and, slightly dazed, I looked around examining everyone looking for visible signs of blood or pain. My eyes swept over them all: Reena, Devon, Rasheed, Trey. It was chaos, and everyone seemed to be midmotion screaming or saying something. Blood started seeping through the hole in Rasheed's shirt in his chest and he fell to his knees. Trey ran to Reena. Devon and I examined each other, breathing sighs of relief when neither one of us were shot. I watched Rasheed take his last breath, for real. I felt for his pulse and everything.

We were sitting out front waiting on the police to get there. Devon felt it'd be best to bring Reena out for the fresh air. I honestly couldn't care one way or the other. All of this just needed to be over so I could figure out what else I needed to do for Taya's service.

"That was my baby who got shot, wasn't it?" she asked in a tiny voice.

"Yes, that was Rasheed." I answered her cautiously, scared of what she was about to do or how she'd react to the news.

She turned and looked at me as if she'd just seen me for the first time all day. "Michelle? Where the hell you been? I ever tell you how I met Rasheed's father?"

Not in the mood for any more of her stories, I held up my hand and said, "I think you have."

She frowned, and went back to la-la land.

Devon had gone all quiet and pensive on me, and Reena just sat there, staring off into space. He seemed like he had a mind full of questions to ask, but settled on staring down at the pavement instead.

The police pulled up, and we were swarmed with activity.

"Someone called; I need to see the person who committed the homicide," a rough voice called out.

I glanced at Devon and he had the same confused look that I did. Homicide? How could he possibly call it that without hearing our side of the story? We looked up in unison as a tall man with the presence of an ominous thundercloud approached us. Everything about him from his suit up to the top of his head reeked of this darkness.

Devon began to step forward and I pressed ahead of him. "I shot him. He'd taken us against our will and I was struggling with him for his gun."

He gave me a gruff nod. "Glad you've decided to cooperate." His hand pressed at the small of my back, pushing me toward a black sedan. "It'll make it easier to request a less severe form of punishment for that actress you shot back at that restaurant. Hopefully she won't press charges."

Actress! Nobody shot an actress. What the hell?

The car door slammed curtly in my face with the ending of that statement. Impossible, they had it all wrong. One of the witnesses must have seen or reported something inaccurately. Reaching for the handle, dread was all that met my fingertips in the sensation of smooth, molded leather. There were no handles in the back seat, and a Plexiglas divider cut off access to the front seats. The man who led me to the car was speaking to Devon, who was holding Trey. They'd turned and he was making hand gestures, pointing toward the hospital. Pounding my fists against the window, I screamed and yelled. It had to be some kind of reinforced glass.

The car shifted as someone got into the driver's seat. I was so busy trying to get Devon's attention I didn't see who it was. The Plexiglas distorted my view of the other side. I clawed at the plastic divider, growled, screamed, and kicked at it, but just like that damn window, I didn't even put a scratch on it. Feeling like a complete idiot, I remembered my cell and jerked it out of my pocket. I had 8 percent of a charge left. That would be enough to make a call or send a short text, but not both. I tapped a quick message to Devon.

They think I shot some actress. Need a lawyer.

I almost snapped that pretty piece of shit phone in half when it vibrated.
Message send failure. No service.

The car rolled for what seemed like forever. It finally stopped moving and I tried to get my bearings. We'd stopped in front of storage rental area. The driver walked over and opened my door.

"We've been ordered to shoot on site if you run."

Nodding my understanding, I timidly climbed out of the back seat. He led me over to a storage unit. The metal door slid up with a loud clanking sound that shook me all the way down to my core. It was a sound that rang of last words or last rights. I peered inside, waiting to see my executioner in there. The only thing visible was a single fold-out metal chair beside what looked like an old card table.

"Sit, this won't take long." The driver spoke in a curt tone.

The sound of the door sliding down in place made claustrophobia set in instantly. The space was small and dank. Mildew and mold seemed to be the scent of the evening. It made me think of spiders, brown recluses, and black widows. My skin was starting to crawl, and I tried to focus on anything but what could or couldn't be in that space.

Thankfully the door slid up just as I was about to lose all my nerve, get up, and start banging on it. He didn't introduce himself or even say anything. Simply strolled in and slid it across the table: thick green paper with fine printed handwriting in blue ink.

"What is this?" I stared at it, straining my eyes to read the wording, afraid to touch it.

"Sign it. It's an agreement." He paused, waiting for me to read it. I didn't move. "It says you murdered Rasheed because we asked you to. We paid you with money from our fund and even gave you the gun he was shot with. There are bank transfer slips, six overall backdated to various points in time. When I give the okay, the money will go into your account and it will look like it's always been there. It's the only way I can help you."

It sounded like the losing end of a deal to me . . .

"I don't understand who are you; what fund am I getting paid from?"

If something went wrong, I'd be signing something saying I conspired to murder Rasheed. There was no way a judge or court anywhere would let me off with that.

"We can't help you otherwise. It's a sinking ship and you're standing on the bow, Michelle. This is your lifesaver."

My hand shook as I scribbled a barely legible version of my name. He clicked open his briefcase, placing the papers that determined my future inside.

"Tell no one. I'll be in touch."

Chapter 25

Secret Agent Man

It was about time spring started showing its ass. I was getting restless with all the cold: gray doom and gloom. You could see all the signs, fresh buds, melting ice, and twitter-pated squirrels. Spring was becoming my new favorite time of year. The air was losing the brisk chill from winter, and we were getting some of the warmer days everyone yearned for minus the humidity and the bugs.

It'd been four months since Lataya's funeral. It was the only thing about those events that I chose to mark on my calendar. She wasn't my baby, but in my heart that little girl would always be my baby. I'd like to think that being with me even for that short time was heaven before Heaven for her.

Devon had been stressing and having a multitude of fits. It seemed like every day he'd get a call from this lawyer or that lawyer with a detail or another bit of information on the case concerning his step-mother. It was hard on his family and tearing him apart. I'h no idea Devon owned the hospital, and every day he was being asked to furnish a financial record for this holding or financial evidence backing that holding. I'd gone online and done some research. I tried to explain they were doing it to all the families, not just him. Every dime she extorted had to be accounted for.

The case was becoming so intricate that he was looking into another facility to move Reena to, and I didn't blame him one bit. Things finally seemed calm enough for me to start working a little more. I took on a manager to help make decisions on major closings, but an absent owner would be a broke owner. I tried to step in on major closings when I could or at least help with properties that they were having problems moving.

Too much turbulence and my ass would get airsick, so I tried to stay put as much as possible.

I'd just landed and was trying to remember where I'd parked my car in the garage. I'd closed on a $4.5 million waterfront property that we hadn't been able to move for a year and was damn excited. The seller was threatening to find a new agent, and we'd moved it just in time. My phone died on the flight, and I cursed when I didn't see my car charger in the car.

Not having my cell was like leaving the house without a shirt on. Frustrated, I slammed the hell out the car door, cursing silently. Those silent curses turned into shouts when my damn car wouldn't start. Opening the glove compartment to get my AAA card a tiny black laminated card fell to the floor on the passenger side. I picked it up and read the silver letters, with, my lunch slowly making its way up throat.

You are activated. Instructions will follow.

Everything stopped moving. The armpits of my blouse and blazer jacket were instantly soaked.

Activated? What the hell was I going to have to do?

A yellow cab squealed to a stop behind my car and I almost fainted from the sound. Dust flew up and engine exhaust hit my nose. The purr of the engine echoed through the garage. I swiveled to look out the back window as the cab driver leaned over and yelled out the window in a heavy accent.

"You get in, now."

He nodded toward the back seat, his black leather fedora bobbing on his head.

I reluctantly got in and he sped off. Arabian music was blaring out of the speakers as we bounced out of the airport garage. I could feel myself getting nauseous as nerves built on top of nerves.

This wasn't the kind of person I was. What the fuck had I signed? Why the fuck did I sign that shit? I didn't even read it; I just scribbled my name because the man in the suit said do it. My dumb ass didn't even ask him for identification.

I couldn't call Devon. I couldn't call the police. I'd felt better with a gun pointed at my head; at least then I knew what the outcome to that would be. He flew down Military Highway and I noted landmarks, car dealerships, IHOP. We got on the interstate going toward downtown Norfolk. He stopped in front of an old office building on Granby Street.

"You're here," he shouted to me over the music.

I looked around, trying to figure out where "here" was. I got out and stood staring at the crumbled front of the building, trying to figure out if I was supposed to just go in or what. The doors swung open and a young woman in a black pantsuit came toward me.

"Michelle, follow me." She turned and walked back inside without waiting.

"What am I doing?" I asked her shakily.

"You've been activated. Follow me for your objective briefing," she replied matter-of-factly.

She led me through the building, up a stairwell, and across a mezzanine. I followed shakily, not sure if I'd make it without falling out first. We walked up another stairwell and we got onto a service elevator. She stood in front of me and I debated trying to hit her on the back of the head like I'd seen in movies. Knocking her out and running. Something wasn't right. I looked to see what button she pressed and in that moment she stepped off through the front elevator door, and my ears went super sonar a split second too late as the back service door of the elevator opened behind me.

Someone grabbed me, and instinctively I slammed the heel of my pump down. The joy I felt at the yelp of pain I'd elicited was short-lived as I whirled around my hand poised mid-throat chop.

"What the fuck, Devon? You scared the fuckin' fuck out of me!" I screamed in his face, punching his arm.

The elevator stopped and the doors in front of me opened onto the main floor of a breathtaking hotel suite. I gasped in awe, my hands flying up to cover my mouth. There were vases of bright yellow calla lilies, pink and white tiger lilies, and birds of paradise, all over the suite.

Devon sucked in his bottom lip turning bright red. "The plan was scoop you up, kiss your neck, and ask if you were ready to be debriefed. Then um, debrief you as in "get the panties, but you went all *Charlie's Angels* on me," he mumbled sheepishly, as he escorted me off the elevator. "It just all worked out so perfect in my head . . ."

"Aww, baby." I grabbed his face in my hands and kissed him.

Devon tried to talk against my lips. "Statistics show relationships that start off dramatically—"

"Boy, I know your ass ain't up in here quotin' lines from the movie *Speed*." I kissed his nose sweetly. "I've had enough drama in one lifetime that you don't need to do none of this, not this. I don't mean the room. I like this part, the room is good. But, all that other stuff . . ." I shook my head. "I can do without that."

He smiled, nuzzling my nose with his. I was thankful when he didn't nuzzle any lower, because all that adrenaline and running around had me wanting a shower. As if he read my mind, he took my hand and smiled, walking not to the bathroom but toward the bed. I started to say something until I saw the Olympic-sized Jacuzzi bathtub not three steps away. But he didn't go to the bath; he went past that.

"Baby? Umm." I pointed and pouted sadly at the inviting water.

"You're not dirty enough for a bath yet." He responded in that authoritative, seductive voice of his, and I instantly got chills.

It's one thing to have a man who knows what the hell he's doing in the bedroom, but you've got a beast of a completely different nature when he ain't scared to experiment. My legs were straddling his face and I'd just gotten his sleep magic number down. So I was working it. Sucking and simultaneously stroking him to the damn finish line. He had the dick game down but, I couldn't lie, the head game still needed work. He needed to learn my sleep magic number. That's when you know exactly how, where, and how many times to lick, suck, or flick. Some might need a nipple twist or their clit sucked hard; some women don't like it sucked they like it rubbed. Whatever it is, you know exactly what the magic number is before that head game puts your boo to sleep. Well, he ain't know all that.

I knew he was in the final stretch. His stomach was flexing and I could feel him swelling in my hand and in my mouth, when I started vibrating. Not a small vibrating, but I almost shot up off him and backed back down. He'd gone and bought a big-ass dildo. I mean, like one that I would have gone and bought myself if he was gonna be gone on a long business trip. I tried to scoot back on it because it was feeling super nice and then "pop."

Oh no, he didn't. I know we'd had the ass discussion. It was off limits.

My ass was plugged and it was vibrating, and my clit was still vibrating, and it wasn't bad, it was just so much vibrating that I couldn't tell if I liked it all at once. So I licked my pinky and slid it in. See how much he liked it. One second I was holding the dick and voila it went from being magically delicious to feeling magically delicious.

"Oh, you wanna play in asses?" He roared, "You forget that I'm the nigga?"

Each word was accented with a pussy-clenching, sheet-tangling, mattress-shifting, power pump that slid me across the bed. It was the worst, best punishment ever.

"Damn! Yes, you are. I'm sorry." I moaned and whined.

Devon stroked my pussy with the determination of a man with OCD methodically stroking a cat. They'd be long and rhythmically deep. I agreed with him, apologized, and probably thanked him in advance until he'd find those bittersweet spots that'd make my legs tremble. All I could do at that point was hold on, and then everything stopped. Exasperated, I clawed his thighs with my nails. Devon grabbed my wrists and leaned forward, pinning them above my head. He kissed me and I moaned against his lips, wiggling my hips, trying to get him to move.

"Tell me what you want," he directed.

When I merely frowned up at him not answering, he pulsed in between my legs, making my walls clench in reflex and my eyes cross. Devon made me aware that no matter what happened on a day-to-day basis, when we got down to us, man to woman, skin to skin, it was okay to want or even like for someone else to be in control. I didn't have to pretend to be unbreakable or invincible. Although sometimes I just liked pretending so he'd try to break me.

"I want you. I don't want anybody but you, baby," I whispered helplessly. I was lost and loving every bit of it.

"Good, now you've earned your bath, and when you're done maybe I'll give you the present I bought you." He grinned and I wondered what the hell he was up to. It was too damn early for a ring. It'd better not be a damn ring. I watched his thigh muscles flex as he kneeled to adjust the water and turn on the jets in the tub. Trey was with Denise so I knew he was in good hands, but I didn't know about this whole surprise business. I hated surprises. People never seemed to give you exactly what you wanted or expected. The room was beyond nice; it was on some all out honeymoon suite type shit. At the moment, the last thing I wanted to do was have a Twix moment on this nigga because he'd popped out a promise, engagement, or even a damn friendship ring.

Devon brought me a glass of moscato once I'd eased myself into the water. He'd remembered that I didn't really like champagne. I was so nervous I downed the glass. You definitely shouldn't drink in hot tubs, It makes the smallest amount of alcohol go straight to your head.

"Okay, no peeking. I promise you'll love me for it." He handed me a damp wash cloth.

Laying it over my eyes, I put my head back with a sigh. The jets were loud so I strained to hear what he was doing. A glass touched my lips and I took a sip rolling my eyes at his attempt to get me drunk. *Okay, more moscato.* He pressed up against me, removing the washcloth. I was instantly teleported back to the hospital. My heart had to have skipped at least five solid beats. She was right there pressed up against me, the girl with Lataya's eyes. The back of the Jacuzzi scraped my back and water splashed everywhere as I panicked and tried to climb out. I was scared to take my eyes off of her to see where Devon was. Her hand quickly flew up, covering my mouth, and she smiled, shaking her head at me.

Where was Devon? Did he set me up? Was he hurt?

Chapter 26

Twisted Sister

"Hi, Michelle. Did you miss me?" she asked.

It was Honey's voice. I was dead certain of that, but it wasn't her face. I squinted at her like a Monet, but aside from her eyes, I just couldn't see the baby-faced bitch I knew. Devon moaned from somewhere behind me, it sounded like the bed. Honey grinned at the sound.

"Oops, I might have drugged y'alls wine a little bit. See after Rah oh, wait, they think you shot me, huh? Hmm, wonder how that happened? Well, either way, it hurt like a mothafucka. I was tryin' to get a refill on my oxy while I'm in the E.R. and I overhear a nurse on her break talkin' all quiet to who? Your boo, Dr. Harrington, on the phone. He's telling her how he's tryin' to find a girlfriend for his girlfriend." Honey explained.

I was starting to feel sluggish and woozy as she talked. So she was Devon's damn surprise. Ugh. He had the worst taste in surprises; I didn't want or need a woman in our relationship.

"Honey? If it's even you. Why would you hurt him, he hasn't done anything to you?"

She didn't answer me, she slowly backed away, taking enough bubbles with her to cover her body. She was staring at me the entire time. My eyes were starting to feel lazy. Not sleepy, just lazy.

"Michelle? I'm not gonna kill you. You'll wish you were dead by the time I'm finished though. When you an' Larissa decided how and what would happen to everybody around you, it was like playin' God and shit right? You ever tried china white? I think we gonna stay here until you love china white more than you love life."

What the fuck is china white? I tried to think of every damn drug I'd ever heard of or seen Ris do or deal with. Honey climbed out of the Jacuzzi, gracing me with a view of her full bare ass. She had a stripper's ass, and then, there they were on her left shoulder, the letters Honey. It was definitely her. A new surge of adrenaline and fear coursed through me, and I tried to get up off the seat before she came back from wherever she was. Devon was laid out across the bed, I could barely see his chest rising and falling. There wasn't anything close that I could use for a weapon except . . .

Grabbing the champagne flute, I slipped it into the water and snapped the cup off the stem against the edge. I ran my thumb across the jagged glass pick I'd created. It could work. Honey came sashaying back from the direction of the bathroom.

"Just in case you wanna' try some sneaky shit, I brought my l'il friend," she announced with a fake accent and a giggle waving a small gun. "Now, come here."

I refused to let the only weapon I had go, it was no match for a gun, but she wouldn't have that gun in her hand forever. My legs felt like rubber as I tried to stand up. I used my imbalance as a reason to turn my back to her, and I slid the washcloth over my glass shank. She walked over just as I managed to climb up and sit on the edge of the tub, guess I was moving too slow for her.

"Look at me, Michelle. It's time to start your new life," she instructed.

I refused, scared she was about to stick the barrel of the gun to my forehead or in between my lips. I sat there, naked and shivering, shaking my head no. She pointed the gun at me and my nostrils flared as I weighed my options. Reluctantly, I did as told and she blew some kind of powder into my face. I coughed and gasped for air, rubbing my eyes and blinking. She started speaking but her voice sounded like she was in a different room, and it was strange but I felt happy as fuck. Like there was nothing wrong at all. I couldn't remember where I was or why, but I honestly didn't care, everything was good.

"That was scopolamine, or devil's breath. You won't remember none of this. Now, we are going to have ourselves some fun."

I watched everything from somewhere inside my body. It was like I wasn't in control of what I was doing; I just gladly did as I was told. Honey scampered away and came back. She laid out all these syringes, pills and powders in front of me and I smiled down at them. She laughed at me and I laughed with her.

"We are gonna play a game. We'll start with the pills and you'll work your way up until you get to the syringes. There's one for you and your boo, Krokodile. It's paint thinner, kinda like heroin, tears your skin to shit, so we'll save it for last. Um, this should be heroin, or it's morphine, I don't remember. But, when your man wakes up, you'll pick a needle, walk over like nothing's wrong, and give him a shot. Okay?" she asked.

"Alrighty. But, what do I win?" I asked.

"You win a fucked up drug habit, and we'll ride to your bank and you'll withdraw some money for me after that you'll go get your son so I can take him with me. He won't want to be with your broke drugged up ass now will he? Isn't that how everyone thought about me?"

"Yes, that is how we thought." I giggled like we were discussing an episode of *Love and Hip Hop* and not my son.

"Okay, let's do some pills or something, my ass gettin' bored as fuck."

Honey took two and handed me two; I did what she did and swallowed them, drinking from the moscato bottle nearby. She threw a robe at me and I slid it over my body, enjoying the feel of the cotton gliding over my skin. Devon moaned over on the bed, so I did as instructed and reached down, picking up a syringe filled with this brownish tinged fluid. I watched him in the setting sun and waited, excited to have a mission. Honey swayed on her feet and I giggled at her. Devon shifted and I rushed toward him smiling, he was waking up and Honey took off in the direction of the bathroom.

"Don't worry. I think this one is the cracker bill . . . crocodile . . . heroin. This one is heroin." I called out to her, straddling Devon.

He opened his eyes as the needle jabbed into the skin of his neck, I started to press the end of the syringe, smiling brightly all the while.

"Nothing's wrong." I told him, just as I was instructed.

Frowning, he swatted me off of him with a growl.

"What the hell are you doing?" He touched his fingers to his neck.

"Nothing's wrong," I couldn't think of anything else to say, it was as if I needed a script.

Devon rushed past me, toward the bathroom, and I followed behind him.

"Aww, what the fuck?" he cursed.

I looked around him, Honey was on her knees in front of the toilet. Well, more like her head was in the toilet. From the looks of it the pills she'd taken didn't mix well with whatever was in the bottle of moscato. She went to vomit, passed out, hitting her head on the way down, she drowned with her face in the toilet bowl.

I had the worst headache of my life the next day. We didn't say anything to the police about her drugging me. Devon carefully put everything in her bag, and luckily for her, they didn't mention any of that in their reports to the media. It looked like an accident and they left it at that. I remembered bits and pieces of what she'd said and I'd laid him out decent for finding a random female to come through in the first place.

As an apology, Devon finally let me have my way and he agreed to let me do teeniest bit of redecorating in his "asylum" portion of the hospital. I told him that after having firsthand experience as an actual guest and an actual million-dollar broker, I was beyond qualified to help make the place a little more antidepressant.

"Devon, I'm not even crazy and I wanted to kill myself after only a week up in here." I laughed.

"That is sea-foam green and it's statistically relaxing," he retorted.

"Mmm hmm, just like your 'statistically dramatic' date that almost put you in the ER? Humph, relaxing my ass."

My first order of business was repainting and redoing the floors. No more of that putrid green, period. We were putting lounge chairs and couches in the visiting areas; no more of that sitting in the cafeteria shit. You treat people like children in a mess hall and they'd act that way. Plain and simple. I'd found some nice landscape portraits of fields and flowers, dreamy stuff that depressed people would feel uplifted looking at. Overseeing the process was a headache as always. I had to keep the patients quarantined to one area, work in another, and keep Devon calm.

"Ms. Michelle?" one of the painters called out. "All this needs to be redone; the wall is chipping."

I wouldn't be able to get that kind of job past Devon. He'd have a fit. Maybe if we did it in pieces. This old place should have been redecorated and primped ages ago. I gave the painter the go-ahead, telling Devon's ass take the day off; his pacing combined with the spot and corner checking was getting on every last one of our nerves. I was pretty sure I caught him with a leveler over a picture.

We'd found a nice place that would take Reena and we decided to split the cost of her stay equally. On nicer days they let their patients go outdoors for a few hours, and I'd decided to personally see if she was settling in okay before we left her in their care. Devon walked with me. Reena was sitting on one of the cement benches beside the rosebushes this place had. I wanted to nudge or punch him and say "see, they have rosebushes." Men don't know anything about what the hell would cheer up a depressed anybody.

"Reena, it's your lucky day," one of the nurses called out from the hospital entrance waving. "Your sister is here to see you."

She approached us, wearing a dramatically huge black Kentucky Derby straw hat, and I shielded my eyes, smiling brightly. The sun was glimmering off all these gold bangles, bands, rings, and such.

I extended my hand.

Let me find out Mona can clean up?

When she gripped it in a firm handshake I immediately snapped it back as she pulled off that hat.

"What in the hell? What the kind of bullshit is this? What are you doing here?" I huffed at her.

All the patients who were outside, started screaming or skipping and singing at the sound of my outburst. One of them even had the nerve to start skipping around us singing ring around the damn roses.

I grabbed Shiree's ass around the neck and held her in a straight-up choke hold. All the gold bangles on her wrist clanged in protest as she waved wildly, flaying her arms, trying to grab me. I wasn't about to get played or taken down by her or anyone else. Not after Honey came and zombie voodoo blasted me in the damn face at the hotel, and especially not after I'd just seen Shiree's ass cozied up with Big Baby and Honey. Rah said he was in love with her ass, too. Oh, no, we were not having this conversation any other way than how I had her ass.

Devon was telling me to calm down, the orderlies were trying to get me to calm down, Shiree was trying to get out my damn arms.

1. "You had the nerve date him or whatever after me and then show up here? You set Ris up? You probably set Honey up that day at the restaurant didn't you?"

"I wanted to pay my respects to Ms. White; it ain't got shit to do with you," Shiree squeaked from under my arm.

Hearing her name, Reena floated over like the world wasn't in chaos all around her. "Michelle, where you been, girl? I ever tell you how I met Rasheed daddy?" she asked.

I rolled my eyes and tightened my grip. "Yes, you have," I snapped. Nobody was trying to hear that mess right now, especially not me.

"No, I always skip the beginning. Let me tell you the beginning, baby."

Chapter 27

Summer, 1986

"Look, how many times do I have to tell you to leave my damn son alone?"

"But it's his baby, I swear. I wouldn't lie about something like this." I pleaded pathetically, but she wasn't trying to hear a word I had to say.

This definitely wasn't what I was hoping for given my circumstances. I'd caught two buses and walked Lord knows how many blocks just to get over here. The sun felt like it was damn near sitting on the back of my neck the entire way, and I only had enough cash on me for bus fare back. I'd stared some poor little Jamaican dude down so hard he'd actually backed up into his shop out of the doorway. Shit, my mind wasn't even on the cash register; if I stole anything up out of there it'd be beef patties and an ice-cold Ting soda.

"I swear, if your little trifling hoing ass isn't wobbling off my porch in the next three seconds, I'll go get Big Bertha. She ain't as nice, and she's way louder than I am."

I hurried up and got my "nine and some change, sweaty, hot, an' ready to burst" pregnant behind up out of there. Mrs. Tessa did not play when it came to three things: her son, the lottery, or her shotgun, also known as Big Bertha.

I'd met Ray when he was interning up at the free clinic on Twenty-eighth Street. No, I was not up in there for no crazy shit. I was actually volunteering. All the crazy shit happened after that. My sister Mona and I had been on our own for nearly as long as l could remember. Our oldest sister, Mirna, had gotten all sanctified, leaving us to do for ourselves. She'd been putting in overtime turning out this deacon's son, and once she'd gotten him on lockdown she acted like she ain't *want anything to do with any of us anymore. She packed all her stuff and moved out to be with him, turning her nose up at us like we was beyond God's reach in the process. Mona did what she had to in order to keep us decent and to keep the roof over our heads. Sometimes that meant doing things that some folk might consider immoral or scandalous, but it made do.*

My sister Mona was nineteen and working part time at the shirt factory in between losing her damn mind the winter that I met Ray and I was going on seventeen. He was hell-bent on making something out of his life, and at that point I was just hell-bent.

I was volunteering, or more like "voluntold", to work at the free clinic as punishment for shoplifting. It was one of those drab gray winter days where the sun sits like a block of ice in the sky, and the wind's so cold it makes your lips burn. I'd been pissed all week about Mona selling my pea coat at the flea market that Sunday. If I weren't trying to keep my record clear over that shoplifting shit, I would've whooped her ass and gotten myself a new one off that five-finger discount.

Inside the clinic I took up my usual position behind the reception counter, ready to read and reread the articles in my Ebony *magazine. It must have been too much for me to ask for a peaceful day. Glancing up, I cringed as a woman staggered in through the door toward the front desk where I sat. Before I could even open my mouth to ask her what she needed, he walked, no, let me rephrase that, he glided in not far behind her. I'd heard about pimps bringing in their girls for the free STD treatments, but I'd never actually seen or dealt with one. The entire concept of giving up hard-earned money to someone else for no reason completely baffled me anyway.*

His floor-length mink fluttered around him in a fur cloud as he sauntered toward me with a smirk on his face. There were so many diamonds on him I damn near had to squint as the lights shimmered off of them in various directions.

He leaned onto the receptionist desk like he owned it, a tea-tree stick hanging out from the corner of his mouth.

He was so close my eyes started to water from the pungent minty scent as he chewed it casually.

"Let me tell you how you're doing today." His voice was smoother than a baby's ass, and equally as soft as he continued. "You finer than fine china, eating off paper plates every night. I already know I'm right, because wrong ain't an option. You been misguided, because somebody sold you a blank map to life, when all you really need is someone to map your life out. Let me get you off this road to nowhere and into show-where. Ho-where. Ho territory making that prime ho fare."

This fool couldn't be serious. "I think your lady friend over there needs help." Frowning, I gave a quick nod toward her. She was leaning against the wall looking worse by the minute.

He didn't even glance in her direction. "Business first, ass last. That's rule number one."

"Well, I don't think she's interested in doing any kind of business, so you can check in or leave." Ray's voice was a deep road block in Frankie's map.

"You know you're addressing Frankie the Ambassador Diamonds, young blood?" Frankie straightened slowly, his jaw flexing around the chew stick.

"I know who I'm talking to, but your title doesn't mean anything to anyone outside of the broken women you exploit."

Frankie Diamonds stared straight past Ray as if he didn't even exist. He flung the lapels of his coat behind him and marched toward the door, angrily yanking the girl up by the arm on his way out.

Up until that point, Ray had all but ignored me anytime we were stuck working together. He was quiet and stayed lost in his head, but there was always something about him that stood out from all the idiots who catcalled at me all day. He was a Venus flytrap in a garden of geraniums, and I just had to know if I put my finger next to him . . . near him . . . on him . . . would he snap. And, snap he did.

It was as if I'd been sleepwalking through life ever since the day Momma left us, and being with Ray was electrifying.

He was that feeling you get when you dream you're falling and you jerk yourself awake. I wasn't about to tell him that though, couldn't have him thinking he had me all wrapped around his little, middle, and index fingers. Even though he did. Truth was I didn't have to tell him anything. Anyone looking at us could see it written all over our faces and in our body language. Our souls were mirrors of the other, and it was seen and felt no matter what we did. You'd think working in a damn clinic with mounds of birth control at our disposal we'd use it, and we did. But it only takes that one time to get caught up in the moment, and it's a wrap.

His parents eventually found out through the gossip grapevine of nosey-ass neighbors and store owners that we were seeing each other, and they had him moved into a new intern position. They'd been molding him to follow in their footsteps and they damn sure weren't about to let him get mixed up with anyone that might get him off track; especially not with someone like me. Ray managed to sneak across town to see me throughout my entire pregnancy. He was probably more excited about the baby than I was.

The problem with young, stupid love is that you never realize you're being young and stupid while you're in it.

When I finally went into labor, it was a muggy summer day in August. Mona was in jail for breaking and entering, and my damn water broke while I was on a bus of all places. When Ray got to the hospital I'd already put his name on the paperwork and dozed off. Not long after he'd arrived, a roar started in the hospital lobby that burst into my hospital room in the form of two angry parents.

"What the hell is this, Ray?" his momma fumed; her face was damn near bright red she was so mad.

Ray was seated in a chair in the corner, holding an ice pack to his neck.

"Son? Answer your damn mother. How could you go against what we said? We forbade you to deal with this girl, and now look at the mess you're in." Ray's daddy was pacing back and forth, his long legs covering the length of the entire room in three steps before he was turning to repeat the process.

I couldn't take it anymore; my body hurt and I was dead-ass tired. They acted like I wasn't the one who had just done all the fuckin' work.

"Excuse me; Ray is still a little fuzzy from his head hittin' the floor. He kinda passed out a few minutes ago. If the two of you would please stop yelling and just sit down, the nurse will be back in a few minutes and you can meet your grand-babies: Rasheed, Rayshon, and Rosalyn."

Chapter 28

Momma's Maybe, Daddy's Baby

It was as if a game of freeze tag had ended and everyone could move again.

"Michelle, can you let my sister go please?"

"Sister?"

"Michelle, let me fuckin' go," she squeaked.

I tightened my grip. "So why you ain't say anything to her at Ruby Tuesday's when she was sitting behind us, Devon? She was right there, squakin' at Rasheed, remember?" I asked him sarcastically.

Devon took a step toward me with his hands out and I tightened up. The orderlies were all over the place, corralling the crazies, but I kept an eye out for one just in case.

Devon sputtered nervously, "I honestly didn't see her, didn't recognize her voice or anything, Michelle. They were behind us, remember, You're tripping right now."

"You really wanna call me crazy again, boy?" I gave him that look that said when and if we got home it was goin' down, and not the type of going down that he'd appreciate.

Shiree tapped my arm. "Chelle, he probably ain't know it was me; my ass had laryngitis. I swear on my life. I was up in there coughing and everything. You had to have heard me."

"I really didn't know. I swear I ain't know it was her, Michelle." Devon said looking at me pitifully.

I looked down at Shiree. In her tight sundress, there was nowhere to hide a weapon except for up in her snatch.

I wouldn't even put that past these trifling-ass heffas these days.

I let Shiree go, throwing her away from me so she'd lose her balance, and she fell into Devon. They were both scowling at me, and in turn I scowled right the hell back.

Devon looked between me and Shiree and started laughing. "She gotta be a keeper if she can whoop my sister's mean ass."

Reena wandered back off and was busy humming back into her rosebush.

Shiree watched Momma walk away. "Sounds like old Reena was getting it in." She laughed and asked, "What she say all them damn babies names was?"

"Rasheed, Rayshon, and Rosalyn; damn, even I caught that and I had you in a choke hold. She was stuck on them Rs, must've had a Reese's. I think they're wrooooong. I don't like any of 'em. But that's just me." I laughed.

Shiree hit *the* ground. Devon swayed where he stood. I was the only one laughing.

Uh oh. Whatever it is, it ain't gonna be good.

"My first name is Rayshon. My dad raised me, Shiree, went to Grandma's. I remember him and Melanie arguing about another little girl he had that went there too, but I never met her. I went to Great Uncle Lowell," Devon whispered.

The orderlies helped Shiree sit up, and she looked a myriad of emotions that I could never begin or even want to understand or explain.

"First thunderstorm. I can hear it already. Y'all hear that? 'How sweet the sound . . .'" Reena asked in a singsong voice, before bellowing out her haunting, memorable rendition of "Amazing Grace."

We all looked up; there wasn't a single cloud in the damn sky.

We were all sitting around the kitchen table silently, with grim, somber faces. No one really wanted to say what the others were thinking or feeling. It was as if we'd drank and partied, finally waking up hung over. Each of us in bed with someone we knew but didn't really know, remembering what we'd done or did with and to each other. Reena was a mouse trapped in a maze of memories. She'd find her way out only to go get lost again.

"Why did she keep Rasheed and not us?" Devon wondered out loud.

Remembering the Frankie Diamonds story, I answered him. "They got chased and split up she could only carry one of you, so I think your daddy grabbed you two."

The Cliffs Notes, minus the gruesome details. That's what I gave them, and they still looked down at the table like I'd stepped on their favorite pet cricket. Shiree was even harder to read and I could understand why. She literally loved and lost her brother.

I wasn't even trying to wrap my head around my relationship with Devon or Rayshon or whatever. Ugh, I shuddered whenever I said or thought of that name. I'd decided to call it a night after the pizza came for Trey. I put on my house sweats, did the movie and pizza thing with my little man, and then we were out.

I woke up in the middle of the night, sweating and out of breath. I was having a nightmare that Devon was Rasheed and he was trying to kill me. Out of habit I turned to Devon and realized I'd fallen asleep with Trey. I quietly climbed out of Trey's little bed and stretched my stiff, sore back.

"I can rub that for you."

I turned around slowly. "How did you get in here, Towanna?" I asked her quietly.

"You didn't answer my calls, didn't return any of my texts. I had to make sure you were good." She shrugged and picked at her fingernails.

"Towanna, where's Devon?"

"On the couch, exactly where he was when I came in," she replied calmly, too calmly.

"Stop playing with me; you know what the hell I'm asking you. Is he alive?"

"For now. I'm not the one who's going to determine how long he lives. You are. So come along; we don't need to get cliché about this shit, either."

"What about Trey? What am I—"

"He'll be safer here. So give him a kiss and let's go."

We walked right out the front door. Past Devon, who was passed out drunk on the couch and everything. The only good thing was I still slept in full preparation mode sometimes. My phone was in my pants pocket, and I looked for any chance to call or text for help.

So much for my macho-man super protection; and what's the point of the damn house alarm if he's not going to use it? Worse than Key's ass.

We drove for about an hour until she finally stopped at the Chesapeake Bay Bridge. The water was pitch black beneath us and the night wind whistled in cold sheets against the side of her SUV. I was too scared to ask why we were there or what she was about to do with me. I just stared at the stars; every now and again a stark white seagull would appear and dive below.

"Get out of the car, Michelle. It's time to get this shit over with."

She got out, walked around, and opened my door.

"Whatever this is, I don't want to do it. I'm serious. I really don't want to. You're right, I'm wrong."

"I'm not the one trying to prove anything. It's your ass. Get the fuck down here and stop acting like a little punk-ass bitch. You done let that nigga twist your mind all the fuck up like that? The dick can't be that damn good."

I climbed out the truck, slamming the door and I walked up to her, yelling the entire way. "Are we really standing in the middle of this fucking bridge having a damn argument over . . . over I don't even know what it's over? So leave my man and his dick up out ya mouth, Towanna."

"Okay now we're getting somewhere. So he's your man now?"

"Yes, he's my man, Towanna. You mad or somethin'? Is that why we here?"

She ignored me and kept going with the questions, her nostrils flaring and eyes raging. "Does he love you?"

She would ask me that after the day we just had.

"What happened? We ain't so quick when it counts anymore. Does he love you as much as I love you?"

I actually laughed and loud, too. "Towanna, you might need to go get checked out your damn self. The hell are you talking about? No one came to the house that night, there were no cars, you were sleep on the couch. It was just you wasn't it? You tortured me for Rah's money."

"Right, you right." She pulled out her pistol.

My phone vibrated in my pocket.

We have what we need. Get down.

That text turned me into a human panic, button and I was suddenly the one pressed for information.

"Towanna, did you kill your partner that night?

She curled her lip in a smirk. "Fuck no. The hell would you—"

"Towanna, shut up and just answer the damn questions. Is your mom's name Lacy?"

"Da fuck? Huh?"

I clenched my fist and literally groaned out loud. "Tell me, hurry up. What is it?"

She started looking at me sideways; she obviously didn't understand but I didn't need her to understand. We didn't have time for the theatrics right now. My eyes were all over the place, scared a helicopter was going to rise up beside us at any minute spraying saltwater everywhere. Lightning lit the sky up and I almost came up out my skin.

"My mom's name is Royce," Towanna finally called out, suspiciously narrowing her eyes.

I ran toward her, waving my arms before throwing myself at her, knocking her to the ground. The sky split open in a crack of lightning and a roar of thunder and down came the rain.

Towanna looked at me like I'd sprouted a nose in the middle of my forehead. "Woman, have you lost your damn mind? What in the world?" she asked me.

"Why does everybody keep asking me that shit?" I smiled down at her.

And then I passed out.

Chapter 29

Orders Are Meant to Be Followed

Iodine, ultraviolet lights, and ointment: I could smell it everywhere and feel it on the backs of my eyelids, prying them open. People were walking and talking around me in hushed whispers. The last thing I could remember was looking down at Towanna in the rain, and then this. I had no idea where I was, where she was or where . . .

I sat up and pain ran through the entire left side of my body. There was no pinpointing where it began or ended. It felt like the skin was tearing and pulling from the front of my stomach to the back of my ribcage.

"She's awake," I heard someone say on the other side of a white curtain.

"How are you feeling, Michelle?" A nurse approached me and checked my vitals.

"I don't know, tell me what happened and I'll figure out how I feel as opposed to that."

"Well, you were brought in with a gunshot wound to the abdomen. The police report says you tried to kill yourself. Did you know you were pregnant when you attempted this, Michelle?"

I sat there with my head cocked to the side as if I'd gotten water in my ear and I were waiting on that one drop to drip its way out. I didn't move, I didn't blink, and I didn't make a sound.

I was what? I was what? I did what?

Even after I told them not to shoot, throwing myself on this woman like she was a fucking live grenade, they did anyway. And when I got hit, they called it self-inflicted and on top of that I was . . .

Not ready to think about that part of the equation yet. Let's stick with A and B: did the FBI or whoever just shoot me and make it look like I shot myself, and where is Towanna?

"Do you have anything to say, Ms. Roberts?" the nurse asked, raising an eyebrow.

"What hospital is this? Where are Devon and my son?"

"Excuse me, I—"

"It's a simple question. What hospital am I in?" I shouted.

The chatter stopped. The makeshift curtain flew open. A bear of a man appeared holding a soiled Dunkin' Donuts coffee cup. I tried to focus and not to stare at the graying box-fade shaped thing growing off his head.

He spoke in a brusque voice. "Okay, Michelle, calm down. I'm Special Agent—"

"About to get fucked up if you don't tell me that what this nurse just told me is a bunch of bullshit."

He drew in a long breath. "You were given an order, a directive. You failed and this is your fault, your punishment, your fuckup. I'm Agent Harper."

"Have you told anyone that I'm here?"

"Not yet, we need you to corroborate the story before we set you out in the world with it. You're stuck here until you cooperate."

"And Towanna?"

"She's being questioned."

"What if I told you that you have the wrong person? Do you think I'd throw myself in front of a bullet for no damn reason?"

Agents I didn't even know were out there poked their heads in at that moment. Looking, listening, ready to hear what I had to say. But, not until I knew Towanna was okay.

They brought Towanna in and she nodded, assuring me that she was okay.

"Okay, Michelle. We can't just have people sitting around without an explanation. This is your show; all eyes are on you right now."

"Melanie Malia took out five genteel wealthy men, one of whom was none other than Momma White's baby daddy Ray, and, on top of that, she somehow got Devon and Shiree in the process. When Momma White told me the story, she said it happened twice. I had to do some research into Lacy's cases."

"What are the names of all the husbands, Agent Harper?"

"Renner, Clark, Kellam, Latharium, Ponce, and Harrington." Agent Harper rattled them off one by one.

"There's a man in the area by the name of Marcus Latharium Bello; he was good friends with Rasheed, goes by Big Baby. He's the only Bello I know and Rah told me they grew up together, how Big just showed up one day, no parents, he just appeared. I never thought about the story until now. Mr. Latharium's son. Momma helped Lacy get rid of him by giving that little boy to the African lady at the shop, kind of a repayment thing. When Lacy picked Ray, Momma refused to do it again."

A few agents had some light bulbs go off and began writing down what I was saying. Good, because I was starting to get tired.

"He has some massage something or another's popping up all over the place. Check into him and his stuff, he's probably hiding whatever it is that Lacy used in plain sight."

There was a rush of excited voices and they exchanged glances.

"I asked to redecorate Devon's hospital after he checked me in, no thanks to you morons. A nurse had mentioned stuff happening on the 5th wing. Devon checks out. I couldn't find anything on him. The only thing you'll find there is that area, his lab, which also houses the electroshock therapy units. Every now and again he has elite and VIPs come and go without check-in or special clearances, but that's expected when they're high-profile celebrities and don't want the press finding out about it.

"And, Towanna. I didn't forget about you. Your momma married three times I think? But remind these good people who she is and who her second husband was."

"They already know. My mom's name is Royce; she didn't know she was pregnant when she did what she did to my dad. Don Cerzulo is my stepfather. May he rest in peace, even though me and him weren't that close."

And then a light bulb went off in my head. "So that's why you're helping them, because you just tie the whole family together, huh? Then when I came in the picture they were all like, find out what I know, so that when a time like right the fuck now came they'd have whatever they needed to get me to help fit everybody the hell together."

"But, Michelle, that's why nothing really happened, and I didn't even have anybody up in the house to hurt you. Angelo didn't even come to the house. I'd asked one of the agents to swab Lataya, and for whatever reason he did them both. When these dudes killed Ennis . . ."

"He drew a weapon on an armed agent and refused to stand down, ma'am."

I didn't see who said it, but that explained poor Ennis.

Towanna sneered at one of the men and went on, "I just wanted to know if you knew anything ASAP so I could be done with the shit. So I staged that whole thing to try to make you talk. That's all, and then you ran all the way out here."

I was starting to feel weak and nauseated. Connecting all these dots to all these different people was really starting to wear me out. The FBI and CIA had tracked down and traced everyone connected to Lacy in some way, shape, or form. I guess the world really does revolve around money. I still had to know something.

"One last question and then I'm done. The agreement I signed said that I killed Rasheed. What did yours say?"

"That's classified, Roberts," several agents blurted out at once.

"It's okay, Towanna, I already know. It said you killed Lania and Keyshawn, didn't it?" I asked her anyway, despite their warnings.

Towanna looked down at the floor quickly, but not before I could see the tears in her eyes, confirming my suspicion.

"That's enough, Roberts. Conditions of your agreements are confidential and need-to-know only. You are relieved and needed no further."

"Well, we might as well show our hands then." I addressed everyone in the room, taking turns looking at them one by one. Some of them looked away, some met my stare with indifference or defiance as I continued, "It doesn't make any sense acting all shy now. Not when we all know who's using who. Tell me again, my options were to sign or what? Sink, right?"

Done with my tirade, I was finally feeling winded and my side was aching. I had to get a point across even if they didn't give a fuck about me making it. They scowled, and Towanna stood there clammed up, looking pensive and hurt. Drained, I lay my head back, empathizing with the pain I knew she was feeling.

"And for the damn record, my last name is Laurel. I've changed it since you don't seem to get up-to-date information. And, you're welcome."

Chapter 30

I Am Relieved

"You sure you wanna do this, Michelle?" Devon whined, looking at me with the stank face.

We were lying in bed enjoying the peace and quiet. Trey wouldn't be home until Sunday and me and my man had ourselves a date. Devon rolled on his stomach, sticking his head under the pillow, ostrich style. I quit fiddling with the button of his pajama top I was wearing and rolled my eyes. Trey might as well have been in the bed with me; the man was acting just like him when he ain't wanna get up in the morning.

"Boy, stop. It ain't gonna be that bad." I smacked his ass.

Biting my nail, I grinned at that bad boy as it bounced in the matching bottoms to my top. I was about to reach over and smack it again.

"Stop smackin' my ass, woman." His voice was muffled under the pillow.

"Huh? What did you say, baby? I can't understand you when you're speaking ostrich," I teased him.

He threw the pillow and snatched me down in its place and I yelped. Giggling, I stared up and him through my lashes.

"Guess we need to work on that language barrier then. 'Cause, I can understand yo' ostrich perfectly fine." He mocked me, "Harder, baby, get it, get it, choke—"

What in the hell, is that what I sound like? Good Lawd.

Slamming my finger up against his lips I shushed his ass. "What I say or don't say in the heat of the moment is not to be repeated. Ever. I made a list of stuff you need to get before our date night. So we need to get up."

There was too much on my to-do list today and ass was not one them. At least not now, definitely after, but now we had shit to do.

"But a double date though?"

"What's wrong with a double date? It'll be fun and I like Nurse Denise."

"How you even know she swing that way? She might just be shy or a late bloomer or something. I know you can't tell because I'm so ruggedly sexy and shit now, but I too was a late bloomer. You might mess around and have her out there embarrassed and shit."

"Look, I think Denise is cute and I also think she and Towanna would make a cute couple. Besides when's the last time you took me out on a date, Devon?"

"Um. The, uh. We go on dates," he eventually sputtered.

I gave him the side eye. "The secret agent hotel doesn't count, bae."

I'd had lunch with Towanna at least once a week since the night I took a bullet for her. I'd told her that she was gonna have to let me shoot her for GP now. It was only fair. We couldn't be best friends otherwise. She'd laughed her ass off that day, reminding me that I'd already shot her. Not sure how on earth that little detail had slipped my mind. I never told Devon about losing the baby. There was no point in upsetting him over something he couldn't have controlled or changed. He would have been hurt for no reason, banning Towanna from our lives, when I still would have gotten over it as I did.

The Feds finally caught up with Big Baby. Turned out he did have that concoction that connected Lacy to all five of those deaths. He'd been remaking it up in his shop in Miami. Shiree was taking it the hardest. Devon said she'd actually miscarried not long after finding out Rasheed was her brother, and I was hoping my manhandling her ain't have anything to do with it. He said it was stress related, but on second thought I think she might have gotten rid of the baby all together. She'd only come by the house once, and that was to say good-bye. She said she was staying in Miami, and then possibly going to Cali.

Trey didn't bat an eyelash, pout, or anything when I'd dropped him off at Denise's nephews on Friday evening. It felt good to have some little boys around his age he could play with. He'd been so excited and it was all he'd talked about all week.

Mommy was excited too. This was going to be the first night in I couldn't remember how long that I was going to have a grown-up dinner and dancing date night with no drama and no bullshit.

I'd gone to at least three different stores and finally ended up around the corner, spending around $450 at Pier One on candles, wine glasses, and vases. I wanted to have a real nice evening before we went out with wine and talking. It would give Denise and Towanna a chance to warm up to each other. I figured given the rare chance they didn't like each other, they would have an escape before we got to the Melting Pot.

"Look, I don't want you hookin' me up with none of your dude's Nurse Ratchet friends," Towanna complained, moping into her Cobb salad.

Reaching over I smacked her elbow.

"This one ain't ratched, trust me. She's cute, thick, an' Towanna wanna thicky, dimpled, hippy girl . . ." I bobbed back and forth, singing to her in my seat.

"Yeah, all right. What's her Facebook?"

That was all I needed. She started grinning sheepishly into her plate. Clapping my hands, I tapped my feet on the floor squealing in delight like I'd just scored myself a touchdown.

"Don't worry 'bout all that. I already showed her your picture. She's all in. It's a double date. We goin' to the Melting Pot. Saturday, fool. So dress cute, pretty please. None of this T-shirt business," I warned, waving my hand over her with my face all furled up.

"Damn. I ain't give her the stamp of approval or nothin'. And what the hell's wrong with my T-shirt? Makes my arms look good. Gun show all day, baby."

Everyone was supposed to be at the house at six p.m. and I'd made our reservations at the restaurant for a late dinner at nine. That would be more than enough time for the two of them to sit around, chat, and play the interview game. Since this was Denise's night and I didn't wanna upstage her date night, I kept my attire simple with a fitted, above-the-knee cream-colored dress and yellow pumps for flair. I pinned my hair up because Devon always liked to call himself messing something up. This was just for him. I'd told Devon if he played nice tonight, I'd let him have his fun losing all my damn bobby pins between carpet and the bed later.

I turned the TV on to one of the Music Choice channels that played a variety of R&B. The entire house smelled like the crisp bamboo and citrus cilantro candles I'd gotten earlier. He did it on purpose, and my head almost rolled off my shoulders. Devon zipped past me into the kitchen. Dolce & Gabbana all over his baahdy, probably even on the top of his freshly shaved head, knowing him. My nose followed my favorite smell until he came into my line of sight, and I damn near jumped the man.

"Negro, where the hell are your clothes? They're gonna be here in a few minutes and you ain't even dressed?"

He bopped over, smiling wickedly. "You have to give me something if you want me to wear clothes tonight. I just said I'd shower and be nice."

I smirked at him. "Fine then, walk your ass around naked. They ain't gonna care. I'm the one getting the show."

Why I thought I'd get away with that answer, I had no idea. I was trying to take the wine out the fridge . . . and then I was pressed hard up against the fridge. My eyes narrowed impishly. Devon was already hard up against my stomach. He was being so bad. But getting so, so good. He started off licking every inch of my pussy. I alternated between holding his head and the top of the fridge for balance.

The doorbell rang and I swear I wanted to cry in frustration. He slid me down, sitting me on the floor, and we butted foreheads. My eyes instantly watered as I fought a sneeze. Pinching the bridge of my nose, I glowered at him, trying to figure out where he was even bending to in the first place. He chuckled and I climbed back into my heels . . .

When the hell did he take off . . .

"See, I told you they'd be here; where the hell is my thong? You couldn't have just pushed it to the side? When the hell did you even take it off? Go get me one out the laundry room!"

When the doorbell rang again, I hurried to answer it.

"Hey, y'all. Sorry, I was trying to open the wine."

You know how people come in and sit at your counter in the kitchen or your kitchen table, Well, that's what I'd planned for the start so we could have finger foods and chat. Bruschetta with tomato and cheese was laid out, different kinds of dip to pair with different kind of wine. I turned to get the wine and wine glasses and ta-da, there's my wonderful thong sitting in the kitchen sink! Hoping that neither of them had seen it I took a plate out the cabinet when . . .

Devon's still in the damn laundry room!

"Excuse me for a second," I said politely, "I just need to go in here and see if Devon's shirt is dry."

"Um, Chelle. You ain't wash our glasses in the sink with them thongs, did you?" Towanna asked with a sarcastic grin on her face.

I could feel the red creeping up my neck. Oh, that was so embarrassing. Sliding my hips through the smallest crack I could possibly make in the door, without letting in any light, I exhaled when I was finally all the way in the room.

"Took you long enough," Devon whispered from directly behind me before picking me up and sitting me on top of the cool laundry of the washing machine. I was struggling with every shred of self-control to maintain my composure and be the adult.

"We can't, they are gonna hear us. You need to get your ass dressed." I grabbed a mismatched sock and shirt from under my butt, handing them to him. "We gotta go out there. This is rude; stop being rude." I slapped his arm.

"They gonna hear you making all that damn noise, not me. They can have their date and we'll have ours. You done already took your panties off for me remember?"

"No, I didn't. You did that—"

Devon knew I'd have argued with him all night in there if he let me. He shut me up the best way he knew how, and I answered with my teeth all in the side of his neck.

Chapter 31

Which Witch is Which?

We were seated at the restaurant, having our first course of fondue. The waiter stood beside the table, mixing everything in the little broiler on the tabletop burner. It was everyone's first experience except for Devon. I shot him a look, daring him to compare my night to another date and he'd be reliving the laundry room experience with his hand. He clammed up quick.

From what I could tell, Towanna and Denise were or weren't getting along. They were both kind of take-charge, so it was like watching a couple of rams go head-to-head. Devon started getting annoyed around the third course, but I thought it was hilarious. I was digging around in my oversized purse, trying to find my phone so I could take a picture. I felt like the worst parent in the world when I found Trey's iPad. He'd specifically asked to take it and I'd forgotten to give it to him. He was obviously having a good time if my phone wasn't getting blown up about it though.

Speaking of phone, I couldn't find it anywhere. There was so much going on I prayed I'd just put it down somewhere at the house. I must have hit something, because the iPad came on at a screen called notepad. It was the screen where Rasheed typed to Trey before he'd died. I shut it off and stuffed it back into my purse. My appetite was instantly gone, and I sat there rigid as a board.

"Bae, you okay?" Devon put his arm around my shoulders, looking over at me concerned but I couldn't speak past the lump in my throat.

"You're cold, here." He took his jacket off, draping it around me.

Towanna tried to get my attention. "Chelle, what's the matter? We can leave if y'all ready to go."

I didn't want to leave, and I didn't want to stay. I felt feverish, but the minute I went to remove the jacket I felt cold again and pulled it back around me. I nodded. I was ready to go.

Denise was trying to call and check on Trey for me since I didn't have my phone. When she couldn't get a call to go out with a full signal, my favorite friends, fear and trepidation, paid a visit.

"Towanna? Remember when we were in that hospital?" I barely whispered my question.

She was sitting behind Devon on the driver side of the SUV, and I barely looked over my shoulder to acknowledge her response. Devon and Denise looked back and forth, trying to figure out what was going on. Towanna nodded ever so slightly.

"I had all these questions. There were so many things I didn't understand. I asked those people question after question. Lania and Keyshawn, they weren't on your agreement, were they?" There was so much sadness and regret in my voice.

Devon frowned over at me in between glancing anxiously at the road. "Michelle, what's all this about? What the hell has gotten in to you all of a sudden?"

We were slowing to a stop at a red light, and I saw the only chance I had. I grabbed the syringe I'd felt in Devon's jacket pocket at dinner, and pulling the top off, I reached back, stabbing Towanna in the leg.

The pistol in her hand fell to the floor, and Denise screamed at the sight of the gun. I was surprised the glass didn't shatter. Devon stomped on the brakes. Towanna stared at me in shock, her eyes taking on that drugged, glazed look.

Grabbing the pistol from her lap, I turned it on Devon. Denise continued screaming like the gun was actually pointed at her.

"Denise, I'll shoot you to shut you up at this point so please . . ." I threatened her, thankful for the immediate silence.

"Devon, you're a psychiatrist with a damn chemistry lab in your asylum. You have people come and go at all hours of whatever on that floor. Rich people who could actually afford cocaine if they wanted it. You keep no record of who comes or goes or when they come or go. I've already dealt with one dealer. I'm not doing this shit again."

The light turned green and he looked at me, hesitating. I pointed the gun, instructing him to drive.

"What you want me to do, baby?" he asked quietly.

I almost didn't know what to say. My throat got this scratchy feeling like I was growing a baby cactus in it, and for a second I couldn't speak.

"You're gonna have to turn yourself in. They're not gonna stop until they have you."

He nodded, but of course it couldn't have been that easy; he wasn't nodding at me.

Do all of these motherfuckas' carry emergency knockout needles in their damn pockets?

I cringed, waiting for the pinch and paralysis that never came. Thank sweet baby Jesus in a manger, even after threatening her with a pistol Denise stuck Devon instead of me. I straddled his lap and pressed the brake, putting the car in park.

"Find Towanna's phone. I know they called or sent her a text. I need to know where to take him."

Just like my phone the day Devon checked it, there were no missed special agent calls or texts. I cursed silently.

"How long does that stuff last, Denise?"

"It depends. It could be twenty minutes, up to an hour."

I did the only thing I could think of. Hell, it worked last time. I hauled ass toward the Chesapeake Bay Bridge. It wasn't super early a.m. like the last time, but there was barely a car out there. I stopped in the middle, and Denise helped me drag Devon, out and then we got Towanna.

"Okay, now you get back in and stay down. I got my ass shot last time."

Her eyes got huge and she went MIA inside the truck.

I pulled out the pistol and fired into the air three times and waited.

Squad cars came rolling up with the lights on, sirens blaring and I was beyond relieved. Devon was still out, but Towanna was moaning. A spotlight turned on, blinding me, and I shielded my eyes.

"Drop the gun. Get down on the ground, with your hands behind your head."

"I need to see Agent Harper." I called out nervously, dropping the gun, and the spotlight immediately shut off.

I was grabbed and thrown into the back of a car. I could see police officer's going to Devon and Towanna. They yanked Denise out the truck ass first. I slammed my head back against the seat and waited impatiently.

"You were relieved, Roberts; what in God's name are you doing here?" Harper blasted his question at the side of the car I sat in. The windows possibly rattled.

"Rasheed left a note on Trey's iPad. Then you guys sent Towanna the message; when I figured it out, I brought him in."

Harper exhaled loudly, leaning up against the side of the car. He was staring at the flurry of activity across the bridge where they had Devon. He'd finally come out of his stupor and was being put into the back of car across the way. Harper opened my door, letting me out the squad car.

"Don't discharge another damn firearm in public. You'd better go make up with that man, 'cause he look some kind of pissed off right now. You were relieved, Michelle, and we meant it."

If I wasn't mistaken, either Harper had given me tender smile or a vexed scowl. It's not like there were varying degrees of emotion to the man's face.

Chapter 32

An Equal Sign
=

Ain't Nothing but Stacked Up Minuses

Devon wouldn't speak to me let alone look at me after the officers released him from the squad car. He'd stood there with his eyes mysteriously hooded by his dark lashes, feeling withdrawn and distant. In the entire time we'd been together, I'd never seen him so angry and cold. I just kept waiting for him to turn around and blind me with that disarming boyish smile or wink at me, but nothing happened. Standing in jaw-gaping wide-eyed disbelief, I watched as he got in the Land Cruiser and with a stony voice suggested that one of "my girls" drop me off at the house. It was as if my best friend had sped off and left me holding the sack on the day of the championship three-legged race. I'd just felt the other end of betrayal's double-edged blade.

Denise had called one of her nieces to pick up her and Towanna, and they'd agreed to let me ride with them. The girls had all decided that drinks were in order after what they declared from beginning to end as "the official hell date of the year." I was outnumbered and outvoted. As bad as I wanted to curl up in a ball and cry, it would just have to wait until later. Of course they'd pick a strip club of all places.

I was sitting in Liquid Blue all the way out Newport News far from where I really wanted to be. My head hurt and my eyes hurt. I was squinting against all these bright blue neon lights that just followed me and magnified whenever I close my eyes. Towanna's buying, so of course the shot of the night was her signature drink, Pixy Stix. After about four of those things I just felt like I was gonna be Pixy Sick. All I could think about was how mad Devon looked and how horrible I felt for trying to turn him in. I mean, in the time I'd known the man, granted, he did put me in his asylum, but he still took really good care of me. It was more than Rasheed or Ris or anyone had ever done for me. He'd never cheated on me or lied to me, and the one time that I should have trusted him, I took him to the Feds and straight up turned his ass in.

There couldn't have been any way possible for me to feel like the world's biggest douche. Until someone thought it'd make me feel better if I got a lap dance. Dynasty spun my barstool around and climbed, yes, climbed on top of me. She'd started grinding all over me and I couldn't breathe because, one, I had Dynasty's double Ds up my nose, and two, I'd started crying. Yes, ladies and gentlemen, there I was, having a complete emotional breakdown in the middle of the strip club. Ass, titties, liquor, and tears . . .

Towanna, the guilty party, pulled me in to the ladies' room.

"Don't cry, man. Everything'll be fine." She patted my back, trying her best to console me.

It was atrocious. I'd started doing this uncontrollable hiccupping thing, like I couldn't breathe but I was still trying to talk at the same time. Through hiccupping and sobs I'd managed to ask Towanna why she was even pulling her gun in the first place.

"Um, because your name was originally on my agreement. I was supposed to kill you on that bridge; you jumped in front of your own bullet, and lived because you asked my mom's name. They figured you knew more than you should. Remember the agent said you tried to commit suicide? I thought you'd gotten a call or something, you invite me on this date with a chick I can barely stand and midway through you go all Stepford wife, then we get in the truck and you go in with the questions—"

"That's because I was thinking Devon's name was on your agreement. Rasheed wrote 'Don Cerzulo told Daddy see Doc' in Trey's iPad. I sat there, piecing everything together, and when we got in the truck and Denise's phone didn't work I thought you were going to kill him. I'd just as well take him in, and I fucked the fuck up . . ." I started crying all over again.

It was a total misunderstanding, except you know neither of them drugged and then literally drug me to the law
enforcement. Towanna was just a lot more forgiving about it
all than Devon was.

He sat in the darkened living room in nothing but his sweat
pant bottoms when Denise dropped me off at three a.m. I was
still wearing my dress from our date night. An empty cocktail
glass was sitting on the coffee table in front of him as he sat
with his forearms resting on his knees.

I stood in the doorway, debating what to say while I closed
it behind me. I settled on keeping it simple. "Hey."

He didn't look up or anything at the sound of my voice. "I
think you and Trey should find a place for a little while. Might
be best that way." He was frowning at the floor in front of him.

Tears clouded my vision, welled up and burned so hot I
wouldn't see my own hand if it were right in front of my face
even if I'd wanted to. I blinked, and they rolled down my
cheeks. There was nothing for me to say. If he wanted me
gone, I'd leave. There wasn't a single thing I could think of to
make up for my fuckup of mammoth proportions.

I got my and Trey's things together as quickly as possible. I
put his key on the table beside the door, and just like that, I
left. Now, I knew Devon was missing from me the moment;
he wouldn't smile for me anymore. It's actually fucked up,
because in these movies we grow up with, the guy chases
his woman down, yelling about how much he loves her. And,
it's usually right about now that he'd do that shit. Because
sometimes they have to watch you leave to realize they really
want you to stay.

Well, some shit just doesn't go down like it does in movies.
Checking my rearview only made me cry harder, and it only
made my heart feel like a worthless block of sorrow sitting in
my chest when I didn't see him there. My phone, which had
been in the bottom of my purse all along, was painfully silent.

My chest almost exploded when it rang. Seeing Denise's
number I was so let down I didn't answer. Towanna called and
I still didn't answer. I just didn't feel like being bothered right
that second. We could chat and I'd let them know what went
down later. I needed to find a damn hotel. I almost threw my
phone out the window when Towanna called a second time.

"Yes, Towanna?" I answered in a watery voice.

"You good? I'm worried about you."

"I'm good, I promise," I lied.

My eyes were so puffy and swollen I could barely see the road. I'd passed at least five hotels but I was so depressed I kept driving just for the sake of having something to do.

Towanna's voice was whisper soft. "You can always come to me."

"What's your address?"

Exhausted, I actually just wound up finally parking in a Wendy's parking lot and reclining the seat. My intent was to only close my eyes for a couple of minutes.

There was a loud tapping on my window, and I blinked and shielded my eyes against the intrusion.

"License and registration, please?" The officer waited beside my car.

"I'm not driving, sir," I called out, looking at him, confused.

"Are you intoxicated? I will have to write you a ticket for public intoxication as well as disruptive conduct, and . . ."

I looked at the clock, and winced. I didn't mean to sleep until almost eleven a.m. Annoyed, I got my shit out. It must have been end of the month and these idiots were trying to meet their damn quotas and shit. Handing him my information, I rolled my eyes and sat back as he walked to his car. He finally came back and handed me my ID and registration and the damn ticket.

Leaning down beside my window he said, "Okay, I'm just issuing a warning this time. This is her, boys."

Two men hopped out the back of his squad car and climbed into the back of my car. I'd gotten lazy and comfortable; the old me would have been ready for something like this.

No, the old you wouldn't have been out here for something like this to happen.

"Drive."

I could feel him staring at me, watching my every move. It's akin to when you're outside and people peek at you through the curtains. That feeling you're in a room and the hairs in your ear vibrate and stand up on the back of your neck.

"We haven't been formally introduced, have we?"

I looked up into the rearview and found myself gazing into eyes the turbulent color of the underside of thundercloud. For some reason, I couldn't help feeling as though I'd seen them somewhere before.

Chapter 33

Sins of the Father

I stared at this silver-eyed stranger and my mind clicked. He sent champagne to Keyshawn at Liv.

Glancing back in the rearview as I drove without directions, I asked him, "I'm sorry, but are you sure we haven't met before?"

"I'm sure we have not met. Pay attention to the road please. So, in case you's wondering, I'm Angelo Testa. Rasheed got some vital info out of my father and killed him. His name was Don Cerzulo. Now, I need you to take me to Rasheed; that info was extremely important. Otherwise, I'll use you and your son to flush him out."

This might not be a good time to tell him neither of those is possible. How do I keep ending up in these impossible, impossible-ass situations? Koala's fingerprints look similar to humans. They're almost identical.

"Rasheed is in the hospital with his momma, but I have the info. Look in my purse, it's on the iPad. He typed it so he wouldn't forget. I didn't know what it was or I would have erased it. Trust me."

Angelo gave me a suspicious glance before digging through my purse. I dropped my phone into my lap, tempted to text Towanna, but I didn't know what to say just yet. I couldn't risk reaching down to put my phone on vibrate and drawing attention to it. So I let it be.

"It's a phone number with the name 'Doc.' I'm setting up a pickup at your house, what's the address? That way if there's any funny business and this shit isn't real, you'll suffer."

I glanced down at my phone and gave him Towanna's address, then quickly sent what was probably the worst shorthand text in history: omw2 ur plc wt angelo 2mt drg dealr b rdy

Angelo called and set up his deal, and I drove toward Towanna's, praying the entire way. When she didn't respond, I almost cried. I was pretty sure I'd died, and hell was reliving your last moment thinking you were still alive. Because, when we pulled up to the house and I saw the empty driveway, I died over and over again. If I'd left, Angelo would have known I was lying about where I was taking him and his supplier. He probably would have shot me on the spot, so I committed to my lie and pulled into the empty driveway.

I was so busy looking for Towanna's car that when I finally saw Devon's Land Cruiser pulling up on the opposite side of the street, I gasped out loud and if I'd had my gun I'd have shot it at him.

"There's your man," I told Angelo, pointing at Devon's truck. I was seething with the most irrational anger. *I bet he didn't even know I'd be here either. Probably feels stupid, too.* I'd started climbing out the car and walking over without a second thought, barely glancing at the black car pulling up in the driveway. Devon got out of the truck. I took one look at his face and almost turned around and ran back across the street.

"Dad? What are you doing out here?" he shouted across the street.

Confused, I spun around, and there was this handsome, older clone of Devon standing at my car. It wasn't Towanna who had pulled up; it was a black Lexus. I'd walked right past him. At that moment, Towanna did pull up, along with the FBI. Angelo was yelling about his narc sister turning on family as they put him into a car.

"Devon, I thought your dad was dead." I looked at him, still completely puzzled by everything I'd just seen.

His face was a complete mask of upset. "I never said that, it's something else you assumed and ran with instead of asking me. I said my great uncle raised me. Pops fell in love and took off with Melanie, her case, for murdering her first five of six husbands, he was the sixth. They were too busy globetrottin' and shit to deal with us. He might as well have been dead though. I didn't want him or her in my life after that."

Getting anywhere with this man seemed damn near ridiculous no matter how hard I tried. Everything I'd accused him of and put him through was all because of his damn father, all because I was too stubborn and foolish to trust a trustworthy person.

I grabbed his hands and he reluctantly let me hold them; he looked everywhere but down at me.

"Devon, you can't make me realize that I need you and then take you away from me. You're the one who said you can fix anything, so help me fix this." My voice broke and tears ran down my cheeks but I didn't hide them. "I can't love you by myself. I didn't want to fall all by myself. You were supposed to fall too." I dropped my head against his shoulder and cried. I'd been refusing to let anyone in for this very reason, and then he came along and—

"I did." Devon's voice was a raspy whisper as he lifted my chin and stared into my eyes. "I did fall too, and I do love you. Baby, please stop crying." He leaned down and kissed my cheeks.

"I'll probably have to get you an autographed R2-D2 jersey to make up for it, huh?" I asked him in a pitiful voice.

"Get me a what, woman?" He looked down at me with the sweetest confused face.

I shrugged. "That football guy you like for the Redskins, RPG. I'll get you an autographed jersey to hang on your wall," I explained.

He made an exasperated sound and started laughing. I didn't get the joke.

"Chelle, it's RG3. And after I figure out what's going on with all this"—he pointed toward his father being put into a car—"I know something even better than can um, hang from my wall," he replied, winking down at me.

"Glad you answered your Bat-Signal, playboy," Towanna called out as she came across the street grinning like a damn fool.

For the first time since all the commotion started, I noticed the letters "FBI" on her shirt.

"You've got to be playing. This whole time, Towanna, really?" I stared at her.

She nodded and kept grinning. "Yes, the entire time. Let's go have a drink and I'll tell you all about it. Feels like I ain't seen you in forever."

"Shots fired, shots fired," Towanna's radio blared.

Devon pushed me into the Land Cruiser and Towanna drew her gun. No one, and I repeat no one, saw the shooter that took Angelo out as he was being put into the cruiser.

Chapter 34

Always Share Your Nightmares

So They Can't Come True?

(Three Years Later)

Most people loved summer. Not me, and especially not in Virginia. The heat and humidity alone could make your boobs and butt combust into sweat the second you stepped outside. My favorite time of year quickly became early fall. Fall was supposed to be a time of year when the clouds brought to mind marshmallows and hot cocoa with a splash of Kahlúa. The crunch of leaves on the ground sounded like cute boots and comfy sweaters. Yet, there was nothing fall-like or cozy about sitting directly underneath the "cook your forehead" hot sun on a Wednesday afternoon during one of Virginia's Indian summers.

Someone had a grill going nearby, and the smell of charcoal and hotdogs in the air reminded me of summer on the Fourth of July. We were sitting Indian style in a soft patch of clovers near the swings. I was glad I'd just worn an old comfortable pair of jeans and one of my Old Navy tees. All these confused-ass heffas in workout gear had taken up all the benches in the shade. All they were doing was sitting around eating snacks and talking on their cells. Not one of them looked like they were trying to scoot over or leave anytime soon.

"Show me which one you're thinking about. I wanna see if her ears bleed." Towanna leaned over, nudging me with her elbow, laughing. Denise sat behind her, arms wrapped around her waist, smiling over her shoulder. Funny how they couldn't stand each other, as Towanna put it.

Some people like to get close to you just so they can say they were close. They really don't care about your dreams or what makes you, you. They just want to be able to tell people on the outside that their asses were part of your inner circle.

Thankfully Special Agent Towanna James wasn't one of those people. After everything that'd happened, I never thought I'd let anyone get near me again, but I'd found genuine friendship with her, and real love and happiness with Devon. They both had ways of making me laugh, and the drama that used to be my life seemed worlds away. Well, except for my usual drama.

"Trey, you'd better put that down. I'm watchin' you," I warned, giving him a stern look and in turn focusing that same gaze on his counterpart. "Paris, little girl. Ah . . . no. If I have to get up and come over there. Don't put that on him. See, that's why he hit you. Trey, pick her doll up. I said I was watching you. Both of y'all just stop, nobody touch nothing. Go play on the slide over there or something."

He gave me a big grin before he went bouncing toward the slide.

Blowing out an exasperated breath, I fanned myself. For a parent, even playing was hard work. I felt akin to child wrangler out here. All I needed was a bullwhip and a megaphone.

"Towanna, I swear that boy is the devil sometimes. He is fa' sho his daddy's child, because that kind of foolishness is not of me." I shook my head. "No, I didn't make all that."

"Stop frowning at the boy, Chelle, he's behaving." Devon plucked a dandelion, tossing it at me. He was sitting on the opposite side of me. Giggling, I tossed it back. I'd never told him what Rasheed had typed into Trey's iPad before I'd deleted it. I debated ever telling Trey. But, I needed to learn a lesson from Reena and not turn into an old woman withholding a century of secrets in my head. Secrets like, "Don't be like Daddy." I had reasons for what I did, and like Devon always said, if I'd asked instead of jumping without looking, well . . .

Towanna snickered. "Yeah, he's a boy, Chelle, that's what they do. They terrorize little sisters and when they grow up they become their bodyguards and best friends. I grew up with two older brothers, remember? Trust me, I'd know.

It could be worse; he could be stealing Paris's tiaras, calling himself the Queen Bitch. Snappin' and twistin'." She chuckled.

"Heavens no." I sucked my teeth and let out an exasperated breath on that one.

"I'll just be glad when the terror, tease, and fight phase is over all—" I'd barely gotten the words out before little Ms. Lataya Paris II came launching her little self up into my lap.

I was stuck trying to find her head out the sudden crash of upside down bright pink and white dress and limbs. She'd face planted, and all I could see were little legs sticking from in between mine. I finally managed to pluck her out without getting kicked in the process, and she was crying and screaming at the top of her lungs, damn near splitting my eardrums. Of course Trey wasn't far behind, proudly carrying a got-damn baby python. I grabbed Paris and hopped up, screaming my own head off.

"Trey, what in the hell? Put that thing down before it bites your ass. Have you lost your mind, boy?" I looked over at Devon to handle what was also suddenly on his feet beside me.

"Hell, no. I don't do snakes," he shouted, throwing his hands up.

"Calm down, y'all, it's just a garden snake. A baby one at that. They're harmless." Towanna went all nature woman on our asses. She got up and took the ungodly spawn of Satan boa constrictor from Trey.

I backed up with Paris in my arms. "If you come over here, on my life I'll get in that car and leave all of y'all asses out here." Just then, a large black bat-looking something or another hovered suspiciously near me, and I went Mayweather on it. Bobbing and weaving, sidestepping and shrieking, all with Paris squealing in my arms.

"Um, it's just a butterfly, Chelle. The two of y'all are a mess. We will never go camping."

"Camping is anti-evolutionary anyway. I don't give a damn. It's a bug. I don't do snakes, bugs, critters, creatures, creepers; anyone who knows me knows that shit. I have nightmares about them things crawling on me and I can't get them off. I'm telling you about it now so it can't happen again."

"And I have nightmares about my wife trying to kill me and holding a gun to my head and drugging me and turning me into the FBI."

Denise, Towanna, and I gasped in unison, and I immediately started blinking back tears and smiling. This fool was on one knee holding up a ring.

"I'm telling you about it now, so it can't happen again. Emphasis on wife. I think we've traced our family trees and learned enough about each other. I want you and the silly, crazy, somewhat controlling woman you are, as more than just my baby momma," he added in a hushed whisper.

Denise took Paris from me because I was about to fall all to pieces as I said yes.

He wasn't gonna ever let me forget that whole drugging, FBI thing either. Devon stood up, pulling me close, and I could hear Trey groaning as he stomped off behind Towanna and Denise so they could set their anaconda free at the edge of the park. I smiled into Devon's face and pressed my nose against his.

"You sure your auntie twice removed on your momma side ain't run a brothel off Hampton Boulevard in 1986? I'm just askin'."

Chapter 35

I

Four Years Ago
Washington, DC

I pulled frigid air in through my nose, letting it fill my lungs, freeze my insides. I'd spent the last week shut away inside a room no bigger than a broom closet. The smell of my own waste still filled my nose. I cringed at the gritty texture of my own filth and dirt crusted underneath my nails.

The wind whipped around me and sent my hair cutting into my cheeks. If I had any sense, I would've dressed a little more rugged, worn something other than leggings and my favorite sweater. It was just some old, ratty, cotton-ball-thick-thing that was the color of coffee with two creams. It wasn't name brand or anything special. But it was one of the last things my dad had given me before we fell out, so I loved it just as much as I hated it. I didn't appreciate the fact that I'd probably die wearing the damn thing. But, it's not like I knew that a week ago when I put it on.

My arms were wrapped around my body tighter than a straitjacket. I clenched and unclenched my teeth to keep them from chattering from the cold and maybe from fear. I'm not sure which one. But I was feeling this sickening, never-ending roller-coaster drop kind of feeling.

Adrenaline sent tremors of terror through my body, rocking my ankles, knocking my knees together. I forced one foot forward, and then the other, shuffling across gravel, tattered cigarette butts, and busted up pennies that might have been wishes. When I couldn't go any farther, I looked out over the tips of my shoes, barely hanging over the gunmetal-black edge of the bridge. Silvery-black waves rippled across the water beneath me. It looked so close and so terrifyingly far that it took my breath away. The pounding from my heart rocked my whole body.

There was a heavy, churning ache in my chest as I guided my feet forward. I opened my eyes long enough to blink. I inhaled, throwing all of my weight forward, curling into myself. Not in my worst nightmares had I ever imagined something like this. I was curling into myself. My nails cut into my skin through my sweater. I hunched forward, plunging through the air like I was trying to split my back open and spread wings before I reached the bottom.

Air rushed into my face, beating against my skin so hard and fast I couldn't get a breath in to scream. My stomach floated in my chest, tingling the same way it did when I rode the roller coasters at Busch Gardens. There were so many thoughts fighting, fading, and clouding my head that holding onto a single one was like grabbing at smoke. All except one—the last one—and it was more of a feeling than a thought. It felt worse than everything I'd been through that'd got me up on that bridge in the first place. It was even worse than the falling in itself.

The scream that finally tore its way up my throat should've hovered me over the water. It should've frozen time, or caught God's ear so he'd hear me and give me a do-over. Regret exploded in my brain, spreading into my soul as I hit the freezing waves like a concrete wall. The shocking cold water instantly numbed my skin, jarred my bones, shaking my insides. After everything I'd done, I was going to die with you in my belly and I'd forgotten . . . Well, no, I didn't forget. I just didn't get a chance to give you a name.

II

March

There was a soft beep coming from somewhere nearby. My heart sent throbbing pulses of pain to my temples that synced with the beeping in my ears. I tried to swallow, but the inside of my mouth felt like sandpaper. All of my body parts were waking up individually. Feeling came back to my limbs one by one in the form of pins and needles as my senses came back.

The smell of onions, Black & Mild smoke, and something familiar met my nose. Somewhere outside my room, a man was speaking in a rough, quiet whisper.

"Yo, I know you ain't *still* talkin' about that shit? How long ago was that job, though?"

He paused to make several long honking sounds with his nose. I gagged as he snorted up and swallowed snot.

"A'ight, well, *if and when* she wake up, I'll let you know so you can have that revenge chat or get that revenge pussy. The bitch probably brain-damaged, but shit, if you wanna talk to or fuck a comatose ho, it's whateva. You the same nigga who was like fuck the spiders, fuck karma. And where that shit get yo' ass?" *That* was the familiar smell I smelled. It was Tariq. He doused himself in Egyptian Musk body oil, and I swear that smell could travel through the walls. It was enough to pry my eyelids open. As things slowly came into focus, a chilly breeze came through a window beside my bed. The unfiltered sunlight hurt my eyes, but it was the best kind of hurt I'd ever felt. It meant I was alive. Everything was bright green with flashes of electric-blue sky. The air felt and smelled like it was the beginning of spring, but that was impossible, because from what I remembered, it was just hot and humid out. It was just July.

Flashes of silvery-black water came rushing up to my mind. Tears welled up in my eyes. All of the hurt and disloyalty washed over me. I survived. Oh God, I'd survived. But something was different. My body felt different. I dragged my hand toward my stomach, squeezing my eyes shut tight. That warm fullness that I'd felt in my belly for so many months was gone. My stomach wasn't even round anymore.

Tariq's footsteps echoed across the hardwood floor. They weren't moving toward me. A bottle hissed open, the cap bounced, making a soft metallic whir before falling flat with a tiny *plink*. Women moaned loud over the sound of sleazy music. He was watching porn.

I fought against the invisible weights holding my body down. Looking around didn't seem to take as much effort as moving, so I concentrated on that. It almost broke my heart to see that the room was damn near empty. There had to be something I could use to help me somewhere. A heart monitor and a clear plastic bag hung beside my bed on one side. I turned to examine the other side of the room, cringing when I realized the oniony smell was coming from my own body. *Well, at least, I know that nigga wasn't getting his kicks by sponging me down every day.*

Moldy dark brown and black water stains marked the ceiling. The dark wood floor looked bare and dusty except for a small worn-out rug by the opened bedroom door. I couldn't see much of the rest of the house from my angle. A small, scratched oak nightstand sat beside the bed with extra IV bags lined up along the top of it. Relief hit me in a wave when I saw the dingy-yellowed cordless phone. Moving took nearly all of the energy I had, but I managed to lean as close to the side of the bed as I possibly could.

The beeping from the heart monitor sped up as I tried to lift my arms. It felt damn near impossible, like one of those dreams where you're half-awake and half-asleep. The volume on the television lowered. I leaned back toward the center as shoes clipped across the floor in the direction of my room. Snapping my eyes shut, I tried to take slow, deep breaths while focusing on the birds chirping outside. I could sense his presence standing in the open doorway. The frame creaked under the weight of his back.

I could see Tariq's face in my head. He used to have a nasty habit of sticking his hand in his pocket whenever he saw me, and that action in itself disgusted me. Someone told me niggas do that so they could stroke themselves whenever they see something they like. He would always stare at me for a second too long with his hand in his pocket. At least he was smart enough not to try anything with me.

Beer sloshed in a bottle. He gulped long and deep before his footsteps disappeared back down the hall. I waited until the television turned back up. This time, I scooted millimeter by millimeter while rhyming the lyrics to "I'm on One" in my head. It was my favorite Drake song, and it was the same tempo as the beeps from the heart monitor. I was beyond pleased with myself when the beeping didn't change its tempo. I called the only person I could trust.

My voice came out in a scratchy croak.

"Shandy?" I said into the phone.

I wasn't expecting to not be able to talk. The thought hadn't crossed my mind.

"This me," she snapped back. "And who the hell is this?"

I almost smiled. That was my Shan, always feisty as hell.

"It's me, girl, Novie," I whispered.

"Oh my God! If somebody's playin' on my shit, I swear I'm gonna find you and—"

"Yeah, I need you to find me. I just woke up. I don't know where I am. Tariq is here."

"Girl, I know where you're at. I came to see you. That fool was trying to holla so hard, too. Lady J had you moved; she said it would be quieter if they put you somewhere other than the house."

I wanted to scream, laugh, and cry all at the same time. It was getting harder to keep my heart from racing. Fresh tears were just waiting to fall from my eyes.

"I need you to go to the Anytime Fitness and get my ho-bag. You still got the key I gave you, right?" I asked.

"It's around my neck as we speak," Shan replied.

"*Nobody* can know that you're going to get it or that I called you," I told her in as firm a voice as I could.

There wasn't enough money in my bag to get me far. I'd pinched off of it way too many times to help Shandy pay a bill or to buy something cute. But there were clothes, a phone with a clean sim card, and an extra ID in there. It was everything I'd need to get out of this shit and get myself together. Daddy didn't like Swiss; he never did. I wasn't ready to face my parents. Not yet, anyway.

Shandy clicked her tongue. "Tariq has been trying to get at me all this time, anyway. Offerin' to take me and the little one to the Cheesecake and whatnot. He ain't gonna be a problem."

I nodded even though Shandy couldn't see me. Hearing about her baby made a wall of toothpicks well up in my throat.

I hesitated just before hanging up. There was one more thing I needed to know

"Shan? My baby? Have you heard anything . . . about my baby?"

I held my breath waiting for her answer. If I was alive he needed to be alive too. This was our second chance, and I'd have to make up for what I did for the rest of our lives. Shandy hesitated. The tension made my pulse start racing.

"Okay, Novie." She said my name in that after-school-special-tone of voice. It was that let's-sit-down-and-talk-so-you-don't-fall-down-tone of voice. "Girl, you know there will be plenty of time to talk about all that once I get you safe and—"

My arm was starting to shake. The muscles in my shoulder were on fire. I slid the phone back onto its cradle before Shan could finish not answering my question. The television volume lowered again. I knew he was coming this time, and he'd see my chest heaving and my body shaking. He'd see the tears running down my cheeks, and he'd either kill me, or let me go, or somehow, I'd escape. I tensed every muscle that I could control as his heavy feet slammed across the floor. The monitor sped up, but I couldn't stop the sound of my heart breaking if I'd wanted to.

And then he stopped dead in his tracks, turned, and went back toward the living room, toward the sound of his cell ringing from wherever he'd left it.

"What up, Shandy? I wasn't expectin' to hear from you. Girl, I'm on watch until tomorrow. Shiiiiiit, for all that, I might can get away for a few hours. It ain't like this thing here is goin' anywhere anytime soon."

I relaxed deep into the thin mattress. Lord knows I loved my homegirl to death. I'd owe her my life for this.

Chapter 36

Where It All Began

A Maine coon the size of a baby lion trekked across the lawn. It found the perfect spot, sprawled out under a tree that provided shade, and yawned. The cat's tail flicked back and forth as it stared lazily up at a baby squirrel lounging on a feeder no more than a foot above its head. *Exactly,* I thought. It was too damn hot for all that running, chasing, and climbing bullshit. Just like it was too damn hot for me to be sitting up in this nigga's car waiting for him to get these damn Erykah Badu tickets from this mystery *associate.*

I waved a club flyer back and forth trying to cool myself down. *Club Tryst. Humph, when did this nigga have the time to go there, and where was I? He probably went with his damn associates.* That ain't even sound right coming from him. Was *associate* the new word of the day on Madden or *Call of Duty?* Where did he pick that shit up from? Javion didn't have associates. He was raised by his grandma in East Philly, he had a bum-ass-squad of niggas, and they lived where bum-ass-niggas lived . . . with their mommas or their baby mommas.

I craned my neck to stare up at the strip-mall-sized mansion in front of me. A fleet of shiny black cars stared back at me. Swiss was up to or getting into some shit; I could feel it. He didn't know anybody with that kind of paper, and if they had it, they didn't get it legally.

I cranked the AC in his Camaro up as high as it would go, running my finger through the frosty condensation that formed in the corner of the windows. He had one of those weird man-obsessions with his car. Washed and hand dried it twice a day, just like his ass, topped off all the levels, covered it good night, fingered it good morning. Okay, I'm exaggerating. But I wasn't about to be sitting with the shit on "midlow and not high, because high runs out the Freon," as he'd say.

I crossed and uncrossed my legs. Drummed my nails along the dash. None of this was sitting right with me. He'd used the word *associate*. I'm not saying my baby ain't bright as day, but niggas don't lie well. It's not in their genetic makeup. This was all starting to remind me of a book Shandy couldn't pull her face out of, where the nigga was inside fucking his wife all while the side chick sat waiting in the car. *Baby Momma,* that was the name of that book. I don't think Swiss would do some shit like that. Nah, not with the way he thirst after this ass and these hips. But you could never tell with niggas these days.

I tried to ease my mind by rummaging through his shit. I couldn't think of any other reason why the nigga would leave me unattended to go in some random's—my bad—some *associate's* house and take forever just to get concert tickets. *Humph. Guess they had to make the paper, mix the ink, and print them out too.*

I rifled through Burger King and miscellaneous takeout receipts in the armrest. As much as he cleaned his car, you'd think he'd throw away some of these receipts. I'd flopped down the driver-side visor when I noticed an old blue something creeping past. The sun reflected off the glass, preventing me from seeing inside. Blinking away sunspots, I fumbled, trying to put the visor back. *It has to be a confused pizza delivery guy or something.* I was so focused on the car I didn't see the bushy spider until it plopped down out of the visor onto my lap. A gas bubble squeezed its way out of my back end, and a screech came out the other as I limbo'd over the center console, screaming bloody murder. I was halfway in the backseat before I realized it wasn't a spider. It was front-row, center stage, Erykah Badu tickets. And the show was starting in less than an hour.

Sweat appeared on my upper lip. Even though it was frosty cold in the car, I was blazing hot and furious. The front door was still closed, and there wasn't a sign of anyone moving around inside the house. A quick glance over my shoulder confirmed that damn blue car was still there too. It'd parked on the street with the front bumper sticking out into the driveway enough for me to see it. Every second made me feel like screaming or climbing out of my skin.

I snatched the keys out of the ignition and eased my French-pedi'd toes back into my gold heels. Swiss was the first dude I'd ever met who found a woman in heels sexier than seeing her naked. He bought more shoes for me than I bought for myself. He defended it by telling me how he loved to follow my long legs down to my pedicured toes peeking out of something sexy. Made him want to tear all up into this more than any lingerie ever would. Thinking about him thinking about me in my heels made me want to tear that fucking door down.

I eased myself out of the car, careful not to slam the door, then quickly adjusted my sundress straps out of habit. *Let me walk in on this fool doing some shit; he'd feel all of this sexy-ass heel digging in that ass. Got me out here sweating and he's probably in there slurping lemonade outta her belly button.*

Sweat made my hands cold and sticky. I hesitated on the welcome mat for a bare second.

The sun-beaten door handle was hot to the touch. It seared into my clammy, nervous skin. If this fool was in here doing something he shouldn't have been doing, there was no way in hell I was gonna ring the doorbell. That would give him enough time to straighten himself up. I was surprised when I pressed down on the handle and it moved easily. Icy-cold air blasted across my face and neck as I eased the door open. I stepped into the foyer. *I am definitely not in DC anymore.*

Tall, bright green bamboo plants lined the foyer. I stared up at them with my mouth momentarily hanging open in awe. Red, green, and gold parakeets chirped and flitted around the tops of bamboo stalks up near the glass-domed ceiling. It was real cute in a Peter-Pan'ish kind of way, but fuck that bamboo and them birds. Where was this fool? I moved across the spotless floor, careful to keep my heels from clicking against

234 Ni'chelle Genovese

the surface. Three long dark hallways spread out in front of me. I headed toward the one in the middle.

My ears were set to super sonar. I wiped my sweaty palms off on the front of my dress when a soft moan caught my ear. I paused . . . listening so hard I gave myself a headache. A second moan louder than the first one set my feet in motion toward the first door on the hallway to my right. *I will kill this nigga and his ho. He got the wrong one if he thinks he can play me like I'm boo-boo the goddamn fool.*

"*Shhh.* It feels good, don't it? I know you wanna tell daddy you like that shit," Javion said with a chuckle. "And I want you to stay just like this."

Javion's hushed voice was followed by the sound of his own low, husky moan. Betrayal stabbed me in the chest. That was *my* moan. That sound was supposed to be meant for me. I stepped into what looked like a small entertainment room. My lips were already forming every word that I was about to pop off at his lying, cheating ass. I've never felt so stupid or so humiliated. So blindly dumb. My mouth opened, but no words came out. My peep-toes peeped the mental stop sign slamming to a halt before the rest of my body got the message. I damn near did a full-front bow.

Her knees were spread, hands planted shoulder-width apart. I blinked, blinked twice, and then I blinked again to be sure the girl I was looking at was the same girl who'd opened the door. She was kneeling on top of the pool table in the middle of the room. Her skin was shockingly white against the black fabric. It matched her long hair piled into a high, messy ponytail on top of her head.

"I thought I told you to wait in the car," Javion's voice was dark and angry.

The girl's eyes were like headlights as they locked with mine. She couldn't have been more than nineteen or twenty. I had to force myself to look past the black tape across her mouth. I felt her degradation, along with my own confusion as I followed the handle of a broom sticking out of her ass like a stiff horse's tail. Javion's hand held the other end of it straight and stiff. A pistol was in his other hand, aimed in the direction of her head.

That couldn't be Javion. My Javion was a teddy bear and an HVAC repairman who listened to Future and fucked me to Jeremih. This Javion looked malicious, like something straight out of a Quentin Tarantino movie. He was sitting in a bright blue and white paisley patterned armchair pulled up to the edge of the pool table. Covering his face was a bright crimson-red ski mask.

His usually cheerful eyes were resentful and hard as he glared in my direction. I was scared to move any closer to this stranger of a man who I felt like I suddenly didn't know. The girl on the table whimpered when his hand shifted.

"Shhh. I know, I know," Javion hushed her like he was soothing a frightened animal. "I need you to hold that for daddy, just a little bit longer."

His eyes were on me all while he talked to her, like this was completely normal.

A deep voice boomed through the house, "That was a good workout! You know the best way to work off that freshman fifteen is to hit the treadmill. Your mom never liked working out but . . ."

The voice traveled through the house, echoing off the walls.

"Ashley?" he called out again.

The girl responded with a muffled shriek.

He was getting closer, his voice was getting louder.

Either the giant was coming down the beanstalk, or my heart was slamming against my chest so hard that it felt like the house was shaking all around me. I automatically looked to Javion for help because I had no idea what else to do, but he wasn't even paying me any mind.

"Ash, you got company? I thought I heard the doorbe—"

The owner of that deep, booming voice stopped just in the hallway. He had to have been at least seven feet tall. His wide-muscled body took up the entire door frame as he stepped forward in a pair of sweats, with sweat raining down his bare chest.

When push comes to shove, I'll take the stranger I know over the stranger I don't know. I instinctively backed myself toward Javion until I was standing a good distance behind his chair. I needed to keep myself a good distance from Javion too. As far as I could tell, he was on the other end of crazy for me right now, his own self. I wasn't trying to be in arm's reach of either one of they asses. Javion sat still and quiet, like he just wanted the nigga to visually eat up the moment, roll it around in his brain, and digest it. That's exactly what happened, too. The man's deep golden tanned skin went sickly pale. His grizzly squared jaw moved back and forth under the blond beard covering it, and his eyes narrowed to slits on Javion.

Javion finally broke the silence. "We gave you an extension, Beau. You missed it. The boss says I need to relieve you of a few obligations. Said maybe that would help you free up the finances to repay your obligation to him."

Beau raised his big meaty hands in the air. His heart broke the second he saw the girl on the table in front of Javion. You could see it all over his face and in his eyes. He was furious, scared shitless, and completely helpless—with no option left but to beg.

"Look, man, you don't have to do this. Please," he begged. "She's my only child. My baby girl." His bright blue eyes were glassy with tears. "I'm so sorry, Ash, baby. Daddy is so fucking sorry," he spoke to the girl on the table his voice shaky and cracking.

Beau raked his hands through his short blond hair, ruffling it into a spiky mess. He was shaking when he talked to Javion. "I swear on my life I'll get you your money. All I've got to do is win my next match. I'm guaranteed to win. I'll have it. All of it, I swear. Take my car, take whatever you need—"

"Not good enough," Javion answered.

Javion stood. I cringed at the pitiful sound the girl made when he twisted his hand holding the broom. This was a part of the game I never saw or experienced. It made the inside of my mouth get that uncontrollably wet feeling you get just before you vomit.

"You have until midnight to pay up," Javion said in a cold, flat voice. "Or I'll be making a trip to baby girl's dorm to finish this. Um, Chandler Hall at William and Mary University, if I remember correctly."

With that, he let the broom drop before turning the gun on Beau. Javion grabbed me by my elbow, calmly marching me toward the front door. I kept looking back, expecting to see Beau running after us with a gun blazing or on the phone calling the police.

"He ain't gonna do shit, so stop checkin'," Javion said as he opened my car door.

My eyes were full of questions, but I was still a little too shook up to do more than sort through my rambling thoughts. *What just happened? What the fuck kind of pervert ties a girl up and shoves a broom up her ass? Is that the kind of shit he enjoys?*

I slid my shades on, trying not to look at the house through the rose tint of my sunglasses. Hopefully, they'd be enough to hide my face if Beau or his daughter were in a window with a camera phone snapping pictures of their attacker. My phone lit up. It was finally charged. I tried to stop my fingers from shaking so I could check my missed messages or log onto Facebook. I needed to do something—anything—to take my mind off what I'd just seen. Javion walked around the back of the car toward the driver's side.

Thudump!

Something slammed up against the back of the car so hard it rocked in place. I jumped in my seat dropping my phone.

"Oh, shit!" Javion shouted.

The worst of the worst scenarios flashed through my head. All that tie-'em-up hostage craziness had my ass so discombobulated, I'd completely forgotten to tell him about the blue car. *God, if this nigga is shot or is stabbed, it'd be my fault.*

Chapter 37

A Complex Electra Complex

I turned completely around in the seat, my nails dug into the leather of the headrest. I was expecting to see blood splatters or five dudes in black wife beaters with crowbars and tire irons. My eyebrows shot up at what looked like a long black weave bobbing up and down. She started screaming down at what I think was Javion on the ground.

"Nigga! I can't believe you! I cannot fucking believe you right now!" she yelled, stomping her foot over and over.

"Tinesha, *stop!* Stop, nigga, you're pregnant," Javion yelled back.

She gave a final stomp. She stopped putting her hands on her sides. Tinesha was huffing like she was practicing her damn Lamaze. Javion hopped up, minus his ski mask. Light brown dirt speckled the side of his face and head. He tried to dust off the front of his jeans.

"Nigga, if you don't calm the fuck down, you about to get everybody caught up out this bitch."

"Nigga, the only person 'bout to get caught up is you and *that bitch*. I told *you,* this baby is yours, and you handle it by hiding from me? You ain't no man—you ain't shit," she huffed, all while pointing in my direction with her chest heaving.

"Get the hell on with that. You out here trippin' over nothing. I'll deal with you later," Javion talked quickly over his shoulder as he marched toward the driver-side door.

"You'll have to back me over to get out of here, bitch! I ain't goin' nowhere until you handle this shit like you're supposed to!" Tinesha stood behind the car with her arms spread out.

"What the fucking fuck, Javion," I snapped as soon as he opened the car door.

Sweat ran down the side of his face. He completely ignored me and started the car, throwing it into reverse.

"Move, Tinesha, I ain't playin' with you," he yelled out the window at her.

I punched him in his arm for ignoring me. I didn't sign up for either one of these bullshit situations. Yeah, he might've helped out with a bill or two and got my hair done whenever I wanted, but it wasn't worth all of this.

Tinesha posted up behind the car. "Hit me then, bitch. You man enough to take a life, but you ain't man enough to raise one? Huh? *Really,* nigga?"

She pulled off a shoe, hurling it at the car. For a pregnant woman who looked about to bust, she sure as hell had a lot of fight in her.

Javion turned the wheel to the far right, punching the gas. The car made a small arc as we backed around her. A few inches to the left and that would've been all she wrote. She gave us the finger so hard I bet she sprained her wrist.

I stared at the side of Javion's head with my arms crossed tight over my chest.

"Novie, that kid probably ain't even mine. She was fuckin' with one of my homeboys who was always doin' his thing on the side. Shit, we got drunk, she made her move, and I hit it a couple of times, but stopped because my boy said they were good. She was being greedy, and I don't do sloppy seconds," he explained. "Then she called me outta the blue a month ago, talking about she's seven months along. Nah, that ain't me. It can't be."

I didn't know who or what to believe. Another woman would explain all the late-night trips and phone calls, but what I'd just seen this nigga do back in that house explained that shit just as well.

"So what if it is your baby?" I asked.

The corners of his mouth turned downward as if just thinking about a baby with her turned his stomach. "If it's mine, and my boy don't kill me for the disrespect, I'll do my part. But it ain't mine. It can't be. I ain't ready for that shit, and definitely not with her."

I wrestled with the idea of him having a baby with another woman. We'd only been seeing each other for four months. It definitely wasn't enough time for me to get crazy attached to him, but it was enough time for me to feel comfortable being with him. I could rock with the idea of us being together for now, but if that baby was his, I'd have to let him go. I didn't want to deal with any men and their unstable baby mommas.

I scooped my phone up. Shandy had sent me a text.

Javion watched me out of the corner of his eye.

I never asked him his business concerning who called or texted him, but he was sure as hell nosy enough to constantly ask me about mine.

"Wha'sup? You got somewhere else to be?" he asked.

"It depends on whether or not you telling me what just went on in that house."

"*Spppsht*. That? That shit was just work," he answered nonchalantly.

I sucked my teeth. "Don't hit me with that bullshit. That was more than *just work,* and you know it."

"All right, Novie. Your boy back there is some kind of UFC World Champ. His dumb ass blacked out, had some kind of posttraumatic fight meltdown and snapped his wife's neck because of steroids. Boss straightened it all out. Kept him out of jail, kept his record clean, let him keep that title belt too, and now that nigga's bitch ass acting funny about paying. It's just work, like I said."

The look I'd seen on Beau's and his daughter's face, I couldn't shake it. Nobody deserved to be humiliated like that.

I crossed my arms and turned so I could face him. "So, basically, you help rich people get away with murder? And you went after his *daughter,* who didn't have shit to do with what he did? If that ain't fucked up." The bracelets jingled on my wrist as the palm of my hand fell hard and fast across the back of Javion's head. If we weren't so far away from my house I'd have gotten out and walked. I slumped back into the soft leather of the seat and stared at the sun dipping in and out of the clouds overhead.

Yes, I was raised in the game, but it was different type of game. Back in the day, Ramsey Evans was one of the youngest dudes in the game; he was a computer hacker who ran dope in and out of North Carolina and South Carolina. His daughter had a thing for *The Hunger Games* and *Comic Con*. They went to every convention every year. She wanted a live deer-hunting contest at one of them. Ramsey went above and beyond and hired the actors from the movie; he even gave people real bows and arrows. Almost caused a stampede when the deer came crashing across the stage waving its antlers, but he paid for a show, so he got one. You had Ewoks, Storm Troopers, and Wonder Women all shooting their arrows, not sure if their target was an animatronic or a real deer.

When it collapsed and the head fell off, people gasped. Ramsey . . . lying there with tape over his mouth so he couldn't scream. His hands and his legs were tied together. Daddy took over after that. That's how he did things. He would handle business like a Nigerian warlord when he needed to. But he never *touched* people's kids. He had boundaries, rules; there was a code of ethics that he followed. Javion left a bad taste in my mouth with his child's play. I couldn't respect a man that did shit like that.

"Novie," Javion said my name like it was an excuse. He sucked on his bottom lip and alternated between watching the road and watching me. *"This* is what I do in order to make these stacks we burn through like kindlin'. It's why I expect you to wait in the car when I tell you to wait in the car. It's not just me; it's a family thing, so I'm with my people. We do a lot of infamous shit for famous and financially privileged motherfuckers like him. Sometimes they ask for more than they can afford, and when they do, we have to scare up their payment."

A family thing, okay. I guess that would explain why I hadn't met or seen so much as a picture of any of his kin. If we weren't trying to take it slow and really build whatever this thing was that we had, I'd have started pressing him about this secret-squirrel family business.

I decided to try my luck. "So, who is this boss that you work for?"

He focused on the road in front of him. "Can't answer that."

"You move weight too? Have you been doing this for a long time? Have you ever killed anyone?" I fired the questions at him one by one as they popped into my head.

"*Novie*," he yelled slamming his hand against the steering wheel. "Chill with the questions. I already told you a helluva lot more than I should have. So let it go. I ain't telling you anything else."

I put my head back against the headrest and closed my eyes, unsure of why I wasn't scared or completely turned off by what he really did for a living. As much as I hated what my dad did for a living, I don't know why I kept falling for niggas who followed in his footsteps.

Chapter 38

The World Is Ruled by Favors and Fools

I parked on the street and stepped out, taking in a deep breath of the city. Summer was just starting to spread her legs after a long, celibate winter. You could smell it in the air, almost taste it on the tip of your tongue. It was that energy that made niggas anxious to get out of the house and into some bullshit. That shit that kept my plate full of cases, clients, and pretty faces needing favors.

The Metropolitan PD was my last stop before calling it a night. I liked to check in from time to time to see who or what had been brought in. I kept at least three officers in my back pocket at every station in and out of the area. They scratched my back, and when it was necessary, I watched theirs.

Dim fluorescent lights lit up the grubby interior of the station. It wasn't nearly as busy as I would have expected for a Friday night.

"Oh ho ho, now, looks like Santa stopped by extra, extra early. Hide your convicts and hide your wives. Genesis Kane is prowling the building."

I'd recognize that Boston-proper accent anywhere. Officer Squatton strutted over, giving me a rough pat on the shoulder. All the legal aides back at the office called him "The Fucksquatch." I'm close to six feet two, and even I had to look up slightly to make eye contact. He was a big, less hairy version of a Sasquatch with a fondness for women who weren't fond back.

I shook his oversized, sweaty hand.

"Squatton, I get a feeling that ugly leer on your face you call a smile means you might have something for me."

Squatton's eyes shifted up and down the corridor uneasily before he motioned for me to move in closer. "I need you to do me a solid."

His mouth barely moved. "See, I got this abuse of authority and misuse of a service weapon thing coming down on me, and I need you to do your thing. But this one is major."

Those were serious violations, so I crossed it off of my easy list. He'd already come through on a couple of big asks for me, so I rocked back on the balls of my feet and gave him the go-ahead.

"Me and my partner were answering a call, see? Prostitution, loitering . . . I don't know, I was gonna figure it out when I got there. Everybody scattered. Rook took the front, I swept the rear. Pretty little thing too, nice tight ass. Might or might not have been hiding beside a brownstone. I let her feel my gun." He ran his hand over the butt of his holstered weapon. "And was about to let her feel *my gun*." Squatton grabbed his junk with a leering sideways grin on his face. "But my rookie partner came crashing through the bushes like a fucking Himalayan pygmy boar. Who the fuck doesn't stand down, when you say 'stand down' on the mic? I ain't even bring her in. Told her get the fuck outta there. Well, she got picked up the next day. But that ain't even the shit-shit," Squatton hissed through his teeth.

Squatton was a dog gnawing on a thick piece of rawhide. He leaned so close, I could see the bloody chewed, chapped, and cracked skin peeling away on his dry lips.

"Outside a hotel downtown, some undercovers were posted up, watching this new kid. A local heavy hitter who's been dropping bodies all over DC. He goes by the name of Face. They see the girl come out of the hotel last night, assume she's either a prosty or a customer. The guys drag her in. She has coke on her. They turn the heat up when she starts hollering about 'the other night.' Sarge is sayin' they gotta look into it. Her name's Saniah Sutton. Tell me you can fix this shit. It's my hands. They the problem. I'll get therapy, go to rehab. I'll do whatever. Just let me retire with a clean badge."

And The Fucksquatch strikes again.

"Can she identify you?" I asked, seriously considering the severity of the situation.

"Eh, she didn't look back, just got up and ran. But all she has to do is say where she was. They know where me and the rook were."

"Show me what you've got and I'll see what I can do."

Squatton grinned from ear to ear. He turned on his heel and led me down the hall with an extra bounce in his step. Hell, I didn't say I would or could do anything. I always say what I mean, and I said I'd see what I could do. It depended on what I was working with.

I sank my shoulders back onto the murky-grey painted wall as I waited in the interrogation room, or the box, as it was called. The lights overhead flickered, making a steady, loud, mechanical hum. A tiny little thing with long, dark, wavy hair falling all over her head covering most of her face was shoved through the door in some in-take pants and shirt so big they looked like they'd fall off her. She was younger, prettier than I expected, with creamy almond-brown skin.

"Tsk, tsk, tsk!" I peeled myself off the wall, pressing toward her slowly. I pulled out a chair, offering her a place to sit. "What would a bad thing like Face be doing with a sweet little thing like you?"

She twisted and untwisted her fingers together, staring at the door like she was about to get ambushed and eaten alive.

"You don't know my brother," she whispered, her voice was shaky and uneven. Her watery eyes shifted over the artificial wooden lines in the cheap table, tracing the dirty cup rings and coffee stains.

I pulled my card out of my lapel pocket. "So let me help you help this brother of yours. What's his name, Face?" I said, easing it across the table. I slowly waved it with two fingers like a white flag, a peace offering. "Genesis Kane. I represent the officer you're filing a complaint against."

"I don't care about that shit. I just wanted to bargain with them so they'd let me go, but it's too late now. I'm not saying nothing about nobody. Leave my brother out of this. He's been so fucking paranoid lately, he don't even sit down to take a shit. As soon as he hears about me being here, he's gonna freak out." She nodded at the scar on my lip. "What's it like living with that on your face?" she asked.

Caught off guard, I didn't have a ready answer. Sometimes I forgot about the twisted sand-colored skin that ran up across the top of my lip. Most people acted like they didn't see it, or they saw it and acted like it wasn't there. I can't think of anyone who just came out and asked about it. I shrugged, "I never really—"

"You don't think about it, right? Because it's not some shit like this." She pulled back her thick veil of hair with confident fingers. The flesh around her left ear down to the bottom of her cheek was scarred, jagged. I almost winced at the pink and brown skin healed over and woven together like a third-degree quilt. "My own brother did this to me. And it's even worse if you're against him. He does it to your whole face, all the way down to the neck. He lets the skin fester and the flies set in and maggots come. That's why they call him 'Face.' Y'all might as well kill me."

I couldn't swallow. My collar felt tight around my neck. I was normally prepared for anything, and I mean anything, but this was so left field. The metal chair legs squealed across the floor. Squatton was right in my face as soon as the door opened.

"What she say? That was the fastest head-fucking you've ever done. What did you tell her? You head-fucked the shit out of her, didn't you?" He was whispering a thousand words a minute, hovering around me like a zealous admirer.

"Not this time. This might not be your night." I wagged my finger back and forth. "You might actually have something I can't un-fuck for once."

Squatton slammed his fist into the concrete wall. His head fell back. He stared up at the ceiling with his jaw clenched, his hand limp at his side. It was probably shattered or broken.

"This can go only one of two ways," I told him. "If she stays here, that complaint is going forward. If she walks right now. No questions asked. All is forgiven."

His Adam's apple bobbed in his throat. Squatton knew either way he was fucked. Even if she walked, the guys building the case would smell something funny. Squatton just so happened to be on duty when she miraculously disappeared. Footsteps echoed down some hallway in the distance, reminding us we weren't the only ones in the building. Air whistled through his nostrils with each breath.

Squatton leaned his head back against the wall. "Hey, Kane, remember that favor you asked me for? Ahh?" He rolled his head back and forth across the wall like a rolling pin.

I cracked the bones in my suddenly stiff neck, left, then right.

"It was a rape case, right? You wanted some evidence to *disappear*," he said in a smart-ass tone.

"What's your point, Squatton?"

His head stopped rolling across the wall; he looked me in the eye. "Now, I need you to make something *disappear* for me. Out of my jail. I'm gonna give you that bitch and everything she came in here with. You sign that book up front. Anybody asks why she walked, I'm gonna say *her attorney* got her out."

A few minutes later, I laid several oversized ziplock bags containing Saniah's belongings on the table.

"Here's your shit. Get dressed and meet me out front. I'll take you wherever you need to go." I laid her things neatly on the table in front of her.

She stopped wringing her hands. Her tongue darted across her lips. She pulled her bottom lip in between her teeth, debating on whether or not this shit was really happening.

"That's it?" she asked.

I nodded. "That's it."

"What do you do, again?" she asked in genuine awe. "Are you an attorney or an angel?"

I chuckled, feeling somewhat redeemed by her appreciation. "I do a little bit of everything," I stated with a wink. "The real question is, what am I not? Now hurry up. I was trying to grab some Chinese before they switch over to that late-night garbage they use for the drunks and after-hours crowds."

Live music floated on the warm night air. It was jazzy, up-tempo, tuba-heavy, something to keep the tourists out spending their dollars. It made the city sound like New Orleans during Mardi Gras. Saniah didn't give the precinct a second thought as she rushed outside in a cream-colored sundress. It clung to her full hips, which I did not mind watching as she walked in front of me. It also showed off the roundness of belly when she turned to take in her surroundings. My eyes lingered for a moment longer than I intended, but she didn't notice. Squatton left out the fact that he'd perv'd up a pregnant girl. The baggy prison clothes had kept all parts of that from showing.

I opened the back door for her, making sure to seat her somewhere in sight. I don't like the awkwardness of strangers riding all up in my personal space. And I never liked someone sitting in my blind spot.

"Where do you want me to take you?" I adjusted the rearview so I could see her face.

She stopped fiddling with her phone long enough to turn these big damsel-in-distress eyes onto me.

"Do we have that whole confidentiality thing like they give them on *Law and Order,* or naw?" she asked.

"Yeah, technically, I can't say a word."

"Yes, gawd!" She dug through her purse. "And all my shit is still here too. *Woop!*" She celebrated, and then she put something up to her nose . . . and snorted. Twice. Wiping it clean with the back of her hand.

This bitch was actually doing coke in my car, in front of me, and she was pregnant.

"Oh, I needed that. Um, Genesis, right?" she asked as she opened the car door. "Look, I'm sorry for getting you involved. Me and my brother are misunderstood; always have been. He would never put his hands on me. I exaggerated a little, and I'm sorry." She sighed dramatically. "It's all about territory. I hear Sammie Knox has way more territory than him or his bitch need." She started rubbing her belly with a slick grin on her face. "I came up with an easy way to get it. Y'all niggas'll do damn near anything for a son, though. For a little prince."

The corners of my mouth turned down into a bitter frown. "Nah, not all of us. Just another hand to slap away, if you ask me."

"That's why I ain't ask you," was her smart-ass reply. She started to close the door but turned back as if it was an afterthought. "Oh, and my face? Car accident. Like I said, my brother's misunderstood. But, thank you for your help. I'll do you a favor and make sure Javion don't fuck you up when he comes back to execute everyone in that police station." She sashayed away, hips swaying, hair bouncing, and an energetic dance to her step. She sidestepped puddles, twirled to the sound of the band, and faded into the night like a ghost.

A sinister shiver ran across the back of my neck. It traveled across my cheeks, tugging at the scar above my lip until it throbbed. Favors. I didn't want shit from them; then I'd owe them something back. I was so sick of hearing that word.

Suddenly, food was the farthest thing from my mind. My gut was filled with anxious, twisting snakes of dread, all knotting together, making my mood sour as fuck. The SUV rocked from the weight of my fist slamming into the steering wheel. I cursed to relieve some of my frustration, but it didn't help.

I could feel that shit. Sense: it with everything in me. The same way I could pick up on a judge who'd lean in my favor, or a juror who'd fuck up my client. I felt it when I'd asked Squatton for that favor so many months ago, and he made the evidence disappear on that rape case, and I felt it now. Only it was stronger. Way worse than before. I'd fucked up, and it was telling me I was going to regret some part of this night. Some part of this shit was going to haunt me for the rest of my life.

Chapter 39

Hello, Kitty

Almond-coconut-scented steam swirled around me, clouding the air, fogging up the mirrors and my view of the city from the sixteenth floor. With a sigh, I eased down into the half-moon-shaped tub that could've easily fit a small swim team. Soft coconut shavings brushed against my skin underneath the bubbles.

I drained the water from my washcloth, draped it over my face, and lay my head back, enjoying my few moments of peace and quiet. The bathroom door creaked open. The sound of the evening news drifted in from the TV downstairs. *"An armed assailant flees from police down H Street after robbing a CVS. A double homicide has police looking for this woman. We'll tell you more at ten."*

I tuned out the grisly news, listening to see if I could hear Elgin trying to sneak in. Elgin was Javion's spoiled rotten, ugly as hell, hairless cat.

"Look here, little freak cat," I grumbled from underneath the washcloth, "leave my goddamn panties alone. Elgin, I swear on my life if I have to get out this tub, I'm gonna snatch you up by your little hairless balls and put you outside with the real cats," I warned.

It still wasn't exactly clear as to *what* he was doing to my panties once he got ahold of them. I don't know if he was eating or shredding the damn things, but every now and again, Javion would find a pair and swear up and down I was leaving them on purpose. Like I was on some kind of female territorial marking spree or some shit. All I know is I'd lost half my brand-new Frederick's of Hollywood collection over here, and I wasn't trying to buy anymore until they had another sale.

Hell, I ain't even *like* cats, let alone men with cats. Javion got a pass because he had more checks on the "date him" side than the "don't date him" side of the scale. He was single, fine as hell, with zero kids, and he had a good job. Shit, on top of all that, he was a straight man in DC, so that got him a double check-plus. So, yeah, I could definitely overlook his creepy panty-freak cat and his hustle for all of those perks.

With that thought, my washcloth was slung off of my face. It landed in the corner with a wet *splat. Mmm, let me find out he ain't playing tonight. Wonder if he wants to pretend to be the dirty plumber again?* The last time we got down in the bathroom, we had to take showers afterward just to get clean. It took every towel in the place to soak all the water up off the floor.

I kept my eyes closed, waiting for him to make the next move. My skin tingled in anticipation of whatever fun Javion had planned for us tonight.

"Humph, looks like I found me a mermaid. Didn't know they made 'em in black."

My eyes snapped open. A woman with a thick New York accent had me scooting to the farthest corner of the tub as I glared up at a different kind of hairless cat.

"Who the fuck are you?" I snapped in her direction, scanning the bathroom for something to cover myself with. "Javion," I shouted at the top of my lungs. *Where the fuck is he?* There wasn't a towel anywhere close, and my cell was in the bedroom on the charger. Elgin tipped in and plopped down at the heels of this colossal cat lady who was either smirking or frowning down at me. It was hard to tell which one since she'd had the kind of plastic surgery that was usually only for superrich and famous people. The kind that gave them all meaty lips and oversized cheekbones with stiff, puffy eyebrows. It was the kind where you didn't know if they were *all the way crazy* or just really confused kind of crazy. It would've made a hell of a difference in helping me figure out whether I needed to get out of the tub and all the way beat her ass, or just slap her around until she figured out where she was.

"Hey, babe, sorry I took so long. The front door was cracked. I think the maintenance guy must've stopped by or . . ." Javion answered on his way up the stairs.

Whatever apology or excuse he had brewing on his lips dropped along with the expression on his face. He stopped dead in his tracks just outside the bathroom door. His eyes locked on the woman standing over me.

"*What* are you doing here, McKenzie?" Javion asked in a cold, flat voice.

She had the nerve to toss her long golden hair over her shoulder before letting out a long sigh, like we were boring her.

"I been calling all night, but you ain't been answering. *Now* I see why. You was obviously busy. Boss man sent me to get your pull for the day. I let myself in."

Javion tipped his head back, giving her a suspicious look. "I've been taking in my own drop for two years. Why would he send you out here?" he asked suspiciously.

Before I could blink, I found myself staring down the barrel of a gun. It came out of her purse so fast, I didn't have time to react.

The water made a solid splashing sound from my jaw dropping down into it. I looked toward Javion with my eyes begging for help.

"You ain't seen the news. Beau, that wrestler and his daughter were killed. Assassination style. Cops pulled your girl's prints from the door handle. Been looking for her all day. Boss man don't know her. He said you're done, and she's dead."

Javion wouldn't look my way. He just stood there, rubbing his hand across the back of his neck. McKenzie was eagerly eating him up in eyefuls. I wanted to tell him to handle this bitch or man the fuck up, but I was too scared to speak.

"A'ight, McKenzie, let me give him a call. I did my job, and I scared the nigga like I was supposed to. He said he'd pay tonight, and we left. If this has to be done I want to handle it. I'll give you twenty grand if you give me five minutes."

McKenzie thought his offer over. She swept me with an ugly sideways glare before stomping away.

"*Mijo*, when you gonna give me a chance? You need to stop fuckin' with these foo-foo-frilly stranger bitches," McKenzie said as they walked away.

Javion's answer was inaudible as they went downstairs. *I know he didn't just let that stranger bitch call me a stranger bitch.* If I was speaking to my dad, I'd have some real hitters out here so fast. Having my life threatened was nothing new, but this whole wanted-for-murder shit had me so hot, it's a wonder I didn't make the bathwater boil. Frustrated and over the whole situation, I got up, sloshing water all across the tile floor as I dripped my way into the bedroom.

Eavesdropping on their conversation didn't even interest me as I made my way down the hall. Javion had just offered to kill me himself. He didn't fight the bitch or curse her out. This nigga was just as bad as the rest. In my book, all men were cowards when it came to stepping up for a woman.

I let out a small gasp when I saw the damn cat propped up on my overnight bag. The way he could creep from room to room freaked me the fuck out. After unceremoniously shoving him aside, I pulled out some jeans and a T-shirt, tugging them over my still damp skin. My sandals were soundless on the hardwood floor as I crept down the stairs and out the door.

How could I be so stupid? First that pregnant bitch pops up, and now this. I should've known he was too good to be true. This was the reason why I was so cautious about letting someone in. This dude wasn't even a top-nigga. My freedom was at risk, and my name was out there, all because of Javion. Daddy would have my ass if he knew what kind of shit I'd let happen. Not cool . . . This was not cool at all.

Chapter 40

Mommy Issues

The next morning, I woke Shandy up, telling her we owed Momma and Daddy a visit. Fucking around with Javion, I was probably gonna need their help, whether I liked it or not.

Every charcoal grill on every back porch, deck, and in every backyard in DC must've all been going at the same time. You could smell the ribs, hot dogs, and hamburgers. As soon as I rolled my window down, the smoky heat pressed its way into the car, swallowing whatever air-conditioning it came in contact with.

Javion had been blowing me up ever since I left. He was doing everything in his power to get into my personal space so he could read all into my headspace. And I just wanted some me-time, and by me-time, I mean time with me and anyone *except* him. A part of me accepted what he did like it was second nature. The perks that came with dating him were unbelievable. It didn't even bother me, knowing that I'd have to watch my back and his. It didn't bother me knowing if something went down while we were together, I'd be guilty by association. And that, in itself, my acceptance and understanding bothered me more than anything.

My parents' place was off-limits to everyone except Shandy. Since Momma had sent me some mysterious 9-1-1 texts and wasn't returning my calls, we were homeward bound.

"Damn, Novie, can you move any slower? Got a bitch titties sweatin' and shit. I need the power of a good turn up in me so bad right now!" Shandy sat in the backseat fanning her double

Fs furiously. She was the prettiest girl I knew, with bright, slanted cat eyes and clear baby-smooth skin. Somebody was mixed somewhere in her family because her hair grew thick and wavy, no relaxer necessary. But if you wanted to see somebody get real ugly, try to throw shade about her weight. I dare you.

Shandy wasn't fat, but she was plumper than what most would classify as thick. She'd been rocking corsets and waist cinchers to sit her titties up and push her booty out before it was even the thing. Don't get me wrong; she was more than comfortable in her skin, but she had no problem snapping if you tried to play her to the left because of it. Another half hour and all of my bestie's NARS foundation would be melting down her chin and into one of the many expensive shirt-dresses she splurged on.

I shrugged. "My bad, girl. I'm just pissed we're here and not hittin' up one of these cookouts."

"It's all good." She stared longingly out the window. "I've got to put in some serious work, though. Find me a sponsor, sling some coochie for cash, or start movin' some serious dope. I was supposed to have two of these houses by now."

I cut my eyes at her over my shoulder. She knew better than to play around like that. Not when my dad was the infamous Sammie Knox. When the streets heard Knox was coming, it was like saying Bloody Mary in the mirror three times.

"Oh, don't look at me like that, Novie. You know I'm just all in my feelings, looking at these pretty houses when I just lost my grant. How the hell am I supposed to pay for my last year of school now? Me and my baby girl need this in our life."

She fussed over Aris Monique Patterson in the car seat next to her. I tried to tell her I don't know how many times, that people wouldn't see Aris and say *heiress*. She'd need an extra *r* or an *e* up in there, but you can't tell Shandy anything once her mind is made up.

"Lawd," Shandy let out a dramatic sigh. "I'm so glad I'm not breast-feeding anymore. I need me a drink and a blunt so bad. I hope Lady J ain't acting funny. You know how stingy she get with her liquor."

I met her wide, worried eyes in the rearview. Momma, or Lady J, as she liked to be called, because *Misses* sounded old, would be all right. "Stop worrying, Shandy. Everything'll be fine."

The tires crunched over the sandy cobblestone driveway through the small forest of pine trees and small oaks toward the four-story glass-front palace that belonged to my parents. Mixed feelings welled up inside me, clawing at the back of my throat. I needed them but hated spending more time than necessary with them. Somebody always wound up needing a favor, and their favors never worked out in my favor. I'd started to say just that as we stood outside the double French doors. I was clawing through my purse, digging around for my spare key. Shandy was busy fretting over Aris in her stroller.

I found it wedged in between the prongs of a fork at the bottom of my purse and made a mental note to clean it out or switch to a smaller bag.

"Ma?" I called out, stepping over a lonely pump with a broken heel. The wall was splattered with cotton candy pink Louboutin polish. Glass shards from the bottle were scattered across the floor. The outside of the house was always plain and simple, but inside, the house looked like a war zone.

"Novie? Hey, boo." She came rushing around the corner with her arms out, all flushed and out of breath. She was stylishly put together as usual, in a light blue dress that stopped just above her knees.

"What are you doing here?" She pulled me into an awkward hug, then grabbed Shandy and did the same.

"What am I doing here? Really? What's up with the 9-1-1 texts, and what in the world happened up in here?" I dropped my purse on the side table by the front door. "Daddy?" I called out. My eyes were searchlights as I scanned the foyer and the main hallway.

"Your dad ain't home, Novie." She folded her hands across her arms saying, how-dare-he-not-be-here, and how-dare-you-question-me, and I-dare-you-to-say-one-more-thing all in that one look.

"Um, Lady J, I think I need to change Aris. Do you mind . . . um, if I use the restroom?" Shandy could sense a family matter like an animal senses danger. She scooped Aris up out of her stroller, resting her head on her shoulder underneath her chin.

"Make yourself at home. Use the one across from the guest room down the hall to the left." She gave Shandy a serious look. "Just keep the noise down, *please*."

I wondered what that was about as she waved Shandy off down one hall before swooping in to block me from going anywhere.

"Okay, Ma, what's really going on? Daddy hasn't answered one of my calls, and he always answers. Did you do something to him? Y'all have a fight?" I spun around her in the direction of the living room.

She was in hot pursuit, trailing after me toward the living room. "Novie, bring your ass here. I need to explain something to you."

I stormed the living room like a one-woman SWAT team. She'd changed all the furniture again. It wasn't the make-you-cringe, we-rich-bitch, pink and gold Versace collection anymore. Thank the Lord. That either went out of style, or somebody she knew had something too close to it. Now it was dark cappuccino-brown, Italian leather ottomans, tall, glossy, floor lamps, brown carpeting. A high-backed leather sofa sat with matching armchairs beside it. But something stunk; it smelled rancid, like old Chinese food and sour washrags. I covered my nose with my hand. Heavy curtains were drawn, throwing the living room into semidarkness. I jerked to a stop in front of the couch, feeling like I'd swallowed a rock the size of my foot. "What the fuck?" I whispered involuntarily when my eyes locked on the pregnant girl shivering on a couch in a tattered, stained sundress. She was skinny as hell, but still very pregnant.

She was hog-tied, with her mouth taped shut, staring back at me for help.

I took a step back when I saw the vomit on the floor in front of the sofa. "What the fuck is this?" I asked. I couldn't even look my mother in the eyes as I pointed down at her. "What the hell is goin' on up in here?" I demanded in a shaky whisper. This couldn't be business related. It was against the rules to bring any of that into the house.

"I told you we needed to talk." There was an edge to her voice that wasn't there before. Fury was exploding in her eyes. "You wanna know what this is?" She chuckled, then giggled, and then she doubled over laughing until she had tears in her eyes. When she finally regained her composure, the venom was back. "Sammie supposedly left on business. *Late* Friday night the doorbell rings. And it's that ho, right there. I don't know what she was on, but the bitch was higher than caviar. Telling me how she and Sammie been together. Showing me a goddamn slide show on her phone. Telling me she's pregnant. She thought she was gonna come up to *my* house. Disrespect me to *my* face. Gonna tell me about *my* husband and the life she about to live with him. *That's* what this is."

"Oh, shit. Daddy did what . . . she came here and . . . oh, damn."

There were always rumors about Daddy's women. I was always suspicious, but I never really knew for sure.

"These new-age bitches," she spat. "They don't understand the levels to this shit." She sneered down at the girl on the couch. "If you trading pussy for the nigga's time and trinkets, you don't come to *my* front door. I'm his *wife. He,* and only he, addresses me. You just another one of Sammie's hoes."

The girl wildly shook her head back and forth. She was saying something, but I couldn't make anything out with the tape over her mouth. And then her body went rigid; her back arched like an electric current surged through the chair. The veins in her neck protruded like plastic straws under her skin. She started squirming and groaning like she was possessed. She squeezed her eyes shut and alternated between clenching her jaw and straining against her ropes. Momma didn't seem the least bit concerned. She checked the hands on her petite rose-gold watch.

"I thought he'd have come home by now. Her contractions are about ten minutes apart," she stated in the most matter-of-fact tone.

Her contractions? I wanted to scream until my throat burned, but I screamed them in my head instead. This was it; she'd finally completely lost it. I knew it would happen one day, and we were there. She wasn't even bothered by the cheating or upset that Daddy might have another baby; she was just upset that the woman had the nerve to approach her.

"Lady J! Lady J, it's Sammie!" Tariq, Daddy's second in command, yelled from the direction of the foyer.

The tone of his voice made the blood drain from our faces. My knees were wobbly as I forced them to steer me in the direction of Tariq's gruff voice as we rushed to see what had him worked up. Tariq read like a brick wall. Outside of working, if it didn't involve weights, weapons, or warfare, the nigga wasn't interested. He never so much as sneezed loud, let alone yelled. Daddy kept him tethered to his side like a two-year-old on a harness. Our eyes met across the foyer as he rushed inside.

Chapter 41

Fake Falls Away, and the Real Gets Realer

Tariq, in all of his Egyptian musk-scented presence, filled the doorway. I had to keep myself in the moment. That smell always took me back. Made my scar ache. His chest was heaving; he bent down, put his hands on his knees, and took a steadying breath. "We were handling business when somebody opened up on us at a light. Didn't see who did it. Sammie needs you to patch him up. We can't risk a doctor's office right now, okay?"

Momma nodded and kept on nodding. She was still nodding after Tariq left to get Daddy. That's when I realized that most women don't start out completely crazy. No, they're usually driven there. The change takes place in the space of an inhale, like zero to a hundred and eighty-three with no seat belt in a two-seater called love. In my momma's case, the driver was my daddy. And as crazy as she was about him, she'd go just as crazy over him, and he'd do the same thing for her, in his own weird way.

She jumped when I reached for her.

"Ma? What do you need me to do?" I asked on the verge of tears, but I swallowed them back.

"You know I'm here too, Lady J," Shandy announced. She scurried away to secure Aris out of the way in her stroller.

Momma's lip quivered before she tightened it. She stopped shaking and steadied herself. Her eyes darted to the door and back. "Go move that bitch to the garage before he knows she's here. I'll have Tariq put him in the back bedroom. We'll just have to deal with her later."

I nodded, pulling Shandy with me. I needed to explain what she was about to see before we got in the living room, and she screamed the roof down on us. Hell, I needed to prepare myself to see that shit again before we got in there.

My stomach pitched. I turned and threw up orange against the far wall and dry heaved until there was nothing left. *Oh my God. What has she done? What did I let happen?*

Shandy turned away, closing her eyes at the sight of the dead with her head turned and her eyes staring through us. They would probably haunt me for the rest of my life. Shandy yanked on my arm so hard she almost pulled it out of the socket.

"Novie!" She got up on her tiptoes staring, fascinated with her body.

I prayed by some miraculous force she was alive, and I'd only imagined she was dead or just looked dead. When Shandy brushed past me, I knew it wasn't the case. I could see it lying there quietly, but I didn't want to believe it. I'd always thought babies were supposed to scream and cry when they were born. Shandy scooped up the slick baby with a look of awe on her face as Momma sailed into the living room with blood on her cheek and the front of her dress.

"How do I save a fool in one room and lose a fool in the other. *Fuck*." Momma cursed under her breath as she tapped her finger against the tip of her nose. "Your daddy is fine. But please . . . Please, tell me she ain't dead."

All I could do was shake my head.

She looked in Shandy's direction. Her finger stopped midtap. It hovered in the air, asking the question on both of our minds. How real was Shandy's loyalty to our family?

Momma crossed the room. "Shandy?" She sounded like they were about to discuss the weather. "You know we've got a lot going on right now. You know we have to get rid of *everything*, right?" Momma reached for the baby in Shandy's arms. The extra emphasis she'd put on the word *everything* was the spark that ignited the tension-fueled air.

Shandy's eyes went wild, her face turned savage. "You ain't takin' Aris away from me! Not again!" She hissed at us, showing all of her teeth, holding the baby protectively in her arms.

"Shandy, that's not Aris," Momma cooed at her. "Aris is upstairs right where you left her. That baby that *you're* holding is a *real* little boy." She talked real slow, as if she was explaining everything to a five-year-old.

And then she turned to me with this soothe-your-savage-friend look on her face, and I threw my hands up, thinking, *I didn't unleash the beast; you did.* Hell, I didn't know what to do, especially since the Aris that we'd left sitting in the stroller in the other room wasn't even a real baby. Yes, Aris looked like a real newborn; she even wore clothes, diapers, and baby powder. But the only person she was real to and had ever been real to was Shandy. People would come up to see her and walk away with the creepy OMG-she-got-a-fake-baby face. Most of our friends understood, and the ones who didn't get it would turn a blind eye or disappear.

Shandy's mom was addicted to OxyContin and alcohol. Swiss ran away before he finished high school. When we were fourteen, her mama pimped her out to one of her boyfriends for pill money. When Shandy got pregnant, her mom said she was useless, and she kicked her out of her house. We took her in; even had her looking forward to having the baby. We were all a little devastated when Shandy lost the baby at seven months. Then Momma got a doll that cost more than a diamond. It was weird in the beginning, but it worked, so we kept going along with it because we thought one day Shandy would snap out of it. The funny thing is, we'd been going along with it for the last seven years. Her momma was in a home for mentally unstable women now. All the drinking and drugs fucked her mind up.

"Okay, Shan," Momma's voice was whisper soft. "You can keep the baby. I'll help you with it, give you everything you need."

Ma, I mouthed silently while looking at her like she'd just grown an extra head and her extra head just said all kinds of bullshit in a foreign language. Shandy didn't need a baby and definitely not one that might be my half brother, whose Mom we might as well be accomplices to murder for. He was living evidence.

But it seemed to be exactly what Shandy needed to hear. She started to calm down.

"Shandy, you'll need to stay out of sight for a little while. And then you just tell everyone he's yours, and we're good. You aren't going to talk about where he came from or how you got him. He's your baby."

We both watched her. The baby whined a little, but he didn't cry.

Shandy furrowed her forehead. She rocked the baby, her whole body swayed back and forth, from side to side, as she contemplated what had been said.

"Why do you keep saying *he*?" She propped the baby up.

He was shiny and slick, covered in another woman's blood and fluids. Shandy displayed his tiny twig and berries with his umbilical cord dangling down the side of her arm still attached to his mother. "*Aris* is a *girl*. Y'all start drinkin' without me?" She scrunched her face up at us like we were the crazy ones in the room.

I pinched the bridge of my nose between my fingers. There was too much going on right now. I could feel a good strong headache coming on. *What the fuck kind of Norman Bates shit were we about to spawn into the world?*

"Novie, go get Tariq. Tell him come clean this mess." She waved her hand in the direction of the couch while pulling me out of hearing distance. "Baby, it's not as bad as you think. People are already used to seeing her with that doll, and she's already a little heavy."

"I'm so done with this family. I really can't cope with you right now, Ma."

"Grow up, little girl," she spat in a sharp whisper. "You have one more year at Howard, and you still ain't picked a major yet. So what? You want to get a job, work until you die? Well, that tuition, those books, your car . . . all of it's paid for in red. We never bullshit you about this life, so you step up or get stepped over."

I traced the patterns into the carpet between my shoes. Her words hurt my pride just as much as they cut into hurt my heart. Shandy had started singing to the baby from behind us. It was something melodic but eerie. I tried to tune her out.

Momma grabbed my chin; she yanked my face up until I met her eyes. They were sad, but they were hard.

"We're gonna need you to do us a small favor."

I knew it was coming. The way the word rolled off her lips. She made favors sound like they were owed and not courtesies.

"What is it?" I had so much attitude in my voice.

Whatever this favor was had to be important. Momma overlooked my disrespect to grab something off the fireplace mantel. Five gold letters stood out on the white card she held up between her fingers.

"That girl had this on her. This attorney . . . Genesis Kane. I looked into him. He's been deputized as a voluntary prosecutor for the district courts when they're backed up. I don't care what or how you do it. You get to him. Find out why she was talking to him, what he might know. I need to make sure your daddy didn't fuck around, *fuckin' around.*"

Chapter 42

King of Hearts

The thick mahogany shades covering the floor-to-ceiling windows slid up without a sound, letting in the glow from the city at night. From up here, you didn't see the buildings or the traffic. You didn't hear the busy heartbeat of the city. I specifically chose this penthouse for the master bedroom's view of the Potomac River. It was the most majestic shit I'd ever seen, a reminder to keep me on my king game. I put all the shit from the other night behind me with a long weekend of uppers, downers, and all-arounders. Scotch, Xanax, hash oil, shit I don't even know. I zoned out on it, my vision blurred, and blood rushed to my head. My other head.

She was butt-ass naked with perfectly perky titties, a gift from her husband. They didn't quite match the age spots on her hands or the wrinkled sagging skin on her midsection, a gift from her son. She wasn't my type in any way, shape, or form. I liked my women with thick hips, dick-sucking lips, and those thighs that a dude could get lost in like quicksand. But I hyped myself up.

I growled, dug my fingers into her hip, making red marks in her flesh. She woke up from a sound sleep as I rolled her onto her stomach. I spread her legs from one end of the bed to the other. Her pussy was still glossy, creamy, full from my earlier deposits. I don't know about most niggas, but I don't like dipping in my own leftovers. Not only did it turn me off, but it made her shit feel like sliding into a bowl of warm Jell-O. I wanted to knock her upside the head, but I grilled her like I'm-about-tear-this-shit-up. My dick wouldn't go down if I wanted it to. I'd taken too many Viagras for that. So I eased inside her, filled her up, fucked her until she begged me to stop, and I ain't stop until she couldn't beg me anymore.

"*Mmm* . . . Damn, I wish I could just roll over and go right back to sleep. But thank you, Kane," she purred with a satisfied smile when we were done. "*Where* were you when I was still single? I swear, spending one night with you beats an entire session at my rejuvenation day spa. I feel like I'm glowing." She stretched, and then scooted in closer to lay her head on my chest. Her hair and skin still held the scent of the Marlboro Skylines she chain-smoked. It never went away, no matter how much expensive lotion and perfume she used, or how often she washed. I hated that scent. If a smell could tell a story, hers would sound like guilty marathon sex in a shady motel on cum-stained sheets. That's why I never delayed the timer on the blinds. If I didn't have anything to focus on, fucking her would be torture.

The combination of stale smoke, sweat, and J'adore Dior filled my nostrils. As my phone buzzed its way across the nightstand, I ignored it; didn't even glance in its direction. I gave her shoulders a warm squeeze. I hid my disgust for her the same way I usually hid my distaste for trashy white women; flashy, loud-mouthed niggas; and laws, in general. I tucked it away behind a façade of fake friendliness. Paula was oblivious, as usual. She placed a warm kiss underneath my chin.

"Somebody else trying to squeeze in already?" She pressed her lips together into a duck-faced pout. "I'm not leaving until you're completely drained, so if you've got more, give it up."

With the tip of her perfectly painted period-bloodred nail, she *booped* the tip of my nose. I moved my head away just slightly. I hated that shit too. I barely touched my own face with my bare hands. And here she was touching my nose and stroking my cheek with her bright whore-red nail polish, flashing at me like a germy warning sign. Only hookers and whores wore red lips or red nails. But Paula Schaefer was listed in *Forbes* magazine as one of the richest women in the world. As VP of Schaefer and Brockman, she could make anyone into anything she wanted them to be. And since I didn't need to be the world's richest man . . . and all I wanted was a small part of that fortune in a fraction of that time, I smiled bright, kissed her on her forehead, and said whatever she needed to hear.

"I think you wore me out. How about you let me have some time off to recuperate?" I got up and headed for my master bath with Paula hot on my heels.

"Ugh! I'll tell you this much, one kid and your bladder shrinks to the size of a fucking walnut. I've got to pee so bad." She sped past me into the bathroom, unleashing a hiss of a stream into the toilet.

I braced my bare shoulders against the wall. "You know there are four other bathrooms in here that you can use besides mine?" I reminded her for what had to be the hundredth time.

"I know. I know. You don't have to be so possessive. Sharing is caring, Kane. Jeez, I couldn't hold it. But I've been thinking and . . . How would you feel about coming in and taking care of the paperwork . . . one day this week?"

The toilet flushed, and Paula was right there, back in front in front of me, hand extended, waiting to shake on making me a partner in the firm. No wash, no hand sanitizer, nothing. I reached for it, wondering how many million-dollar deals went down over some sorry sex and a pissy handshake. The sooner we made this partner thing official, the better off I'd be. It'd take me a minute to figure out how to break things off, but the idea of sending her husband an anonymous tip wasn't looking that bad.

She got dressed while rambling about whether she should have red, white, or some new amber wine at a dinner party for her husband. I'd just be a member of the bachelor's club for the rest of my life. You marry a woman, and then she plans all of your parties and vacations with the nigga she's fucking. I'll pass.

"Kane," Paula called from the doorway, "I've got the paper for you, and doughnuts."

"Doughnuts?" I rarely ate doughnuts, and Paula didn't eat anything white. Something to do with good carbs and bad carbs, or I would've told her to keep and eat the doughnuts. Instead of making a big deal out of it, I said thanks and endured another smoky good-bye kiss.

My phone buzzed its way across the table as I was making my way back inside. I was in such a rush to answer it, I missed the last step. Bile rose up the back of my throat. The muscles in my stomach shuddered. The Dunkin' doughnut box was lying on its side on the floor right next to my foot where I'd dropped it. And if you followed the glossy globs of congealed blood that trailed out of it for about a foot, you'd find the fat, bloody-red pig's heart that'd rolled out of it when it fell.

It took me an extra hour to pull myself together enough to clean that mess up. This wasn't the first one, but it was the biggest. It'd started small with what might've been a mouse or a canary heart, and every so often, I'd get another one. I just never knew when or where. Why didn't I call the police? *Because I'm not a fucking snitch.* I was an attorney with a long and buried past that I didn't need or want anybody digging around in. It was most likely a crazy fuck-buddy-turned-friend who wasn't happy with the new status. All it'd take was some new dick, and she'd forget about me and terrorize that nigga with her gory heart story. Or she'd show herself. Either way, I had real shit to take care of.

On top of that, the texts were from Fucksquatch. It was urgent, and he wanted me to meet him at the station in an hour. We always kept our meetings to the ten p.m. time frame. After shift change, they were on a skeleton crew until morning. I checked my watch, wondering what the hell else he could have gotten into in a few days. Knowing him, it'd probably be in my best interest to get out there sooner than later. But if this shit had anything to do with Saniah's complaint, he was on his own; my work was done.

I parked in my favorite illegal spot next to the hydrant in front of the precinct. Squatton needed to make this quick so I could get into the office and sign those papers while they were still on Paula's mind. The moment the door closed behind me, I knew something wasn't right. But it was too late to turn back.

"And here's the man of the hour. Genesis Kane. Am I right?"

A pile of bloody massacred cops lay behind the dude who'd stepped forward. The ones that weren't dead yet were lined up along the wall. Four men who I would've mistaken for computer technicians stood behind him with grim faces. Their Polo shirts and khakis were covered in too much blood; their posture was too aggressive for some IT work. I had an idea who he was, but I wasn't 100 percent.

There wasn't any point bullshitting. "Okay, I'm here. What do you want?"

He tossed Squatton's phone in his direction. It clattered to the floor in front of his shackled feet. Squatton had a look in his eyes like he was about to shit a freight train. He doubled over, making a sound that was somewhere between a laugh and a desperate wail.

"Where the fuck *is my sister*!" He slammed his fists into his forehead, dragged his hands down his face like he was trying to pull off his skin. His movements were jerky, mechanical, as he stormed toward the front desk and grabbed the bloody hunting knife off the counter.

The pack of officers shifted behind him mumbled, cried . . . prayed.

"On my life, you better start spilling secrets before I start spilling blood," he demanded. He moved in on a stocky female cop. "How many of those liars, I mean lawyers, out there know your secret, Kane?" he asked.

What secret did this bottom-feeder think he had on me? This nigga was on that Pablo Escobar. That scared the truth out of you or would draw blood until you told a good lie. That was my first thought. Thinking on my feet was how I made my living. The legal game was worse than being a fake fortune-teller. People lie to stay alive, and you don't have any choice but to learn the truth about them from their actions, their mannerisms. And this nigga didn't come across as a territory-hungry power-thirsty alpha nigga. I played to that, didn't ask any questions, or give him any decisions to make. And prayed that I was right.

"Saniah, right? I helped her get out of here. So give me a little time to check on her. I just need a few days." I sounded a helluva lot calmer than I felt. Sweat was starting to soak through the pits of my shirt.

He stalked the floor in front of the desk.

"She called me." He pointed the knife at his head. "She told me about you. My sister, Face."

The tip of the blade pointed at me.

I wasn't paying attention to a word he'd said or was about to say. "Your sister Saniah . . . is Face? Not you?" I asked. That was one for the record books. That scrawny little pregnant chick was taking over the drug game, scaring these cops and street niggas out of their turf all because they thought she was her brother. The pieces were still clunky, but they were all starting to fit together: her scar, the name; the only piece missing was her.

It was as if he hadn't even heard me. "For whatever reason, my sister likes you. But Face always liked keeping weird shit in jars, like ladybugs and butterflies. I should fuckin' kill you. But today ain't your day. So go. But you owe me, Ladybug. Remember who you owe."

Chapter 43

Always Keep a Spare Tire

Two vodka cranberries later, and I was still tossing and turning. Every time I closed my eyes, I thought about Beau and his daughter, or the pregnant girl and the baby boy who Shandy was hell-bent on raising like a baby girl. I felt sick to my stomach. Out of all the sick and fucked-up shit that my parents had done over the years, that was the worst. The one person who I'd normally talk to, Shandy, was caught right up in the middle of it.

The bright green numbers on the clock beside my bed changed to three a.m. I gave up on sleep and got dressed, and then I just started driving. That always helped me sort shit out. Every set of headlights that came up in the rearview had my chest thumping and my hands sweating. I should've asked my mom to help, but the timing was off. I cracked the windows, settling on a satellite radio station that played mostly old-school R&B. I just knew those blue lights would come flashing after me. I grabbed the pack of Newport Lights in my armrest. No one knew I smoked. Not even Shandy, my bestie/roommate.

The match flared, filling my nose with the smell of smoke and burning sulfur. As weird as it sounds, I loved the smell of burning matches, and I hated the smell from cigarette smoke. The end of the cigarette glowed bright red as I took a long, slow drag. I could feel some of the nervous tension leaving my body as I exhaled carefully, blowing a stinky cloud of smoke out the window. I'd become a pro at smoking and keeping the stink out of my hair and clothes.

I called my other bestie, Denise. We were so much alike that we got on each other's nerves. She was cool as hell, but she'd talk about you like a dog the second you turned your back. Aside from Shandy, Denise was the only other person who could maybe talk some sense in to me at a time when my life was making no sense at all.

"What's wrong, Novie?" Denise yawned extra loud and long into the phone. "I'm answering in case this is an emergency. But I'm hanging up if you need me to get out of my bed and leave this house." She went off as soon as she picked up the phone.

I let out an exasperated sigh into the phone. "Dang, girl, I ain't even said anything. Why every time I call something's gotta be wrong? I was just . . . um." Well, damn, maybe I did only call her when something was wrong, because I was drawing a blank trying to think of another reason. "I was just being nosy; can't sleep. What did you get into tonight?"

"You ain't fooling nobody, but anyway, girl, I tried to get something up in me, but I'm about to fire this nigga Stephen from my little lineup."

I took another pull from my cigarette, digging through my mental Rolodex of Denise's fuck-buddies and random-run-bys. There were too many nameless faces for me to narrow it down. I drew a blank. "Fire who?" I asked, blowing wispy white smoke into the air.

"Stephen. The little white guy I been talkin' to from my job. I told you about him, the new supervisor with the dick-bulge. I've been trying to find out if he packin' or just *packin'*, like stuffing that jank with socks or something, but that nigga stay bringin' me chicken for lunch. I mean, yo, what the hell he think? All black people just like chicken?"

I did my best to keep from laughing. "Heffa, since when did you stop liking chicken?"

"Huh? I ain't say I don't like it. I love that shit. But that nigga just be bringin' it to me all unsolicited and whatnot. KFC, Chick-fil-A, Church's—that's all I get. I'm over it."

I giggled into the phone. I don't know what was funnier, hearing how mad she was about the chicken, or hearing her call this white dude nigga the whole time. That was my girl, though.

"Oh, and I used all that coconut oil you let me borrow," she continued. "I found this little recipe on Pinterest for a hair conditioner. That stuff works, and Heather said it smells good, too. Can you give massages with that shit? I'm gonna get her to rub me down."

"Hold up, who the hell is Heather? Girl, I'm gonna make some picture flash cards of all your *friends*. I can't keep up with who you're into, or who's getting into you. Is that the new girl you're talking to? You, Chicken Little, Hannah Montana, and whoever else ain't about to be using up all of my stuff for whatever it is y'all do," I warned her.

"Why you gotta play like that, Novie? Her name is Heather. But what the hell are you doing heading to Javion's?"

"No, I'm going somewhere else."

"Wait, I knew something was up with your little phone call. What's the matter? You been spendin' every weekend up in your little love nest. And now you goin' somewhere else? Do I need to get my little cousins to fuck him up, with his young-looking ass? Oh, let me guess. He lied about his little age? I told you that nigga was a twenty-five-lie. What is he, seventeen, nineteen?"

I bust out laughing. He really was a very, very young-looking twenty-five. I gave Denise a quick recap of my day, leaving out the part about Shandy and the baby.

"Well, damn, how are you going to get all that shit cleared up? You can't turn yourself in. There's no guarantee that they'll believe you," Denise pointed out the obvious.

I took a deep breath, paused, and exhaled my answer into the phone.

"I'm going to Krypton."

"Oh, *hell* to the naw. I know you ain't talkin' about *Kryptonite*, Novie."

I cringed even though she couldn't see me. The tone of Denise's voice said one hand was on her hip while she gave every word with a self-righteous head wiggle.

"Kryptonite in the flesh," I answered weakly.

"I'm coming to get you, because your ass is obviously on somethin'. That nigga is off-fucking-limits. Sammie is gonna kick your ass, and he's gonna skin that nigga alive when he finds out what you're up to."

My teeth tugged at my lower lip. Just thinking about Swiss put a smile on my face.

"That's why my dad ain't gonna find out," I answered in a smart-ass tone.

There was also a chance that Swiss could help me with my problem, since I didn't get a chance to ask my dad for help.

"Novie, miss me with all that. You are way too forgiving after what you went through . . . and that nigga . . . You've always been *too forgiving*." She took some of the harshness out of her voice. "I know you still have your little feelings for Swiss, but does Shandy know you're still messing with her brother? Family or not, Swiss ain't never been shit, and never will be. Girl, we were barely out of high school. How many men go around fuckin' they baby sister's only best friend in the *whole world*, just to fuck her over? Only my no-good, bullshit brother would do that. You had to let go of a man, but she let go of family behind that shit. Wrong is wrong. You shouldn't pick something up after God's smacked it out of your hand."

Yeah yeah yeah, I know. I was always deeply grateful but guilt-tripped, knowing Shandy was loyal enough to cut her own brother off. She was obviously stronger than I, I thought. I couldn't cut him off completely, and every time I did, I somehow found my way back or he found me.

I cleared my throat. "You know I was just having a moment. Talking to you about all that actually helped. The moment has passed." I lied to get her mind off the subject.

The line beeped in my ear. "Speak of the devil. Javion's callin' me. Probably to apologize and clear all this up. I'll let him buy us a few new Michael Kors purses or something before I fully accept his apology."

"Yasssss. That's my bitch! I need a new clutch, too. Make him get one in pink boa or some exotic shit. Hit me back if it sounds like he can't fix this," Denise all but oozed into the phone.

Instead of answering Javion's call, I turned my phone completely off. It only took me six sticks of spearmint gum and thirty minutes to make the drive from DC to Woodbridge. My jaw was sore from chewing so much gum, but I didn't want to get to my destination smelling like Smokey the Bear.

I promised myself a smoke on the way back home, and that eased some of my anxiety.

If there was one thing my momma always told me, it was to make sure I kept a spare tire. My palms got hot and sweaty on the steering wheel at the sight of Swiss's muddy work truck sitting in the driveway. I gave my hair a quick check in the mirror. The steam from my bath knocked all my curls out, leaving me with no other option than to tuck the sides behind my ears.

The front door swung open as I walked up to the house. He stood in the door in a pair of oil-stained coveralls barely hanging around his waist. Despite my conversation with Denise, I couldn't stop the smile from spreading across my face. Swiss was my spare tire. We'd been off and on for the last three years, but we could never claim each other, so we'd fall together, and then we'd fall apart. Swiss always called it an *understanding*. I called it stubborn denial.

"I missed you, Novie-star!" Swiss sang out my name in his deep, raspy voice returning my smile. "Am I off punishment?"

His thick bottom lip was drawn in between his teeth as I climbed the last step toward him. I stepped into the heat of his body, inhaling the smell of him. It was masculine, metal, motor oil, almond butter, and sweat. His locks were loose, hanging down the middle of his back, brushing against my hands wrapped around his shoulders.

There was a low rumble in his chest when he pulled back and cupped an ass cheek in each hand. He slowly dragged me toward him the way a bulldozer pulls earth. He parted my lips with his and fucked my mouth with his tongue. Shockwaves danced across the tops of my teeth. He stole my breath and breathed it right back. It was some kind of tantric CPR. Swiss was the only man in the world who could tell me exactly what he'd do to my pussy without ever saying a word. When I was panting, soaking wet, and wobbly, cool air replaced the heat of his lips.

"You can't be leavin' a nigga like that," he said in a quiet voice, pressing his forehead against mine.

"I know," I whispered. "I missed you too."

His warm, gingerbread-colored eyes stared hard into mine. He seemed more bothered or hurt than usual. I was stubborn, always put up a fight, and he was trying to figure out why I was throwing in the towel so easily this time. My eyes felt hot thinking about everything. I'd been working extra hard at avoiding him. The last time we were together, I felt myself falling for him, and I panicked. Swiss swore that he was ready for me and a family, and that he'd tell my dad everything. He said he'd quit working for the family, get a regular job, and it'd be us. I was the one who got cold feet. I did what I had to do to move forward, and then I turned all my attention toward Javion, hoping he could erase Swiss's name off my heart. But Javion was only good for keeping my mind busy. All his kisses and caresses couldn't make my body stop yearning for Swiss. As long as Swiss was in the picture, my mind and my pussy would never align with the same guy.

I stared at the goose bumps rising along his chest. They matched the bumps that circled his dark nipples. "I'm kinda sort of in trouble," I told him.

He tilted my chin up with his thumb. The corner of his mouth quirked up into a half smile. "So I heard through the underground gossip line. Don't even worry about that bullshit. I'll handle it for you."

Chapter 44

The Fairer Sex Never Plays Fair

Now that that was taken care of, I could focus on another pressing matter. I pressed my hand against Swiss's chest, urging him backward into the dark living room. The contact from his bare skin radiated through my fingertips, down my wrists, and through my elbows. He pinned me back against the front door the second it closed. His lips rained kisses down the side of my neck. We were getting a semicool breeze through the window, but it wasn't enough to keep me from breaking into a sweat.

He peeled me out of my T-shirt, covering my skin with kisses as he went.

"It's a li'l humid in here. My AC on the fritz. That's what I've been working on," he said while unzipping my jeans.

"I know you're still good with those hands."

He kneeled to tug my jeans down over my hips, past my thighs. "I had to keep myself busy since you weren't around for me to feel on."

I tangled my fingers in his soft locks, tugging them just a little. "Are you too tired to work on this, or no?" I asked.

My jeans hit the floor. Swiss wrapped one of his hands around my neck. It wasn't enough to choke me, but it was just enough to make me want more of him. He'd come close to kissing me before backing away in the sweetest form of torture I'd ever experienced. I let him know how much I liked it by dragging my nails along his back.

He had a way of taking complete control of me whenever I was with him; my mind, my body, and my senses. His finger blazed a ridiculously slow trail of heat up my inner thigh. The pressure building in between my thighs was so much it was almost painful. He was slowly parting my lips, teasing me at first, letting his finger explore the soft, sensitive skin around my already throbbing lips. I was already wet and ready. Swiss growled when he felt it, returning his finger to my mouth so I could taste myself. He licked my lips as he shoved two fingers deep inside me, and I swear I almost exploded right there on the spot. Before I could get too close, he kneeled between my legs. I squirmed underneath the hot slickness of his tongue running up my inner thigh.

"You know I ain't never too tired for you," he answered.

His hands were in all the right places at the right time. He palmed my ass, squeezing each cheek in alternating rough circles. My hips moved with him, circling toward him. Swiss buried his face in between my legs. He inhaled a long, deep breath, letting me feel his nose and the air he was taking in brush against my most sensitive parts. When he exhaled, he groaned. And it was a long, hoarse, deep sound that said, *I missed you, and I want you,* all at the same time. It rumbled against my clit and sent ripples of feel-good up my body that shot all the way up to the hairs on top of my head.

My panties dug into my skin before giving away with a loud rip. My legs were already feeling shaky, and the nigga hadn't even touched me for real yet. The last time I came good and hard it was by my own hand. Swiss closed his eyes, rolling his tongue across my skin slow and steady. His tongue dipped into the liquid heat between my legs and the world stopped. Swiss slurped and sucked up my juices until I couldn't hear anything except the sound of him enjoying his meal. I could feel electric points of light at the roots of my hair. They surged down my spine, arching my back, ending at my feet and shooting out of the tips of my toes. This nigga was my tour guide as I rode the tip of his tongue. He dragged me closer to the edge, sucking my clit slow and steady before flicking it with his tongue. Before I could dive off the edge, Swiss stood. The heat from his hands scorched my skin. He palmed my ass, sliding me roughly up the length of his body.

I wrapped my legs around his waist, locking my ankles together behind him. He crushed my lips with his, and I kissed him back with the same fierceness that he gave me. He was just as long and hard as I remembered. Before my mind went completely blank, I couldn't help thinking briefly about how he'd spoil me, paying hundreds to get the best tables and the best seats whenever we'd go out. But this dick right here was the best seat in the world to me.

I don't remember falling asleep, but I drifted in and out through most of the night. It was muggy and Swiss's big-ass body was like a damn furnace. He had me tucked into his side with his arm draped across my bare hips, but as sweaty as I was, I was too comfortable to move. I'd had plenty of arms hold me, but none of them felt exactly right. Not like this did. *But* unlike every other time where I'd run back to Swiss with the hope that we'd work and be okay, I was coming to the realization that if I wanted to be happy with him, I'd have to do it in secret, or lose my father's respect.

The bed shifted. Swiss leaned over me, bracing himself on his elbow. He ran the tip of his finger over my eyebrows, tracing their shape. It was all good until he headed toward the tip of my nose, tickling me. I scrunched up my face, and we laughed as I tried to wiggle myself away. That got him growing hard and hot against the side of my thigh. I was trying to pick the perfect moment to ask him for help. Every minute I waited was a minute wasted. I'd gotten picked up when I was fourteen, so my prints were in the system. It wouldn't be long before I got found out. I reached down, giving him a soft good morning pat.

"Ahh, just because you're up, you think I wanna be up too?" I teased him.

"You the early bird. You know yo' ass was already up. Plus, I've got the best seat in the house right here waiting for you," he teased me back, placing kisses on my shoulders that led up to my lips.

I smiled at the nickname I'd given him from years ago. It was something I did with all of my boyfriends. In my opinion, naming a man's dick was like taking sole proprietor ownership of that bad-boy. Especially if he started calling it the name you gave it, you all but trademarked it.

Swiss leaned back, putting all his attention into plucking at a frayed thread on the sheet.

Something was on his mind. I didn't have to press him for details, though.

"How my sister been doin'? I mean, y'all really think she's gonna be all right with a . . . a . . ." Swiss was always hard to read. He was never one for showing his emotions. His face was blank, but the tone of his voice was distant and sincere.

My mouth opened and closed a few times. Loyalty to Shan made me clam up. She would have a fit if she knew where I was, let alone talking about her. But he'd never asked about them before. The least I could do was ease his mind.

"Shandy is gonna be fine. She has Momma to help her, so I'm guessing the two of them will make it work. Some chicks are made to be mommies." My voice caught in my throat. I turned away from him, focusing on the clumps of black dust piled along the edges of the ceiling fan blades. Yeah, Swiss and me always fell back into place, but not once had we ever talked about what displaced us to begin with. That was the bad part of the movie we both skipped over, because neither one of us wanted to watch it.

Swiss grabbed my hips, pulling me in close. His mango-lime-scented locks washed across my face, tickling my cheek. The fresh stubble on his chin was scratchy against my skin as he buried his face in my neck. My arms instinctively went around his broad back. I distracted myself, pretending my finger was a tattoo needle. I absentmindedly wrote my name over and over in his skin, hoping it would sink in and imprint on his heart the way his name was tagged all over mine.

"I am so sorry," Swiss's voice was muffled against the side of my neck.

My body stiffened, my finger stopped mid-O. I'd heard him, even though I didn't want to. Five years was a long time to wait for an apology. It never ceased to amaze me how my eyes could water just a little and drain every ounce of wetness from my mouth. He let me push him away from me. Tears that I didn't want to cry, that I shouldn't even have had, left, sliding down my cheeks. I dragged the sheet up toward my chin like a shield, glaring at him out of the corner of my eye.

Clenching my teeth against the tightness in my throat, I said what I'd practiced in my head over a million times for five years.

"Nigga, I was only eighteen, and you left me. I was pregnant and you—"

He reached for me, "I know what I—"

"Do not interrupt me!" I couldn't hold back anymore. I let go and reared up, slamming my fists into his chest, slapping his face. He could have stopped me, but he didn't. My nostrils flared wide, my eyes were glazed over from tears and years of things unsaid. I wore myself out and stopped to catch my breath. We both sat back on our knees, facing each other. Red handprints formed all over his chest and shoulders.

"You don't know *what* you did!" I screamed into his face, jabbing the tip of my nail into his stony cheek. "*I* had to find somewhere to go to get an abortion where nobody would know who I was. *I'm* the one who stays up at night wondering if I did the right or the wrong thing all because I was too scared to do it without you." I hopped to my feet, standing no farther than a breath away from him.

Swiss was so sick with guilt he couldn't even look me in my eyes. He should have been weighed down with all the guilt—the one wearing all the emotional scars, not me.

I clapped my palms together circling him. "You should have manned up and taken care of us. Nobody else. *You!*" I screamed in his face. My throat was raw from yelling, and I wanted to—I *needed* to make sure my words sank into his dumb head. I took a breath to calm myself down.

Ever since I was thirteen, I'd been training at commanding Daddy's soldiers. Yelling was the attention getter, but quiet storms raised fear; they were memorable. Ignoring my nakedness, I got down in front of Swiss, planting my elbows on my knees. I gave him the same disgusted look Daddy gave dudes when their count was off or they got caught trying to skim off the supply. He shifted in place, his eyes drifted from mine to the floor and back uncomfortably. His hood ass understood that shit.

I let out an exhausted chuckle.

After all these years, it was finally out there, hanging in the air mixing with the dust, our sweat, and the lingering smell of sex. I hated him for being a coward, and I hated myself just as much for still loving him. The air mattress hissed as I dropped back onto it, tired from venting. Swiss's shoulders slumped forward. He moved like gravity was working against him as he dropped down next to me.

"Don't . . ." I started to argue when I thought he was leaning in for a hug. He laid his head on my stomach, facing away from me. I stared at the top of his head in disgust. I wanted to fight this out. I didn't want to feel bad for making him relive his lowest moment.

I could feel cold, wet spots from his tears on my stomach, but I refused to acknowledge them. I'd cried an ocean and three rivers altogether. His fifteen crocodile tears wouldn't kill him.

"Now that we've finally aired out our issues, do you think we can do this for real this time?" he asked. "Sammie'll be good as new in a couple of days. He can get someone else to watch his back, and I can tell him that I'm in love with you."

My heart jumped up into my throat. I was still trying to process the whole list of shit we'd just thrown into the air. I wasn't ready for this kind of talk.

He finally turned to face me with this sad but hopeful look in his eyes. It made it hard for me to look at him.

"You know what I mean, Novie. Can we do *us*? Be together? All my boys got wives, and they on their first or second seed. I'm tired of these sometimes situations we stay having. I want this all the time. I want *us* all the time."

The sun filtered through the blinds, making long bright dashes across the shadowed parts of the room. Silvery flecks of dust whirled in the sunlight. I stopped staring off into space, turning my head toward him and angling my chin down. I was all of a sudden self-conscious about blowing my morning breath in his face. The man was a freak of nature. He never had dump-truck mouth in the morning, not even after a night of drinking. My breath would probably be like that too if I swore off red meat, junk food, and wine like he did. But none of that was happening, the same way I couldn't see us happening. Our past felt too cracked and too weird now.

We could never be like we were before. He'd admit it too, if he wasn't going through last-man-standing syndrome. All his friends were wifed up, so now he thinks he wants to be wifed up too. I tried to wrap my mind around the right words to say.

"Knock, knock, woman." He tapped his finger against my forehead. "All those thoughts you got goin' on up there right now, can you let me in on 'em, because that face of yours don't hide a thing?"

I cracked all of my toes twice before stretching my limbs one by one. Swiss flopped back onto his pillow with a sound that could've been a chuckle or an irritated snort.

"Why can't we just do this like we're doin' right now? Like we usually do? And if it works, it works," I blurted out.

"And if it doesn't work, we fix shit and work on it until we get it right? *Right?* Is that what you're saying?"

That wasn't what I was saying at all. That meant we'd technically be together, which I still wasn't sure about. Even though he was finally saying the right thing, he was saying it all the wrong way. I couldn't tell if this had anything to do with love or caring about me. I needed to know that he wasn't just tired of being the odd man out when it came to his friends. That I wasn't just his safety net.

I got up, making a big deal out of searching for my jeans to avoid his eyes.

"Yeah, something like that," I replied over my shoulder. I didn't want him to see the lie on my face as I gave him my walk-of-shame answer. I could only tell so much truth in one day. I'd have to find someone else to help me out. Swiss was too emotional and unpredictable. And here I thought I was the woman in the situation. Guess not.

I was walking toward the front door when it swung open so hard it bounced off the wall. A gloved hand reached in, stopping it before it could bounce closed.

My mind instantly jumped to the one time where Shandy and Denise made me marathon *Police Women of Broward County* with them. We watched eighteen episodes of fools running from the police, and now I understood why they did it. My fight-or-flight instinct kicked in, and the only option my brain kept giving me was to run. I knew clear as day that I didn't want to go to jail or prison.

Chapter 45

Woman to Woman

I knew that if I saw any part of the troop of officers that were outside waiting to swarm toward me, instinct would send me running for the hills. I, instead, went against everything I felt, and waited with my eyes shut and my hands raised to show I didn't have any weapons. I didn't want to take any chances at having the cops think I was any more of a threat than necessary. These days, it didn't seem to take a whole lot to get killed instead of apprehended.

My eyes snapped open at the dull thudding pain that shot through my left cheek. I caught her out of the corner of my eye drawing back for number two, and I sidestepped just in the nick of time. It was the same bitch who'd gone off on Javion earlier.

"I knew it! I goddamn knew it. I'm out here carrying your fuckin' baby, and you playin' me like a fuckin' idiot. Who the fuck is—"

The pause only lasted for a split second, but it was long enough for me to see that she'd recognized me too, and long enough for Swiss to get ahold of her arms. He pinned them down to her sides while I swallowed the words I was so tempted to yell. They settled in my stomach like a big rotten potato. *Swiss,* my Swiss, was the homeboy Javion was talking about. My Swiss had been messing around on me the whole time I stayed away, messing around on him.

If I decided to tell it, all the truth would fuck up this lie she was trying to keep up.

"Tinesha! Chill the fuck out. You are out of bounds right now," Swiss yelled down at her.

She was so short she had to be half midget or some shit. Javion I could kind of sort of see dealing with her, but not Swiss. I rubbed my jaw. It wasn't broken, and all my teeth felt intact, but I could taste my own blood, and that pissed me off. If this bitch fucked up my face, I'd fuck up her little midget ass.

A shadow filled the doorway. "Get your hands off my sister, nigga."

I turned toward the front door ready to square up, if need be. A taller version of Tinesha stepped in. They had the same bad sew-ins. She was bigger and meaner looking than her little sister, but that didn't matter to me. What did matter was the sight of the toddler perched on her hip. I'd tried to imagine Swiss as a baby plenty of times, but there was nothing like seeing his mini-me with everything from his eyes down to his chubby, fat feet. He couldn't deny that little boy if his life depended on it. His hair was braided in thick plaits that ended halfway down his back.

It felt like my lungs collapsed. Not only did he get this heffa pregnant, he already had a baby. And after all this time, he never bothered to tell me. Those were supposed to be our babies. I felt myself deflating as I stood there. The girl holding the baby gave me a disgruntled look with her nose scrunched up.

Swiss was still contending with his baby momma. "Tinesha, stop hittin' me. We ain't together and you know it, so stop with all this bullshit," he growled down at her.

"So we wasn't together when you was in my bed on Wednesday or Thursday night? We wasn't together when you fucked me Friday morning before you left my house?" she yelled.

I couldn't believe my ears or my life. How do two completely different niggas fuck the same ho and let me down in less than two days? And in that same time frame, I find out my daddy ain't shit either. Men ain't shit, I swear they ain't. I didn't even see any point in bursting Swiss's bubble and telling him Javion might be the baby's daddy. He would figure all that out in due time.

"Tinesha, I'm gonna go get Brandon's diaper bag. Li'l nigga smellin' ripe as hell right now," the sister announced from the doorway.

Nobody heard her except for me, and I hoped she'd take as long as Swiss needed to get her sister calm. There was no way I'd be able to fight her off. She looked like a one-hitter quitter.

"Fuckin' don't mean we together, nigga. We was both horny, and we handled that. I been told you about getting all in your feelings," Swiss told her.

Tinesha glared from Swiss, to me, and back again. She propped her hand on her hip, throwing her words around with as much venom and spite as she could.

"Okay, Mr. Tin-man. So this is the bitch who supposedly got your goddamn heart? All right. Let's see how bad she want that rinky-dink rusted motherfucka after I put that ass on child support. I'm gonna take all your fuckin' money," she spat at him before stomping toward the door. She gave me the ugliest, nastiest look. "Thank you for freein' me of this nigga," she spat at me. "You are more than welcome to wash his stank-ass boxers and clean the dirt from underneath his crusty-ass fingernails. And he gave me trichomoniasis, but that probably came from you anyway. I am so over this bullshit."

Tinesha stomped to the door toward the sound of her baby crying from somewhere outside.

"On your knees with your hands up. We've got the place surrounded." The amplified voice crackled through the loudspeaker. It penetrated the walls, pinging my eardrums, turning my heart into a lump in my chest.

I exchanged glances with Swiss before shaking my head at myself with my tongue in my cheek. These niggas were gonna be the end of me.

Chapter 46

Peter Piper Picked a Partner

Tinesha's sister stood by with a smug look on her face. It was fairly obvious that she'd gone outside to call the police. Who knows how many news stations my picture was probably broadcasted all over. An officer's hand roughly mashed the top of my head, shoving me down into the back of a squad car. The handcuffs cut into my wrists as I met Swiss's eyes through the window. He'd stopped arguing with Tinesha long enough to give me a pitiful look. His eyes said he was sorry, but I didn't need his apologies. It was pretty obvious who his loyalty was with.

One phone call home and my dad would have me out of this bullshit. The thought made me lift my chin ever so slightly. I was determined not to need him or anyone. They owed me for all the bullshit they'd put me through, and that would be a debt I'd never collect. They needed to regret their choices for the rest of their lives. I took slow, deep breaths to keep from crying. The back of the car smelled like Fritos, Claiborne for Men, and coffee breath. The smell turned my stomach. I hadn't killed anyone, but I knew this was the smell of my freedom slipping away.

The officers were huddled in front of the squad car. They were arguing over something. A few stomped away, arms swinging and all red in the face. It wasn't long before a Range Rover with dark-tinted windows rolled to a stop on the street a few feet away. Half the officers nodded respectfully, the other half spit at the feet of the man who climbed out of it. He said a few words to one of them. All eyes turned in my direction in the backseat. He casually walked over and opened the back door.

"You must be Novie," he said in a voice deeper and richer than hot caramel. "I hear you're in need of an attorney."

I couldn't believe my ears, but I didn't want to start thanking my lucky stars too soon. I eyeballed him up and down, taking in his tan flat-front slacks and the burnt-orange cashmere-silk vest peeking out from underneath his custom-tailored blazer.

"I might need one," I answered suspiciously. "The real question is whether I can afford one."

"They got you for a double homicide, right?" he asked casually, leaning with his foot propped up against the side of the car. He squinted up into the tiny bit of sun shining through the billowy clouds before turning his attention to Swiss and Tinesha arguing on the front porch. His cologne cut through the curry-scented hell I'd been sitting in. It was warm, peppery, and very masculine.

"A friend of mine called me and asked if I'd do this as a favor. I take it that you aren't the type to take handouts."

"I'm not. And I don't do that whole sex for favors mess, so you can keep it moving, if that's what you want." I made a big show out of sitting back hard against the seat. It hurt my wrists like all hell.

"Okay, Novie, one of my legal assistants hopped up and moved to New York without any notice. I've got a big workload and no time to go through the hiring process. I will pay you and take a small percentage to cover my expenses if you'd like to do it that way. Sound like a fair trade?"

The cuffs on my wrists were cutting off my circulation, sending pins and needles dancing through my fingertips. That shit sounded too good to be true, but it sounded a helluva lot better than working on the phones all day making cold calls to sell alarm systems. If all I had to do was sit in a stuffy office typing up memos to get myself out of this shit, then so be it.

"You have a deal," I stated in a firm voice.

"Looks like you picked a good day to start a new career," he announced with a grin.

I tried not to, but I couldn't help staring at him as he moved past me to address the officers. Attorneys didn't move like that, like predators. They thought like them all day, but Genesis seemed powerful and dangerous. He moved with purpose in confident, smooth strides. Like a tall, Guilty-by-Gucci-smelling panther. *Mmmmph.*

I was surprised when I was un-cuffed and released.

"Sorry for the confusion, ma'am. You're free to go," the officer stated.

The lawyer rocked back on his heels, clasping his hands behind his back. He flashed me a bright smug smile.

I rubbed my wrists to get my circulation back. My eyes traced the shape of his lips, curiously following the thin, jagged scar. It twisted the tip of his full upper lip into a tiny sneer that faded where his mustache ended beneath his aristocratic nose. Now *that* is a man. I tugged the tip of my tongue between my teeth. *Okay, Screw Face,* I thought, tilting my head to the side slightly interested. My stomach did high-speed somersaults at the idea of showing him my screw face. *Mmmph. Know my ass needs to stop. Javion would try to snap him into four pieces with one hand.*

"Okay, wait, hold on. Is that it?" I asked him quietly so the officers wouldn't overhear me. "You say a few words, and we're all done here?"

"Yeah, you are free and clear, and you'll need to be at work tomorrow. We start at eight thirty."

He handed me a crisp white business card. Gold embossed letters spelled out "Genesis Kane, Attorney-at-Law." It was the same card Momma had given me with the office address and his contact information listed beneath it. Well, shit, Momma must've had someone call in a serious favor, because my luck was never this good. I blessed him with a bright smile. Let that nigga be jealous for a change. My ass was over being the caring one.

GENESIS

Chapter 47

Girls, Girls, Girls, Girls

My steps were a little heavier as I walked into the office the next morning. No one knew exactly what went down at the Twenty-third Street Precinct, but the word was getting out about Javion and his boys. Even without his sister around, Javion was still making a name for himself, and for me as well. You can't have a station full of cops go down, and I be the only lawyer who walks out. It left a bitter taste in my mouth, not to mention the tension I was getting outside of the office. I went to help out this Novie girl, not knowing if I was going to get shot or locked up in the process. Hopefully, she'd be better in the office than the last assistant I'd hired on a lookout. If I said it once, I'd say it again . . . I hate favors.

Work was usually my personal sanctuary from the world outside. The entire building was made out of this sunglasses-dark tinted glass. You could never tell if it was sunny, gloomy, cloudy, or raining. It always smelled like the inside of an expensive car dealership. Like soft leather, Colombian coffee, and frigid, filtered air.

I stood in the hallway, staring at the empty space beside the sleek black ampersand on the marble wall. When I signed those papers, it'd say "Schaefer, Brockman & Kane." Brockman was a silent partner that I'm almost certain didn't exist. I gave myself a mental pat on the back as I shoved my hands deep into the pockets of my fireplace-ash-colored Van Heusen slacks. The key fob to my new company car sat heavy on the inside. It unlocked a fully loaded Audi A8 parked in my very own personal parking spot. Paula was slicker than I thought. She'd already had it delivered and waiting for me.

I was still excited despite the gloomy circumstances. Five years ago, a nigga like me would've needed a lawyer before I would've become one. I didn't care about shit like slacks or attorney meet-n-greet golf outings. And I for damn sure didn't know the difference between a fairway wood and a hybrid, any more than I knew the difference between the Aventador and the Murciélago. None of that shit mattered to me back then, but the old me was dead.

"You should be proud. You've earned it." Paula came sailing toward me in a ruby-red pantsuit. Her Skippy-glow was on ten this morning. That's when a woman tans so much, her skin looks peanut butter brown all year-round. It always made me think of Skippy Peanut Butter, and crave a PB&J.

I tilted my head in greeting to one of the legal assistants passing by as Paula gave me an awkward *we-not-fuckin'* pat on the back before nodding toward her own name on the wall.

"I can't believe you're young enough to be my son and I'm making you partner," she joked, displaying perfectly straight Chicklet-sized pearl-white teeth. She was ageist to the core. Paula broke out into hives if you put her in the same room with anyone over the age of fifty-five. And she'd slit you open, bathe in your blood, and eat your spleen without flinching if someone told her it'd take five years off her face.

"I don't know if that's a compliment or a complaint, but I'm a conceited man, so thank you," I answered.

"Ah . . . well, we've been soooo very . . . um . . . busy earlier that I forgot to say thank you for filling in at that symposium last month. As much as I hate going to Catalina with my husband, I hate speaking at those fucking things even more," Paula chuckled.

"Not a problem. *Anything for a partner,* right?" I asked, giving Paula a wink. Those were her exact words to me when she needed my help making a rape charge discreetly disappear from Kharter, her oldest son's, record a few months back. He was home from Harvard and didn't know how to handle rejection from a bagger at a grocery store he thought was gay. Kharter stalked him and followed him home from work. Broke both of his arms and the guy's nose before he raped him. A charge like that would've put a blemish on the family's smudge-proof image. As much as that gay shit repulsed me, I fixed it, with Squatton's help.

Paula gave me an appreciative smile. She tapped the manila folder tucked under her arm. "I just need your Johnson . . . err, umm, your John Hancock. I need your signature—"

"Genesis Kane, my mothafuckin' ass!"

Paula and I both turned toward the sound of a woman screaming at the top of her lungs in the main lobby.

"Tell that fake-ass, dead-beat, lyin'-ass nigga to come out here!"

Not today of all the fucking days. The corners of my mouth turned down. I suddenly found myself preoccupied, straightening my Burberry cuff links as my mind zipped through a Rolodex of voices. As familiar as she sounded, I couldn't place that voice to any of my current sidepieces. No one in their right mind would come up in my place of business acting like that.

"I'm going to ask you to leave before I have you removed."

I could already hear Tangie, my no-nonsense body-guard-secretary corralling the woman out of the building.

Paula's finely arched, pale yellow eyebrow made its way up to the top of her botoxed forehead. "Um, is there a problem, Genesis? I hope we haven't misgauged your fit here at Schaefer and Brockman?"

My nostrils flared. I'd worked too damn hard, put my dick at risk popping too many Viagra, and put in too many real labor hours for someone to unravel it all in seconds. Paula was the only decision maker, like most of that "we" shit that came out when the legion of voices in her estrogen-powered brain was irritated.

I cracked the stiff joints in my neck left, then right. The lobby had grown quiet, but there was a storm of unspoken tension beating up the air between us.

I blessed Paula with an award-winning, bullshit, fake-as-fuck smile. "Not at all, partner. Maybe *I* misgauged some good cognac and bad company, but that was a long time ago. *Absence* makes the *heart* grow jealous . . . You know how that goes. It won't be happening again."

I straightened the lapels on my jacket, knowing good and well that I hadn't misgauged shit. My boy Foreign rounded the corner as I was about to make my way to the lobby. We stopped shoulder to shoulder. I checked the corridors to make sure none of the legal assistants or admins were out or within hearing distance before approaching him.

"Who the fuck was that?" I asked in an anxious whisper.

"Hell if I know. Tangie got her teeth into her before I got out there. But you been holding out on me, man?" he asked, punching me in the arm. "When did you build up the stable? But take a lesson from the master. You need to keep them in their place or *put them down* when they act like that."

Foreign gave me a serious, pointed stare. "Wait, did you get another one of those fucking bloody heart things?"

I looked away, disgusted with myself for telling him about it in the first place. Even though he was my boy, sometimes he didn't know when to let something go.

Foreign slapped his palms against his forehead. "Oh, fuck me. Do you think that was her?"

"Look, I'll take care of it, Foreign. It'll get it handled one way or another." I began making my way toward my office, signaling the end of the conversation. "Oh, and I've finally got a new legal assistant . . . to replace the last one. It's starting to get tedious retraining a girl every time we lose one, so this one is *off-limits*," I warned him.

Foreign grinned from ear to ear. "Off-limits to who? Me or *you*, playboy?" He aimed his index fingers at me like two pistols. "It's all good. I'm gonna be busy doing you a solid, taking care of your crazy lobby bitch problem. Tell Chief we about to go hunt us a wabbit."

I ran my teeth across my bottom lip. There's always some-body somewhere warning a nigga, telling him to watch what he does and who he brings up when he makes it. I put my boys Chief and Foreign on as private investigators. Now not only was I responsible for the trouble my dick got me into, but I had to account for their dicks too.

I had a better idea for a project to keep Foreign from terrorizing my staff.

"Foreign, find Chief. There's a missing girl I need you to find. Saniah Sutton. She'd mentioned something about Sammie Knox. You might want to see what you can find there first."

Chapter 48

Mue Make Your Money

I dressed in the most legal-looking outfit I owned. High-waisted black slacks with some suspenders and a button-down blouse, completed with a pair of black heels made up my outfit. I arrived at Genesis's office on H Street. It was busy this time of morning, especially during the week. You had to keep it moving or get bum-rushed by homeless folk and con artists begging for money. I pushed my way through a group of guys in suits and sunglasses marching toward the Metro, clutching their briefcases.

Both Swiss and Javion had been blowing my phone up all night, but my only focus right now was impressing Mr. Kane on this new job I'd landed. Every fifteen minutes or so, another text would come through. Javion had a million questions about where I was, what I was doing, and were we cool. Swiss was apologizing, begging for my forgiveness and understanding. The only thing they had in common is that they were both sorry as fuck.

I pulled my hair back into a tight bun, leaving a little out in the front for a small bang. I stopped to use the side mirror of a car on the street to check my face before I went in. Turning my head from side to side, I admired my almond-brown skin. My hair framed my heart-shaped face, accenting my high cheekbones that were so much like Momma's. Lip gloss made my already full lips look a little too full, not a good look for the office, so I grabbed my Burt's Bees honey lip balm. My nerves had been all bunched up between my throat and my stomach all morning. I'd been doing everything from meditating to chanting. I even tried tantric breathing, and I think you're supposed to be having sex when you do that. It took a shot of Henny with a Listerine chaser and coffee before I was able to get myself dressed.

Aside from the one summer where I'd volunteered at the YMCA in high school, I'd never worked in an office. The few jobs I had worked were retail. Shandy was gonna stay at the house with Momma for a little while, so I had the apartment all to myself, and the silence I usually craved was driving me crazy. I'd googled, binged, pinged, and tinged every fact I could find about the legal business. I even watched every show on Netflix, Hulu, and Vudu that had a lawyer in it.

The office building was the only bronzed glass building on a street full of concrete giants. I was outside the front entrance trying to calm myself down. I went statue-still with my hand barely on the handle, watching the woman go off in the lobby. She was four-foot nothing, wearing a black pencil skirt and gold blouse that flared at the wrists. I had enough sense to step back out of the doorway. Sure enough, her little heated ass came tumbling out in a blast of cool air. She stood there, facing the building with her mouth balled up and her hands folded in front of her like she was expecting Genesis to just come out to see her.

"What the fuck you staring at?" she snapped, without turning to look in my direction.

"Um, I'm not trying to get all up in your business, but did I hear you say Genesis Kane was a liar? I mean, he's lawyer, so, hey. But the thing is, I kind of work here now and I just wanted to know—"

"That sounds an awful lot like a question somebody trying to get all up in my business would ask," she replied with a smirk.

There were malicious flames in her eyes as she came toward me, jabbing the air, swinging some kind of gold medal.

"Look, *I'm* not crazy. *I know my husband.* He likes to play his little games, but I ain't playing. So you go up in there and you let that bitch-ass nigga know Tima said"—she slapped her open palm against her chest—"I will pull up every brick in this city to bury his ass. Eye for an eye, G for a G."

The look Tima gave me before she hopped in her illegally parked Hyundai Genesis was so spiteful and dead-ass serious, you'd have thought I did something to her little mean ass. Yeah, I'd give Genesis the message from LDYG4EV, according to her custom plates. She looked a little Genesis-crazy to me. *Who goes to work and almost gets beat down by the boss's psycho ex-whatever on the first day?* That's got to earn me some brownie points or something.

When I finally got the horse's hooves to stop pounding through my chest, I walked in and started my first day of work.

The double glass doors opened soundlessly as I walked into what looked more like a high-end boutique, rather than an attorney's office. If this nigga didn't tell me that he had a decorator come in, then he was definitely going on my gay list. The lobby consisted of two blocky, cream-colored sofas. In between them sat a rectangular glass table with yellow and white candles on glass stands. Earthy green eucalyptus trees were placed in different places throughout the lobby.

I followed the walkway that was lined on either side with crystal clear glass windows and drawn white blinds.

An older lady ran up on me from around a corner.

"You must be our newbie," she said. "Ms. Deleon, I presume?"

"Yes, but you can call me Novie."

Even though I was nervous as hell, I gave her a bright smile, which the heffa didn't even bother returning. She actually rolled her eyes, spinning on her high goldfish-orange heels to go back in the direction she came from.

"I'm Tangie. Kane is expecting you. And you're late," she called out pointing up at a large glass clock on the wall that read 8:35. "Your attendance is tracked. It determines whether you will continue on with this firm. Eight occurrences means termination. One to fifteen minutes late and that is a quarter of an occurrence. A missed workday equals one full occurrence."

I pulled out my cell as the numbers changed from 8:29 to 8:30 on the screen. If this was what I had to look forward to, this job was already looking like bad news.

I was marched past a small open area with five desks, all with identical staplers, tape dispensers, and inboxes. Four of them were occupied. I assumed the one on the end was to be mine.

Tangie gave me a brief drive-by introduction. "That's Robert, Bobby, Beau, and Mavis."

No one looked up. They sat with their faces buried in their wireless monitors. Genesis's office was around the corner. The doorway was built into a large wall.

"Nice to see you again," Genesis announced with a genuine smile.

He looked just as good as I remembered, and smelled even better. After Tangie was dismissed, I took a seat in front of his desk. He had an edgy but intelligently sophisticated look. Like he could roll a blunt, discuss world politics and investing, all while sipping Cognac over ice. His eyes roved over me a few times, making me squirm uneasily in my seat.

"The office gets a little stuffy. Let's take a quick walk," he said.

Genesis began walking in the direction of Chinatown. "You'll be helping me by going over my documents for cases and making sure my *I*s are dotted and my *T*s are crossed," he said. "I give bonuses for every case we win, and most of my clients are people you'll recognize from television or movies."

My phone whistled from somewhere in my purse, but whoever it was would have to wait. Opportunities like this didn't just pop up every day for someone who was homeschooled by drug traffickers. I'd learned math measuring harvest bales. Daddy was so obsessed with knowing the laws just so he could break them, he had stacks of law books and encyclopedias worth thousands. He didn't believe in doing anything on the computer, so I studied those things old school with a pen, paper, and a dictionary.

I had to hit the sidewalk double time to keep up with Genesis.

The armpits of my button-down were getting damp. Trying to stay side by side with Genesis had me feeling like I could barely talk. "I was at that house, but I didn't kill anyone," I told him. "I'm just wondering if I'm qualified for the caliber of work that you do," I answered in between breaths.

Genesis slammed to a stop.

"Swiss is one of my best guys. When he said he had an old friend that needed my help, I didn't question him. But I need to know the particulars," he said in a perfectly normal I-jog-or-do-extreme-cardio speaking voice.

The comment he'd made caught me completely off guard. *Why would Swiss be some lawyer's best guy, when he was already Daddy's guy?*

"Were you sleeping with him?" he asked.

I probably gave myself away when I couldn't look him in the eye, but I wasn't about to own up to it.

"I don't know why that matters," I said breathlessly.

A small smile tugged at the corners of my lips. So, Swiss had actually helped me out this time. He hadn't left me out there to fend for myself like I'd thought. Maybe he was worth keeping. But if it wasn't for his aggravating baby momma and her sister, I wouldn't have needed Genesis's help to begin with.

"Novie, last year I kept Swiss out of prison at least a dozen times. But he kept it one hundred with me on all sides. I just need to know if my go-to guy has some conflicting drama that might affect his work here. His son's mother is already a handful; she'd send that nigga away for life if someone so much as offered to pay off her payday loans."

I shook my head, still trying to catch my breath. "No, I'm not messin' with him. But I don't think who I *do* or *don't* sleep with is any business of yours." My tone was a little snippier than I intended, but it was only because he was irritating me. It really wasn't any of his business what I or Swiss did, even if he was in the business of saving people's asses from prison.

Since he wanted to be all up in my personal business, I took it as a good time to share some of his.

"Tima, she said she was your wife. She said she's gonna kill you," I blurted out without warning.

Something flashed behind Genesis's bright golden-brown eyes. Distrust, or maybe even anger. But it was there, and then it was gone.

"My *what?*" he asked like he'd suddenly forgotten how to speak English.

"I ran into her on my way in. Not sure what it's all about, but she was not happy with you. She actually said she'd pull up every brick in the city and bury you, G for a G. I think I got that right. I probably should've taken notes or something."

Genesis clasped his hands behind his back. I was certain that I'd let my damn mouth talk me out of a good thing.

"A good attorney always has a good argument." He admitted this with a smug smile curving his lips. "I can already see that you lose your mask when your feathers get ruffled. We'll have to work on that. But Tima was someone I dated who couldn't handle it when I didn't want to date anymore. That's it."

Before I could ask what that meant, he draped his arm across my shoulder in that macho way men do their home-boys when they agree to disagree and be cool. God, he smelled like cedar and spicy pink pepper, like he'd just gotten out of the shower.

"I honestly think you'd be an asset to any firm out here. You didn't break under pressure. I need a new source of inspiration. A new muse. I'd rather have someone like you on the team than working against it."

Relief surged through me. I even felt a little conceit coming on at being called a muse. That was a new one. I'd never considered myself a man's key to success, but I'd take it.

"Also, I prefer yellow Post-its. Fine-point pen in black when things can't be typed up, and you need better clothes. Attention to detail is one of my pet peeves. C'mon," he directed, nodding toward the Macy's across the street. "We've got an eleven a.m. with Farrah Harper. You can't meet her dressed like that."

Well, damn, I knew my wardrobe needed a little updating, but was it that obvious? I thought I looked decent enough. Probably should've spent more time hitting it with the iron, but it still wasn't bad.

Genesis placed his hand at the small of my back, nudging me forward. *Damn, I didn't even get to sit behind my desk or ask if I had benefits, and this nigga was all in my business knocking my clothes? What's gonna be next?* All these specifications and minute stipulations were making me apprehensive. But it's not like he ran one of those dime-a-dozen e-businesses. It was time to step my game up. All of it.

***

After hauling out close to $3,000 in pencil skirts and button-down blouses, we were finally on our way to meet Farrah. Genesis had surprised and impressed me by picking out some of the hottest combinations in life. That man was more than welcome to dress me whenever and in whatever he wanted to, especially if he was footing the bill.

I'd changed into a Mediterranean Sea-colored skirt with a fitted sleeveless silk blouse in bright coral pink with blue splashes. Even my pumps were on point. They were covered in what looked like wet paint splatters in the same colors as my skirt and top. I don't know why I'd always been so scared to try something other than black or grey. If Shandy could've seen me, she would've oooh'd herself to death because I was "snatched to the gods," as I'd heard her say. I even got a nod of approval from Genesis, with his overcritical self.

We pulled up in front of Farrah's office building ten minutes early. I checked my texts while we waited. Genesis synced his schedule with the office while listening to Drake's new album. It seemed out of place. He didn't come across to me as a hip-hop head, but who was I to judge.

Swiss called four times before he finally texted, saying it was over with Tinesha. He wanted to know if we could do dinner. Reluctantly, I agreed.

I massaged my fingers against my left temple in small circles. We weren't even a day into seeing each other again, and he came with what felt like five years' worth of drama. Call me a glutton for punishment, but now that Swiss was all *into me,* I really wasn't sure if I was feeling him. The *oomph* was gone. The thought of him didn't get me excited, scared, or nervous. Thinking about him actually felt draining. Before, it was like gambling. I never knew if I'd beat the house or lose everything. Now, with it all laid out in front of me, I wanted to look at other options. I needed to make some side-by-side comparisons.

"You should wear blue and coral a lot more. Softer colors work with your skin."

I jumped at the sound of Genesis's voice. I was so lost in my head, I'd forgotten he was even in the car.

"They did a study," he went on. "Brighter colors are supposed to make you look friendlier, more likeable. It really works." He tugged at the orange and lavender bow tie around his neck as if he was proving a point.

He seemed so content and pleased with himself. I'd swear I was sitting next to my daddy if I didn't know better. Whenever he had to show me why his way worked better, he'd have that same cocky, what-did-I-tell-you expression.

Worry lines creased my forehead as I picked at the hem of my skirt, like the material was suddenly not good enough for me. I wasn't even about to let Genesis feel like Father Superior. "I don't know if peacocking's for me. You know, looking bright and flashy so I'm likeable to all the other birds isn't really my style. Black is subtle, and it's always in. I'm gonna have to think about all this frilly, pinky, girly stuff," I teased him.

Genesis gave me a tight nod. "Whatever works for you, then. I'm just an ordinary nigga with an extraordinarily successful multimillion-dollar law firm who deals with successful women all day. What would I know about aesthetics or styling?" He turned to stare out the window.

And so we entered into the silent, stare-out-the-window portion of the drive.

The car rolled to a stop. Genesis rubbed his hands together, clapping as the chauffeur walked around to open the door.

"Game time, Novie. You ready to do the damn thing? I already know you are. Let's get it."

He didn't wait for an answer and was out of the car before I could blink. His sour or irritated mood at my comment about the clothes was gone just as fast.

And I could see why, as a white silk-draped tornado spun out of the house before we could get to the first step. She pulled Genesis in for a tight, intimate hug, letting him know that her sister, Farrah, had to step out, but *he* was welcome to come inside and wait. I didn't miss her emphasis on the words *you* can come in either. Genesis's rushed instructions for the driver to take me back to the office let me know exactly what was up with that.

NOVIE

Chapter 49

Amu$ement$ Can Make That Money Too

I sat in bumper-to-bumper traffic with my new clothes piled high in the backseat. You can't tell me there isn't something in car exhaust that causes amnesia. I swear, every evening I'd see the reason why I should be taking the Metro, and then that shit would be long forgotten by the next morning. By the time I got to my overcrowded apartment complex, I was dead-ass tired.

Denise was standing behind her car in her parking spot next to mine as I pulled up. She yanked my door open before I even had a chance to put the car in park.

"Heather is gonna kill me, put me in a shallow grave, and dig me up so she can kill me all over again!"

"Aww, hell, what did you do?"

"I can't find Hennessey nowhere! I was counting when that nigga Stephen called to smooth shit over. I swear I was only on the phone for like five minutes. Maybe ten minutes, I don't know, but it wasn't that long."

She threw her hands up in frustration.

"Um, have you been day-drinking without me? And when did the liquor store stop selling Hennessey?"

Denise rolled her eyes and stomped her foot. "No, woman, I lost Heather's daughter!"

Both of my eyebrows shot up to the top of my forehead. I didn't know Heather had a daughter, and I know she couldn't have entrusted Denise with a live, little person. She could kill a fake plant. And, yes, fake plants can die. Try not dusting one for a whole year and you'll be burying it in your trash can.

I took a deep breath for both of us. "Okay, calm down. What's her name, and what does she look like?"

"Hennessey, um, she's short. She had on a pink tank top and shorts. Or, shit, I think it was a purple T-shirt and a jean skirt," Denise stammered. "Hell, I don't know. I've been babysitting a five-year-old blur. That little nigga don't stay still for shit. *Hennessey!*" she shouted through the parking lot.

I put my hands on her shoulders to get her focused attention.

"Dee, did you drink Hennessey today, or am I really about to look like a stoned up alchie walkin' around here yellin' for some Cognac?"

"Her name is Hennessey! She's a little yellow thing with funky-colored eyes. Lawd, I don't even remember what her hair is like. What if the police want me to do a little sketch with one of those murder artists? I've gotta call Heather. No, I can't. I cannot tell that girl I lost her baby. This is what happens when you pop molly with a white girl. You get fucked in the ass by your girlfriend's boy-boo and you lose kids and—"

"Y'all did *what?* You can tell me about that later. We've got to make moves. If she was snatched up, we need an Amber Alert, the police need to know, and so does her momma. You're a hundred percent positive she isn't in the house?"

"She's not in there. We got locked out when I was going to check the mail. I left my keys somewhere in the house. We were just gonna play hide-and-seek until you or the maintenance man showed up."

I pulled out my phone. It was time to call in some help before we waited too long and lost all chances of finding Heather's daughter.

"Oh, shit, oh, shit!" Tears rolled down Denise's cheeks.

She held her phone up, shaking it extra close to my face. Heather's picture was bright on the screen. I snatched the phone from her hand.

"Hey, Heather, this is Novie. We' have a little teensy tiny problem. We lost Hennessey playing hide-and-seek."

Denise was staring hard in my face, biting the tip of her fingernail. I put the phone on speaker so she could hear.

Heather sighed into the phone. "Novie, are you guys indoors or outdoors?" she asked. She didn't sound the least bit worried about the fact that we'd lost her little girl.

"We're outside in the parking lot right now," I answered.

"Is Dee's car there?" Heather asked impatiently.

Denise and I both turned to look at her little red Nissan Sentra parked beside us. Unless Hennessey could fit up under the seats, she wasn't in there.

"Yes, it's here," I answered her. "But—"

"I've told that little girl *a thousand* frickin' times . . ." Heather mumbled under her breath before answering. "Novie, go tap on the trunk of the car."

I raised my eyebrows at Dee and did as I was told. I walked to the back of her car, tapped three times with my ear near the trunk like I was thumping a damn watermelon. We both jumped back when the trunk flew open with a burst of giggles. Hennessey popped up, holding Denise's keys in her hand.

"Little girl!" Heather yelled through the phone. "You are getting the business when I get off work. You'll stand in the corner until your legs fall off. Do you hear me?"

Hennessey's June bug bright green eyes filled with tears. Her expression dropped. She let out a tiny, pitiful, "Yes."

I apologized to Heather. Denise helped Hennessey out of the trunk. I rolled my eyes to the sky and back. In the event we'd had to get the police involved, she would've had us all jacked up. This little girl had on a yellow shirt with blue jeans. How she got pink or blue from that beats me.

An hour later I was standing in the Denise's kitchen, me in my fuzzy house pants and my favorite Duke T-shirt, and Denise in a blue adult onesie with bunny ears, like the weirdo she was. Hennessey had gone to bed right after dinner as punishment. Denise poured overflowing shots of apple Crown Royal for us both. We were on our third round.

"I hope this whole babysitting thing isn't about to become a habit," I told her.

"Girl, my babysitting days *and* my Molly days are over. I'm not made for this kind of shit. I swear, if Heather didn't lick me like a—"

I held my hand up for her to stop right there. "Eeew, too much information. I don't want to hear about any of that." I lowered my voice so the little ears in the other room wouldn't pick up on my convo. "Tell me about all this nasty shit that you're into all of a sudden."

Denise gave me a serious look. Well, as serious as she could in her onesie.

"Heather works hard for her paychecks, and she parties harder. Novie, she has niggas who will bow down and be our table while we eat. They be down there the whole time we're eatin' dinner or whatever. White, black, Asian. These niggas like that shit, and Novie," she put one hand over her heart and raised the other like she was swearing on a Bible, "Hand to the sky, no lie. They pay her money—money, TVs, she even gets that green crack. We got some medicinal shit called Padussy from this one nigga, and I swear the blunt fucked me because I was knocked out."

"You can officially never say a word about anything I do. Y'all some freaks."

Denise stuck her tongue out and bounced her shoulders. "We some paid freaks, though. You are more than welcome to come work with us. I'd cut you in at fifteen percent of my fifty. You don't smoke or pop pills, so you can help deflect dicks from goin' up my butt when I'm lit."

Laughing, I flung a grape across the kitchen table. It bounced right off that heffa's forehead.

"I will *pay you* fifteen percent if I can avoid having to see any part of what I just visualized in my head in real life," I choked out between chuckles.

"Novie, I swear if you could see some of the men and women we fuck with, you'd stop laughing and climb onboard the butt-hole bandit wagon. They be finer than sugar."

When we finally stopped talking about Denise's sexcapades, I gave her a rundown of my first day at work.

"Well, at least this Genesis Kane is startin' off on the right foot," Denise said with a satisfied nod. "Do we need to run him through the little daddy-database before you decide to hop all up in his bed? Heather can probably see some shit in the computer. You know the DMV got all kinds of records on niggas these days."

"Girl, no, I don't need y'all to look into or look up anything," I told her.

As tempting as it sounded, I wasn't about to be one of those women who damn near stalked every man that came into her life. Even though it did sound like it would save me a ton of time by weeding out the no-good idiots early.

"So, hypothetically, if she was gonna look, umm, what alls would she be able to see?" I asked before shaking my head. That was the liquor talking, not me. "See how you be tryin' to start shit? That right there's the reason why I don't tell you anything," I scolded her.

We took our shots while my phone almost buzzed itself off the table.

"Awww, is baby J callin' to apologize?" Denise asked, while reaching for my phone.

I snatched it up before she could get to it, taking off in the direction of the bathroom.

"Hello?" I answered as I eased the door closed.

"Novie?"

I leaned back against my bedroom door, pissed that I'd even bothered to answer.

"Hey, Momma. What's up?" I asked.

"Look, some guys have been asking about your daddy. I already heard you're working in that office, so what have you found out?"

"Today was just my first day. There isn't much that I can do in a day."

"Well, I need you to hurry up. Something's going on, and it doesn't feel right." Her voice was whisper soft.

"When I have something, you will too. I can't rush in and mess up, or I'll get thrown out."

Not to mention I wouldn't get to hang around Genesis's fine ass either. I hung up before she could say anything else.

I was lost in my thoughts when the phone rang, flashing Genesis K.

What could he possibly want?

Bad enough I was a little tipsy. If he was about to give me some shit to do in the morning, I'd need to focus.

"Novie, I'm on my way to pick you up. We need to head over to Farrah's," he ordered.

I giggled into the phone. "Good evening to you too, Mr. Boss Man. I thought I was off the clock, so I was doin' grown-up shit, like drinking. I can't go."

"Can you name any other job where you get paid to party?" he asked.

"Umm, party planner, club promoter, DJ, liquor repr—"

"That was a hypothetical question, Rainman. Get dressed. Put on that Rimondi cocktail dress we picked out, the red one. It'll be perfect."

Chapter 50

Cinderella Dressed in Yella

Genesis gave me the evil eye while his chauffeur opened the door for me to get in. We needed to get one thing straight up front. My mother and father were not here. The last time I checked, I was very capable of dressing myself. To prove my point, I'd purposefully put on a canary-yellow dress with a low dipping neckline and plunging back. It was about a year old, but it still fit just right, hugging my hips, accenting my mermaid frame.

He chuckled as I adjusted myself in the seat beside him.

"Interesting choice," he stated dryly.

"Thank you. This felt like me, like it'd be more comfortable," I told him in a sarcastically chipper voice.

I knew I was doing too much. Trying to hide my nervousness made me feel even more clumsy and nervous. My clutch tipped over in the seat between Genesis and me. Lip gloss, loose change, and an emergency cigarette spilled over the leather seat. Genesis reached down and picked up the cigarette.

"You didn't strike me as a smoker. That shit's nasty."

He tossed it out the window without any thought. I considered diving out the back door and hitting the cement rolling at sixty miles per hour just to get it back. So what if he thought it was nasty. It wasn't his place to decide what I'd do with my body or my habits.

We made the rest of the drive from my place to Farrah's in silence. My eyes were glued to the window. I was silently pouting, pissed that he threw away my last smoke. *Who does that? Who the fuck does that?*

Now that I didn't have one, I was sure I'd need it. We rolled to a stop in front of a place called Fuerté. The building was made to look like a miniversion of the Roman Coliseum where the gladiators fought. It even had the crumbled part where half the upper wall on one side had fallen away. I'd seen it on E! and heard about it on *TMZ*. They had all these superstar chefs, and only the best of the best are there. Regular people had to spend at least a thousand just to get a table, when celebrities and all the beautiful people got in and dined for damn near free.

Red carpets and paparazzi lined the walkway in front of the restaurant that also doubled as a lounge. Men and women stopped to pose, flashing teeth almost as bright as the cameras flashing around them. Others rushed toward the limo-black tinted doors to get in as quickly as possible without being photographed.

I noticed everyone walking in was dressed in various shades of red and burgundy. Genesis smirked down at me as he helped me out of the car.

"If you're colorblind, I can have a stylist come to you from now on if it'd help. Red seems to be the color of the year, so there will be more Red Parties. Otherwise, just go with my selections," Genesis said.

He adjusted the red vest underneath his tux and straightened the matching red bow tie at his neck. If I could choke him with that bow tie I would have. I stood out like a poorly dressed thumb in my dress that was the wrong color and several seasons too old. At least my face matched the theme of the night since I turned about thirty-five shades of red from embarrassment.

Genesis made introductions to a few of the people who were walking in with us. A few men stopped to watch me walk past while the guys with dates snuck peeks at me out of the corner of their eye. I plastered my best smile on my face, deciding to make the best of an embarrassing situation. All the nigga had to do was tell me that the party had a color theme. That would have made a lot more sense than just ordering me to wear a certain dress.

My irritation at Genesis slipped my mind once we got inside the building. The lights were so dim they might as well have been turned off. All of the booths lined up along the walls with silk red draperies that could be untied for privacy. Some of the booths had tables, others had chaise lounges in front of cozy fireplaces with hot pink and purple electric flames.

Loud, trancelike music thumped in my ears. I fought against the urge to reach out and touch a giant metal lotus blossom. It was almost as tall as me sitting in the middle of the room with real flames shooting out of the center. A naked man slowly walked past, making me gasp when I realized he was covered in flames from the neck down. I could see other flaming men and women moving carefully through the crowd.

"He's covered in a special kind of gel," Genesis spoke into my ear. "We had to bring it in from Taiwan. It's illegal, but legalities don't stop us from getting whatever we want."

Someone mentioned how Farrah had gone in for tonight's party; she'd spent close to a million. Shit, the last thing I'd do with a million dollars was set some people on fire. I was staring hard, trying to figure out what the lotus flowers were made of when someone caught my eye through the flames on the other side of the room. *Swiss*. What the hell was he doing here? He winked at me through the flicker of the flames. He'd pulled his locks up on top of his head in a tight ball. He looked good enough to eat and ride.

I still hadn't forgotten that he'd gone and had a baby with another bitch, but it's not like we were together. Holding that against him would have been similar to him holding Javion against me. Life happened, and he just so happened to have made life in the process.

"Novie, this is Farrah Harper," Genesis interrupted.

I managed to pull my eyes away from Swiss to meet Farrah.

"Farrah, this is the newest addition to the team," Genesis introduced me cordially.

Farrah wasn't anything like I'd expected. The friendly faced stocky woman walked around me looking me up and down. When she finally stopped in front of me, she gave me an approving nod.

"They'll never see the likes of you coming," she said, reaching around to smack my ass.

"Um, thank you . . . I think," I answered.

Genesis coughed under his breath, giving Farrah a wary look.

She waved his warning off. "I take it you haven't filled our little doll baby in, have you, Kane? Let me do the honor," she announced proudly. "Novie, that man beside you supplies half of the free world with every form of substantial sin you can think of."

I was beyond confused by what the hell she'd just said. Genesis was a lawyer, a really good and a really expensive one from my understanding.

Genesis's hand rested in the small of my back. He leaned close to my ear. "She's right. We aren't here to celebrate. We're here to pick up a shipment. Farrah supplies the stuff, and we move it. I need you, because I don't have a sexy smart-mouthed bombshell. Do you know how many ball players, rappers, and politicians we can lock down with you on the team?"

I looked at Genesis like he'd sprouted a second head. If I wasn't going to sell for my parents, there was no way in hell I'd sell for this nigga. He was out of his damn mind. I motioned for him to lean down so I could talk without yelling all my business.

"I'm not doing this shit. You can find somebody else," I said into his ear.

Genesis straightened up and stared down his nose at me.

"Novie, I can make those prints reappear faster than you can get through those doors. I told you that my service came with a price. This . . . and staying away from Swiss, is all I ask."

My lips worked themselves into an angry thin line. *Stay away from Swiss? Staying away from Swiss wasn't an option, and it didn't have anything to do Genesis.*

Farrah sipped from the champagne flute in her hand. She tipped it back, emptying the glass in one gulp. As if Genesis could sense the fury welling up inside me, he grabbed a champagne flute from a passing server.

"Let's toast to our newest girl, and her journey to becoming as successful as our best guy," he toasted with a smile.

I couldn't believe this shit was happening to me. This was some straight-up television entrapment-type shit, and there was nothing I could do to get out of it. I excused myself to the ladies' room. Maybe there was a window or something I could jump my black ass out of. I'd already run once, so doing it again wasn't impossible. It would just be harder this time around since I didn't have thousands stashed away in a locker at a bus station.

Chapter 51

Model Millionaires Are Rare

I was too pissed off with Genesis to do more than throw the champagne back down my throat as quickly as possible while I searched for the ladies' room. It took everything I had not to bolt for the front doors. If I was going to get out of here, the bathroom or a back-door was my best bet. I'd figure out how to deal with Genesis once I was away from him.

A surge of jealous heat ran through my body when my eyes found Swiss again. He was smiling down into the face of a beautiful woman wearing a dress that didn't quite reach the middle of her muscular thighs. Jealousy should have been the last thing to hit me. Especially since he'd been dealing with her consistently, and I honestly didn't have anyone because I consistently compared everyone to him.

I'd moved into a less-crowded section of the building when a hand covered my mouth, yanking me behind a curtained wall. I screamed, but it was muffled behind somebody's hand.

"Shhhhh, I just wanted to see you."

Javion's voice brushed against my ear. He spun me around, slamming his dry lips against mine. I pushed against his chest, leaning away from him.

"What are you doing here? And you're the last motherfucka I want to see," I spat at him. "Surprised you ain't laid up with Catwoman right now. Nigga, you're the reason I'm in this shit to begin with."

"C'mon, girl. Ain't nobody checkin' for McKenzie. Why would you think I had anything to do with settin' you up?

I wouldn't do no shit like that. Boss man gets whatever he wants, Novie. He been had his eye set on you. It was only a matter of time before he stopped watchin' the picture and tried to get in it. There ain't shit I could do to stop him."

"What do you mean set his eye on me? If you know what the fuck is goin' on, you need to help me, Javion!"

Despite my resistance, Javion pulled me toward him, holding me close against his chest. I would've kneed him in his nuts if my dress wasn't so damn tight.

"I've got to get out of town. I refuse to work for that nigga anymore. I sold off the last of my package, and I'm gonna use it to set up my own shit in L.A. Come with me. He won't look for you out there. Come with me, Novie. It'll be you, Mr. Weasel, and me. We can start over, live without anyone watching us," Javion pleaded pitifully.

Little did he know, I honestly didn't have an affinity for Mr. Weasel anymore. I only gave him that name because he snuck into this pussy like a little weasel when I was emotionally distraught. Under normal circumstances, I would've never given Javion the time of day.

But for a split second, his offer did sound good. It sounded like a way to escape Genesis and his illegal drug bullshit. But I couldn't bail on Shandy, and even though I was being told not to, I couldn't stay away from Swiss. Now the thought of not having or seeing him was making me realize how bad I wanted him.

"I can't go, Javion."

"What do you mean, you can't go? You mean you can't go tonight? Yes, you can. You ain't gotta pack shit. I'll take care of everything." His voice cracked; he sounded like he was on the verge of an emotional meltdown.

I leaned in, giving him a soft peck on his chin. Yes, every kiss begins with "K" and sometimes "K" could stand for keep 'em coming, but right now, it stood for keep it moving. This way, I wouldn't have to come up with any flowery excuses or bullshit lies to cover up the truth behind the matter, which was, I didn't want to go. Apparently, still, that wasn't clear enough. Javion dipped his head lower toward mine. I put my finger up to his lips.

"What are you saying?" His words vibrated against my finger.

I stared at a point just behind his ear. I was trying to say everything without saying anything. And I think he was finally starting to hear me loud and clear.

Javion's face clouded over. His grip tightened painfully on my arms.

I looked down in disbelief at his whitening knuckles, his fingertips digging into my skin.

"I just gave up everything for you!" he hissed into my face, shaking me so hard my teeth knocked together.

"Nigga, you'd better let me go. I didn't tell you go and do that dumb shit," I lashed back when he finally stopped shaking me.

He shoved me away from him so hard I lost my balance. My arms flailed, searching for something to grab. Thankfully, the soft shag carpeting broke my fall. Javion was on top of me, straddling my waist, clawing at my throat before I could recover.

"You fuckin' bitch. Die, you stupid, fuckin' bitch! You ain't worth shit!" he hissed.

Flecks of frothy white spittle formed at the corners of his mouth. It sprayed from his lips. My fingers clawed at his hands around my throat. Nobody knew where I was, and I'm sure even if they did, with the curtains closed and the loud music, they wouldn't know I needed help. This was a different kind of feeling from when I jumped from the bridge. I'd chosen that ending, so I still felt in control, even though I was helpless. All I could feel now was this pitiful helplessness and anger over not being big enough to whoop this nigga's ass. His face was going in and out of focus as my lungs begged for air.

"Da fuck!" Javion yelled, falling back.

I coughed, rolling to my side to get away from him when I was scooped up into strong arms.

"You know you've got a thing for attracting the crazies, right?" Swiss whispered down into my ear.

I relaxed into his chest. "With my track record, that means you're crazy too."

"I'm the craziest out of all the crazies. *But* I'm crazy about you," he murmured.

As bad as I wanted to thank him, I wanted to get air past my raw throat and into my chest.

He pulled the drapes closed, sitting me down in the chaise lounge a few feet away from where I was attacked.

"Stay right there. I mean it," he ordered before disappearing through the red drapes.

I was massaging the tender spots on my throat when he returned. I don't know where the tears came from. One minute I was fine, and the next, I was just overwhelmed with the fact that I'd almost gotten killed. Swiss sat down behind me, positioning me so I could lay across his chest.

"Thank you," I told him in a watery voice.

"You know I have to go, right? I've got to get that body out of here before somebody finds it. Kane thinks I'm about to run a delivery across town."

I nodded against his chest, leaving big black smears on his red dress shirt from my mascara. Good thing I didn't have on a full face of makeup, or he'd be walking out of here looking like he had a mask on his shirt.

There was a shaky hoarseness in my voice when I tried to talk.

"I'm not mad about your little boy or the fact that your side-ho is pregnant," I said quietly. "I am mad at all this bull-shit I've been sucked into. And the fact that I've got this nigga suddenly controlling my life."

Sobs rocked me to my core, making my entire body shake. Swiss slid his fingers underneath my chin, nudging it upward so I could look him in the eye.

"Novie, it ain't as bad as you think. A nigga might see sixty or seventy thousand a year out there sitting in a cubicle fuckin' with Excel five days a week. But that ain't for us; we ain't got university degrees, Novie. I got a master's in this street shit, and you got a Ph.D. I keep a low-profile crib and a low-profile life because my baby momma would cut off her own leg to get to my paper if she knew I had millions. I just want to see my li'l man grow up happy and healthy, I want you to be a part of that."

I would've scoffed at that last part if my throat didn't hurt. *He wanted me to be a part of his baby momma drama? Umm . . . no.* Tinesha would make both of our lives hell just for shits and giggles.

I shook my head against his chest. "Genesis said I'd distract you. He threatened to release my prints to the police if I don't cooperate."

"Novie, Genesis will only know what you want him to know. I make close to two-mill a year. This shit is superlow risk for that kind of dough. Imagine once you get in and see how shit operates. You'll probably figure out how to flip three times that."

I leaned back, giving Swiss an extra hard, extra thorough look. What he was saying sounded too good to be true. The only sour side of the deal was that I'd either have to cut all ties with Swiss, or sneak to see him until we decided to cut all ties with Genesis.

"Okay, Swiss. I'll do this shit, but if that heffa hits me again, I'll break her face."

Swiss's face broke into a wide grin. The corners of his eyes crinkled while he laughed. He leaned forward, giving me a soft peck on the same cheek that his baby momma'd punched me in.

"Yeah, she snuck you with a good left jab, but you took it like a champ. You do know the two of us together are smarter than all the world combined, right? I say we do us, get this paper, and if you want to be done at any point, just say the word and we're out of it."

I bit the inside of my lip. Two against one sounded a helluva lot better than me against the world. If my daddy had never interfered in the beginning, Swiss wouldn't have abandoned me. He didn't abandon me when I showed up needing help, so I felt safe going into this with him as a secret ally.

"Let's do this shit," I announced with a smile matching his.

He was on the brink of giving me another one of his dangerously slow kisses when the red satin drapes billowed in toward us. I jumped, letting out a small surprised squeak. Genesis slammed through the drapes. He stood in the middle of the booth, looking back and forth between Swiss and me.

I'd been so caught up in my conversation with Swiss that I hadn't even noticed that the music had stopped. The soft murmur of hundreds of hushed voices met my ears. My heart hiked across the inside of my chest in spiked cleats. *Oh, shit. How much has Genesis heard?* I knew I was gonna need that damn cigarette.

Chapter 52

The Art of Allowing

I couldn't tell if Genesis was going to kill us on the spot or wait until later when he had some privacy. His face was dark and stony as he stood in the booth.

"Everyone's evacuating. Someone found a body in the men's bathroom," Genesis announced.

He gave Swiss what looked like a disgusted stare down before turning his eyes to me.

"Shit," Swiss cursed, pushing himself up off the chaise lounge. "I walked in on your boy Javion, roughin' her up. You know I black out a little when I get too worked up. One minute I was here, and then it was like I blanked out and snapped. Next thing I know, he was lying on the floor with a broken neck," Swiss told Genesis.

I looked at Swiss with different eyes. What happened to the man I used to know? The old Swiss would've knocked Javion out or cracked a few ribs. He wouldn't have killed him. Or maybe he would've done it, and I was just giving him too much credit.

Genesis's expression didn't change as he spoke to Swiss. "Get out of here before you get found out. I'll take her home," he said.

Swiss's eyes held an unspoken promise as he looked toward me before leaving. Once he was gone, I realized I was all alone with the intimidating Mr. Genesis Kane.

"Are you all right?" he asked with what sounded like concern in his voice.

"Mm-hmm, just shook up, but I'm good."

The tenderness in his voice caught me off guard. It was weird to see him acting like a normal, caring person. He helped me up from where I'd been sitting. A deep frown creased his forehead when he saw the bruises on my arms and my neck.

"I told you to stay away from him. Swiss can't focus on the mission in front of him when there are distractions. Now he has a body on his hands because you didn't listen."

I glared at Genesis. "*I* didn't listen? You'd be picking my body up off the floor right now if it weren't for Swiss. He saved me, and you weren't anywhere around to help."

"Novie, Swiss is not who you think he is. This isn't the first time I've said it, and I know I can't be the first person to tell you leave him alone. This time, I'm saying it because it's for your own good."

No, Genesis was actually third in the line of anti-Swiss conversation. My daddy had the number one spot, and Shandy followed him up behind in second. The conversation I'd just had with Swiss replayed in my head. Genesis's legal-beagle ass was probably superintimidated just being around a real dealer/hit man. If he knew half as much about Swiss as I did, he wouldn't be worried about anything.

I pasted a fake smile on my face. "All right, I got it, Genesis. No more Swiss. I understand."

It was close to two a.m. when I finally walked into our dark and empty apartment after yet another long, silent car ride with Genesis Kane. That man seemed next to impossible to peg down. One moment, he'd be cool, and the next minute, he could be obstinate and rude. I wonder if he treated his momma like that. That's if he actually even *had* a momma. If somebody told me he'd been raised by a pack of wild boars, I'd believe them.

I poured myself a shot, hoping I wasn't expected to actually get up, get dressed, and then roll into an office first thing in the morning. That shit was definitely not going to happen.

Tangie could take that occurrence policy and shove it up her ass. I wasn't even in the mood to pick out my work clothes or log into Facebook. I kicked my shoes off into the living room, groaning as my toes stretched out into the carpet.

I was in the middle of a silent debate on exactly which details I could or should share with Shandy. She wasn't going to believe half of the shit that happened, but I needed to talk to someone. First things first, I needed a shower. I undressed, wincing when I saw the four long reddish purple bruises that wrapped around my neck. I couldn't believe Javion had really tried to kill me. I'd never seen him look like that before, not even on his worst day or when he was at his angriest.

Pushing away my thoughts of Javion and Swiss, I hopped into the shower, lathering up, letting the scent of vanilla orchids and blue coconut water ease into my pores.

Suddenly, the shower curtain peeled back—I dropped the bottle of soap.

"I got real dirty tonight fighting with my bare hands for the honor of this fine-ass chick I seen at the spot," Swiss announced.

I let out a relieved breath before throwing my loofah at his face.

"Y'all are gonna give me a heart attack with all this sneaking and popping up shit. How the hell did you get in here, Swiss?"

Our shower was big enough to fit one person comfortably, but if you put two people in there, it got crowded quick. Swiss's body swallowed up most of the space as he stepped in, grinning.

"You don't give me enough credit, Novie-star. I'm not the same nigga who ran off years ago. I learned a lot, and I'm better than what I used to be."

"Well, before you get all comfy, I guess I should tell you that Javion and Tinesha were fuckin' around behind your back."

Swiss kissed me so slow and deep I was dizzy when he finally stopped.

"I know. That's why I broke his neck." Swiss grinned like the cat that ate the canary.

"Nigga, you ain't got no shame! So you already knew she was cheatin' on you?"

"Yeah, me and her was talkin' until I found you again. I cut her off, and then you left, so I got her back. She kind of figured that I had someone on the side, so she started playing me. Guess I let it happen to keep the peace. So I could see my li'l man and see you. As long as she was busy stressin' Javion, she wasn't stressin' me."

"So you know the baby might be his, right?"

"Yeah, I know. But Brandon is here now, and he is mine. He's my only concern until she has the baby. I'll deal with that bridge when I get to it."

It felt conflicting to see Swiss stepping up to his responsibility after he'd abandoned me so many years ago. But he was right; he had changed, and that made him sexy as fuck.

"Let's go to bed," I suggested.

"Novie? I know you didn't get in your little bed with all this water all over the bathroom floor."

Shandy's voice dragged me out of the dream I was having. I groaned, blinking to focus my eyes. Bright light streamed in through the window. A baby cried from somewhere in the front of the apartment. Swiss snored in his sleep beside me. *Oh, shit! I forgot he's here.*

"Bitch, what in the world did you do last ni—" Shandy stood in the doorway of my bedroom.

Her eyes were wide and round as she looked over at Swiss sleeping beside me, then back to my face.

I gave her a weak smile. "Hey, Shan. Look who I found. It's Kryptonite."

Swiss pulled himself up, tucking a pillow between his back and the headboard.

"Hey, little sister. You look like you're doin' all right."

Shan obviously didn't see the humor in the situation. She whirled around, stomping out of the room.

"So I'm your Kryptonite? And that's supposed to make you Superwoman or something," Swiss chuckled.

"Not now, boy, she's pissed. Shandy?" I hopped up, wrapping myself in the comforter.

Shandy was in the living room with her purse on her shoulder and her keys in her hand.

"You have lost your fucking mind bringing him here, Novie."

"Shan, it's not what you think. He isn't the same. He's nothing like he was back in the day," I reassured her.

"Whatever, Novie. I'm just mad that I rearranged my whole life to help you move forward, and you go right back."

Chapter 53

Sex Kitten Vs. Sex Panther

I finally dragged myself into the office two hours late. With Shandy acting the way she was acting, it was best to leave her be until she decided to come around. Swiss, on the other hand, was not being cooperative at all. I had to insist that he not show up out of the blue like he did, but he wasn't trying to hear any of that. The only way I could keep him from showing up was by promising that'd I'd head over to his place after work.

The other paralegals who I'd decided to start to calling "Bobby" and the rockers were all surprisingly quiet as I passed.

My lip curled up in complete disgust as I stopped just short of my desk. Old, moldy, cobweb-covered cardboard boxes filled with folders had been stacked all across it. I threw my purse into the top drawer, scanning the neon green Post-it note attached to my chair. *Relabel and file by year and alphabet in the archive room ASAP—Tangie.*

As if she could hear me reading her note, she bobbed over, parking herself in front of my desk. "You're a little late getting in here this morning, aren't you?" she asked, nodding in the direction of the clock. Her shock-blond Afro wig bounced around on her head. I'd figured out the fact that Tangie was a twenty-three-year-old mean girl trapped in a sixty-five-year-old woman's body. She was petty, spiteful, and had a jealous streak from hell.

Her red, black, and green curled nails drummed across one of the boxes on my desk. I hated her nails and her nail polish.

Why couldn't she pick one color instead of a different color for every finger?

I gave her a nonchalant shrug, pulling out some folders to work on. I didn't know I was supposed to work every hour on and around the clock. I almost got strangled to death, and I didn't get in until two a.m. That sounded like a legitimate reason to run late to me.

Tangie huffed and puffed before she hightailed it to her dungeon beside Genesis's office.

"Your hair looks really cute today, um, Novie, right?"

I looked up from the folders to see everyone staring expectantly. No, my hair actually looked like shit. I didn't have time to do anything to it except pull it back into a bun. Bobby complimenting me on it confirmed it, though. Those hating he-heffas probably wouldn't bat a fake eyelash my way on the days when I was on point. But let me look a little rough, and they were singing compliments my way.

I picked the Bobby closest to me to respond to.

"Thank you, Bobby. It was one of *those* kinds of weekends. I have been in la-la land ever since," I replied giving him a bright smile.

He ran his finger in slow circles around the lid of the Starbucks cup on his desk. "Oh. So, I guess you didn't hear about the client we have coming in today?" He ran his eyes up and down the length of my outfit.

I slow blinked from Bobby and his fashion bullshit back down to the stack files.

"It's Farrah Harper, honey, the wealth consultant. Who knows, that whole peasant look you got going on just might work in your favor," he blurted out, swirling his finger in the air in my direction.

Farrah's job title sounded like a bunch of bull to me. A wealth consultant, really? The way people just made up jobs these days was hilarious.

I couldn't help it. I had to ask. "What does a wealth consultant do?"

Bobby shook his bobble-head before exchanging looks with his underling bobble-heads. They were on the verge of a meltdown at the fact that I didn't know something that was obviously bobble-head common knowledge.

"She gives people these life-makeovers. And I mean *life*. They come out with better money, friends, social status—basically, turns shit to sugar. She was on *Oprah* and *Dr. Phil*."

They all nodded in unison. It was pretty obvious that none of them were associated with Genesis's illegal after-hours business. After the night I had, nothing about Farrah was impressive to me. She was just another boss who I had to contend with.

"Novie?" Tangie shouted down the aisle. "Genesis wants to see you in his office. *Now*."

I stiffly rose from my desk to go find out why I'd been summoned.

Genesis's office was an interestingly strange mixture of Japanese masks, legal books, and stuffy, old-man furniture. It even smelled like him with a hint of old library and leather books in the air.

"I think we got off to a rough start. I would like to take you to dinner after work, to get us on better ground."

It just seemed like it would've been weird if I was standing outside the boss's office waiting to go out, so I sat at my desk scrolling through different Twitter feeds. I let Swiss know I'd be a little late just to keep him from popping up at the house. Farrah had finally left Genesis's office after spending close to two hours demanding copies of miscellaneous documents. Outside of our illegal partnership, she acted as if we didn't know each other, and that was fine by me.

No one was even slightly suspicious about why I wasn't on my way out. Even Tangie's militant behind barely glanced my way when five o'clock rolled in. She was probably just anxious to go climb back under whatever bridge she'd hobbled out from.

Genesis finally came by my desk. He looked surprisingly cheerful. I was getting used to the serious scowl he always had.

"How do you feel about sensory deprivation?" he asked.

"I have no idea that I even know what that is in regards to or how I'd feel," I told him with a puzzled look on my face.

"Doesn't matter." He rubbed his lips together. "We'll figure it out today. I'll pull the Porsche around."

Genesis driving himself anywhere was like hearing that Batman could put his draws on without Alfred.

He pulled up to the front of the building in a silver Porsche truck.

"Is the lady ready to step out of her comfort zone and figure out what she likes this evening?" he asked with a mischievous lift to his voice.

I chewed the inside of my mouth, anxious to find out why this place put him in such a good mood.

"Oh, wow, I always thought Porsches were these expensive little, eensy-weensy cars made extraspecial for dudes with little eensy-weensy tender-bits," I replied.

"Woman, you keep thinking like that, and you'll miss out on some of the biggest thangs life has to offer."

Well, damn. I can't argue with that.

We made small talk on our way to the restaurant. It was nice to have a decent conversation with someone. I was telling him about Heather's daughter and the whole trunk episode when he gave me a strange look.

"So, your best friend who you live with is a lesbian?"

"No, I mean, yes, but no. She likes a little bit of everybody," I told him.

Genesis got quiet. He seemed to be digesting that bit of information.

"So, has she ever tried to get at you?" he asked after several long, silent seconds.

"Who, Shandy? Hell no, not since high school."

The look he gave me made me feel like I needed to explain. "I mean, she was just figuring out that she liked women, and since we were besties, she tried to come at me. But no, that's my girl; that's it."

Genesis drove us to a restaurant called Dans Le Noir. We walked in through the front door into a small hallway. I didn't know if I was going to step into a strip club, circus, or a pit of deadly vipers. Genesis grabbed my hand. His skin was comfortably warm. His long, smooth fingers gave mine a squeeze as we stepped through the curtains together.

I gasped as we stepped into complete and absolutely ear-shattering darkness. It was the kind of pitch black that made your ears instantly sensitive. Panic started to swell in my chest. I couldn't find a single point of light to focus on. No matter how hard I tried, I couldn't get my eyes to adjust. The only thing that kept me sane was Genesis's hand in mine. I knew nothing bad would happen as long as he was with me.

Slow footsteps approached us. They sounded too heavy to be a woman, with a shuffle and a lag in between each one. It's a damn shame that I could pick all of that up, but if you take away one sense, the rest really do get better. It was someone coming to greet us, and he was just in the nick of time, because I was ready to drop to the ground and crawl for the curtains.

"Welcome, guests. My name is Louis. I'm your server this evening, and I am happy that you two have chosen to indulge your senses and dine with us tonight." The greeter's words were hinted with spearmint gum and what might have been vodka. It was hard to separate the smells coming from his mouth from the smells surrounding us. But I could definitely make out what I thought was vodka. Hell, if I worked in a pitch-black restaurant, I'd probably grab myself a shot or two from the bar.

Genesis tugged on my hand, and I shuffle-stepped in line behind him. I was scared I'd trip over the back of someone's chair and land on the floor. I couldn't tell where the rugs ended or began. They could've at least put in a little lighted walkway like the shit at the movies. I wonder how many lawsuits this place saw in any given week, because this shit was dangerous.

"How the hell can you see, Louis?" I asked the server.

"Ah, ma'am, most of the staff wears night vision goggles. Some of them are actually legally blind, so nothing extra is required."

There was a quiet hum from a thousand different conversations going on around us as we were led into the dark dining room. Not only were my ears extrasensitive, but my sense of smell was surprisingly keen all of a sudden too. I could smell everything from the red wine sloshing in glasses to the scallops being sautéed in white wine and rosemary somewhere nearby.

Louis took my hand from Genesis and pressed it onto a chair so I could sit without falling flat out onto the floor. He also showed us where our water glasses were sitting and the placement of our napkins and silverware. I listened to the soft tilt of his French accent as he read the menu to us. Everything sounded beautifully put together. I ordered pepper brined chicken with honey garlic sauce and sautéed greens with banana peppers. Genesis got the jerk chicken with pineapple salsa. Louis took our orders, leaving us to the dark.

"What do you think so far?" Genesis asked.

Now his voice could ooze over me without the distraction of my other senses. It was like warmed-over salted caramel, smooth and rough but still very sweet to my ears.

"So far, I think this is one of the craziest things I've done since I've been in DC."

He laughed. It was a soft sound from somewhere beside me that sounded like genuine humor.

"Novie, I can think of over a hundred things crazier than this for you to do," he said with his voice barely above a whisper.

There was something so intimate about being in the dark that made it feel like we were alone, even though there were probably a dozen other couples within a few feet of us. We sat and sipped wine while we waited for our food. Mine was sweet and tangy. I could taste all of the blackberry accents, and even a little cinnamon.

"Novie, we have the same wine. I think your taste buds are shot, because I taste cherries, chocolate, and maybe a little black pepper."

I giggled at his description. "Sounds to me like you're tasting that cologne you wear. You should try to drink it without breathing in through your nose," I suggested.

"Or I can taste it right here," Genesis whispered.

He'd managed to slide his chair all the way over until he was sitting beside me in the dark. His lips were only inches away from mine. I could feel the air he exhaled on my chin and cheeks.

"Taste what, right where?" I asked in a whisper equal to his.

He answered by grabbing the back of my neck and melting his lips into mine. My heartbeat stutter-stepped in my chest.

This was so not supposed to be happening, yet I wasn't doing a damn thing to stop it. Our tongues touched and entwined in a seductive, slow dance. He was right; his kisses tasted like cherries and chocolate with a little spicy pepper.

The pitch black of the restaurant made me feel daring and even a little raunchy. For all I knew, everyone around us were either tonguing each other down or fucking at their dinner tables. I could hear what sounded like a soft moan somewhere off to my left. To my right, forks clattered against a plate. And right in front of me, Genesis was keeping a calm, cool exterior, all while giving me searing hot kisses. I curiously slid my hand down into his lap. There was no way this couldn't be affecting him the same way he was affecting me.

I could feel him smile against my lips as I patted him, straining against his pants.

"Well, hello, to you, Citizen Kane," I murmured against Genesis's lips.

"Citizen Kane? I think I like the sound of that. Say it again and squeeze him a little."

This game we were playing had me melting into a puddle right where I sat. Good thing it was dark, because my panties and the seat were going to be sopping wet whenever we got up to leave. Genesis pulled away, and I gasped when he came back. I closed my eyes, even though I didn't need to. He held an ice cube in between his lips, and he ran it across my shoulders, down the front of my neck. I let out a tiny yip when it dropped in between my breasts.

"Is everything okay?" Louis asked from somewhere over our heads.

That fool had probably been standing there the whole time, enjoying all the various freak shows that were going on.

Genesis squirmed in his seat beside me. "We are fine, thank you."

"Perfect. Your meal will be out shortly." And with that, Louis left.

I sighed, enjoying what smelled like white wine and rosemary over chicken. Everywhere I turned, there were smells to paint pictures in my head. Genesis leaned forward. It was amazing how well I could sense his body heat and hear him breathing. He poured wine into my mouth from his. It was shockingly cool compared to the heat of his mouth. A trail of wine ran down the corner of my mouth, and he caught it with his tongue. The heat from his fingers grazed my inner thigh as he slipped my soaking wet panties to the side. My teeth sank into his bottom lip as his finger dipped into the dripping honey pot between my legs.

Serving trays clanked nearby. I could hear the servers coming our way. I tried to close my legs, but Genesis wouldn't move his hand. Our food was set out and Louis explained what was what and where. Genesis strummed a steady rhythm with his finger. Spicy Jerk chicken, strum, pineapple and mango salsa, strum strum. I didn't hear a damn thing the man said after that. My mind was only on one thing.

When the servers disappeared, my senses were reeling from the exotic-smelling food heightened by the darkness and the slow lull of Genesis's hand. He pulled me toward the edge of my seat, dipping his fingers faster and harder into my pussy. A quiet moan slipped out of my mouth before he kissed me deep and hard, claiming the sounds of my moans as his.

Swiss had never done anything this exciting, and Javion had damn sure never gotten me anywhere close to the heights Genesis was taking me—and with a damn finger at that. He stroked until I could feel the walls closing in. I was standing right at the edge, ready to fall into oblivion—and he stopped.

"You didn't ask me if you could cum yet." His voice was dark with excitement.

I blinked several times, feeling empty and cold from his retreat.

"Okay, I'm sorry," I whispered leaning toward him. "I didn't know I was supposed to ask. Can I cum, please?" I fidgeted in my seat, crossed and uncrossed my legs. I settled on pressing my knees tight together.

"Well, I can't say no when you ask like that."

His hands were on my hips, quietly directing me to stand up. Cool air brushed against my bared ass as my skirt was cinched up around my waist. My knees almost gave out when he slipped my panties to the side, burying his tongue deep into my pussy. I found the back of my chair in the dark and held on to it for dear life. He licked, sucked, and lapped at my center until I could feel the dampness running down my legs.

I tasted myself on his lips when he rose up in front of me. He lifted my leg, wrapping it around his waist. I don't know when or how he freed himself from his slacks. But I felt every hard, hot inch of him as he pressed forward and upward, driving deep in one fluid motion. My arms wrapped themselves around his neck. I dug my nails into this back, burying my face in his shoulder to muffle my gasps and moans. We rocked together somewhere in the middle of the dark restaurant with people eating and chatting around us. Genesis stroked me over and over with the scent of red wine on our breath and the pineapple mango salsa on his dinner plate flavoring the air around us.

My legs started shaking. I wanted to scream his name. I pressed my lips against his ear, remembering the lesson he'd just given me a little while ago.

"Can I cum? Please, make me cum."

He answered me in strokes, going deeper and faster. I moved my hips in unison with his until we were both shaking and ready to explode. Pulses of light quaked from my pussy, sending beacons of light up throughout every nerve in my body. The lights danced in front of my eyelids and exploded in little flashes. As far as I knew, we were the only ones in the building. All my senses were dialed into the pulsing heat pressing upward between my legs. Genesis breathed against my neck, stroking my skin with his lips and sometimes his teeth. It sent me over the edge. I bit down into his shoulder—hard—getting a mouthful of suit jacket as our worlds exploded together. Genesis had to hold me up, else I would've hit the floor. That had to have been the hardest, longest climax I'd ever had in my life.

Afterward, I carefully eased down into my seat. Genesis handed me the handkerchief from his shirt pocket so I could wipe my legs. Never would I ever have guessed that his well-dressed, starched, and pressed legal ass could put it down like that and in a place like this. I had a lot to learn when it came down to judging people's characters.

Novie

Chapter 54

Candy Kane

Genesis dropped me back off at the office two hours later. We exchanged a few good-bye kisses before he handed me a padded envelope.

"This is for a special client. I'll call you by ten with the drop-off info. We need to make sure he's still interested. Oh, and I would like it if you came by my place afterward."

Genesis winked and my blood was set on fire all over again. After the way he'd dicked me down in the middle of that restaurant, I'd go or be wherever he wanted me to. Good food and an even better fuck had me ready to lay it down. Swiss was too unpredictable. The chance of him showing up if I canceled our dinner plans was too risky. When Shandy was in bitch-mode, nobody could be happy until she got out of her funk. Seeing Swiss would only make her extend that shit.

It was only seven thirty so I headed to Swiss's place while trying to come up with an excuse to roll out at ten when Genesis called. Worst-case scenario, I could make up something about Shandy babysitting and needing help because Hennessey was sick. Nothing short of Jesus' Second Coming was going to keep me from getting to Genesis and getting part two of my dick-down.

Swiss was already home and dressed when I got there.

"Hey, you." I slipped my arms around his waist.

He kissed my forehead and frowned down at me.

"You look different. Did you get your eyebrows done or something?" he asked. "You smell nice too. Is it something new?"

My heart paused. I'd forgotten about Genesis's cologne. I'd been smelling and resmelling it in my hair on my way to Swiss's.

"I had to ride with the Boss man to see Farrah. He freshened up his old-man funky cologne on the drive." I told my lie, pulling away from him. The guilt I felt in my stomach was unexpected.

"This shit isn't gonna work," I complained to cover up my sudden lack of interest in doing anything with Swiss. "I can't work with that nigga all day, and then run and do all these crazy-ass jobs whenever he and Farrah snap their fingers. I'm tired, and I don't get any kind of rest."

Swiss, being Swiss, was sympathetic and understanding as usual. He ran his hands up and down my arms.

"We can stay in. I'll run you a bath, get you a drink. Take your mind off things."

Ugh, Swiss's way of taking my mind off things was not what I wanted. Genesis started this fire, and *he* needed to put it out.

I was pulled out of a good dream by my phone buzzing from somewhere in the bed. It never mattered what kind of grip I had on it when I fell asleep. It always wound up somewhere crazy, like under my leg or behind my neck. The buzzing stopped. With one eye open, I carefully peeled Swiss's arm from around my waist to feel around for my phone. It was tucked under his side.

I sighed and stared at the missed call. Genesis could really work a damn nerve when he wanted to. He was supposed to call me before ten, before I got stuck being the good girlfriend and playing house. Yet, here it was going on two in the morning, and he was blowing up my shit like he'd lost his damn mind after I'd just seen him at dinner.

Swiss groaned in his sleep. I froze, only moving again when I could make out the steady rhythm of his breathing. He was normally a lighter-than-light sleeper. I chuckled. He probably would have snapped to attention if I hadn't gotten him fucked up off shots of 1800. Desperate times called for desperate measures, and I just wasn't feeling the whole staring-into-each-other's-eyes, love-sex thing tonight. Not when I'd been promised an "a-cock-alyptic" dick-down, and that was the exact wording Genesis used. Half a bottle of tequila couldn't even get me in the mood for Swiss, not when I was thinking about Gen. So we had an hour-long drunk conversation about I can't remember what until Swiss passed out.

I slid the phone under the blanket to text Genesis back.

I was asleep. What happened to ten o'clock?

He texted me right back.

I'm sorry. I got caught up. You know Citizen Kane can't tell time, though. I won't tell him it's not ten o'clock if you don't. ☺ 125 Bloom Court.

A smug smile curved my lips. He'd used the name I came up with for his dick. Now I could officially say that I had myself a legal dick.

I glanced in Swiss's direction. He was out cold. I could probably leave and act like I'd gone into the office early. He usually didn't question my work hours so long as I didn't get too crazy with it.

Okay. See you in thirty, I replied.

My phone buzzed again as I tiptoed to the bathroom. It was a video message of Genesis biting his lower lip, stroking Citizen Kane into all of his thick and long glory. It was prettier than I'd imagined.

You better hurry up. I already started. Bring the envelope.

I made the twenty-minute drive to his loft near Union Market in a record time of eight minutes flat. I felt like a movie star from the moment I pulled up. There was free twenty-hour valet just for visitors, so I didn't have to worry about parking. And I'm sure Genesis kept them all content by tipping well whenever he had cash in his pocket. I handed my keys to the valet and stood in the heated roundabout so I could admire the thirty-story glass-front building. A pudgy little doorman with greying hairs sticking out the sides of his red and blue hat held the door for me.

My heels clacked across the cream and gold marble floor. It was a maze of glass etched in green bamboo separating different seating areas. Floor-to-ceiling bubble tanks churned water and changed color with the electro-swing music playing in the background. They must have bought their lobby music from the same place as Forever 21 or Express because the music made me feel like I should've been shopping.

"Good morning, Ms. Deleon," the front deskman greeted me in a cheerful voice.

The fact that he already knew my name before I could say anything was creepy, but very impressive.

"Mr. Kane has asked that you join him on the roof. I can have someone show you up if—"

"It's okay, thank you. I'll find the way."

Genesis texted me before I was even two feet away from the receptionist's desk.

Open the envelope in the elevator and follow the directions.

My face felt like it was on fire as I rushed toward the elevator. I didn't want everybody to know who or why I was coming to visit. And what was he doing on the roof, I wondered as I stepped into the gold-mirrored elevator. I'd thrown on a simple pink and black medallion print wraparound dress. The only thing holding it in place was the belt tied around the waist. I squinted around the lightning-forked gold veins in the elevator's mirrored walls to check the wings of my eyeliner before opening the envelope. There was a small index card and a fancy pink and silver e-cigarette. The card read, *"This is better,"* in barely legible handwriting. Something told me it was Genesis's.

I had twenty-four floors to go, so I puffed on my new e-cig a few times. It was definitely different than my emergency cig. The lack of smoke was a plus, though.

Somewhere in my coat pocket my phone started vibrating. I pulled it out as the elevator stopped on the top floor. The picture I'd saved of Swiss smiled back at me. I hit the volume button to stop if from vibrating. Maybe he deserved something better than what I could give him, because I knew I deserved something better than all the grief he'd given me.

The doors swept aside, and I climbed off the elevator, making sure to tuck my new toy back into the envelope. When I looked up, my mouth damn near fell off my face.

Genesis stood naked, wearing nothing but the night air.

"Our client cancelled, and Citizen Kane was starting to complain," he called out.

Either the roof was too high or I was in shock. I swayed where I stood at a sudden feeling of light-headedness. Purple lights lit up the pool behind Genesis. It made deep dark shadows that breathed and stretched across the roof. I was suddenly aware of every piece of fabric on my body. My dress felt like silk against my skin, and the breeze that flowed across the roof felt like angels' kisses.

As much as I wanted to turn around and get back on the elevator, something kept me swaying where I stood like a wild rose in a rainstorm. I couldn't take my eyes off of Genesis or the bizarre scene rolling out in front of me. This nigga knew I was coming, yet there he stood—with two naked hoes on their knees in front of him. The backs of their black weave brushed the ground behind their bobbing heads. They fought over his dick like two kids trying to lick the same candy cane. I giggled. I actually giggled. Technically, they *were* fighting over a "candy Kane."

A third girl was behind him running her nails down his back to his round ass, and even further downward to his calves. She'd go to the bottom and start all over again. The envelope fell out of my fingers. It hit the ground with a soft slap. Genesis reached back, smacking the girl behind him hard on her ass. Ironically, none of this was bothering me. I should've been back on that elevator as soon as I saw what was happening, but I was still there. Heat swirled between my thighs. Genesis motioned for me to come to him.

I shook my head no, watching the world turn into a hazy blur of crystal blue pool, purple lights, and brown shadows. Something was in that e-cigarette, and it wasn't nicotine, not with the way I was feeling.

"Come here," Genesis ordered. He pointed at the ground in front of him.

Jealousy crossed my mind, but so did something else. Competition. I walked toward him with the meanest look I could make, considering I couldn't feel my face. My fingers undid the belt at my waist. My dress slipped off my shoulders, down my back, pooling into a colorful puddle behind me.

Genesis's hand wrapped around the back of my neck. He surprisingly found the spot that I never told anyone about in less than four seconds. A nigga could get me to do anything just by breathing on that spot. And now his fingers were swirling in the short hair that grew there. The feeling made my knees weak.

"You like your new e-cigarette?" he asked in a warm, slow voice. "It's better for you. Cannabinoids. Weed without the smoke; stronger and healthier."

Shit, my boss got me high. I would probably never be able to say that again in this lifetime. The chicks down in front of him didn't even acknowledge me. They slurped and sucked at what I considered to be my Citizen Kane. I was surprised but too fuzzy-headed to react to the tattoos covering Genesis from his collarbone all the way down to his thighs. He pulled my head toward his, taking a kiss and stealing my breath at the same time.

When he pulled away, he looked at me with proud eyes.

"I bought them for you, but you took too long," he said.

I wasn't worried about the other women anymore. I wasn't worried about anything except getting his full attention and his body to myself. My nails drifted down his chest to his navel. I let my fingers tangle in the hair of the girl closest to me. Genesis had better not get used to no shit like this, because this was going to be my first and last girl-girl-girl-girl-guy get together.

Genesis groaned. It was deep and throaty, and it sent chills down the back of my neck. That was my groan. He needed to be making that sound for me. I moved to push myself in between the girls in front of him, taking the girl's wig with me. It must've tangled on the ring I always wore. She popped Gen's dick out of her mouth.

"Damn, bitch! It took me two hours to pin that shit just—" she stopped.

"Just so you can talk shit to me at home, and then sneak around, fuckin' my nigga?" I asked Shandy, poking my index finger hard into her forehead. The bitch beside her stopped what she was doing . . . and I wasn't even surprised to see Heather.

"Heather, you need to let that nigga's dick go. Now," I warned her.

Shandy was the last person I expected to see. Being high didn't help me focus, and it didn't help me stay calm. The more I reprocessed the sight of her sucking his dick, the more disgusted I got. The bitch behind him didn't even have the decency to stop what she was doing.

"Eh . . . hmmmm," I cleared my throat trying to catch her attention.

"Novie, if you don't calm the fuck down," Genesis interrupted. "I paid them to come out for a client. Me and you were gonna have us a peep show. He cancelled, and I figured we could have some fun."

"I can't believe y'all. This shit is what you consider *fun?*" I aimed all of my outrage at Genesis.

"Shit, we ain't even got to go through all of this," Shandy butted in before he could answer. "We can take what we've made and call it a night, sir, or Kane, or whatever your name is," she said to Genesis.

"Nah." Genesis shook his head with his lips turned down into an ugly frown. "I will give y'all five times your normal rate if you'll stay."

"Nigga, that's twenty thousand," Shandy sputtered.

I looked at him like he'd lost his ever-lovin' mind. I know this nigga wasn't about to pay Shandy and her crusty side chicks that much money. Shandy had the potential to do damn near anything for a dollar. Her mouth fell open at Genesis's offer; she didn't even need to ask Heather what was up. That bitch was already reassuming the dick-sucking position.

"Only thing missing is you." Genesis pointed at the ground in front of him.

I didn't need this shit, and I damn sure wasn't about to share. He must've sensed the hell I was thinking about raising. His face went hard and cold.

"I didn't know you knew them, Novie, and they weren't cheap to begin with. I want you to experience this. Being among friends should be a plus for you."

He pulled me toward him and held up his hand for me to open my mouth. I took whatever he was offering, letting it melt on the tip of my tongue. *Fuck it.* That was my last thought before I let myself be blindfolded. I felt weightless. There were hands and mouths all over me. The nigga didn't miss a beat. He held me up against him. Fingers and tongues ran up and down my back. Lips sucked on the back of my neck. I tightened my legs around his hips, wrapping my arms around his neck . . . the excitement, the thrill of having so many women around us when all he really wanted was me, fueled for a heat-seeking missile that was about to explode inside my pussy.

Kane palmed my ass in each hand. The heat from his long fingers seared my skin as he guided my pussy up and down the length of him. My head fell back, a soft moan leaving my lips. I was flying, floating, and about to cum, all at the same time. I could feel every inch of skin, every throb, and every muscle. This nigga was fucking me into some love. I chanted the words over and over; even though I was trying to stop myself, I couldn't keep from saying it.

Genesis groaned against my lips. "*Mmmm-hmmm,* you love this dick?" he asked.

I sighed, whirred my hips harder against him, trying to lock him inside me forever.

"*Ahhhhhh,* I love you. I love your dick. I love everything," I moaned back.

My walls contracted and closed in around him. It hit me like a flash flood that started in my pussy, working its way outward to my fingertips and toes. I couldn't breathe, couldn't hold myself up. Eyes closed, I let myself float on each wave as it came in.

Chapter 55

Inspector Gidget and Inspector Gadget

Shandy and Heather were both sitting at the small bar that stretched across the kitchen cabinet. We normally used it as our dinner table, but it was currently covered with papers. A couple bottles of red wine and empty glasses sat between the two of them. I dropped my keys somewhere on the couch and kicked off my shoes.

I could tell they were up to something just by looking at them, but everything was still awkward after our night with Genesis. It was next to impossible for me to look Heather in the eye, considering I now knew what she tasted like. Shandy was the only one acting like everything was fine and dandy.

"I'm still mad at you, but now that I've got ten grand, I could care less what you do, girl. I'm keeping your fifteen percent, though," Shandy said. "That nigga is paid out the ass, and he love him some you. Go bat your eyes, he'll give it to you."

My eyes narrowed suspiciously. "What the hell is wrong with you two? That's the type of shit y'all be out there doing? I still don't know how I even feel about what went down or the way it went down last night."

"Well, we feel fine about everything we've done. Your little boo-thang is a freak. You better hold on to that. Good-looking, good sex, and he got paper. It ain't gonna get any better, Novie. If you don't stay with him, me and Heather already agreed on sharing him," Shandy joked.

They were still looking suspicious to me. Knowing them, they'd christened my bed or my bathroom. The two of them sitting there together just had this look like something nasty or sexually explicit transpired somewhere sacred, or where I eat maybe.

A slow grin spread across Shandy's face. The last time she got that look was when we worked together in this small office, and she'd started using the company card to stock our fridge.

"So, Heather and I have been doing a little investigating into your Genesis Kane. Even though he gave us a little fake name. He said he was Trent Santora when he booked us," she announced.

Heather nodded. "I had one of my girls run him through the database at work and—"

"You did *what?*" I snapped at her. My temper instantly went through the roof. "Shandy, I told you I didn't want to check into him or have you check into him," I reminded her. "Y'all get prostituted for one night, and now all of a sudden you want to start running checks without anyone's permission?"

"Technically, I didn't do anything. Heather did all the work." She pointed her thumb in Heather's direction, averting her eyes away from me.

"I didn't want anyone checking into anybody. How did I not make that shit clear?"

Silence filled the air as neither one of them could answer my question.

"Well, we did find something you might really want to know," Heather spoke up.

Even though I was miffed, my curiosity got the better of me. "Okay, so what is it?"

Heather handed over a sheet of paper, and I waited for her to explain.

Chapter 56

Home Sweet Home

Monday should've been an awkward, part-two, day, but Genesis surprised me by calling in sick. I'd managed to avoid Swiss all weekend, but I could feel it in the air. He was bound to pop up sooner than later.

The office wasn't the same when Genesis wasn't there. Tangie seemed a lot more social than usual. The Bobbys were all on ten. They'd shown me every dance, cute shoe, and every outfit they came across, all while stalking their crush's Instagram. Mavis was the only one who was still quiet and all business as usual in her corner of the office. I was disappointed when I texted Genesis and he didn't answer. I still felt some kind of way about sharing him with my friends, and then being ignored or avoided. Maybe he was feeling some of that "morning-after" shame too.

Genesis didn't come across as the type of man who would feel ashamed about anything, though. I flagged Tangie down during her coffee refill.

"Do you know where Mr. Kane is?" I asked her in as nonchalant of a voice as I could manage.

"Not sure; the boss doesn't have to let anyone know if he's going to come into work," was her snippy reply. She softened it up a little when she saw the disheartened look on my face. "He probably has a bug or a meeting. I heard his voice mail in his office replaying messages. He normally calls and checks it when he's out and about working."

"I see." I tried to think of a quick lie to throw her off. I was too new to be checking for the boss like that. "He'd mentioned Farrah was coming by, and now I feel stupid for dressing up for the occasion."

Even though I was irritated, I'd dressed up just for him. Now I was irritated at him missing the chance to see me all dressed up.

"Well, if it'll make you feel special, you can entertain the auditor I'm expecting to arrive any minute now. I need to go make sure we shredded everything."

My eyebrows flew up at that.

Tangie cackled an old witchy sounding cackle. "Just messin' with you, baby girl. I'm going to touch up my lipstick. If it's the same auditor we had last time, I need all this," she ran her hands dramatically over her hips, "to be correct. The sight of that nucka' sent my menopause into remission."

Tangie tipped away in her leopard print pumps, wiggling and giggling to herself. What in the world did she expect me to do to entertain this so-called auditor? What if he started asking questions, I was the wrong person for that considering the inside knowledge I had concerning Gen's finances.

"Hello?" someone called out from the small lobby at the front. Metro-Bobby popped up to escort her in. He came back moments later with a woman dressed like Agent Scully. She peered down at me over her glasses when they stopped in front of my desk.

"This is Novie. She'll be assisting you until the office manager Tangie is available," he announced, before going back to his desk.

"Hi, Novie." She said my name with so much attitude in her voice I did a double take.

Her hair was slicked back into a tight curly ponytail hanging halfway down her back. I couldn't place her face or her voice until I saw the rounded bump under the front of her suit jacket. My breath caught in my throat.

"Tinesha?" I asked in an unsure voice.

A slow smile spread across her face; it looked the same way the Grinch looked when he stole Christmas.

"The one and only. It seems like our world keeps gettin' smaller and smaller," she replied in a fake polite voice.

Lord, this can't be real. This has to be some kind of joke or some shit.

She eased down into the empty chair in front of my desk. Gone were the purple sprig-a-sprags and all the *ignance*, yes, *ignance* that she normally showed up with. Tinesha must've gotten a Ph.D. in chameleon business and life tactics. She had whoever had given her a real job completely fooled, because I'd seen how foolish she could get.

She looked around the office with her nose turned up, taking inventory and making assessments on the worth and value of everything Genesis had.

"So, this is where your nigga-thieving ass works?" she asked as she looked over the Bobbys who were all busy with trying to look busy. They weren't even fooling me.

When she was done with her visual assessment, she settled back in the chair and folded her hands in her lap. "I didn't take you for the type to hold down a real job. I figured you were more like a professional side chick."

This bitch has some nerve callin' me a side chick with all the dirt she has piled up in her yard.

I smiled at her so hard my cheeks burned. "Funny, and I was just thinking the same thing about—"

"Did you know, *Novie*, that when the IRS audits a business, we're just looking for hidden assets, misreported earnings, and fraud."

Oh no, this heffa is not going for the jugular and not on some play shit. Genesis's business doesn't have anything to do with the beef she has with me.

"All I need is one teeny-tiny mistake, and, by law, I have to make an *adverse opinion*." Her words sounded more like a threat than an explanation.

I prayed that Genesis had all of his shit in order. Swiss had said she didn't know about his dealings with Genesis. But if even one number didn't line up with another, I don't think she'd need to know anything about it. She'd raise enough hell in her own way.

The plush leather desk chair I was sitting in might as well have been a stack of heated cement blocks. I shifted uncomfortably. I had no idea exactly what an adverse opinion meant, but it sounded like something that would hurt Genesis more than it would hurt me.

"What do you want?" I asked.

Her top lip scrunched up toward her nose. She squinted at me through the lens of her glasses.

"Well, for starters, I want *you* to keep your damn mouth shut. You say a word to Swiss about Javion, and I'll make sure I find something to shut this bitch down."

Shit, it's way too late for that one. Hopefully, I could catch Swiss before he opened his fat mouth and told her anything I'd said.

"Second," she continued in a hushed voice, "I want to know where the *fuck* Javion is. The last time I talked to him, he said he was leaving with a bitch named Novie De-la-di-da. His phone is going straight to voice mail, and you're still here, so . . . ?"

"So what if I don't know where Javion is? What if I haven't seen him since the day you stomped him down outside of his car?" It wasn't a lie . . . Well, half of what I'd said wasn't a lie. Last time I'd seen Javion, he was dead. It never crossed my mind to ask Genesis or Swiss what happened to the body or the cover story for the body.

"Then you'd better track him down, or the IRS will make your life hell. People get audited all the time; they go to prison for tax evasion. Have you filed all of your prior year returns? Oh, wait, it doesn't matter. They will disappear if I need them to."

Tangie might be mean as hell, but I can say one thing . . . Tangie is no parts gangsta. On any given day, she kept the whole building on lockdown, and now her old rusty hind part's MIA when I need her to come to my rescue.

Tinesha wasn't done. "If Javion reaches out to you, make sure *you* reach out to *me*. I'll be in touch. And so you know how serious this is, I've already seen a glitch in Mr. Genesis Kane's information, and you are the deciding factor in what I do with that."

Tinesha wasn't even all the way out of the office before I started blowing up Gen's phone. He wasn't answering any of my calls or the texts I'd sent. Something was wrong. Something was definitely wrong.

***

After my visit with Tinesha, I was in panic mode. Initially, Tangie wasn't too enthusiastic about letting me leave early. Her mind changed real quick as soon as the word *flu* came out of my mouth. She shooed me out of the office in a lemon-scented cloud of Lysol, mumbling about a flu epidemic. I needed to get in contact with Genesis before Tinesha did something stupid. Hopefully, he'd be able to give me an idea of what I could tell her to throw her off. It would be nice if I knew what the fuck she'd found, though.

I'd started to make my way to Gen's loft, but Shandy and Heather's tip about this "mystery house" kept running through my mind. He'd never mentioned another house. It made me wonder if he lived there with some kind of secret family. If he was home, he could be gone by the time I left the loft and fought traffic to get out of the city. My best bet was to head out of the city first and work my way back in.

An hour later, I was standing in one of the richest neighborhoods in the city with my heels glued to the rust-colored cobblestones underneath 'em. I'd parked a few blocks away so I could take a minute to get my mind right without having my car spotted. Since I wasn't supposed to know about Gen's place out here, I didn't want to risk him recognizing my car and not answering the door.

All the gusto I'd felt earlier shrank away as I stared at houses lined up as high as mountains. Each one bigger and badder than the next, like I'd stepped into my own episode of *Real Housewives*. Even the sidewalks looked expensive as hell with cobblestones instead of cement and fancy silver lamps lining the streets. Their tiny flames flickered, getting brighter as the sun started to set. I definitely wasn't in Norfolk, Virginia, anymore. But that was the last place I wanted to be anyway.

My insides were shaking like Jell-O shots at a sorority party. It didn't make sense for me to be feeling this kind of nervousness mixed with anger. But considering how many times we'd been together, Genesis had only taken me to his loft once or twice. *Yes, that's it.* Shit, and even then, it was late as hell, and I was too damn tipsy and too busy trying to get some ass to take in the details. He'd never felt the need to mention his house.

This was all Shandy's and Heather's fault. If they hadn't run his name through the system, I wouldn't have been dying to figure out why he had so many addresses. And since he wasn't at the office or taking my calls, this felt like my only option. What was he hiding? Nobody hides something like a house unless they've got somebody up in that bitch.

I shook my head at myself and took a shaky pull from my stress Newport, twisting my lips as I exhaled so the smoke would blow into the wind. I should've borrowed one of Shandy's wigs, just in case he was outside and I chickened out; then, I could make a quick escape unnoticed.

I dropped my half-smoked cigarette, crushing it under my heel as I marched toward my man's house. The oversized gift bag I'd made for him was balanced in the nook of my arm as I dug through my much-hated purse. I had this thing down pat. Sanitize the hands, follow it up with the fresh lotion, and pop a stick of gum. It all must've worked, because not once did anyone ever complain.

I stopped in front of the address I'd memorized forward and backward. There were a few lights on inside, but I couldn't tell if he was home. My fingers locked around the handles of the gift bag in a sweaty grip as I marched up the circular driveway toward the Swiss archway of the front door. Now, we'd finally see about Genesis and this so-called *flu bug*. In my defense, it was only right that I check in to make sure he was really suffering . . . and really alone.

My plan was to peek in, and if all looked good, I'd just make that ass some chicken soup and hot toddies until he was too full and drunk to complain. Yes, this was probably all parts of wrong depending on how you looked at it, but he *was* my man, and as Genesis liked to say, *if it ain't sneaky, it ain't freaky.*

I propped my ear toward the door listening for the TV, or movement, or some bitch whose ass I'd have to whoop in case he was, after all, lying about everything. It was dead silent. *Girl, if this ain't the craziest shit you've ever done.*

After a few quick glances up and down the street, I pressed the doorbell. It let out a deep, loud dong, like a church bell. *You are wrong for this; he's probably sick as a dog, and you done popped yo' ass up over here. Mmmph, mmmph, mmph. Bet not get me sick, I know that much.* I held my breath, praying he'd appreciate this and not be mad. That he wasn't laid up with another bitch, cheating.

The sound of the lock turning sent my heart slamming into my chest. The door opened slow as all hell. Yo, my nerves and the excitement had me hopping from foot to foot, running in place like a jogger on a street corner. As soon as there was a gap big enough for me to fit through, I slid in without invitation, smelling and looking at everything I could see from the front door. It was warm cinnamon and apples, black forest oak wood flooring, and from what I could see, bulky, masculine furniture.

Genesis was standing to the side, one hand still on the door handle with the other holding up the *New York Times*. His face was plastered to the paper as he focused on whatever he was reading. He was wearing a long red robe like the ones boxers wear before they step into the ring. The hood hung low over his head, nearly covering his eyes. I tried to hone in on his face under the shadowy hood. The corners of his mouth were turned down in an ugly frown. I knew that look. It meant something was wrong; either he'd lost money on his retirement account, or a stock had dropped. There was no telling with him, but whatever it was, he wasn't going to be in a good mood behind it.

Suddenly, I realized how stupid this whole idea was. I should have at least called first. Now, here I was, uninvited and invading his space. My eyes shot around the foyer, looking for a place to hide while I tried to figure out if I could run my grown ass back out the door before he saw me.

"Where's your key, baby?" Genesis murmured in a low, distracted voice. "Guess you changed your mind about going to the—"

He looked up from his paper with confusion flashing across his face as we locked eyes.

My face scrunched into a wince, smile, and a cringe at being caught red-handed snoop-checking up on my man.

"Hey, you," I whispered back.

"Novie? How did you know where to find me?" he asked, sliding the hood of his robe back off his head. This made the front of the robe fall open, showing off the grey and black tattoos covering his smooth brown skin from his collarbone on down.

I stared up at him, momentarily speechless. That's how it felt when I saw him after any kind of hiatus. Our silent stare down came to a stop when his words finally registered in my brain. *Wait, did he say "baby" when he didn't even know I was at the door?*

All of the love, care, and attention I'd put into his gift bag was out the window. I let his gift bag hit the floor.

I marched right at him shooting electric sparks from my eyes. My index finger was already raised in accusation.

"Who were you calling *baby* if you didn't know it was me?" My voice was surprisingly calm, even to me, as my finger made invisible quotation marks in the air. "And what . . . *What* did she forget? Humph, I know how y'all DC niggas do. Is it even a *she*? I know for *damn sure* the word *key* won't about to come up outta your mouth," I snapped with my voice going up three octaves.

I was so pissed I could feel the pistivity rising up off of me like heat waves.

Genesis snapped the newspaper he'd been holding shut, methodically folding it in half before tucking it under his arm. He was probably trying to bide his time while he worked up a lie.

He let out an irritated sigh. "Are you done?" he asked calmly.

My eyes narrowed on him like a target. *No, this nigga did not have the nerve to look and sound perfectly healthy.*

"Kane!" An irritated woman's voice ricocheted through the house. "Kane? If that's my pizza, check and make sure it got extra sauce on it. Last time it was burnt *and* there wasn't no sauce," she screeched from somewhere upstairs.

My eyes widened and my head went on swivel. I looked from Genesis to the stairs and back. Shit, hopefully, I'd give myself whiplash so I could sue his ass. I ain't know exactly where that ho was, but she was about to catch it. *I know this nigga ain't got another bitch up in here.* I closed my eyes trying to find the words that would drop a man dead. He must have seen what was coming.

Genesis shook his head at me. "Calm down, Novie. There's a logical explanation for all of this."

"*Psht*," I hissed at him. "Logical, my ass." At this point even his calm demeanor was pissing me off. "You must logically think I'm an idiot."

"Kane? I'm gonna drink the last Naked juice. I don't feel like driving to get ginger ale . . ." her voice trailed off.

My gaze shifted slowly from Genesis's blank face up the winding staircase. They stopped dead center on this light-bright heffa standing on the balcony. She was wearing a black boxing robe similar to his, and it didn't look like much else underneath it. My blood ran so hot I got a headache and started sweating, all while picturing my hands around her throat.

"Dang," she talked like she didn't have a care in the world. "Why didn't you say you were having company? I hope you ordered enough pizza for everybody, because I ain't sharing my shit." With that, she turned and walked off.

My jaw dropped. I launched myself toward the stairs with tears blurring my vision. This couldn't be happening. Genesis's arms snaked around my waist, yanking me back against his chest. He became a human straitjacket, wrapping his arms around mine, pinning them to my heaving chest.

"Let go of me! You *smell* like you been fuckin'. Got that bitch's scent all over you. I swear on my life I'll—"

"You swear what?" Genesis barked down at the top of my head.

I was let go for the quickest second before his fingers dug into my shoulders. He whirled me around to face him. I was eye to eye with the tattoo of a sugar skull painted over a woman's face. She was beautiful and eerie at the same time. In the beginning, I didn't really think about it when he said sugar skulls honored someone who's passed. But the fact that he wouldn't tell me about this woman who meant so much to him he'd put her face on his body starting making me jealous little by little.

I refused to look up at him. I didn't want him to see my tears or how much he'd hurt me. My jaw was clenched so hard my teeth hurt as I settled in for a staring contest with his tattooed lady. She stared out at me from the middle of his chest; her empty eyes laughed at me.

"Well?" Genesis asked quietly.

My nose was running, and I couldn't remember the question.

He used the sleeve of his robe to dry my face, and he even wiped my nose.

"Novie, you might as well come on in, sit down, and have a drink with me. I was trying to wait for the best time to talk to you. There are a few things I was scared to tell you about myself . . . about my life."

GENESIS

Chapter 57

You'll Never Lose Women Chasing Money

Novie was a piece of fucking work, and that was an under-statement. She had all her five feet of nothing squared up like she was ready to battle. She didn't even consider the fact that she'd just invaded my space and my privacy. She was the one who'd spied, gotten my address, and then showed up uninvited. It amazed me how women could go looking for some shit, and then have the nerve to be hurt when they step in it.

Kenisha was still watching from the balcony. I avoided looking in her direction altogether. She was either getting a kick out of this, or building up her own arsenal of shit to come at me with later. Even if I asked nicely, Kenisha wasn't about to budge an inch so long as Novie was acting hostile. My home protects home first, and in the event I needed to get dealt with, she'd do that when it was just the two of us. I ran my fingers across the hairs on my chin and nodded toward the living room.

"Why don't we go sit down and talk about all this?" I asked in as calm of a voice as I could manage.

I didn't keep up nor did I put up with drama or dramatic episodes. Novie gave me a slow nod. I led her into the other room with the sound of Kenisha sucking her teeth from above. We sat across from each other, and her big brown eyes were shimmery with tears and hurt. She angrily crossed her arms over her chest while she glared at me. I seriously debated on just cutting this shit off completely. I'd never had a woman physically track me down, show up at my house uninvited, and invade my space like she just did. If I'd wanted all my cards on the table, I would have put them all out there. I operated the way I did to fend off the charity cases and chameleons. Once someone knows your worth, it gets harder and harder to figure out if they're down for you versus your assets.

"Who is that woman, Kane?" Novie asked in a small, angry voice.

I was momentarily at a loss for words. My own name sounded strange to my ears. She never called me Kane. I was always Genesis or Gen. She was still sexy as fuck, though. Even when she was mad as hell with her nostrils flaring and her hair swinging everywhere all wild. It was rare to see honest, raw emotion. Everyone in my world from the police, to the other attorneys, to the clients were all so calculating and manipulative. I rarely saw *real* feelings. The realization made me bite the inside of my lip and fake an ear scratch so I could look away to hide my smile. When I turned back, I was composed and ready for whatever.

NOVIE

Chapter 58

What Had Happened Was

"Kenisha, come down here for a minute, please," Genesis hollered through the house.

I didn't want to meet no damn Kenisha or hear any bullshit excuses. I wanted the black-and-white honest-to-God truth.

The girl lazily waddled into the living room like she'd just been summoned to a hearing.

Genesis introduced us. "Novie, this is my niece, Kenisha. My brother got himself locked up, and as her next of kin, I stepped up and took her in. We've been getting along pretty well. Kenisha, this is Novie."

Kenisha looked me over curiously with her nose turned up like a little pug. She pointed between the two of us. "Y'all got a thing or somethin'?" she asked Genesis.

"Yeah, somethin'. I just wanted the two of you to meet face-to-face. That's all."

Kenisha rubbed the side of what I could now see was a belly underneath the huge boxing robe. "Okay, well, this baby's foot is in my ribs, so I'm gonna go lie down and wait on that pizza."

When she was upstairs and out of hearing distance I turned to Genesis. "She's pregnant? How old is she? How far along is she?"

His face looked older than usual; worry lines creased his usually smooth forehead as he ran his hand back and forth across his chin.

"She's sixteen. Been staying with me since she was fourteen, and I don't know shit about raising girls. I stayed home today because she's been having early contractions, gas, or Lord knows what. But she said pizza would make her feel better. I never know when to do what with her. She isn't even supposed to be pregnant, not on my watch, but all the lying and sneaking around, the attitudes, and know-it-all-ness. She's like a miniature version of you."

I punched his arm, forgetting how angry and embarrassed I was just seconds ago.

"Nigga, I am *none* of those things. Don't be mad because I have my own opinions and need justification for bullshit."

I wanted to punch Shandy and Heather in their nosy faces for this one. I'd gone and run up in this man's house looking like a lunatic. What if Kenisha would've answered the door, or if Genesis hadn't stopped me before I could get my hands on her?

Genesis eyed the goody bag sitting in the middle of the floor. "Did you bring me a surprise, or is that where you keep your gun, Inspector Gidget?"

"I brought you some get well soon rations, but now I can see that you don't need them."

Genesis smiled as though he appreciated the gesture. He offered me a tour of his house, showing me everything from an indoor heated pool, to a full gym and sauna. We stopped on the third floor in a room that could've been a home office or a library. I followed Genesis out through white, billowy curtains onto a large balcony made of blinding white stones. Big bottle-shaped vases were carved into the sides of the walls, made out of the same white stones as the railing and floor. They were piled with tropical orange and red hibiscus. A hummingbird zoomed by, taking my breath away. I'd never seen one in real life before, only on TV.

Genesis sat down at an all-white patio table. Deposition papers, his laptop, and cell were all strewn about across the table. I had to keep reminding myself that he was still a smart and very reputable attorney. Outside of work, in his element, he could've passed for anything. An actor, a rapper. I looked at him wondering if I'd ever get to know the man behind all of the masks.

"I was downstairs with Kenisha all morning. Glad it didn't rain, or I'd be out shopping for new electronics."

I used that opportunity to fill him in on Tinesha's visit to the office, as well as her threats.

Genesis didn't even seem slightly fazed by that information. He stared out into the woods that surrounded the edge of his backyard. Dirt trails split in at least five different directions through the trees. They were either hiking or dirt bike trails.

"Tinesha isn't going to be a problem. I'll send a little birdie her way just to make sure we've got all of our bases covered. Thank you for keeping an eye on things. I'll be back as soon as I know Kenisha's good."

My phone rang. I dug it out of my purse, but not before Genesis could see Swiss's face flashing across the screen. I wasn't fast enough.

Genesis's face went stormy. "I thought I told you to stay away from that."

His voice was so low and quiet I could barely hear him over the sounds of the birds chirping in the trees around us. I silenced Swiss's call, giving Genesis my undivided attention.

"And I told you that it's *not* what you think. *He's* not whatever it is you're thinking. You fucked my friends, yet you have the biggest problem with even the thought of me fucking one of yours?"

"Swiss is no friend of mine!" Genesis roared, jumping to his feet, flipping the table.

I jumped, sidestepping his phone as it slid across the ground. This was not the type of reaction I'd expect from someone who did regular business with another dude. There had to be something more behind Genesis not liking Swiss than he was telling me. If Genesis wasn't going to tell me what I needed to know, that only left one other person for me to talk to.

"I need to talk to you," Swiss blurted out as soon as I answered the phone.

"Okay. I'm leaving the office now. I just need to run home and freshen up and then I'll head over. Your women better not touch me or my car, Swiss."

NOVIE

Chapter 59

Step Up Or Get Stepped On

I rushed home and after a quick shower I was finally ready to relax and let myself breathe. Swiss was waiting for me to come scoop him up so we could have a "talk." We'd been so hit or miss lately. Well, I'd actually been missing him on purpose. Genesis was always on my mind, taking over my thoughts. It was time for me to let Swiss go, and I wasn't sure how he was going to take it.

I almost didn't make it out of the house on time since it took me close to forever to remember where I'd put my keys. I needed to start laying them in one specific spot when I got home. They were in the dish by the front door where I normally never put them. But with Heather and Denise and Shandy all planning a weekend in, it should have crossed my mind to ask one of them where they were instead of searching for an hour. They all seemed to share some kind of extreme OCD that involved moving and rearranging things that did not belong to them.

Whoooo hooo! I swung my hair, loving the way it felt as it brushed across my shoulders. One hand was up through the moon roof, with my fingers snapping on beat to the stars and the streetlights. I whipped Genesis's Jag through the streets, swerving around taxis and traffic like I was in the Daytona 500. Swiss reclined in the passenger's seat with a bottle of champagne in one hand and a bottle of Hennessey White in the other. He'd said Genesis had picked them up for him.

For Genesis to be as hell-bent against Swiss as he was, he sure did a lot of nice things for the man.

Swiss tapped my shoulder. "Girl, slow this bitch down. You weren't that late scooping me up. Damn, we can still make the movie. We comin' up on a red light. Here." He held out the Henny.

I took the bottle with a smirk, lifting it to my lips. He was trying his best to get me fucked up, but I'd just wind up dropping him off and go see my babe. Every red light brought another round of shots as we hooted at the parade of women crossing over the crosswalks. I was getting further from sober and closer to having to pee.

"What is this grudge Genesis has against you?"

Swiss took another long, deep swig from the bottle. "Novie, why does it feel like this nigga's name keeps popping up every time I'm around you? Can we leave work at work for once?"

"I need to know, Swiss. I want to make sure he doesn't try to do anything to hurt you. It's not some kind of regular shit; it's like a full-out raging *I hate that nigga* grudge."

"He has more to worry about what I would do to him. It's a pheromone thing, or fuck if I know; maybe he's trying to get at you and it's just some plain old nigga bullshit."

"It's deeper than that, Swiss. He acts like he can't stand you."

"If that nigga feelin' some kind of way, he'd better to step up before he gets stepped on. He's always cool as cream when I deal with him. As long as my pockets stay right, I'm fine with it."

Giggling, I watched Swiss fumble, trying to put the cap back on the bottle.

"Nigga, you really can't drink, can—"

Bam! Thoomp! Thuddump!

The words were knocked loose from my brain before they could leave my mouth. Droplets of rain sprayed me in the face as I jerked forward before slamming back into my seat.

Oh, fuck, I've been shot.

Dazed with my head spinning, I looked over for Swiss. It was either dead silent or I couldn't hear anything over the ringing in my ears. The passenger-side door was sitting wide open. He was gone. He'd actually bailed on me again.

Everything slowly came into as much focus as it could with all the shots I'd taken. People were running around the car.

They reminded me of silent movies or mimes the way they were pointing, gesturing hysterically, and pulling out their phones to take pictures. Cameras flashed by the dozens. I was hit so hard the trunk had popped open, slamming into and breaking the back windshield. My door was yanked open. A little Filipino man looked me over with an anxious expression.

"Somebody called an ambulance. I saw everything, but I couldn't get the plate off the car that rear-ended you," he said in a shaky voice. "Just hold on. You're gonna be okay. You were wearing your seat belt but . . ."

He looked away from me, staring off and down the street at something. I followed his line of vision. It was then that I saw streetlight folded into the hood of the Jag. It wasn't even raining. Blood ran into my eye. Swiss was lying half on the sidewalk and half in the street. I could see him clear as day without the windshield. His leg was bent at an unnatural angle. I slammed my eyes shut at the big jagged bone that had torn through his jeans sticking out of his thigh.

My Bluetooth announced Denise was calling.

"Answer," I called out in a weak voice. "Dee, me and Swiss were just in a car accident," I blurted out before she could say anything.

An ambulance pulled up in a blur of deafening sirens and red lights.

"Novie? What happened? Are y'all okay? Where are you at? I'll come out there," Denise asked a frenzy of questions through the speakers.

"Somebody hit me, they pushed me into a—"

Suddenly I couldn't be heard over all the police officers and firefighters swarming around the car. They even got up to run over from where they'd been huddled around Swiss in the street.

"We've got a Code 4 back here! Code 4 on a kid in the trunk," one of the EMTs shouted over all the chaos.

"Novie? Did he just say a kid?" Denise screamed, her voice echoed through the speakers, bouncing around the inside of the car.

"Oh my God, is Hennessey with her? Is she okay? Did you tell her we looked everywhere for her?" Heather was chanting and panicking in the background.

I lay my head back against the headrest, wishing I was the one lying in the street instead of Swiss. Tears slid down my face. Hennessey's little body dangled lifelessly from a paramedic's arms.

"Novie! We've been looking for Hennessey for the last hour! She wasn't hiding in the car, was she? Answer me, Novie!" Shandy begged over and over for an answer.

My throat constricted until I couldn't speak. It all made sense now. Why I couldn't find my keys. Why I'd heard three thumps . . . one when I was hit, another when I hit the post, and the last thump was a tiny person being thrown around in the trunk of my car.

"Get out of the fucking car now," officers started shouting.

Lights were put on me. They were so bright they made my head spin. Guns were drawn, and the officers posted up around my car like I was some kind of criminal.

"I don't think I can move," I cried out the driver's side door with my hand shielding the light from my eyes.

It felt like my arm was being pulled out of the socket when I got yanked out of the car and thrown down onto the ground, right there in the middle of the street. Glossy golden motor oil ran down the pavement. It puddled where I lay. It was sticky and hot against the side of my cheek as someone's knee went into my back, pressing my face into the cracked black asphalt. Broken glass scraped my cheek and poked into my chest through my dress as my arms were cuffed behind me. A lonely blue and white shoe sat on the ground underneath my car.

Tears slid down my cheeks, burning the scratches on my face. I should've never been drinking and driving in the first place. There was nobody to blame for any of this except myself.

There was only one person I knew of who could get me out of this, and I had no idea if making that call would save me or sign my death certificate. First Javion, now Swiss. I'd single-handedly disposed of Genesis's number one and his number two guys. He'd probably let me rot in jail, or he'd make my life so hellish, jail would seem like a walk in the park.

Chapter 60

Alpha Dog

To the chagrin and dismay of more than a few officers, it was easier for Genesis to get me out of jail than I thought. The DUI and double homicide charges all but disappeared before my hand could put the crusty phone in the station down onto the receiver. Genesis gave me his word that everything would be taken care of, and from what I could tell, he'd kept it.

A few hours later, I was climbing into the back of the Lincoln Town Car that'd arrived outside the jail. My eyes were red and sore. I hadn't stopped crying since the police had put me into the car.

"Novie, I swear you could put CIA operatives and hired hit men to shame if you ever decided to expand your résumé," Farrah chimed from the backseat.

I jumped in surprise. I wasn't expecting her. Genesis had given me the impression that he'd be coming to pick me up. Disappointed, I climbed in, giving Farrah a weak smile. Talking wasn't at the top of my list right now.

"It wasn't what I'd intended, I promise," I assured her.

She handed me a miniature bottle of Perrier. I accepted it, even though I hated that mess. It tasted like carbonated yuck. I'd rather just drink regular water.

"Well, now with this tragic turn of events, I've found myself in need of a new captain. A new number one. I've looked into your family, Novie. The Deleons have a solid reputation. You come from good stock."

I frowned, trying to see Farrah's eyes through the oversized shades on her face.

"My family and I had a falling out. But I'm sorry, Farrah; blame the concussion. I'm kind of confused," I admitted. "I, um, I thought Genesis was your go-to person. The boss, or your number one guy, I guess I should say."

Farrah scoffed at me. "Who, Genesis? Oh, how that control freak would love to be the man in charge." She laughed. "That's a good one. Genesis Kane as a boss? Not hardly. He's my legal muscle, the reason we all stay damn near untouchable. Genesis has helped cover up dirt on behalf of the police department, city council, even the mayor. If they ever decided to be uncooperative, well, I'd pretty much own the city. But no, Genesis has never been in charge. Swiss was my burly Alpha warrior. He was my number one, my go-to man." Farrah let out a sad sigh. "And my go-to fuck. God, sex with that man was better for my body than Pilates and water aerobics combined."

Fizzy lemon-lime water went down the wrong pipe, making me choke and sputter.

I dabbed my watery eyes with the back of my hand. "Sorry, wrong pipe," I muttered after I'd gotten my composure.

Swiss and Farrah . . . What the fuck? Well, damn, who wasn't Swiss fucking?

I almost punched the seat in front of me. This shit was more than I was ready to face or process right now.

"So, Novie, back to my question. Do I trust an outside source to come in and pick up where Swiss left off, or do I give you that position?"

Okay, this was definitely way too much for me to process. I'd just killed a man and the daughter of my best friend's girlfriend. Those two deaths hanging over my head were making my stomach reel. By now, Heather and Shandy had been contacted, and I still had them to deal with. How do I apologize for accidentally killing someone's child? How could I make that up to someone? All I really wanted to do was crawl into a hole and never crawl back out.

"Farrah, can I have some time to think. It's just that all of this was kind of traumatic. I just need to get my bearings."

"Sure. As bad as Genesis wants the title for himself, I'm giving you forty-eight hours to come to grips with reality. You've taken out my two best guys. If you don't take this offer I can't say that I will have much further use for you." The lines around Farrah's lips wrinkled as she pursed her lips together. It made it look like she had a little pink-sour asshole poking out of her face.

I nodded my understanding.

It was pretty clear that my only option was to accept her offer or she'd renege on one of my get out of jail free cards. I'd never been good at ultimatums. The last time I was faced with one, I tried to kill myself. But this time, the thought of being in charge, running things, hell, even running Genesis, didn't seem as bad as it sounded.

The car rolled to a stop in front of an Enterprise Car Rental.

"We have an account here. Genesis has already set you up with a car," she stated.

Half an hour later, I was leaving the rental office in a compact blue Prius. This had to be Genesis's way of punishing me for Swiss's death. It still felt too soon for me to go home and face the aftermath that I knew was waiting so I called the devil himself.

"How many times had I told you to *stay away* from that nigga?" Genesis growled in the phone without saying hello.

"Now you don't have to worry about that ever again, Genesis. It's been handled permanently!" My voice broke.

I'd been holding in guilt on top of resentment on top of anger at myself. Saying the words out loud made me feel the impact of what had happened. Swiss's sons would have to grow up without a father, and Heather would have to go on without her baby girl. I pulled over to the side of the road. None of this felt right. Why did God let me live over and over again?

"Where are you at, Novie?" Genesis asked.

"Somewhere near Enterprise," I sniffled into the phone. "I pulled over."

"Well, stay there. I'm coming to get you. We can go get your mind off of things."

***

An hour later, Genesis and I were going shot for shot at a brewery not far from where I lived. Genesis had gotten us a cozy corner table away from the crowded bar so we could talk. Even though I didn't have any kind of an appetite, I ordered steak fries since he insisted I put something in my stomach with all the alcohol. The waitress brought out my fries, hovering over Genesis for a moment or two longer than necessary to make sure he was good. When she finally left, I turned to him, juggling a bite of the piping hot fried potato between my teeth and my tongue.

"Why did you lie to me? You let me think you were running everything," I asked once I finished wrestling with my food.

He didn't even look shocked or caught off guard by my question. Genesis stopped twirling the toothpick that he'd been tossing from side to side in his mouth. He laid it neatly on the side of his napkin.

"If you know what's what, then I'm guessing Farrah has already spoken to you," he said.

"Yes, and she wants me to take Swiss's place."

Genesis scooped up his shot glass. "Let's take another shot, and then I'll tell you everything."

Tequila burned its way down my throat and chest. I almost gagged the shot back up. It reminded me of why I hated it in the first place. It was Genesis's choice, so I didn't complain when he ordered it, but boy, my head and stomach were surely gonna complain in the morning.

"I didn't lie. I never said I ran anything. You assumed that part. I've worked with Farrah for a good number of years. I was only twenty-five and fresh out of law school. She was my first client, and I lost her case because I was inexperienced. When she got out and wanted to start over, I helped her because I owed her one, and I saw her vision."

"What? Let me find out the wealth consultant was on her Martha Stewart back in the day," I blurted out in shock.

"Yeah, and she brought your boy Swiss in a couple of years ago. He made shit happen, and he did it fast. Got territory covered, mapped out who we could deal with, who we could work for, and . . ." Genesis pointed in my direction. "He figured out who could be useful to us."

"Useful?" I gawked at Genesis. "Useful, like how? This was all a bullshit fluke. If that shit hadn't went down with Javion—"

"Novie, if it wasn't the shit that went down with Javion that made you cross our paths, it would've been something else. Swiss's mind had been made up about pulling you in way before you ever knew what you were being pulled into."

And just like that, what little appetite I had was gone. I threw a half-eaten fry back into the basket, rubbing my fingers together to dust off the salt.

"No. Genesis, I'm telling you that you must have misunderstood something somewhere. Swiss was—"

"Novie, Farrah wants to tap into the medicinal marijuana industry. Swiss insisted that he knew a woman who could do more than all of our efforts combined. Said he had *intimate knowledge* of you." Genesis scowled saying the words *intimate knowledge* like they left a bitter taste in his mouth. "Swiss had guys watching you and your apartment for . . . I don't know . . . a year, maybe longer. You even got a few phones he had preloaded with spyware. He knew where you went, who you saw, and what you were doing. Javion was originally one of the guys gathering info on you. He didn't know why he was doing it, but he fucked up when he crossed the line and used what he knew to get in your panties."

Genesis stopped to tell the waitress who'd wandered back over we were good. I too declined her offer for water and another shot. I was still in shock. This was all way too much to process in one day. *Javion had been watching me?* Now it all made sense, why he knew so much about me and how he seemed to remember it all so effortlessly.

"I know this sounds crazy, and it's probably too much to tell you considering what you've been through, but you deserve to know the truth."

"Did Swiss tell Javion to shove the broom up the daughter's ass too, or was that all Javion?"

Genesis shrugged. "Either way it goes, if you hadn't left your prints on the front door, Swiss was going to plant them when he went back to slit Beau and his daughter's throats."

"Would he have let me go to prison if I told you no when you approached me that day?"

The grim look on Genesis's face made my stomach turn.

"I had enough cash on me to buy the entire Eastern shore if that's what was needed to get you out. I was told to take the money to a field and burn all of it if you declined."

I slumped back in the hard wooden chair with my mind whirring. I ran from Swiss and the drug game, just to get sucked back into it all over again. There was no way I could work for Farrah. Too many people had already died because of me, and I wasn't about to get any deeper into this shit than I already had.

Genesis touched my hand across the table. "That's why I kept telling you to stay away from him."

"So that's the reason why you were doing things for him? You were his errand boy? Hell, the champagne and Hennessey we'd drunk were—"

"They were items he requested. You can't find Hennessey White in the States, but I know a guy. The same goes for the de Brignac. For a hood-ass nigga, Swiss had good taste. Look at his choice in booze, to cars . . . women."

I ignored his little suggestion at the end. There were still too many unanswered questions, and my heart was still too heavy for me to get distracted that easily. "So what happens if I tell Farrah that my answer is no? Do you turn into the bad attorney and go out planting seeds all across town to get me locked back up?"

"Turning Farrah down isn't an option, Novie. I'll protect you for as long as I can, but you know a lot of damaging details. She won't trust you not to talk. Bottom line, you need to choose between working with us . . . or disappearing. Forever."

Chapter 61

The Only Thing Stronger Than Another's Love Is Another's Hate

I tripped over something as I walked in the front door of my apartment. Something was always out of place, or laid down and forgotten about. The extra key to the Prius Genesis rented for me clanged loudly onto the coffee table in the living room. Hearing them clank onto the table brought fresh tears to my eyes. Hennessey probably stood at the window by the front door, popped the trunk, and then ran to get in, dropping my keys into the dish by the front door. I didn't even know to look or listen for her in there.

It was almost three a.m. Genesis and I drank until the bar stopped serving liquor. Both of us had an early morning to get ready for, so he'd dropped me off horny and drunk. I left him the valet key so he could have someone drop off my rental. I was really hoping he'd take me to his place and fuck the sadness out of me.

I regained my balance while trying to focus my blurry, spinning vision on whatever was lying on the floor trying to kill me. Suddenly, the corner lamp came on with a loud click. I jumped so hard it's a wonder I didn't get scared sober. I whirled in the direction of the light, blinking against the bright light.

"I didn't sign up for this bullshit, Novie."

Shandy was sitting on the couch balancing a vodka bottle on her thigh.

"Hey, Shan," I whispered.

She stood up almost nose to nose with me, forcing me to look into her eyes flashing with pain and fury. Her hair was pulled back into a loose ponytail, giving her more of an angry teenager look versus a grown woman.

"Nah, Novie, don't 'hey' me. I told you to leave well enough alone. I told your ass not to get mixed up with my brother again."

She slammed the bottle down on the wooden coffee table, like a judge slamming a gavel. "You didn't listen, and Denise doesn't have anything because of you. Heather can't stand the sight of her. My brother and Hennessey are gone. I'm tired of living my life as Novie's crutch. You have to go. Tonight."

A confused frown creased my forehead.

"Go? Are you putting me out?" I sputtered. "Where am I supposed to go, Shandy? Girl, you know I don't have anywhere or anyone else."

"There are mad shelters out there. Pick one! You can sleep under the little desk in your office for all I care. I'm done giving a fuck about you!" Shandy stomped her foot. She flung the vodka bottle at the wall behind me. It left a big gaping hole before hitting the floor and rolling. "I had to call and explain to my momma that her son is dead because of you. She won't even take my calls anymore. I know my momma wasn't shit, but she and Swiss were all the family I had, Novie. You've still got all your family *and* your side nigga. Just go. Somebody will feel sorry for you and try to take care of you like I did."

My drunken mind jumped from plan to plan, explanations to lies, to the absolute truth behind her words.

"Shan, you don't mean that shit. You can't even afford the lease on this place by yourself—"

"Since when has someone else's ability to do or not do been a concern to you?" she hissed at me.

My eyes dropped to the points of my silver studded pumps. I was doing my best to hide the anger building up inside me. I'd lost. I'd been hurt in all this too, and she was putting me out on the street like I wasn't shit. After everything we'd been through, this is how she was treating me?

"Shandy, I am so very, very sorry about—"

Her hand flew up, cutting me off.

"Do you lie to fool *you*? Because you ain't fooling me. Sorry, yes—yes, you are a sorry excuse for a woman, but you ain't contrite." Her voice was shaky and low, but her words were acidic. "I moved, I started over. I didn't have to, Novie. I *really* gave up everything to help you."

She circled around me, stopping just behind my right shoulder.

"And you couldn't give up one thing for me. Your selfish ass just couldn't leave my brother alone, and now he's dead because of you! I fucking hate you, and I hope you get everything you deserve!" Her argument ended with her screaming in my ear.

She stepped back in front of me with her hands clenched into tight fists. Tears ran down her splotchy red cheeks. Everything she'd said was true, but I couldn't admit that to her, and I couldn't be stuck out on the streets either. She brushed past me, toward the dark bedroom.

This wasn't the plan. I was so mad I could barely breathe. My breath was ragged and choppy. I should've died in that crash, nobody else but me. Genesis should've let me go to prison and serve time as punishment. I didn't deserve to be out. But it's not like I did it on purpose. Shan couldn't stand Swiss, and she barely like Hennessey, and knew it. Her anger was inexcusable.

I marched toward the door where my things were sitting in sloppily organized little piles. She didn't even have the decency to let me get my stuff together myself. I snatched up as much as I could carry in one trip. One of Genesis's flunkies had gotten my car to the apartment in one piece. If I put my shit in the rental I wouldn't have to deal with her neighbors staring at me.

It was quiet outside as I rushed to get my things in the car as fast as I could. Three trips later, I was down to my last few items. I'd just finished putting my suitcase and laundry basket in the backseat, and all I had left was my favorite perfume and a few toiletries. I was almost at the car when the toe of my pump caught a crack in the pavement. My eyes went wide, and it was either going to be the perfume or me, so I let that shit go. The black bottle hit the ground, shattering to pieces. I teetered, reaching for anything to catch me and getting nothing. Before I could brace myself, I flopped forward, hitting the ground hard as hell.

White-hot pain seared through my chin. My right wrist felt like it was broken or sprained. I sat up slowly, trying to see if anything else was hurt. It felt like water was soaking through the front of my turtleneck. *Great, I fell in sewer water. I'll probably grow a third nipple now.*

I'd barely gotten my shaky, wobbly legs to hold my weight when I noticed the red stain on the front of my sweater. Blood was dripping from a big open gash in my chin. I pulled out my cell and dialed 9-1-1.

"Nine-one-one, what's your emergency?" the operator asked in calm, mechanical voice.

"Yes, ma'am. I, um, I need some help. I'm bleeding really bad."

The throbbing in my chin fell in sync with my heart. Every throb sent blood dripping and pain shooting through my face.

"Ma'am, where are you and what happened?" the operator asked.

My voice was shaky and breathy. "I just . . . um."

My mind went blank. Maybe the fall knocked something loose. I probably had a concussion. I stared at the thin white clouds that my breath made in the air. Each one disappeared like the thoughts in my head.

"I got in a fight with my roommate." The words spilled out before I could stop them. Once they hit the air, I knew it was too late to take them back.

"She hit me. I fell, cut my chin." My voice was shaky from the cold and from the pain in my chin, but it made me sound scared and desperate.

"What's the address, ma'am? I have officers and an ambulance on the way."

I gave the operator my address and moved to sit on the stoop in front of our unit. Back home, I might have bled to death before help showed up. Shit, I'd just started arguing with myself over whether the red and blue lights flashing in front of me were real because they got to me so fast. An EMT rushed toward me with three police officers trailing not far behind. I was moved into the back of the ambulance, where I told them the same thing I told the operator. The officers gave each other a look before going toward the apartment.

The third officer stood just outside the ambulance. "Ma'am, one of your neighbors had called in a noise complaint not more than ten minutes ago. They heard some yelling and whatnot. One of you is gonna have to leave here tonight. Just say the word, and we can press charges, file a protective order, do whatever we need so you're safe."

On the outside I was dazed and frazzled, but inside, I smiled.

I nodded to the officer. "Yes, I want to press charges. She'll probably try to kill me since I called you. I don't feel safe."

The officer hoisted his pants up, giving me a stern nod. I could hear Shandy's voice as they dragged her outside toward a car. She sounded furious. The EMTs gave me a shot of something to dull the pain. The world moved in slow motion after that, and I tuned everything out and drifted to sleep.

Chapter 62

When Love Is a Hustle

After the night I had, it's a wonder I woke up at all. I was in the emergency room, two hours late for work. The cut in my chin wasn't as bad as it looked. I didn't even need stitches. It was just a meaty spot, and according to the EMT, I was a gusher.

Genesis left me the longest, most drawn out voice mail.

"Sorry for getting you drunk and being the bearer of sour news. They won't be checking for you in the office today. I know what the deal is, so you've got the next two weeks off with pay if your answer is yes. Just make sure you call before your forty-eight hours is up; there's a lot of work to get done. A lot to fill you in on. I'll be in a consultation all morning, so don't call me unless it's an emergency. Talk to you later."

I skipped over a message from Officer Whoever who took my statement last night and called myself a cab. I'd deal with the police and last night's drama later. Right now, I just needed to figure out how I'd get a new car and work my way into a new place.

I smirked to myself as I inched down an empty alley off of H Street.

It was almost ninety degrees out, and the sky looked like we were about to get a good thunderstorm. Both of those issues worked in my favor. The Prius's engine rumbled and puttered in complete disagreement with the temperature outside. I gave the shiny leather dashboard an understanding pat. "I know, baby. You too wacked for this shit. And that's exactly why Momma has to retire you so she can get a new baby," I cooed to the car.

The breeze whipped through the alley, kicking me in the face, tossing around my shoulder-length spiral curls as I climbed out of the car. The ground was covered in dirty puddles and potholes. The first few drops of rain fell down from the sky. They clung to my feathered lashes. This was not the day for me to have my hips cinched into a pencil skirt and five-inch heels. But in the words of my momma, "It was a woman's job to look and smell amazing at all times, and a man's job to make sure she's got whatever's necessary to keep that shit up."

The thought made my shimmer-glossed lips curve into a small, devilish smile. I took a deep breath, leaned down, and counted. *VS2, VS1, VVS2*. Yes, I used diamond clarities to amp myself up. Going from very small inclusions to very, very small inclusions built up my courage. When I got to *FL*, flawless with no imperfections, I rammed my pocketknife into the driver-side tire wall, twisting the blade until there was a huge open gash. After doing the same to the back tire I hopped back inside, cranking the heat up as high as it'd go.

Semiwarm exhaust-scented air gusted back at me. I didn't even bother with turning the AC up any higher. This Prius acted finicky as hell if it was set colder than seventy when it was hotter than eighty degrees outside. I paused to breathe in through my nose and out through my mouth. That bag was a hair away from getting dumped out of the damn window. It was one of the more recent gifts Javion had given me, with a fancy name I'd never even heard of.

In all of his logic, he thought that hardly ever seeing me with a purse meant I didn't have any nice purses. To the contrary, if you could find any nigga with even a teeny bit of paper to his name, you'd find every purse you've ever wanted. Or didn't want, as was my case. There was a box in my trunk full of nothing but purses and clutches. But at least I *knew* who made those.

Slamming the purse down on the seat, I made a mini eye-roll. My phone hadn't gotten lost in my tote-along black hole. As soon I could do away with it without Genesis noticing, that pink python "stuff-trap" would go right in the bag box, or I'd sell it online.

I was having a silent auction in my head over how much it'd go for as I pressed the word "Gen" on my phone. I'd planned out just about everything except for what I'd do if he didn't answer. But, Genesis could be so predictably logical that him not answering might have made this a little more fun.

He answered just as I predicted, placing me on hold in place of saying hello.

"Novie," Genesis sighed into the phone, "you didn't check your voice mail? I told you not to call unless it's an emergency. This better be important. I'm in a consultation with a client," he whispered in a rushed voice.

"I know. I'm sorry. I didn't know what else to do. The car started driving funky so I turned down this street and *bam* . . . two flats. So now I'm stuck in this alley behind some old abandoned hotel. I'm scared it might have been some kind of bum trap or something. Maybe they strand tourists so they can break into their cars. I'm scared one might run out of nowhere and—"

"I'll send out a driver and tow truck. It has insurance, and I think we even got you the roadside assistance."

His tone was a lot softer, even though he still sounded a little short to me.

I turned on my damsel-in-distress charm to kick things up a notch.

"Can't you just leave real quick and come get me? I've got this thing when it comes to riding with men I don't know. What if I get one of the crazies?" I spoke slowly, choosing my words carefully since I wanted something.

Every word had to be deliberate and precise. I was a chameleon, changing and adapting to whatever he wanted.

I could hear low voices and papers shuffling on the other end before the line went completely silent. I checked to make sure the call hadn't dropped. His name was still there, and the call counter was still going. See, that kind of rude buffoonery right there is what had made me exercise my most extreme levels of patience. Genesis was always good for randomly muting the phone at any point during our convo. It was always to *uphold his lawyer-client confidentiality,* or so he'd say. As far as I know, he could be laid up, trying to make a quick escape to carry on the call so I or whoever else wouldn't hear anything. Even if it was business, he was still rude and inconsiderate by the way he went about doing it, and that habit was one he'd need to break out of.

He unmuted the phone, making a sound that was somewhere between a groan and a conceding sigh.

"All right, I'm on my way. Send me the address of whatever's nearby."

I did as I was told with a knowing smirk on my face. Just like I thought, he would answer, and he would come get me. *Don't call unless blah blah blah, my ass.* He might run it in the courtroom, but I ran my relationships, no matter who I was with.

No more than thirty minutes had gone by before my stomach was growling. It was a little after eleven, and the bagel I'd had for breakfast was long gone. Genesis and the tow truck driver both showed up before I could make up my mind about whether or not Slim Jims get old. I'd found one crammed in the back of my glove compartment, but Lord knows how long it had been in there.

Genesis came over to open my car door, sending all my doubts and love requirements swirling away. Seeing him felt like a mixture of waking up on Christmas morning and opening a box of Ferrero Rocher chocolates. His dark brown blazer was open, showing off his gold, tan, and yellow vest. It tapered at the waist, flaring over his broad shoulders, and all I could think about was unwrapping and nibbling at all the chocolate that I knew was underneath.

He glanced into the backseat. "Why does it look like you're moving your—"

"Oh, it's nothing. A pipe burst in the apartment above mine and flooded me out." I didn't want to sound like a charity case or make him think I was trying to beg my way into his life. A lie just seemed to sit better with me than telling him Swiss's sister put me out on my ass.

"I see. Well, I had to reschedule the Morelli consultation. I'm billing seven seventy-five an hour for that one. I think somebody owes me a little face time." Genesis winked down at me with a slick grin.

The mention of "face time" would've normally made me melt on the spot. But I was under more stress than any normal person should have to handle.

Genesis checked to make sure the tow truck driver was out of hearing distance. "I think you should stay at my loft. Let me take your mind off of things. Get you wet while your apartment dries out."

"Really, Genesis, why do you always have to be so nasty?" I gave him a sour look for being so inconsiderate to my emotional state. I wasn't made for or used to this type of shit.

"You'll get used to this business, and when you do, you'll realize that there are casualties. There will always be casualties in our line of work, and you have to know when to let go and get on with shit."

At the end of the day, I needed to live and make a living. Who would it really matter to if what I did was legal or not? Swiss said he was sitting on top of millions, and if I was the girl that they'd wanted from the beginning, then maybe it was all worth a shot.

"Okay," I gave Genesis a tight nod. "I'll do it. I'll take Swiss's place. And for starters, no one works under me who I don't personally choose and approve of."

Genesis started to question my request. This wasn't something that could be argued over; it wasn't a bargaining unit. If my ass was gonna be on the line, I didn't want any weak links or weak niggas on my team. Javion never would've made the cut, and Swiss never would've been in charge of any unit I was overseeing. I needed loyal and reliable people in my corner who would take a fall for me, rather than let me fall.

Chapter 63

Road Runner

I tossed and turned all night. The penthouse didn't feel the same as my apartment with Shandy. I didn't have the sounds of city traffic to put me to sleep at night; the walls were supersoundproofed to the point where I couldn't even hear the neighbors.

Genesis had gone home to make sure his niece was okay. His absence gave me time to busy myself, organizing my things and putting my stuff away. In less than forty-eight hours, I'd gone from a woman torn between two lovers to a murderer set free, and now I was a boss.

I was trying to figure out what to eat when Gen called.

"You have work to do for Farrah. Meet her at M Street and Fifty-eighth. Don't be late."

My work was never done, and the days always felt crammed with stuff to do or someone to follow up with. I did as I was instructed, meeting Farrah at one p.m. on the nose. She handed me a small box with specific instructions.

"They're a bunch of Swedish filmmakers. Weird fuckers, if you ask me, but they buy a fuck ton of coke whenever they're in town. Cosimo, Constantinus, and Eckhardt are going to pick you up. Get into the backseat on the passenger's side and hand the passenger this box. He'll hand you $50,000. Take ten off of that and bring me back forty."

I sat in my car listening to the radio, watching the space where the Swedes were supposed to pull into. Not even a full hour had passed before a black-on-black Jeep pulled in with blacked out windows. The license plate read "Direct4You." If that wasn't the film producers, I didn't know who else it could be. The driver-side window rolled down, letting dense weed smoke filter through the gap.

"You Farrah's girrrrl?" he asked with a hard roll on his *r*'s. If I had to imagine what Swedish men would sound like, that was definitely it.

"I am." I smiled, holding up the small white box. It was about the size of a shoe box, but it felt like an eight-pound bag of sugar.

"Climb in, will you? We can't have you out there in the broad daylight and such."

I did as Farrah had instructed, making sure to get in on the back passenger side. No sooner had the door closed before one of the guys snatched the box out of my hand. I was thrown back against the seat as we took off with the tires squealing. The guy beside me smelled like two-day-old beer and blue cheese. He smiled, flashing me with a wide gap between his front teeth.

"Farrah didn't say this was part of the exchange," I told him.

"Eh, we're going to get your dollops. I don't keep thousands on me for carrying-around money. It's right up this way, not far," the driver called back.

He stared at me through the rearview. I was momentarily taken aback by his eyes. They crinkled at the corners like he was always laughing at a funny story or a joke. Farrah was going to be missing twenty thousand if I survived this joyride. Boss or no boss, she wasn't going to be sending me on shit without a proper heads-up.

The Jeep bumped and bustled through the streets as the guys passed around the box of cocaine. They'd snorted so much I'd started worrying that maybe this was a setup. A few more twists and turns and we veered off a side street into a wooded area. This wasn't part of the tour. I inched my hand up to the door handle and pulled. Either the child lock was on, or it was rigged to only open from the outside, because it didn't budge.

The guy beside me who I'd figured out was Cosimo leaned toward me with a creepy leer on his face. I screamed as he grabbed both my wrists. This was it. This was my time. I was going to die in a car in the middle of nowhere, and nobody would know where to find my body. Constantinus leaned over the passenger's seat, throwing a dark hood over my head. It smelled like rotten potatoes and mildew.

I squirmed and fought until something sharp pricked my leg and my world went black.

My nose was itching, but I couldn't scratch it. I moaned. There was the worst throbbing pain in my head. It felt like I'd been out drinking all night. I opened my eyes, trying to remember what the hell had happened. Straw, real live straw, was strewn across the ground all around me. To my horror, my clothes were gone. I was shivering on the ground, suddenly realizing how cold it was, and my arms were tied behind my back and my feet were tied at the ankles.

Either Cosimo or Eckhardt started talking to me from somewhere in the dark.

"Hello, my little mermaid."

"You mean Sleeping Beauty, idiot. The little mermaid was half fish," Constantinus answered.

"And she looks like a half fish with her legs tied like that. Hose her down again."

I snapped my eyes shut against the feeling of the water spraying over me. It was so cold I'd started to scream, but the water went into my nose and mouth, making me regret that decision. The ground underneath me was turning into a muddy pool. Long, dark earthworms began to slide up from the dirt. They thought it was raining and time to come out. I tried squirming away from them, but they were everywhere. As I struggled to sit up, I was yanked into a sitting position. Cosimo pulled me by my shoulders, forcing me to stand.

He whipped a knife out of his back pocket and cut my hands free.

"Now, we will hunt you. Whichever one of us catches you gets to fuck you first." He winked before whispering, "Let Daddy Cosimo catch you. I'm hung like a stallion. You won't feel nothing else after I get through ripping you apart."

The other two men called to him from outside. The sun was setting, casting an orange glow cross the sky. The trees all around us were shadowed and dark. Nobody was going to catch me. I'd chew out his jugular if I could get it.

My hands were untied. I stood in front of them, shaking, naked, and filthy, with the barn off to the side, and the woods at my back. They did more coke off the hood of the car before turning on the headlights. I held up my hand to block out the lights.

"Run, rabbit! Run!" one of them shouted. "We'll even give you a head start."

I turned, running toward the woods, behind me. Their laughter was getting further and further away. When I passed the barn, I acted like I was going into the woods but I ran around the side, watching them do more hits of coke off of the hood of the Jeep. They gave each other high fives before they each broke off into the woods in different directions. Once they were out of sight, I sprinted with everything I had toward the Jeep. My hands were shaking so bad I could barely get the door open. Once inside, I frowned at the video camera sitting on the dashboard. It had been recording for the last two hours.

There wasn't any time for me to figure out who was who or what was what. I turned the key in the ignition and peeled backward down the dirt road, throwing mud and rocks spraying. My clothes were in a ripped pile in the backseat, so I was forced to drive naked. When I was closer to the city I slowed down enough to grab my phone. I called Genesis.

"I was just kidnapped and tortured and—"

"Let me guess, was it three Swedish guys?"

"Yes, and I'm driving to your place right now. I don't have any clothes. I'm naked."

"Hold on, hold on, Novie. They didn't give you your clothes back?"

"Give me my clothes? Nigga, they just threatened to rape me in the woods if I got caught. I'm sorry if I didn't wait around to see if they'd politely hand me my shit."

Genesis chuckled in the phone, and I wished he was in front of me so I could ram the truck into his smug face.

"Novie, there should be a video camera on the dashboard. They're film directors. They like to do these dumb-ass gag reels with retarded scenarios. Constantinus, I think, is the one who likes to dress up like a zombie or an alien and go running out into the woods after you. They might have switched it up so that just as you think you're about to get raped or killed, he comes crashing up on your assailant. These things sell big overseas."

"What? They do what?"

"Yeah, I thought Farrah explained all of that."

"Farrah didn't explain a damn thing. And I was naked, completely, fucking naked. I'm still naked, and now I'm driving a stolen Jeep with God only knows what kind of contraband in it."

"Just come here. I'll handle it. Everything will be fine. I know it's not funny, but I think you're probably the first person to get out of the woods. I'm sure I'll be getting a call from Farrah when the guys hike themselves to the nearest gas station."

"If this is the type of shit I have to look forward to working with you two, I quit. It's not worth my sanity."

Chapter 64

First Response

I was starting to get that lightheaded, queasy feeling that had been hitting me on and off for the last few weeks. Something in my gut told me to pick up a pregnancy test on my way back to the house. I grabbed a four-pack just to be on the safe side. Whichever result I got, I wanted to be certain of. Genesis had said several times that he didn't want a baby. If that was the case, I needed him to be just as adamant about wearing a damn condom.

The house was empty when I walked in. Genesis wouldn't be home from work until later, and Kenisha was staying at a friend's or a boyfriend's, I wasn't sure which one anymore. I threw my jacket on a chaise lounge in the front sitting room and kicked off my shoes. My eyes rolled at the filth Kenisha had left in the kitchen. The black granite countertops were covered in random empty cookie containers and halfway closed chip bags. The juice and half a rotisserie chicken was left sitting out. She even left the damn mayonnaise sitting out on the counter without the lid.

I know this heffa hasn't made a sandwich or whatever and left this shit like this. It didn't make any sense for me to be on a constantly shortening leash when Genesis let that girl get away with murder.

Grabbing a cucumber and tomato out of the fridge, I sliced them up into a bowl with a splash of vinegar. This is all I'd been thinking about all day. I cleaned up whatever I used, leaving the rest of that mess exactly as I found it. Let Genesis clean up after her. My behind was ready for a hot shower and a good hour-long nap. Since neither of them liked anything I cooked, I wasn't even going to waste my time trying to find a recipe to impress their fucked-up taste buds. They could order a pizza or get something from that new service that delivered damn near everything under the sun.

I'd started toward my bathroom when an idea stopped my feet. Genesis always spent so much time in the bathroom with the door shut tight. I could stare under the door and see him pacing back and forth, or he'd be in one place for what would seem like forever. I tiptoed into his immaculate bathroom. Everything was in its place. The floor and mirrors were spotless. I looked in the medicine cabinet, disappointed to find nothing but Motrin and allergy pills. The linen closet was actually in the bathroom. I opened the doors wide and stared at his pristine, perfectly folded white sheets. All except for one at the very top. I had to use the second step as a foothold, but after I pulled myself up, I found it. It was a poetry book, or a journal of some kind, sitting on the top shelf underneath a crooked towel.

I turned to page one. Genesis's handwriting immediately leapt off the page.

Chapter 65

In the movies, the nigga always dies first. Those were my exact thoughts as I stood on the upper level of the parking garage beneath the downtown hospital. Ladybug, my tactical exploration robot, had run herself into a dead spot. I couldn't remote control her from the surveillance van, so, of course, me and myself, aka the only nigga, had to step in for a closer look. Technically, I wasn't the only nigga. There was my boy who was out sick, Warren, the blue-eyed bandit who we called Foreign. His moms looked like Weezy Jefferson, and his pops looked like Red Foxx. We swore up and down that nigga was the milkman's baby. If I was thinking, I would've stayed home and called in sick too. A day at home with a whining woman and an even whinier baby didn't seem so bad compared to the day I was having.

The garage was silent as a tomb and hot as an oven. There were eight of us working the FBI Explosives Ordinance field office in Norfolk, Virginia. Overtime was becoming a popular subject with all the work we'd been getting thrown our way lately. Let's just say, it takes a real special motherfucker to run in and finger fuck an explosive when everyone else is running away. No one could do what we did, or understand the rush you feel from death hissing down the back of your neck.

My hand wandered aimlessly to my left side, to where I kept the five-pointed Gold Medal of Valor in my pants pocket. They give it to agents as recognition for extreme acts of heroism. It was awarded to my pops when I was nine. He was one of the best too, before he got killed in the line of duty.

Now his medal went with me on all my bomb-runs. It was a good-luck thing. Morbid, I know. But it made me feel like he was watching over me, bringing me some guidance.

It had to have been working because I was still alive. Earlier, the calls had started coming in one by one. Protocol required us to send at least two techs out to oversee bomb disposal, but we had all been dispatched to different locations. So far, all the other locations had come back as false alarms. I sure as hell hoped this was one as well. Sweat stung my eyes, forcing me to squint through the hazy visor of my blast suit. It was ninety pounds of fire-resistant Nomex and Kevlar.

"Jarryd, what do you see, son? My neck been bothering me all morning." Peterson's voice crackled through the two-way com in my headgear.

He called everyone son, even though most of us were in our late twenties, and he wasn't any older than forty-five. He'd been through more than any of us, even did a short stint in Kuwait until he got caught in some crossfire. The only thing holding that nigga together was metal pins and grit; 148 of them ran up his spine. He always complained about his neck hurting right before some shit popped off. Hell, I trusted Peterson's neck better than any bomb-sniffing dog.

I squinted through one eye, keeping the other closed. I always forgot how hot it got inside these suits until my black ass was back inside one, cursing because we didn't have the newer air-conditioned ones.

"One minute, sir. Right now, I can't see shit for my own sweat."

My heart was karate-kicking the inside of my chest, making my breath come in short, garlic-scented spurts. Lunch had consisted of garlic-knots from a little hole-in-the-wall Italian spot that we went to every Friday called Feldecci's. They were always on point, but I don't think there was anything on the menu that wouldn't leave your breath humming for the rest of the day. That wasn't the worst of it; the real problem was me. I was shaky and unfocused from slamming back Monster energy drinks to compensate for lack of sleep. This wasn't the kind of job that allowed for a nigga to not be well rested, but try explaining that to a crab-assy bundle of constant tears and shit.

My new baby boy, Jarryd Junior, was eleven or thirteen weeks; hell if I know. I can't keep track of that shit. Tima'd been celebrating everything from his first shit to his first sneeze. Let me know when that little nigga hits one, aka twelve months, so I can crack a beer or something. Since the day he was born, I hadn't eaten, fucked, or slept the same. How was having a baby supposed to be this big joyous occasion when all it did was managed to erase all the joy out of my life? Now there was just constant pressure to earn more and buy the best of everything. When I wasn't working or stressing about work, you'd think I'd get to relax, but, nah, I was expected to spend every free minute with that little nigga.

We had the biggest house in one of the best neighborhoods, and now she had this grand delusion of getting an even bigger house in a neighborhood the director of the FBI probably couldn't even afford. All that shit was starting to make me bitter and cynical. I'd even googled whether it was normal for a man to hate his own baby. It didn't feel natural. All the sites said I was most likely suffering from some kind of male-postpartum depression. Fuck that, I'm a damn man. Men don't get depressed or upset. Only a woman would write some bullshit like that. Men get angry; we get mad, and if I was feeling any kind of way, I was pissed the fuck off. Not fucking depressed.

Tima used to draw a nigga baths at night with candles and wine. She used to cook four-course dinners, and now she be on this four-day dinner routine. That's what I call it when she makes some shit and stretches it out so we have it every day except Friday. Back in the day, a nigga was taken care of. I ain't mind handing over a paycheck or buying her anything under the sun when I wasn't eating spaghetti four days a week. I wasn't mentally prepared for this life of baby talk, baby proofing, and baby bullshit.

"Son, are okay in there?" Peterson sounded on edge. "Akins is on his way back since his call was a false alarm. We can bring him in if you aren't up to snuff. I'm sure the new baby is wearing you down."

My mind was all over the place. I'd started to tell Peterson I wasn't on my A-game, but I manned up. Nah, there was no way I'd admit to getting mind-fucked by an infant. Unlike parenting, I'd been doing this type of stuff my whole career. Everybody can't do what the fuck I do. Niggas run screaming out of the places I voluntarily walk into.

"I'm solid, sir, just hot as fuck in here. This ninety-degree weather ain't helpin'."

I flexed my fingers, hyping myself up as I maneuvered through rows of cars toward the crumbling column in the center. Ladybug sat waiting in a puddle nearby. I removed my ID badge from the utility holster on my side and inserted it into her driver. "Don't worry, Lady, you just sit here and watch me work. I'll be right back." Yeah, I talked to her like she was a real person. I talked to anything with artificial intelligence. If there was ever a robot uprising, your boy would be safe. I'd tried to explain that shit to Tima, but she'd just get pissed off. Let her tell it, I talked to my machines more than I talked to her or my own son. You damn right; my machines had enough sense not to talk back.

Ladybug's system recalibrated with a series of loud clicks and whirrs. NASA held the original patents for her design. She was made for exploring planets and collecting samples. We kept a lot of the original specifications so she could run on autopilot or remote control. After her reboot, she'd automatically trek back to the recon van.

"All right, Ladybug, you watch my back." I gave the metallic claw on top of her canister a fist-bump before moving on.

I checked the numbers on each column until I got to the one with D8 stenciled in faded red letters. The red paint flaked off the side. Someone had made a 9-1-1 call saying there was a suspicious object sitting in front of it. I squashed the fear gripping at my insides and cleared my dry, scratchy throat as I laid eyes on it.

"Sir, this is some devilish but beautiful shit. Are y'all getting this?" I angled my head to make sure the camera mounted on the side of my visor could pick everything up. "The detonator has a bilateral release trigger. One side is an explosive, and

I'm talkin' citywide radius. But the other one is some kind of haz canister, and I don't know what the fuck's inside it," I replied, anxious to either get out of there or get to work.

Peterson made a deep, gravely sound in the back of his throat. It was a cross between a grunt and groan. I'd heard it before. A year ago, I'd been awarded a Congressional Gold Medal for diffusing a similar situation near the Federal Building downtown. It was a lot bigger and nastier than this one; anything could have set that shit off.

"Well, all right, Jarhead."

Peterson called me by my old nickname, making me feel more like my old self and less like the old man I was being forced to become. Before I joined this bomb squad that my wife wanted me to quit, I was a marine specializing in explosives. My ace back then was a goofy nigga named Chief. He saved my ass so many times and vice versa, we swore if one of us ever hit the lottery or got rich, we'd come back for the other one.

"Don't stand there clutchin' your nuts, split some wires," Peterson ordered. "I don't know about your house, but it's wet-mouf-Wednesday up in mine. I've got to get my ass home before the old lady has too many mojitos. She's sloppy and slobby after three. My balls don't take too kindly to cold drool," he barked in what was an obvious attempt to lighten up the tension in the air.

Everyone was holed up in the surveillance van topside watching the feed from the camera mounted to my head on a closed-circuit network. Every time I diffused a bomb, I'd fast-forward to afterward in my head. I imagined myself celebrating in some big old encouraging titties. I didn't celebrate at strip clubs anymore; you get a wife and a kid and somehow, everything that was once a reality became fantasy. But the sooner I got this over with, the sooner I could throw back a cold beer and maybe talk Tima into giving me some head.

The headgear was making it too hard for me to focus. I'd sent my spare drones out for repair. Budget cuts had everything stuck in a holding pattern somewhere. Ladybug being out of commission meant I was the damn drone today.

Even though it was a stupid move, I removed my headgear, placing it on the ground beside me. Peterson's voice was a muffled string of what I could only imagine to be f-bombs and curse words. He could string together words that'd make you feel lower than dirt and more useless than shit.

The air was still and thick with the smell of exhaust and concrete. Sweat poured down the back of my neck. Normally, adrenaline rushes would send me into a calm, methodical trance. But that wasn't happening today. I sucked in a few shaky lungfuls of air, hoping it'd squelch my nerves.

I knelt as carefully as I could in front of the white tank with death flashing all over it. The device wasn't wired like anything I'd ever seen before. A sinking panicky feeling started to roll itself around in my gut. My brain was processing everything at warp speed, connecting lines and wires to switches. This wasn't your normal, everyday device. The orange-tinted lights of the garage reflected off the flawless chrome valves. Every piece of metal was perfectly polished. There wasn't a fleck of dust or an oily fingerprint anywhere on it. It was finely detailed all the way down to the wooden crate it sat on top of. I tried to get a look underneath it for a fail-switch.

If I didn't have perfect 20/20 vision, I might've missed the clear wire running along the underside of the device. It was thinner than fishing line and slightly shaking, which was weird because there was no breeze in the parking garage. A hundred questions drifted through my mind as I rose on shaky legs. Peterson needed to know about this. I was reaching for my helmet when I saw something out of the corner of my eye. My eyes locked with his; dread filled me to the core of my being.

"Don't move," I said in a calm, quiet voice.

The man standing across the garage stared back at me. His yellow Polo shirt was dirty and ripped around the collar. Blood ran from his nose, and his left eyelid was swollen to about the size of an egg. What the fuck is he doin' in here? They said the garage was all clear.

I edged toward him, trying to figure out if he was a victim or the perp. I followed the line from where it started to where it rested in his bloody hand. His eyes were panicky and glazed with pain, but he didn't make a sound. If he yanked or dropped that string, we were done.

I decided to skip protocol and reason with him. There wasn't going to be any time for me to call this in.

"You don't have to do this, man. I'm sure we can solve whatever the problem is reasonably."

Sweat gleamed on his forehead. A nasty purplish-blue knot was forming at the right side of his temple. His lips barely moved. "Run."

In antiterrorism training, they teach you to remain calm and give whoever it is whatever they want.

I held up my hands. "All right, man, in a minute. Tell me what you need and I'll go get someone to help."

"I didn't do this. I . . . I woke up in the trunk of a car. They busted my hand up and made me hold this wire . . . I can't keep holdin' this."

His Adam's apple bobbed in his throat. There wasn't going to be enough time for me to get topside and bring down help. Ladybug was still sitting where I left her booting up. She weighted eight hundred pounds; there was no way I'd be able to get her over here fast enough.

"Okay, okay. Just stay calm. I'm gonna make sure that both of us will walk out of here." My words sounded way more confident than I felt.

I inched my way closer, mentally running down the odds. Can't cut the wire, can't remove it from his hand. Can't guarantee there'll be enough time to diffuse the device before he drops the wire. This is a lose-lose situation.

"Evacuate the hospital. Let me die." His words were breathless, urgent gasps.

"We've already done that, my dude. Everybody's gone except you and me. I got this, I'm not about to let you die."

I was finally close enough to see his hands. How he managed to hold anything was an act of God himself. His fingers looked like they'd been run through a sausage grinder. I made an effort not to wince or make a face at the white bone sticking out where his index finger should have been. Every nerve, every cell in my being was screaming for me to get the fuck out of there.

Blood-splattered papers littered the ground, indicating some kind of a scuffle had gone down. A wallet laid open at my feet. I picked it up, scanning over his driver's license. His name was Genesis Kane. I gave him a friendly, encouraging smile. Hopefully, I could bring him around, give him a sense of security by using his name. Maybe it would rehumanize him if he heard it. Maybe it would give him some hope.

"I'm Jarryd," I introduced myself. "How about we work on getting you out of this mess, Mr. Kane. Can I—"

A blinding yellow flash lit up the garage. It shook the ground and the concrete pillars. The sound of the blast pounded against my eardrums. It felt like an oven had opened behind me as heat rushed against the back of my neck and head. Something told my brain they were flames, but it all happened in a frame of time too short for me to react to. I felt searing heat, jarring pain, and weightlessness, and then I didn't feel a thing.

When I finally managed to open my eyes, I thought I was dead. Dust tickled the hairs in my nose. It felt like there were layers of it crammed up there. My ears wouldn't stop ringing, and my eyes burned like I'd dipped my head into a pool of saltwater. I drifted in and out of the darkness, waking up in small enough stretches to feel a new painful sensation in a different part of my body. I couldn't tell if I'd been asleep for a few minutes or a few months. It took several minutes for me to realize I was lying down in a hospital.

The television was the first thing to break through the dull ringing in my ears. "The FBI have recovered the body of one of their own from the blast zone. Investigators have now identified the human remains uncovered not far from where investigators say the device detonated. Special Agent Bomb Technician Jarryd Keening's ID was found close to the center of the blast radius. There were no other casualties, although several bystanders on the street were injured."

I stared blindly at the TV, barely able to make out the face of the woman reporting the news. What looked like Peterson's ugly mug darkened the screen. He recited a prewritten speech about how good of a man I was. How I was a fallen hero who'd made him proud.

What the fuck? Why would everyone think I was dead? I wasn't fucking dead! *I tried to sit up and fell back from the pain that shot through my shoulder.*

A cheerful nurse breezed into the room in a blur of pink scrubs and caramel skin.

"Good morning, Mr. Kane. It is so good to see you're finally awake. Now I'm gonna need you to behave and be still."

Wincing at the pain now shooting from my shoulder to my forehead, I sat still so she could tend to me.

"What happened to me, how did I get here?"

"Genesis, sweetie, you were caught up in an explosion and found by some volunteer search and rescue workers who found you outside of a parking garage. They flew you in from Norfolk. You're in DC, sweetie."

Did she just call me Genesis? What the fuck? *Why was she calling me by that other guy's name? I opened my mouth to correct her. My name was Jarryd Keening. I had a wife and a new son I couldn't stand. They were home waiting for me in my house with the mortgage that I was struggling to pay. Tima was probably beside herself crazy, grieving over this mix-up, planning my funeral.*

My thoughts stunned me into stupefied silence as the nurse tended to my wounds. She examined my collarbone, nodding to herself before tending to a bandage that I didn't even know was wrapped around my head. As the gauze unraveled, I tried to do the same with my hazy memories. Seconds before the explosion, I'd picked up Genesis Kane's ID. The force of the explosion must've thrown me out of the garage. Without my helmet latched on, it most likely knocked me out of my blast suit. Since I was supposed to be the only man in the garage, when they found the other man's remains inside, they must've assumed it was me. Everyone had just assumed that I'd died, and why wouldn't they? They had a body, my ID, and since I was the idiot who went against protocol, they didn't know anyone else was there.

That little slip on my part could cost me my career if I contacted my command now. I'd lose everything and probably get blamed for the death of a civilian too, all because I was trying to be the hero.

The nurse leaned across me, chatting away with her titties not more than an inch away from my face. "You should know that you've been very well tended to these last few days. You won our finest patient award." She giggled flirtatiously. "It's been hell keeping all the other nurses from trying to steal my best patient."

Inhaling, I hid an amused smile. She smelled like ripe, juicy peaches drizzled in honey. It'd been a minute since I'd gotten a compliment from a woman other than Tima. We bomb technicians stayed tucked away at the office or out in the field. We didn't get to "flex on 'em" like the boys in the penguin suits did. I mumbled a low thank-you for the compliment.

"Not that I was snooping or anything. But your IDs and stuff were all charred up. The only way we could identify you was by your Bar Association card. Um, may I ask what kind of lawyer are you exactly? Because I've got all these damn speeding tickets, and I probably can't afford you, but I really need a good stiff lawyer to help me out."

Her hands left the bandage wrapped around my head, making their way down my chest toward my lap. I'd dated Tima faithfully for three years before we'd gotten married. Five years of fucking the same pussy had my Johnson leaping to attention at the thought of getting rubbed up and possibly falling into some new pussy.

"You keep doin' what you're doing, and I'll be any kind of lawyer you want me to be." The lie slipped out of my mouth so easily I couldn't believe I'd said it. But she was sliding her fingernails up my bare thighs, getting closer and closer to the tent-pole sticking up in the middle of my hospital gown. Her fingers felt like Heaven warmed over when they finally wrapped around me.

I had to keep that shit going. "But to be completely honest. I practice tort law, and I do the whole trial thing too. You know, I've never lost a case," I ground out through some shit I'd heard on a commercial through clenched teeth. I probably wasn't even saying it right or using it in the right order.

But shit, it was the truth . . . granted I ain't never had a case, let alone stepped foot into a courtroom. She ain't need to know all that.

This would be the day Jarryd Keening would officially die and Genesis Kane would be reborn. I just needed to let Foreign and Chief know where I was. We were about to initiate a DC takeover.

Chapter 66

Discovery Channel

I dropped the journal. It hit the floor with a loud slap. A picture of a little girl named Janay with a snaggletoothed smile floated out of it. HAVE YOU SEEN ME was plastered along the bottom in faded yellow letters. Genesis, I mean Jarryd, or whatever he wanted to call himself, wasn't even a real attorney. No, no, no. I backed away from the book like it was on fire. What kind of man would just leave his wife and son? I was shaking my head in disbelief. He was probably just writing some kind of fictional short story and was too embarrassed to be seen doing it by the light of day. But Tima was real. She was at his office my first day on the job.

I picked up the journal and the picture with unsteady fingers. *That nigga probably had an entire harem of women and kids that he'd just wipe out whenever it was convenient.*

The lights automatically clicked on, offering me dim guidance up the stairs toward the bedroom I slept in when I wasn't sleeping with Gen. I still wasn't used to it or all these fancy features that Gen's house had. Probably never would be. Once inside my room, I decided to take some quick action. I reluctantly stopped eating long enough to take my pregnancy tests into the bathroom. They all needed three minutes, and if this wasn't the longest three minutes of my life . . . While I waited, I grabbed a Post-it note from the box of things I'd brought home from my desk. At least Kenisha would know from me personally that the way she left this house was unacceptable. The note I scribbled out for her was straight to the point. *Clean up after yourself.*

It was short and simple, and it would probably send her little spoiled ass through the roof. Kenisha's bedroom was the size of a small palace, complete with vaulted ceilings and a balcony that stretched the length of the back of the house. Unlike Genesis's balcony, hers had two reclining lawn chairs with a large multicolored umbrella set up above them. *I really got the short straw on the room selection. My shit doesn't even have a bay window, and it's half the size of this shit.*

My nose turned up at the clothes strewn all across the floor and bed. Half-eaten cereal bowls littered her vanity. Her closet and drawers were half open with clothes and underclothes hanging half in and half out. How did she ever find anything in here? I wandered over to her closet, stepping over candy wrappers and empty Twinkie boxes. It was like a Forever 21 bomb went off, and all of the clothes landed in and all over her room.

This was ridiculous. My momma would've taken every piece of clothing I owned. She would've held them all hostage or given them away until I learned to keep my shit neat. There wasn't even a clear place to put a note. Not one where she'd see it. There was so much shit everywhere it would just get lost. And then I had an aha! moment. Her little conceited ass stayed in the bathroom. I'd just slap this bad-boy up on her bathroom mirror right at eye level. She wouldn't miss that.

A noise from downstairs made me pause. Panicky and suddenly nervous about getting caught, I waited, listening to see if it was a door closing or maybe just a car on the street. Genesis usually headed straight for his office when he came in. He'd put his stuff down, shuffle through the mail, and finally make his way upstairs. Kenisha was a different story. Sometimes she'd fly into whichever bathroom was closest. She'd sit in there, peeing like a baby pony with the door wide open. Then there were times when she'd come directly to her room with an attitude from hell.

I rushed around a pile of shopping bags and empty shoe boxes stacked near the foot of her bed heading toward her bathroom. It usually took her an eternity to climb those stairs. They'd slow her down, giving me just enough time to get my note in place. My toes dug into the plush carpet; even the carpet in here felt softer than the rest of the house. It was like walking across cotton ball fluff. Thankfully, the door to her bathroom was cracked. I'd be able to slip in and out faster this way.

I'd started to just stick the note on the door itself when I saw them in the mirror. The lights were off, but there was enough late-evening light coming through the bathroom window to illuminate them in grey and blue shadows. Genesis's hand was pressed over Kenisha's mouth. His face was hidden in the side of her neck. They looked like some kind of silent, horrifying painting standing against the far wall of her bathroom. Genesis's pants were around his ankles, his dress shirt strained against the muscles in this back. Kenesha's turquoise sundress was up around her waist, her eyes were shut tight. One of her legs was thrown over his arm as he maneuvered himself around her swollen belly, pumping in and out of her quietly.

Half-eaten tomatoes and cucumbers rose in my throat. The horror of what I was seeing made me shake all over with disgust and outrage. The note fluttered from my fingers, landing beside maternity panties on the floor. They looked torn, like he'd ripped them off of her. What was he doing home when he told me he was staying in the office late?

My brain fired a thousand different courses of actions in a matter of seconds. All of them led me to the same blocked wall. Genesis had too much power. He could make me disappear for what I'd just seen. That wouldn't give me any time to help Kenisha. It wouldn't give me a chance to get her, and myself, away from this monster. He'd be outraged; he'd deny what I'd seen, or worse, he'd kill me on the spot.

The only direction my feet would move me in was backward out of the door. My vision was too blurry for me to see my way. I sagged against the walls, using them to guide me as I staggered back toward my room. That poor girl, that poor, poor girl. I couldn't get the image out of my head. It twisted my stomach into bubbly knots until I ran into my own bathroom, heaving vomit on the way. The spasms were so hard it felt like the veins were going to break through the skin in my neck.

The sides of the toilet were icy cold against my fingers while I prayed this shit would hurry up and be over. When there was nothing left in my stomach, I fell back exhausted, sitting on the floor with my back up against the bathroom.

Too weak to do more than lean forward, I snatched the edge of the hand towel hanging off the counter. Pregnancy tests clinked onto the hard tile floor all around me. My stomach lurched again, but there wasn't anything left in it. Each and every single one of those tests was positive.

Chapter 67

Stockholm Syndrome

It was dark when I finally opened my eyes. I'd either fallen asleep or passed out on the bathroom floor. My body was stiff and sore after being on the floor for so long. My knees were wobbly as I tried to stand. I turned on the cold water, watching it rush down the drain with my life and my faith. How did I let myself get fooled into caring about a man like that? There were so many questions running through my head. I rinsed my mouth out with cold water from the sink before splashing it over my face. This felt like a nightmare I couldn't wake up from.

The sun had finally set, and the bedroom was dark as I walked out. It was somewhere near ten. There were no missed calls or texts on my cell. Even though I was avoiding him, I don't know why it bothered me to know that Genesis hadn't bothered to check on me, nor had he asked me to come sleep with him last night. I know if he'd gone downstairs, he'd had to have seen my coat or *the note!* The note I'd written had fallen and landed on the floor. He must've seen it, or maybe Kenisha saw it. He probably knew that I'd seen him. Hiding in the dark security of my bedroom felt like the best answer after I tipped over to quietly lock my bedroom door. I used my phone's flashlight to find the letter opener I'd packed in my workbox.

The bed creaked as I climbed onto it fully clothed with my letter opener clutched tightly in my hand. I didn't know what to expect or what to do. All of this worrying could have been for nothing. But, now I had a new problem. I had a baby to protect, and Kenisha was somebody's baby too. Now it was up to me to get all of us away from Genesis. My pillow was soaked with tears by the time exhaustion sank in. I crashed into a restless sleep filled with running shadows fucking and Genesis yelling.

I jerked awake with the sun streaming through the blinds smacking me in the face, feeling like I hadn't slept at all. A wave of nausea sent me scrambling to the bathroom. I dry heaved until my throat was raw and my stomach muscles felt sore and strained. This was a whole new experience. I didn't have a single day of morning sickness when I'd gotten pregnant with Swiss's baby. That shit felt like it was a whole lifetime ago. All the old chapters of my life combined didn't have anything on the pages I was writing with Genesis. *How the hell can I even approach him about a baby after seeing what he's done to Kenisha? What if we had a daughter? What if something happened to me and she was left with him?*

There was no way I could get rid of my baby, not again. But now, I'd have to live, knowing I'd made a child with a monster. He didn't even seem real to me after what I'd seen. Nothing about Genesis felt real or genuine. I stared at myself in the mirror with unseeing eyes. Where was Shandy when I really needed her? I hadn't heard from her at all since the night I packed my shit and left. Revenge felt good in the moment, but now a million questions came up whenever I thought about her. Aris hadn't even crossed my mind when I did what I did. And I had way too much pride to call and ask her if they were okay. Without Shandy, without Denise, there was no one for me to confide in; there was nowhere for me to run and hide until things felt safe.

A knock at my bedroom door scared the devil out of me.

"I'm in the bathroom," I called out in a shaky voice.

"I hope you slept as well as I did. I'm making us all breakfast, so come on before Hungry Jack eats everything in the house," Genesis yelled back.

I didn't have the strength or the will to respond. There was no way I'd be able to face them both together at the table. Let alone eat anything. I dawdled for as long as I possibly could, taking an extralong shower, washing my hair, and scrubbing my body over and over. I dabbed foundation under my eyes to hide the dark circles. There was no erasing what I'd seen; there wasn't going to be any looking past it. I'd have to find a way to address this, and then I'd have to deal with the outcome.

Genesis was still bare chested, wearing nothing but blue sweatpants when I walked in. He was just setting down plates stacked high with blueberry pancakes, fried potatoes, and scrambled eggs. All of it made my stomach turn. He gave me a big bright grin as he walked over to kiss me on my lips. I turned, giving him my cheek.

"Think I might be coming down with something," I blurted out.

"Well, I've got plenty of juice and vitamin me to help you get over that."

The look of disgust that wanted to spread across my face almost broke through, giving me away. Thank God he'd turned to tend to a pan full of strips of bacon on the stove. Kenisha waddled in holding the small of her back. I looked her over from the top of her head down to her bare feet. Nothing on her looked out of place, bruised, or roughed up. She was wearing a sunny-yellow and green Mumu wrap. It pushed the tops of her swollen breasts up until they looked like they were about to spill all out of the damn thing.

"Thank you for cooking because I'm about to fuck up everything on this table," she announced just before trying to ease down into a seat.

Genesis dropped the pan of bacon he was tending to rush over to help her ease down into the chair. I watched them closely from where I stood by the fridge. There were no signs of awkwardness, disgust, or even shame as Genesis touched the small of her back. My eyes were waiting to see if she'd flinch or shy away, if he'd react sexually and try to hide it. But they were all business as usual. I probably had more jealousy and disgust to hide than either of them did. Kenisha even smiled sweetly at him, thanking him for helping her with her chair.

I excused myself to my room, claiming I didn't want to get Kenisha or anyone sick. The poor girl was probably suffering from Stockholm syndrome, or he'd brainwashed her into thinking what he'd done was normal.

The sooner I could be alone with her, one on one, the sooner she could answer my questions so I could help get us out of here. How we'd leave and where we'd go I didn't know yet, but I would do something. I sat in my room, staring a hole in the wall. When I heard Genesis go into his bedroom, I ran to find Kenisha. She was still in the kitchen with a half-eaten strip of bacon in one hand and massaging her boob with the other.

"I can't wait to get my body back. These thangs right here hurt like all hell, and it's worse if I try to put on any kind of bra."

I scooted into the chair beside her and gave her a polite but timid smile.

"I saw you two in the bathroom yesterday," I rushed into my speech before I lost the nerve. "Kenisha, no matter what happens, I want you to know that you have somebody on your side. Genesis is the adult, and you're the child. He will be punished for what he did. I'll make sure of it."

The bacon fell out of her hand, clattering to the table as her eyes glazed over. Her bottom lip quivered.

"What are you gonna do?" she asked in a little voice.

"Whatever I need to do. So long as you're safe, I don't care. He's going to go away for a long time. Okay?"

She nodded quietly, with tears slipping down her cheeks.

"After I figure out a few things, I'm going to get us away from here. I need you to go upstairs and get your hospital delivery bag. Make sure you have everything you need. We're leaving tonight."

Genesis whistled as he made his way downstairs. I gave her hand a gentle, reassuring squeeze before I slipped out through the dining room toward the stairs. Genesis had no idea what he was in for. I waited by the stairs listening, trying to figure out which part of the house he was in. There was no way I could face him and not give myself away.

"She knows, and she said she'll send you away," Kenisha's voice was a rushed pleading whisper. "You said having her here would make our lives easier, that we wouldn't have to worry about anyone figuring us out, and she knows, Kane."

"Don't even worry about that shit, babe. You go wherever she tries to take you; act like everything is fine. Nobody's gonna hurt you or my baby. I'll handle it," Genesis answered in a dry, emotionless voice.

I almost fell out right where I stood. I was wrong. I was so *very, very* wrong, and now it might cost me my life.

Chapter 68

Going Home

I took the stairs two at a time, locking my door behind me. My heart was beating so fast I felt light-headed. As bad as I wanted to break down, throw shit, hell, throw both Genesis *and* Kenisha, this wasn't the time. There was an old gym bag underneath my bed. I grabbed it and began slinging clothes into it as fast as I could. There was still time for me to save myself. Genesis was waiting for me to run with Kenisha, but if I left without her, it bettered my chances of getting away.

Genesis shouted through the house that he was leaving for work. He was trying to keep up appearances, which was fine with me. It gave me time to get my shit together and get out. Kenisha thumped up the stairs.

"I'm going to pack and get my stuff together, Novie," she shouted through my bedroom door.

I didn't respond back. I waited until I heard her bedroom door slam shut before I grabbed my bag and crept down the stairs. There was only one place I could think to go. Hopefully, my presence was still welcomed. My heart hurt, my spirit felt crushed. That nigga played me with his sixteen-year-old niece, right under the same roof as me. If this wasn't the most shameful, disrespectful shit I'd ever dealt with, I don't know what was.

Thankfully, Kenisha's bedroom was on the backside of the house. I put my car in neutral, letting it roll down the driveway quietly. I didn't put it into drive or crank the engine until I was safely in the street. Genesis's house loomed above me. It didn't look like home anymore. It looked like a cage of lies, a stronghold of secrets and insecurities. I started driving home, to my real home. It was the only place I had left to go.

It was almost dark when I pulled up.

After a deep breath and several Visine drops in my eyes, I climbed out and walked up the cement steps onto the front porch from my childhood. The doorbell was loud enough for me to hear it chime outside as I pressed the button. Chairs scraped against hardwood flooring, followed by heavy steps in the direction of the door. The front porch light flickered on. I squinted against its brightness, waving at whoever was looking through the peephole with a fake smile glued to my lips.

"You finally decided to climb up out of Genesis Kane's ass. You must be in trouble." Daddy opened the door slowly with a sour scowl on his face.

I wrung my fingers together, feeling how it felt when I was eight all over again.

Momma walked up behind him. "Who the hell's at the door at this hour . . . ?"

Her face lit up when she saw me through the storm door. She pushed Daddy out of the way and launched herself through the door.

"My baby girl is back! Oh my God, look at you, baby. Hug your mother, girl."

She pulled me into a hug so tight I could barely breathe. Happy tears welled up in my eyes as I hugged her back while staring at Daddy over her shoulder. It seemed like no matter how right I thought I was, I was still choosing to side with the people who were the worst for me. I'd done it consistently from day one with Swiss, and I was still doing it now. Genesis was just another notch on my bad call list.

It was time for me to learn how to forgive. I owed my parents the mother of all apologies. They'd only been trying to protect me, and now I could see it for what it was, because I would do the same thing for the little girl or boy that I had growing inside of me right now. I stepped out of my momma's arms, giving my daddy a cautious glance. One side of his lip slowly cracked into a lopsided smile. His eyes were sparkling with tears that he wouldn't shed because he was a rock, and rocks didn't cry.

He hugged me, picking me up off the ground, swinging me back and forth in his arms before he set me down with a kiss on my forehead. He knew something was wrong, and he also knew that he'd given me the tools and the mind-set to deal with just about anything.

"Doesn't matter what it is. You know it'll get handled, baby girl," he said in a gruff voice.

I nodded in agreement before shuffling past him into the living room. Egyptian musk hit me square in the nose before I even had both of my feet in the door.

"Hi, Tariq."

He was sitting on the couch in the semidark living room with the remote in one hand and a blunt in the other.

"Welcome back, Nono," he called out, using the nickname I went by as a kid.

I shuffled in the direction of my bedroom, suddenly anxious to get some real food and some much-needed rest. It was safe here. If Genesis tried to send anyone out this way, Daddy would respond with an army of niggas.

Everything was laid out almost exactly as I remembered it. Momma had changed the color scheme of the kitchen from peach and blue to black and red. All of the carpets were now a blended light oatmeal color instead of the deep navy blue that used to run through the whole house. Momma was going a mile a minute about everything from the day she realized I was gone up until the day she'd called me. I was so tired I couldn't hone in on a single word. My mind was ready to recharge.

"Okay, Momma. In the morning, Momma, I'll tell you and Daddy everything, I promise. I just need to get some sleep, okay?"

I smiled at the collection of stickers I'd stuck all over the outside of my bedroom door back in the day. Momma had obviously thought against redecorating it. I recanted that thought as soon as my hand turned the knob.

"Baby, before you get upset or whatever, let me explain." Momma walked into the room and stood with her arms spread wide.

Gone was my queen-size bed and armoire, a small red Corvette-looking thing with a mattress on top sat in its place. My armoire was replaced with a tiny red and blue desk. The baseball glove-shaped lamp sitting on top of it cast shadows across the whole room. I couldn't step inside until I knew what was going on.

Momma walked over and held my face between her warm hands. "We named him Justus. You kept saying it over and over when they first dragged you out of the water. It seemed like the right thing to do."

My eyes ran back and forth over hers. I was trying to make sense out of what she was saying and what I was feeling. The questions all lodged themselves somewhere in between my brain and my mouth. They fought their way through my sub-conscious mind. *Is she saying what I think she's saying? Did my son survive, and then die, or did they make him a room and give him a funeral?*

"Please, Momma, just tell me what this is."

"Come here, Novie," Daddy spoke from behind me.

My legs felt like they weighed a ton as I moved toward him, questioning him with my eyes.

"Bryan Novellus Deleon just turned four not too long ago. They saved him, Novie, they saved your son."

I always thought the women who fainted or hand-to-forehead swooned in those old-school romance novels were always full of shit. That was up until I'd gotten the most shocking surprise of my life, and my world went black.

When I came to I was laid out on a bed in the guest room. One of Grandma's old brown and burgundy quilts was pulled up to my chin. The house was so small that the acoustics were damn near perfect for eavesdropping. I stared at the light coming from underneath my bedroom door, listening to everyone arguing over and about me in the kitchen. It was obvious that I wasn't the only one with mixed emotions about being back home. And I had a son. He'd lived all these years without me even knowing he was alive. I'd been beating myself up and mourning a loss that never happened. They should've told me.

On the one hand, I could feel hatred swell up in my heart toward them. They knew the guilt ate me alive, but they let me stay in that state of mental purgatory. All it would have taken was a word, a phone call. I was robbed. My baby was robbed. There were so many parts of his life that I'd missed and would never get back. I buried my nose in his pillow and inhaled. He smelled like Swiss, or maybe that's how I wanted him to smell. I curled into a ball, and I cried for the baby I had who I didn't even get to name.

"You need to tell her when she wakes up," Momma said in quick whisper.

I sniffled into my baby's pillow and calmed myself down so I could listen. The clink of a bottle let me know that the men were taking shots. Momma was most likely having a glass of wine since she never drank hard liquor.

Tariq cleared his throat loud. "I don't think we should say anything just yet. She's obviously been through a lot. Might need a minute just to adjust to all this."

"And when she starts asking for him, what do we say?" Daddy asked.

"You'll say whatever's true," I announced as I walked into their argument about me. "So who is the 'he' you're talking about? And where is my baby boy?"

Their eyes all dropped in unison. I got an unsettling feeling in the pit of my stomach. I know they hadn't made a fit out of telling me Justus was alive, only to finally admit that something had happened to him.

"Tell me what happened!" I slammed the side of my fist against the wall.

Momma set down the glass of wine she'd been sipping. "Novie, sweetheart, you might want to sit down."

"I'm fine, just tell me whatever it is that y'all are trippin' over."

"A month ago we were celebrating Bryan's birthday. I invited all the neighborhood kids over. We even had a few extra ones crash the party, but there was plenty of ice cream and junk food to go around so I didn't even—"

"Ma, just tell me what the hell is wrong."

She wrung her hands in front of her. "I tried to tell you when I called awhile back. See, the thing is, his daddy came asking for him a while ago. We couldn't deny him the right to see his son. He'd visit off and on, but something wasn't ever right with that nigga. Then he stopped visiting altogether. Shandy brings this little boy named Aris to Justus's birthday party. They were playing and getting along, and next time I looked, they were gone," she ended with a teary sob. "That bitch stole my grandbaby. We got guys looking everywhere, and nobody knows anything."

For the second time in one day I almost fainted, but anger kept me standing my ground. Swiss knew! He knew about Bryan the whole time, and that's probably what he wanted to tell me too. I never in a million years would've expected the person who I called sister, who I loved like a sister, to play me to the left.

I looked at my parents and Tariq sitting at the table.

"We will get Bryan back. He has to be here, so he can meet his little brother or sister." I patted my still flat belly with a small sad smile on my face.

This time, the chair slid across the floor and a glass hit the ground at the same time as my momma.

Chapter 69

No Justus, No Peace

One thing at a time. A woman can only deal with one thing at a time. Genesis was still in the forefront of my mind, but now I also had to deal with the issue of my snake-in-the-grass ex-best-friend. Shandy was crazy. She had to be. She had the nerve to take my child. We didn't judge her or pass her off to the next person. All we'd ever done was treated her like family. What happened between me and Swiss, and what happened to us was our business, not hers. But she wasn't going to make me feel guilty for the rest of my life about an accident that took the same person away from me too. Family forgave each other, but bitches did bitch-ass shit. They'd clap and run for cover when you clapped back.

I waited until Momma was back to herself an hour later. Daddy and Tariq had gone to check on the latest harvest. They needed to stay on top of this new crop of guys or they'd take too many breaks and take twice as long to bundle up the product.

"Momma, you know Tariq helped me escape, right?" I asked her.

She shifted the icepack on her forehead, giving me a confused look. "No, he said he was jumped when he stepped out to go to the grocery store. That you had some guys waiting to rescue you."

I laughed. "Shandy might be as loud as a group of guys, and she might even eat like that. But no, he wanted to holla at her so bad she distracted him so I could get away."

Realization set in on her face before the words were fully out of my mouth.

"We've had a few guys watching her momma's place. They were trying to find Swiss just in case the story his momma got was fake."

"No, Ma, he really did pass away. I was driving the car when it happened. But Shandy, she was pissed at me for a whole 'nother reason. If she didn't go to her momma's house, there's only one other place where I'd look for her."

"Your daddy and Tariq are gonna be gone for at least another hour."

I climbed into the passenger's side of my momma's Chevy Blazer.

"When are you gonna upgrade this thing?"

She smirked at me. "That's why all those young fools get caught up. Nobody looks for somebody who does what we do driving this," she pointed out.

Momma was right. The reason they'd stayed under the radar for so long was because they worked smart, and they weren't flashy. I knew all that shit too, but being around niggas who made flashy dumb moves made me forget all my training.

"What is he like?" I asked after a few minutes to break up the silence.

Momma smiled at nothing in particular. "He reminds me of you when you were that age. He's extremely smart; he knows how to work his iPad and pick the movies he likes. One time, I told him not to go out the gate and to stay in the backyard and play. When I came back, not even ten minutes later, he was on the other side messing with the roly polies. That boy has a smile that makes my heart melt. When I asked him what he was doing out in the yard, he said he didn't go through the gate. He climbed the fence."

I couldn't wait to meet this little person who sounded like he was the best parts of me and Swiss all rolled into one little being. A part of me was worried about how I'd get him from Shandy and whether he'd like me once we met. I didn't even know if I'd be a good mommy or where we'd go after this. We wouldn't be staying at my parents' forever. In the space of a night, I'd gone from no babies to having a toddler and a baby. My life had a crazy way of never going the way I expected.

It didn't look like anyone was home when we pulled up at Tariq's place. There weren't any cars in the driveway, and no lights were on inside. Genesis called my phone, making us both jump.

"Girl, you still got that damn thing?" Momma grabbed my phone slamming it onto the dashboard before snatching the battery out of the back and throwing it out the window.

"If whoever you're running from has even a lick of sense, they can track you. Get a new phone and a new number."

I hadn't even thought about it. But knowing Genesis, if he was calling now, it was only because he'd realized I'd left him and his precious Kenisha. The reality of my life was slowly starting to sink in. I was about to be a real full-time single mom with two kids. But I'd also been kidnapped, shot at, beat up, and I survived a jump from a bridge. As scary as being a single mommy sounded, it was nowhere near as scary as all of the other shit I'd survived. For the first time ever, I could honestly say that I was ready to take on the world. And Shandy was my first stop.

The plan we came up with really wasn't much of a plan. Momma was gonna go up on the porch and ring the bell and knock like she had an emergency and was looking for Tariq. We only hoped that Shandy would answer the door. I pulled the blazer off, parking down in front of a house a few doors down. I made sure I had the keys and all before creeping around the side of Tariq's place. There weren't any lights on at the front of the house, but there were plenty on around back. The doorbell echoed through the house, and I stood on my tippy-toes to peek in between the small crack between the blinds.

It was the room from my nightmares. The one I'd laid in for months while Tariq watched over me. Shandy's silhouette was all of what I could see at first. She climbed off the bed, taking the sheets with her, leaving some dude naked on the bed. I squinted to see where she was going . . . but not before I saw my daddy sit up on the bed. I dropped into the bushes beside the house with my heart in my throat. I could hear movement from the window on the other side, and I eased up. Tariq had a handful of wheat-colored hair wrapped around his fist. Sweat poured down his back, pooling in the dip above his ass. Heather's head was tossed back; her eyes were closed in ecstasy. There were two identical cribs in the room with them, and my heart stopped in my chest. I know these niggas were not fucking in the same room the babies were sleeping in!

Momma was on the porch knocking and ringing the hell out of the doorbell. I slid around the side of the house and caught her attention.

"Abort mission," I whispered, scared that she'd spook Shandy into running with the kids.

"Huh?"

"Shhhhh. Abort mission." I pointed in the direction of the Chevy.

The woman had the nerve to shake her damn head at me.

"Yo' daddy will bring Tariq out here so we can handle this shit," she hissed at me in a sassy whisper. She pulled out her phone dialing Daddy's number.

I cringed.

"What the fuckin' fuck," Momma blurted out from the front porch.

Daddy's phone had started ringing from inside the house. "Footsteps in the Dark," by the Isley Brothers played loud and long in the house.

Momma hung up, and the song stopped. I leaned against the side of the house. Shandy was the worst kind of friend a bitch could ever have. I probably wouldn't even get the chance to kill her for all the bullshit she'd done. Not if Momma got her hands on her first. I didn't know what to do with myself. I stood waiting, but was completely unsure of what I was waiting for.

NOVIE

Chapter 70

Allow Me to Reintroduce Myself

My blood turned to ice water in my veins. A hand closed over my mouth and something was thrown over my head, and handcuffs were tightened around my wrists. Rough carpet scraped up my arms and elbows. I hit whatever it was so hard it hurt my ribs.

Metal slammed shut, and I was rocked into motion. I lay still and listened, trying to figure out who'd grabbed me and where they were taking me. Whoever it was stayed quiet, but I could hear someone nose-breathing from the passenger's seat, so I knew if I tried to do anything, there would be two people to contend with instead of one. The tires rumbled across the road. We were moving fast from the sound of it. I rolled across the back on a sharp turn. The darkness of the hood over my head and the motion of the van or car was starting to make my stomach turn. When we finally stopped, someone grabbed me by my ankles, sliding me out of the vehicle. I kicked and fought back until I thought I'd pass out from doing so much.

"Are you finally gonna put in some work, or do I have to do this job too?"

I knew that voice. The question came from Genesis's number one dick rider, a nigga everybody called Foreign. We already had enough bad blood between us. He yanked the hood off my head. I wasn't trying to catch anymore, so I buried my chin in my chest, avoiding his gaze. He walked over to post up near his partner Chief standing beside me. We both knew that this *"job"* Foreign was asking about really meant me.

I almost laughed out loud at how stupid I'd been.

Chief shifted his weight from foot to foot hesitating. He either had to piss some kind of bad, or he was avoiding the question.

Foreign rolled his eyes and hissed through his teeth. "Move out of the way with your old soft ass. I got this, just like everything else. But you buying me a cheddar bacon burger from Five Guys when we get done."

Foreign looked *foreign,* like his name, with dark autumn-brown skin, pretty, naturally curly hair that he kept cut low on the sides, and vacant ice-blue eyes. They were glassy, empty points on his face that would've fit better on something without a conscience, like a snake or a cat. Permanent dark circles under his eyes made him look half man, half raccoon. Something about him had always made me uneasy. He just came off as shady, the type that'd steal from his boys and ask you to hide that shit when they came looking for it type of shady.

Chief backed up so Foreign could take over.

Foreign's dirty nails dug into my elbow. It didn't make any sense for a man as pretty as he was to come off so dusty and unpolished, but he did. Maybe he thought his good looks exempted him from maintaining good hygiene.

Foreign reached into the back of his waistband. *Don't cry. You better not fucking cry,* I chanted over and over to myself. They weren't about to run back and tell that nigga how I cried and begged for my life or for him to have a change of heart. The tears still marched down my cheeks, even though I told them not to.

Dread was tearing me up inside as I watched him go for his pistol. He waved it, motioning for me to turn and face the other direction. The nigga slid in, pressing himself up against my body until the short prickly hairs on his cheek brushed against the side of my face.

"You know how baaad I been wanting to put something up in you? Just to see what made you *sooooo* fuckin' special," he admitted in a deep, ragged whisper. "Damn shame it's gotta be this hot lead instead of this hot pipe."

I exhaled the air I'd been holding, relieved when he stepped back, pressing the heavy barrel of the gun between my shoulder blades. "Don't be scared, Heaven or Hell awaits," he cooed.

I almost turned around to laugh in his face. I'd spent so much time playing hide-and-seek with the devil that I wasn't even scared of Hell anymore. Hell was empty. All those devils and demons had been right here the whole time.

"I'm gonna make this as painless as possible, but I don't want brains on my van. So walk," he demanded.

His orders were accented with the poke of the barrel into my back.

Daddy had taught me more about guns by the time I was five than most people learned in their entire lives. Between the DEA's drug raids and other dealers, he was so paranoid that he kept guns hidden all over the house. It was safer to show me how to use one, than to have me find one that he'd forgotten about and accidentally shot myself or someone else. I'd never been scared of a pistol, just scared of being at the wrong end.

Daddy would always tell me take a deep breath to steady my aim before sliding my finger onto the trigger. So now I waited, listening for that breath that meant a bullet was on its way. All I could hear was the swooshing of waves underneath me; they crashed against the rocks as my heart pounded against my ribcage. Air shot through my nostrils in quick, erratic spurts. It seemed like I could hear everything except Foreign. I could barely make out Chief, eerily reciting what sounded like the Lord's Prayer. And that's when I heard it. The shift in the air as the pistol rose from the middle of my back toward the back of my head. Foreign inhaled a slow, shaky breath through his mouth. His calloused finger was steady as it slid across steel.

It wasn't supposed to be this way. But my dumb ass had to be a part of Genesis Kane's world, a world he manipulated to get what he wanted, no different than the words he manipulated in the courtroom. Genesis, who didn't have anything in his life that he didn't have a use for.

The first shot split the air; bullets zipped by my face, and they were so close I felt the heat in passing.

"Stop!"

The sound of Genesis's voice brought relief . . . along with a whole new source of terror.

I couldn't stop shivering. Every part of my body was shaking.

He walked toward us. It only took him a few quick long strides to get to where we were standing. When he stood in front of me, I was too disgusted, too ashamed of his sin to even look him in the eyes.

Foreign jotted over to Genesis's side. "You came to watch this one happen live and direct? You wanna do the honor? Pull the trigger?"

Genesis's shadow stopped at my feet. I watched the dark shadowy version of him on the ground. He shook his head, holding his hand up, silencing Foreign. In his other hand, he held something else.

"You're pregnant." Genesis didn't ask, he spat the words like poison.

"What difference does it make to you?"

He threw the pregnancy test down at my feet. I'd forgotten all about those damn things. When I looked up, he was running his hands over his head.

"I don't know what the fuck it means. I told you I didn't want kids."

"Why not? You scared you won't be able to keep your nasty hands off of them?"

No sooner had the words left my mouth than I found myself on the ground with Genesis standing over me, blocking out the sun.

"Nah, I want kids. Just not with you."

Even though I thought he was disgusting and foul, his words stole my breath. Chief and Foreign looked at each other and shared a smirk at the harsh way I was being handled.

Genesis snapped his fingers. "Put her somewhere. Somewhere nice and cozy so she can have the kid. And when it's here, you let me know."

He stood in front of me and leaned down until his face was a hair's space away from mine. "You trying to take my baby girl from me? You gonna watch me take that motherfucka from you, because I do not give a fuck about you or it."

I watched Chief shake his head out of the corner of my eye as Genesis stormed away.

"Man, shiiiit," Chief said over the wind with what sounded like regret in his voice. "We ain't never did no pregnant bitch before. Seem like some bad juju-type shit, like killin' a spider in the house or steppin' on a grasshopper. Typa shit you don't think about that'll come back and fuck you up later."

Gravel scraped against the black pavement under the heel of Foreign's scuffed Jodhpur boot. "Yeah, well, if it's in my house or if it fits under my boot, I'm squashing it," he spat in Chief's direction. "I don't believe in juju, karma, luck—none of that. I control what *I* control. And it can't be all that bad if we're making bank. You heard what Kane said. Let's just find somewhere to put her until it's time. Gotta be somewhere good, too. She knows too much." Foreign directed his frost-blue gaze down at me before glaring back at Chief. "She knows too much about *all of us now*, you included," he said with a sneer.

Yeah, I'd learned a lot about their fake asses, and I hated every single thing about them. From the way they'd all played me to the left, right, down to the way they'd all betrayed me.

Either way it went, Genesis Kane was going to kill me.

Justus

Washington, DC, 2031

That's it? That's all there is? My fingers held the brown leather journal in a death grip. The dingy reddish-brown splatters on the page blurred and came back into focus. Maybe it was blood. I ain't need nobody to tell me that it was my mom's. My fingers avoided those spots like they were acid. They were scattered across the page running over flowery handwriting. I tried to convince myself that they were old juice stains or hot cocoa. I read my mother's words again. *Genesis Kane is going to kill me.* Tears burned my eyes, and my heart pounded away in my throat. When I got to the last word, I slammed the leather book shut with both hands.

"Justus?" Aris yelled through the house. "Boy, what are you doing? Bryan is about to blow out the candles on his cake."

She cracked my door, peeking into my bedroom without knocking. Something I'd told her a thousand times not to do, but she never listened. It felt like Aris was always watching me for some reason.

"Damn, I'll be there in a minute," I barked back, throwing one of my J's toward the door. My brother's birthday wasn't as important to me as what I'd been reading. Not right this second, anyway.

"My bad. Didn't know you were in there having you-time. Wash your nasty hands and hurry up," she snapped before closing the door.

I looked at Aris in a whole new light now. There was a reason why her voice was deep for a girl, and she was always pissed off and strong as fuck too. Aunt Shan tried to say it was because she hadn't gone through *the change* yet. I think part of it was because Aris was mad. She didn't have any of the boobs or the booty that the chicks in school had. That was fuckin' with her worse than the change itself. The other part was Aris was as much of a dude as I was. We all took the same sex-ed classes. She probably didn't understand why she had a dick but had been treated like a girl his whole life.

Aunt Shan had always told me that my mom had abandoned me and Bryan, but she hadn't. Her name blared at me in letters etched deep into the cover. *Novie Deleon.*

I shook my head, swinging tears across her journal. My vision blurred. *That couldn't be it. Nah, there was no way the story ended like that.* But deep down, I knew that was the end of her story. I could almost sense it. My insides felt like they were vibrating from the years of grief and sadness. I'd shoved all those bullshit emotions that came from not having my mom deep down into my gut. The feeling swelled up inside me, made me rock back and forth on the edge of my bed like the addicts I'd seen in the park. I couldn't tell if it would swallow me whole or make me implode from the inside out. I'd never felt anything like it.

"Justus, your BP level is abnormally high," the mechanical bitch's voice sounded off from my wrist.

I clawed at my life tracker bracelet, trying to rip it off.

The bracelet made its usual annoying warning blips before announcing, "Your Aunt Shan has been alerted."

Getting it off was pointless. I don't even know why I tried.

Rain tapped against the window outside. I sat with my legs hanging over the side of my bed, bracing myself because I wasn't ready to face the fact that my pops the murderer and my Aunt Shan were just as foul.

The life tracker wirelessly signaled for him, sending a message to the life tracker he wore to monitor mine. She'd be busting up in here in about zero-point-three seconds like this bitch was on fire. These fucking bracelets were un-fucking-re-movable, and they tracked every-fucking-thing . . . my mood, where I went, what I ate, and what the fuck I did. Mine was mostly for a heart condition I'd had ever since I was a baby. Everyone thought I'd grow out of it by now, which sucked because I hadn't. Dying didn't scare me, and neither did having a janky heart. Why the fuck do they make us pick our career path and start training fresh out of preschool anyway?

Nobody takes the kid with the fucked-up heart, especially not when it comes to playing sports.

Even though I was only sixteen and already six-three, Aunt Shan was just happy she had an excuse to keep me out of the "legal slave trade," as she called it. She wanted me to be a lawyer like my father so fucking bad, and he wasn't even a real lawyer his damn self. That isn't even what hit me the hardest. Now, I knew the real truth. I knew if it wasn't for him, I probably wouldn't even have this heart condition. And I probably wouldn't have gotten passed over to play basketball.

Now my heart was pounding so hard I could feel it booming in my forehead.

"Justus?"

Aunt Shan yelled for me, shouting through the house. "Son, are you all right?"

Nah, I wasn't all right. I'd been wronged from day one. Shit, from *before* day one, when my mom was standing there for both of us. I felt full but hollow as fuck, pissed off, and sad at the same. I couldn't believe it when I'd found it. A real book, written by hand, and not only that, it was written by my mom to me. It'd taken me almost a month to read it, especially since we streamed books now. I wasn't about to get caught dead walking around with an antique book tucked under my arm.

I'd found it in a crumpled cardboard box in the back of the garage behind some old tires. Aunt Shan had either forgot it was in there, or she wasn't trying to touch it. It was covered with spiderwebs, dust, and rat shit, with the words *Novie's Stuff* scratched out and *Trash* written underneath.

The tightness in my throat made it hard to swallow . . . hard to breathe. The walls were closing in on me, and I wasn't even allowed to leave them. It cut me to my core to know my pops had done so much wrong in his life when I wasn't allowed to do anything. No socializing, hanging out—no dating. That's exactly why nobody knew anything about the one person I needed right now. I sent Asa a message to come scoop me up ASAP. If I didn't get out of this house, I'd lose my mind or snap.

"Justus, are you good? What's going on?" Aunt Shan bust up into my room looking panicked and freaked out. Sweat was pouring off her forehead.

I hated that they could do that, just come in and out whenever they wanted, but she'd taken the lock code off my door back when I was six. I had a seizure, and no one could get in.

I flopped back on the bed and stared up at the ceiling. "I'm straight. You know this bracelet trips sometimes."

"Better to be safe than sorry. Let's at least go take your vitals, Justus."

She started to come toward me, and I couldn't stand it; I couldn't stand her. The thought of being around her, having her near me, made my chest tight. My name didn't even mean anything anymore. What did that nigga know about Justus? Nah, I wouldn't be able to fake this, not when I knew what I knew.

I jumped up, knocking her hand away before she could touch me. "I said I'm good. I'm goin' out," I gritted the words through my clenched teeth.

"Where the hell are you going? And who the fuck you raisin' up at?" she roared.

I sneered. This bitch didn't deserve my respect, and after what she did, she didn't deserve an answer for my disrespect either. My hands felt like they didn't belong to me as I grabbed things and started throwing them into my backpack.

Aunt Shan stepped everywhere I stepped, stalking me, watching me.

"So now you think you too grown to answer me, boy? You ain't too sick to catch one."

Still no answer. I gripped the closet door handles, imagining her neck, my pop's neck in between my fingers as I flung it open. The door derailed from its track, slamming into the wall and falling to the floor.

Aunt Shan grabbed my shoulder, spinning me to face her. Her fist was raised. She'd never beat me the way I'd seen her beat Aris. She'd never even hit Bryan, and he was always doing crazy shit back in the day. Aris caught the worst of it, and now I directed every ounce of hatred, hurt, and anger that I had in me toward her. It was like the wind left her sails; her fist came down, and she took her hand off my shoulder. She deflated right in front of me.

"Just tell me what's wrong, baby. If you're in trouble, I can fix it. Whatever it is, I won't be mad."

"You helped killed my mom?"

There . . . I'd said it.

Her eyes dropped to the floor. It looked as if I'd punched her hard in her doughy gut.

"Why did he give me to *you?*"

She didn't even have to answer my question. The way she'd reacted was answer enough. I went back to grabbing some of my things.

"Baby, there's a lot you don't understand and don't know. Your mom . . . I gave up everything for her. She took so much from me."

"So you took everything from me!"

When I threw the hood to my hoodie over my head, I didn't look back, and she didn't stop me.

Fat, cold raindrops smacked me in the face as I marched across the street toward the silver truck sitting at the corner. I tried to let my feelings roll off my back with the rain and tears rolling off my cheeks.

"Hey, you," Asa called out as I climbed into the truck cabin.

I wanted to answer, but I couldn't say the words that had been filling my stomach ever since I read them. Asa could sense that something wasn't right with me.

"What's the matter, Jus?"

Asa was trying to look through me, but I didn't need that shit right now. I grabbed the back of his neck, pulled him toward me, and I kissed my man like the world was on fire. His lips tasted like Dr. Pepper and spearmint gum. He moaned before pulling away from me.

"Aww, shit . . ." Asa whispered.

His eyes were staring past me, over my shoulder. I didn't have to turn around to know what the fuck was back there. Wind rushed against my back, rain pelted against the back of my neck. The door to the truck was yanked open. I was snatched out by the hood on my sweatshirt. The wet pavement skinned my palms as I fell backward.

I caught a glimpse of Aunt Shan's face as she rushed past me with her teeth bared and hands clenched. She barreled past me into the cabin of the truck. She looked possessed.

"Keep your fucking hands off my fucking baby! Don't bring that nigga around here. You promised! You fucking promised!" Aunt Shan howled at Asa.

Her elbow was flying back; she landed blow after blow. Asa wasn't even defending himself. He was probably in shock. My life-tracker bracelet started beeping and kicking off warnings. All of my levels were off the chart. It made Aunt Shan's go off too, and she turned to look back out at me, still holding a fistful of Asa's collar. And I launched, using that moment to yank her backward out of the cabin of the truck.

I hopped in and slammed the door almost catching her fingers.

"Go . . . go . . . go! Drive, nigga!" I smacked the dashboard, trying to get Asa to move his ass and get us the fuck out of there.

Aunt Shan stood on the sidewalk, staring after us. I watched her in the side mirror until she disappeared. I'd always been afraid of coming out, afraid of telling the world that I didn't feel anything for women. That I actually liked men. Now she saw the truth for herself.

It was quiet as fuck as we splashed through the streets, heading toward the highway. Silence sat between me and Asa like a thick curtain. The quiet was good. I wasn't in much of a talking mood. Asa always knew when to talk and when to stay quiet. Must be something that comes with getting old. Not that my boo was old, but he wasn't in high school. I don't even know if he graduated high school, but he was old enough to be my dad, and I didn't give a fuck. We needed to figure out how to get my life tracker off, or someone would always be able to find me.

After a few minutes, I broke the silence. "Asa . . . I found this, and I read it." I held up the journal I'd been hiding for so many months. No one carried books anymore, not real ones anyway. Everyone streamed anything that was written or typed. Any books that still existed were worth a grip, and they were either in museums or art galleries. Bryan and Aris would've joked me for the rest of my life if they'd seen me with it.

Asa's eyes went wide as saucers. The truck swerved.

"Where did you get that shit?" he asked in a strange whisper.

"Found it. Tucked in a box full of Mom's shit." I sucked in air like I was drowning. "My dad killed her. She wrote it, and she said he'd kill her. I think Aunt Shan helped. She's been lying to me for all these years."

Asa took a shaky breath. "I never told you this, but me, your dad, and your Aunt Shan go way back. I love you, and I loved your dad. More than life itself. But he has always had a way of looking at something and only seeing what he wants to see in it. Your Aunt Shan's the same exact way."

"Like how she only sees me as a lawyer?" I asked in a dry voice.

"Yeah. Something like that. Let's take a drive and I'll explain."

I pulled my soaked hoodie over my head and sat back.

"It all started with Tima. Your dad's first wife." He cleared his throat. "Your dad's name was Jarryd back then, and he worked with me on the FBI bomb squad. I found out Tima was cheating on him with some wack-ass lawyer from an office in Downtown Norfolk. I did what any homeboy would do. I looked out for my boy's best interest. Yo, I told that lawyer leave well enough alone, but he didn't want to listen. So I set that nigga up good. Called in a bunch of scares all over the place to keep the bomb boys busy. The only real one was in that garage. But somebody must've seen me comin' or going. Because your dad somehow got sent out there seconds before it went off. He wasn't supposed to be anywhere near that explosion. But I made that bomb, and I was one of the best bomb technicians, so it was perfect. Nobody would've been able to stop it except me. My heart was in the right place. I wanted to tell him for years, but he'd never seen it like that. So I never told him. And then he took that nigga's identity. He became this Genesis Kane, and every time he loved someone it made my heart bleed. Your mom was smart. She figured him out. And she probably figured out the bloody hearts I was sending him, too. But he never saw me. The nigga just looked right over me."

The wheels were spinning, but there were certain things that they kept kicking back at me, making my brain slam on the brakes.

"If you knew my mom, why didn't I see your name in her journals?" I asked, curious about the way Asa seemed to be hanging onto these stories about my dad.

The truck sped up. Rain tapped against the roof and the windows. Traffic went by in a blur.

"Li'l nigga, I care about you the same way I cared about his rusty ass back then. The only difference is that I actually love you. Fell in love with you. I followed around behind that nigga like a fuckin' puppy, and I would've done anything he asked me to if it gave me a chance to get closer to him. He wanted to get rid of you; he said it over and over. When he saw you, he started acting weird. That nigga wouldn't have given me the time of day, no matter what I did. My boy Chief suggested that we give you to Shandy, but it didn't even make a difference."

My pulse thumped hard in my neck. I didn't even see this nigga for who he was, and he'd been sitting right in my face the whole time.

"*You're* Foreign." I didn't ask. I accused him of that shit.

My man, my boo, the dude my aunt Shandy called my Uncle Asa, was Foreign with the electric-blue eyes, permanent dark stubble, and rough demeanor. He wasn't even a real uncle. I'd felt so sick to my stomach with guilty and disgust, I couldn't eat for a week after the first time we hooked up. Every time someone said something to me, I was paranoid that they could see my dirty secret, that I was gay, and that I snuck out three and sometimes four times a night to fuck my Uncle Asa in his truck around the corner from my house. This secret perversion I was carrying around with me.

"Yo, just take me back," I commanded.

Foreign, or Asa, or whoever he was, ignored me. He sped up until the odometer was over a hundred miles an hour. His eyes were glued on the road.

"Nah. We not goin' back. You know how many years I waited? I dealt with his wife, his girlfriends, side bitches, and baby mommas. I waited and waited for that nigga, but he was too homophobic to just let shit happen. And now I have you. Justus is mine. I have his heart."

He finally looked at me. There was so much crazy in his eyes that I couldn't figure out how the fuck I hadn't seen any of it before. His hand was warm as he reached over to squeeze my knee.

"You love me, so you'll forgive me, and you'll accept this. You're mine."